THE
KOVALENKO SECRET

BOOK 1 of 2

By Philip L. Rettew

DORRANCE
PUBLISHING CO
EST. 1920
PITTSBURGH, PENNSYLVANIA 15238

Dorrance Publishing Co
585 Alpha Drive
Suite 103
Pittsburgh, PA 15238
Visit our website at *www.dorrancebookstore.com*

ISBN: 979-8-88729-132-1
eISBN: 979-8-88729-632-6

THE
KOVALENKO SECRET

BOOK 1 of 2

PREFACE

"We believe that getting killed for the cause of Allah is a great honor, wished for by our Prophet. As he once said: I swear to Allah I wish to fight for God's cause and be killed. I'll fight and be killed and fight again and be killed. Being killed for Allah's cause is a great honor bestowed upon only the very best Muslims. We love this kind of death more than you love life. The hearts of Muslims are filled with hatred towards the United States of America and the American president. The president has a heart that won't listen to words because the American government is an unjust government. It has committed acts that are extremely unjust, hideous, and criminal. They (innocent civilians) are not exonerated from responsibility because they elected their government. We do not guarantee their safety. America boasts that it is still powerful, even after successive defeats from Vietnam to Beirut, from Aden to Somalia."

The above is a real and accurate quote. It is not fiction in any way whatsoever. It is not taken out of context. It *is* the context. It assumes that fighting, including deliberately taking human lives for a religious objective is the only proper or most admirable way to live. It assumes life after death. It assumes that God exists, and that man understands what God's 'cause' is. It is based upon a belief that paradise awaits him who fights to establish Islam as the only universal religion. It is what Osama Bin Laden said in 1997 at an undisclosed location in Afghanistan via a translator to CNN journalists Peter Arnett and Peter Bergen in the presence of photographer Peter Jouvenal. It represents at least one important and concise philosophy at the heart of the modern age of extremist Muslim terrorism. It is also subject to serious fundamental debate.

The following story, on the other hand, is fiction. It is intended to provoke at least entertaining awareness of, if not serious thought about human nature, life, culture, the current condition of the human species, and its future in the age of terrorism.

CHAPTER 1
Thursday, June 5, 1997

**** CAMBRIDGE, MASSACHUSETTS ****

Among the Harvard faculty seated on the stage to the right of the speaker's lectern, Professor Isaac Blaustein, Professor of Religious Studies, leaned ever so slightly toward Philosophy Professor Teodor Michalik on his right, and whispered, "That one, Rahmani... at the end of the first row. He is the one I told you about. He is *dangerous!*"

Secretary of State Madeleine K. Albright was speaking from the outdoor stage on this partly cloudy, 78-degree day.

"Unlike Marshall's generation, we face no single galvanizing threat. The dangers we confront are less visible and more diverse–some as old as ethnic conflict, some as new as letter bombs, some as subtle as climate change, and some as deadly as nuclear weapons falling into the wrong hands. To defend against these threats, we must take advantage of the historic opportunity that now exists to bring the world together in an international system based on democracy, open markets, law, and a commitment to peace...."

Professor Michalik was sitting in a row with other distinguished Harvard professors in their ceremonial academic robes as the commencement exercises continued with more words of wisdom from the upper echelons of the prestigious university, a few remarks from students, and then the long traditional procession of graduates of the Harvard-Radcliffe Class of 1997 to the stage. Most of those young people bore irrepressible smiles of accomplishment and hope for the expected endless bright future ahead of them. With pride and optimism etched into their faces, they mounted the stage and filed past the

1

president of the university as he handed out degrees and offered congratulations as someone announced their names over the public address system. Some of them would become teachers. Many would go on to law school or medical school. A few would lose their way. Some would join the military. Many would go on to business schools and then enter the business world. Many would become financially successful. Others would cast aside the material world. Many would find meaningful partners in life. Some would find true happiness. A few would struggle emotionally. One of them would eventually attempt to subdue an entire country.

"… Joseph J. Quinn, Bachelor of Arts…, Thomas J. Rachman, Bachelor of Science…, Shamir Rahmani, Bachelor of Arts…,"

Shamir was not smiling sincerely, like most of the others. Only for the sake of appearances, he shook the president's hand mechanically, unlike those before him who offered genuine firm handshakes. Then with a straight face, he continued to march in a single file with the other graduates as they returned to their seats.

Professor Michalik nodded subtly in polite acknowledgment of his colleague's comment without much, if any, notice from anyone else. More names in alphabetical order flowed in steady cadence from the public address speakers until the traditional procession ended. Commencement was over. Life and death would begin again.

CHAPTER 2
Tuesday, September 11, 2001

**** Manhattan, New York ****

Cynthia Rubenstein was waiting for her friend at the North Cove Yacht Harbor on that beautiful and memorable bright sunny day in southern Manhattan. She was a guest of family friends about to take their yacht out for a daylong cruise south along the Atlantic coast. She heard the unusually loud screaming roar of jet engines but could not immediately determine the direction from which it came. Then, suddenly the roar stopped with a simultaneous thunderous explosion that permeated southern Manhattan. She looked up toward the east at the result of the impact of American Airlines Flight 11 just seconds after it had crashed into the north face of the North World Trade Tower tilted slightly counterclockwise–port wing down, starboard wing up. While still transfixed in horror watching the aftermath 15 minutes later, a man with dark hair jumped from above the flames through an open window on the west side of the building. He was one of about 200 who deliberately or accidentally fell from the skyscrapers that day. For about 10 seconds, he descended in apparent slow motion, in an almost graceful cartwheel through a prolonged but unalterable period of fate obedient to the universal law of gravity. Before she turned away, she could see just enough detail to note that he was wearing a blue shirt and a red tie–the same color combination her husband Seth had chosen early that morning.

His fall had started with a private decision at the conclusion of an unknown period of intense awareness of inevitable vital danger from the impact and explosion between the 93rd and 99th floors just below him. The subsequent fire, rising heat, and increasing smoke triggered man's greatest fear: full and absolute awareness of his immediate and unavoidably fatal personal future. His only choice was between two certain outcomes: burning alive in excruciating pain or leaping to an instantaneous death upon impact with the concrete more than 100 floors below at about 150 miles per hour. He must have wanted to exert his own final control over his death rather than succumb to it without even a futile defiant fight. That one final decision completely consumed his character and beliefs with questions and no answers before he jumped.

Cynthia? Jane? Existence of God? Honor? Belief? Truth? Life? Death? Life after death? His soul? Fate? Evil?

At 9:03, less than three minutes later, United Airlines Flight 175 slammed into the southeast corner of the south tower. By 10:28, both towers had collapsed. Many bodies would never be recovered.

CHAPTER 3
Friday, February 25, 2005

**** MONTAUK, NEW YORK ****

For the last time, after 1,263 days of heartache, Cynthia summoned her only child to her bedside in her comfortable secluded home at the end of Deforest Road overlooking the peaceful Atlantic Ocean.

After a simple and familiar conversation, the young woman rested her hands on her lap as she sat back in the rosewood Rococo parlor chair next to her mother's bed and said with unfamiliar desperation, "Mom, I have come to the point in my life when I must know the truth about how Dad died. You know you are dying. I know you are dying. Doctor Katzenbaum told me. You asked me to come here for a reason. I know you have been keeping something from me because you did not want to hurt me or lie to me in any way. I know where Dad worked. I know what happened on that day. Now, before it is too late, I deserve to know what is in your heart. I have *his* genes in me as well as *yours*, *his* blood as well as *yours*…. Now, I must have the rest of him–the truth that I feel you still keep within you–if I am ever to find peace of mind. Mom, it may no longer matter to you…, but it matters *very* much to me."

Tears began to fall from her dark eyes as her mother sighed in familiar reflection of that day.

I never had the opportunity to know my parents' last thoughts. Should I let her, even force her to live without knowing what I believe? I cannot be certain, and yet I have mourned his loss every day with the belief that it was Seth. I could never decide not to believe it. I never wanted to believe it. It was not a choice! It was a conviction– an undeniable feeling deep inside my very being. There was never any evidence one way or another. His body was never recovered. Without belief, there is no life…. Life is never as pure nor as perfect as we would wish it to be…. And yet we bravely try to shelter our young from the recurring ugliness and unexpected evil and darkness of life. Is my conviction to be the 'truth' that she needs to know?

The memory was still clear. She did not choose to have that memory. It was involuntarily seared into her psyche. She could always recite her memory but without her conclusions.

The emotional momentum of the moment drew her eyes to her daughter's tearful eyes, as she said in final peaceful resignation, "I saw a man with dark hair jump through a window above the fires in the North Tower. I could see that his shirt was blue and that he was wearing a red tie."

Jane knew where her father's office had been. She had seen the live television pictures of the burning towers. She knew her father's favorite colors. Her tears rushed down her cheeks and then onto her still clasped hands upon her lap as she lowered her head in final acceptance. Then, she made her decision. Within seconds, she sensed that her mother was no longer there. It was now clear to her what she would do with the rest of her life.

**** SCHIPHOL AIRPORT, AMSTERDAM ****

The largest diamond heist in recorded history included uncut diamonds worth as much as $118 million in US currency, during a simple truck hijacking. Two weeks before, the thieves had conducted a test run in a stolen KLM cargo truck. At least one of them broke into the freight area at Schiphol airport and verified that everything was in order. Then on this date, wearing stolen KLM uniforms in another stolen KLM truck, the thieves drove directly to another truck carrying diamonds intended for a flight to Antwerp. With many witnesses, the brazen team forced the drivers out of the second truck at gunpoint, made them lie face down on the ground, entered the truck, and drove away. Since the thieves obviously knew which truck to target and how to obtain KLM uniforms, police suspected inside collusion. Diamond merchants who lost millions in precious stones still blame the airport's poor security. That heist was the second time in six months that thieves had infiltrated the cargo terminal, according to the British Broadcasting Company. Investigators have not recovered the gems and have not identified the thieves.

**** *Long Island, New York* ****

A month after she had finally settled her family's affairs, Jane Rubenstein left her home in the early evening for the last time. She had financial security, a new purpose in life, and a new name–Anat–the Semitic goddess of war. She took a taxi to JFK International Airport in plenty of time to board Delta Airlines Flight 468, which departed on time at 10:59 P.M. After 11 hours and 11 minutes in the air, the plane landed safely in Tel Aviv.

CHAPTER 4
Wednesday, April 7, 2010

**** WASHINGTON, D.C. ****

Leah Cummings had been the homecoming queen in her senior year at York-town High School in Arlington, Virginia, but was merely very attractive at Georgetown University, depending upon how she chose to dress, and how she arranged her long honey-blond hair. She was a good student and maintained a double major in Economics and Political Science. She was an 'army brat,' and had lived in 10 different countries as her father, now four-star Army General Michael Cummings rose through his career. Because of that worldwide experience during an early age and into her teens, she had acquired respectable facility in six languages and a smooth, culturally adaptive manner that refined her maturity to a level of sophistication beyond her years. Her father had in-sisted and ordered in his uniquely military-paternal manner during her early teens that she become proficient in the martial arts because he never wanted to learn that someone had assaulted or injured his little girl when he was away from her. So, over the years of intense practice and training, she had indeed become proficient–*very* proficient in self-defense.

At the CIA, however, she found her niche. She got the job on her own merits, with no political or influential 'assistance' from her father. After a series of traditionally secretarial and clerical positions at various governmental agencies, her career, if not her life, was going nowhere fast. Then she re-sponded to a hint from her last employer over six years ago at the Securities and Exchange Commission who was uncommonly sensitive to her apparent lack of fulfillment in her work. He was also quite astute and aware of the power structure within the I-495 beltway around Washington, D.C. to an extent that comes only from knowing an unusually substantial number of people, maintaining mutually useful relationships, having a superb memory, a ready smile, and *never* burning bridges–or playing with 'matches.'

One day before leaving her office after a routine discussion, he took her aside and said in a sincerely paternal manner as he handed her a note, "Leah, call this man at the CIA. He is as honest as they come, and he will tell you whether you have what it takes for a career in the agency. I have been watching you very carefully during the last six months or so, and I do not see the fire or the sparkle in your eyes that I once saw. You deserve better than this place. Call him. I believe you would find a much more interesting and challenging opportunity there. Please believe me when I say I am *not trying* to get rid of you! I just hate to see you struggle so much for self-fulfillment!"

She looked at the note–*Roy Cander, 202-476-1399.*

She had an independent foundation and did not want favors or condescending, chauvinistic attitudes from others polluting her self-image. He went as far as he believed he could go in trying to help a bright young woman too proud to ask for assistance. However, occasionally even the young, proud, and capable could use a little help. She was almost stunned that a stodgy, potbellied old bureaucrat in Washington would have the sensitivity and selflessness to care about her life and career. Leah made the call an hour later and took the extremely unusual offer of an interview late Monday afternoon.

CHAPTER 5
Monday, April 12, 2012

She kept her makeup deliberately minimal and simple. She was looking for a personal *future*, not a personal *relationship*. She dressed in a presentable smart navy-blue business suit and drove her bright yellow 2009 Chevrolet Camaro to the new Central Intelligence Agency Headquarters building in Langley, Virginia. She left her car in the visitor's lot and walked in a low-key manner, making sure she did not inadvertently invite more than the usual masculine interest in her figure. At the appointed time after registering as a visitor in the lobby, she knocked firmly on the door adorned with the brass nameplate of 'Roy Cander' at precisely 5:30 P.M.

A warm baritone voice responded, "Come in–it's open!"

She opened the door and followed through with a simple business entrance and a measured half-turn, closed the door behind her, and then turned to face the source of the voice. The sight of him sparked all her mental synapses.

Oh my God…! You do exist after all!

The handsome, six-foot, three-inch tall Roy Cander stood up at his desk and slowly walked around it toward her with a brilliant white-toothed, intriguing smile set in a classic strong Hollywood face with only a few small young creases. His deep blue eyes caught her attention. He was wearing a colorful tie with a white shirt that did not completely obscure his muscular form. He had no corpulent pot-bellied love handle arrangement hanging over his alligator belt. His medium-length hair was as black as could be for a Caucasian–

wavy, and disobedient to a part on his left side. He smiled easily and carried himself in a confident but natural athletic manner. He was 41 years old but looked like he could not have been much older than she was, and yet he could have faked appearing younger without much effort.

He held out his right hand to greet her as he gestured with his left hand to a comfortable modern cushioned green armchair opposite his maple wood desk, and said, "Please, have a seat!"

She put a temporary lock on her emotions, as she shook his firm but warm hand. Then she got a faint whiff of his cologne, glanced at his pectorals, exhaled subtly, and sat down in the chair.

Your name is really 'Roy Cander?' You deserve something more exotic or intriguing to go with your... sex appeal!

"I'm glad you could make it at this rather late hour, Miss Cummings!"

Still descending, but only slightly, from the unexpected high of meeting an unusually handsome man, she smiled and said nothing, but nodded just to continue the introduction, unaware that her eyes reflexively may have betrayed her inner soul for just an uncontrolled instant.

He continued in a business manner, "I know traffic will be a pain by the time you leave, but this really is coincidentally the only time I had available. Now, what is your interest in working for the CIA, Miss Cummings?"

What? No mental foreplay? No softening me up? No come-on? No pick-up line or implied request for the fastest path to my underwear? Impressive!

She swallowed physically and mentally before continuing, "Frankly, I have been underappreciated and limited in my access to ladders of professional advancement. I have a confident facility with six languages, proficiency in self-defense, physical and mental stamina, and a verifiably sincere patriotic lineage. I want to put my energy and talents to work in effective efforts to get the bad people to heaven–or wherever they really go–so the rest of us in this country can live in peace and harmony. I have recently decided that the CIA is the organization that most likely should be able to appreciate my talents and abilities and put them to good use."

He mused to himself: *No nonsense, bullshit, or politically correct attitude. Direct, confident, and honest.... I like that!*

"Miss Cummings, I am going to cut to the quick. The agency needs mentally tough women who can exercise unique female physical and mental capabilities in situations in which male agents too often cannot succeed. Our adversaries have a wide variety of moral standards and cultural characteristics that could easily interfere with the conduct of our missions in certain circumstances if we are not flexible and creative enough to overcome our own biases. We need people who can put their personal philosophies aside when necessary to accomplish the larger objective. Now, how do you feel about that?"

"If you are telling me I will have to sleep with the bad guys–or even the good guys–then you really need to look for someone else."

However, you might persuade me to make an exception in your case!

"If you are asking me whether I can literally or figuratively kill another human being, then the answer is yes, I *can*. My father made sure I learned how to fight and use firearms efficiently at a relatively early age."

"Miss Cummings…, neither I nor anyone else in this organization will tell you to sleep with anyone, nor imply or expect that you should. We are interested in your experience, intelligence, and creative instincts as they apply to the accomplishment of the goals and objectives with which we are tasked–nothing more, and nothing less. Every agent we train brings unique abilities and talents to the job. We try to maximize the entire team effort with creative genius, and we do expect responsible decision-making in the achievement of our goals. There is nothing unique about this job compared with any other employment regarding the boundaries our agents chose to respect between personal and official conduct. The fact remains, however, that women have different abilities from men, both within and across cultures. We have a job to do, and we expect to use every tool and means at our disposal in the achievement of our goals. We cannot falter because of incompatible personal moral beliefs and behavior patterns. Sometimes, the stakes are simply too high for mistaken personal priorities to influence our tactics and actions within a particular theater of operations."

Well…, at least he's direct!

"If I understand you correctly, Mr. Cander, you are telling me that the accomplishment of the goal takes precedence over how I achieve it, correct? Or, put another way, 'the ends justify the means?'"

"Yes, Miss Cummings. That is the way most of the world in which we live and operate really works, whether we like it or not. The bad guys do not have any objections to that philosophy, so if *we* do, then the bad guys have the advantage. Not only is that not acceptable, but too often it becomes unnecessarily and sometimes unexpectedly fatal to good people you may never have heard of, seen, or known."

He already perceived in Leah many of the qualities he wanted on his team to defeat the likes of those who would fly large commercial airplanes into tall buildings. He had a particularly strong distaste for the philosophy of suicidal destruction of life, property, and culture. Fighting those who would give up everything in questionable service to an untested 'true' belief with highly dubious rewards was particularly challenging and difficult... but necessary.

"Despite what I said, I'm going to ask you to 'sleep' on it, and then give me a call in a couple of days to let me know your thoughts."

She could not completely hide her smile as she said, "I will indeed 'sleep' on it, and let you know my decision."

I will also remember your phone number!

It is not every day that any employer, let alone the CIA, wants a particular person to work in an organization. Sometimes, however, it just works out that way without apparent rhyme or reason. Sometimes, the right person is simply in the right place at the right time. Not everything in life has serious, obvious, comfortable, or completely logical explanations. Sometimes understanding is irrelevant, and rigorous training, reflex, intuition, luck, or gut reaction is the only path to success, or another breath of air, or another heartbeat.

After she returned to her apartment, she 'slept on it' for the next six hours. Leah Cummings made her decision to take that daring next step into her uncharted future and join the Central Intelligence Agency.

CHAPTER 6
Friday, April 13, 2012

Leah completed her one-year CIA training in a respectable fashion. Despite her lack of superstition, she noted with an internal smile this 'Friday the thirteenth' date of her graduation. After another 6-month period at Langley, she started her first overseas assignment in the United States embassy in Karachi, Pakistan, one of 294 physical embassies, consulates, and diplomatic missions around the world.

**** Mᴏsᴄᴏᴡ, Rᴜssɪᴀ ****

Tickets were available only at the box office of The Moscow New Opera Theater at Number 3, Ulitska Ryad, near The Hermitage Gardens in Moscow. People gathered in lines longer than normal to purchase tickets for this evening's opening performance of Tchaikovsky's Evgeny Onegin. This performance featured the newly promising talent of a 24-year-old young woman of striking physical beauty playing the part of Tatiana. Recent rumors among the elite patrons of the arts in Moscow suggested that she was indeed exceptional. Many of those patrons were willing to depart from the stuffy reputation of the Bolshoi and venture out to see the reportedly refreshing young Karina Kovalenko. By the end of her performance that evening, all 708 people in that theater–the full capacity–would remember her for the rest of their lives.

CHAPTER 7
Thursday, July 17, 2014

**** *HONG KONG* ****

The international world of law enforcement had not yet learned about Umar Kasana. Just after 5:42 P.M., a man dressed in black bought 10 boxes of Godiva Mexican dark chocolate at the Godiva chocolate shop at the Hong Kong International Airport for approximately $70 in United States currency. Each box weighed 2.8 ounces and measured 3.75 inches by 3.77 inches by 0.54 inches thick. He returned with his purchase to Hotel Novatel Citygate at 51 Man Tung Road, Hong Kong, where he had been staying on the 23rd floor for the last three nights at $116 per night. He placed the package of chocolate on top of the dresser, removed his clothing, and then went into the bathroom and showered. Within the hour, he went to bed and readily fell asleep.

CHAPTER 8
Friday, July 18, 2014

The Hong Kong International Diamond and Gem Exposition at the Asia World Expo next to the Hong Kong Airport ended an hour ago. Just after 7:10 P.M., a man dressed in a black suit and black shirt with no tie walked out of the men's room with a felt pouch in his left jacket pocket. Then he calmly walked out of the building into the warm clear air and hailed a taxi. After a car arrived, he entered the back passenger compartment and told the driver to proceed to the Novatel Citygate Hotel. However, after he arrived in his room, he did not retire for the night. By 8:15 P.M., he was working deliberately and carefully at the desk in his room to remove the outer paper and inner aluminum foil wrapper of one of the 10 chocolate bars. Then, as if he were an experienced surgeon, he created cavities from the underside of each square section of the dark chocolate candy bar with a warmed dental scraper. He carefully placed two diamonds into each cavity that would fit without compromising the integrity or appearance of each section of the candy bar. Although the gems were of varied sizes, no stone was too large to fit completely hidden in one square of chocolate. Then he repacked each chocolate cavity with some of the chocolate shavings and smoothed the surface with a small metal spatula and the scraper heated with the flame of a cigarette lighter. Periodically, he rinsed off the spatula and the scraper with hot tap water. Then he carefully rewrapped the candy bar in its original aluminum foil and outer paper wrappers, and then refolded and secured the packaging with small applications of Loctite fast-drying glue. He continued this procedure with another seven chocolate bars until

16

he had hidden all the diamonds inside the chocolate bars.

By one minute after midnight when the planet Mars had set in the western sky, he had finished placing all 222 stolen diamonds inside eight Godiva chocolate bars. Each of the seven bars contained 28 gems, and the eighth bar contained the remaining 26 stones, leaving the rectangular chocolate section of that bar without any diamonds in it. Each candy bar had 14 sections–four rows of three square sections each, and the remaining row with one square and one rectangle equal to two adjacent squares. He carefully marked the remaining two unaltered bars with a minor scratch on the white letter 'G' of the word 'Godiva' on the outer gold-colored wrapper so he could select and open it if necessary, during a possible thorough customs inspection. Then he stacked the bars with the two unaltered bars at the top, and the partially filled bar fifth from the top, and then secured the entire stack with a green ribbon wrapped twice around each side and tied at the top. Eight of those 10 bars of chocolate now represented a street value of more than $9,400,000 in United States currency. All 10 easily fit into his carry-on luggage on his next flight to Narita International Airport near Tokyo. The chance of not biting into a diamond contained in that package of 10 bars was about 20.7 percent. However, since he had identified which bars did not have gems inside, the chance of his biting into a diamond was virtually zero. No one in the entire world could know that the future of us all could depend upon whether a Japanese customs official would decide to bite into one or more of those chocolate bars.

**** PESHAWAR, PAKISTAN ****

Shamir Rahmani started his journey to Boston from Bacha Khan International Airport in Peshawar, Pakistan at 7 P.M. local time on an Airbus A320. He would endure two stops before arriving in Boston–one in Abu Dhabi for five and a half hours, and the other in Dublin, Ireland.

**** DUBLIN, IRELAND ****

A dour-looking middle-aged Russian man with a professionally useful bland facial expression arrived at the Dublin airport at 12:25 P.M. local time. He had deplaned from Aer Lingus Flight 331, an Airbus A320 that had left Berlin, Germany at 11 P.M. local time earlier that day. He had spent his flight time in aisle seat 34C in economy class without speaking to any other passengers. No other passengers spoke to him. When he was not napping, his facial expression discouraged approach or conversation. However, his occasionally furrowed brow betrayed an active mind, but not active enough to understand that a financially independent young woman with wavy dark hair who had also boarded the same aircraft in Berlin had been following him carefully with intuitive interest.

CHAPTER 9
Wednesday, April 8, 2015

After carefully packing his carry-on luggage along with the candy, Umar left his room and took the elevator to the lobby, exited the building, and then hailed a taxi to take him to the airport. After successfully passing through the inspection area, he boarded Vanilla Air Flight 304, an Airbus A320-200 at 3:35 P.M., due to arrive at 8:55 P.M. at Tokyo Narita International Airport. He occupied seat 14K of business class, next to the starboard window about halfway between the cockpit and the starboard wing. Again, he avoided any conversation beyond appropriate minimal responses to airline personnel.

At 9:27 P.M., the tan leather Coach bag on the conveyor belt entered one of the x-ray scanners in the customs area of Narita International Airport. One customs official noted the dark image on his computer monitor representing what looked like a cubical object, and quietly said something to another customs official next to him. At the other end of the conveyor belt, another official picked up the bag and took it to a nearby table, simultaneously beckoning the man in black to join him. The official indicated that the passenger should open his bag. With absolutely no change in demeanor, the man in black quietly stepped up to the table and calmly unzipped his bag as if he had just arrived in his hotel room. The customs official carefully watched the face of a man far more experienced in human deception and self-control than any of the prior several hundred thousand passengers he had seen pass through that inspection point in the last 12 months. Then the official moved a few articles of clothing in the bag and looked at the stack of Godiva chocolate bars. He looked up into

19

the handsome, dark, dry, cool unemotional face of the human equivalent of a shark and sustained a sudden minor fleeting tinge of fear. After a moment of hesitation, he indicated that the passenger should untie the package and open a bar of chocolate. The other man coolly picked up the top bar and opened it. The official motioned with his hand that the passenger should turn the candy bar over. The official's eyes narrowed as he scrutinized both the candy bar and the other man's face. The packaging appeared original and unaltered, as was the chocolate candy inside it. After several seconds, he had put the passenger through enough stress to reveal typical evidence of deception or criminal intent and had seen nothing to arouse his suspicion further. He pointed to the open Coach bag and indicated that the passenger should replace the candy in the bag and leave the customs area. The man in black was now free to meet his next customer.

**** LONDON, ENGLAND ****

The Hatton Garden Safe Deposit Company at 88-90 Hatton Garden sustained a burglary of precious gems and metals over the Passover and Easter weekend with an estimated value of about $298 million in United States currency. Police investigators were unable to determine the identities of all five of those presumed responsible, and evidence from video surveillance equipment in that area has remained within the police department, so the perpetrators could not know whether authorities had discovered their identities. Police arrested a father and son pair but could not immediately identify an unknown man in black clothing seen near the crime scene. The thieves had used some heavy equipment to break through the 18-inch-thick steel walls of the safe, bypassing the door to the vault. Investigators surmised that entry to the building had occurred as early as several days prior to the heist–perhaps as early as April 2. Police also suspected that a suspicious and diversionary underground electrical fire had been set deliberately in the basement of a nearby building to distract attention from the robbery. Although police later apprehended the man in black, they discovered that he had a solid alibi, and released him. MI-6 agents in Hong Kong had observed him at the Hong Kong Airport and verified his presence with the aid of several airport security videos at the time of the London theft.

**** *SAN FRANCISCO, CALIFORNIA* ****

Karim Samad had just received the long-awaited three-word e-mail message from his 'uncle,' Shamir:

'It is time.'

He was a 29-year-old Syrian carpenter on a sacred secret mission. He supported himself by working in his trade and took various odd jobs in San Francisco as they became available during the last three years. He also collected a modest monthly allowance from Shamir to ensure that he could maintain an innocent, inconspicuous, and stable existence if work was unavailable, so he could stay off the welfare rolls, where he would acquire an unwanted public identity. Physically, he was unremarkable beyond having a dark complexion and a neatly trimmed beard. He stood about five feet, nine inches in height, and weighed 165 pounds. In a multi-cultural environment like San Francisco, he was unremarkable.

He began his part of the plan with a visit to the Rent-A-Wreck office at 2955 Third Street just a few blocks west of San Francisco Bay. He leased a well-used red 2006 Ford F-350 pickup truck. After completing the rental paperwork without attracting unwanted attention, he took the keys and left the counter quietly to find the truck in the parking area. He found it quickly in the first row of vehicles. It had several rust holes in the rear side panels that looked like someone with absolutely no regard for form or beauty had spray-painted it carelessly many times with assorted colors of Rustoleum paint, leaving the surface without finished reflective quality. He opened the door, got behind the steering wheel, closed the door, and started the engine. With one final look around the parking lot to reassure himself that no one was watching him with unusual interest, he started to drive north to 25th Street and then turned west toward the entrance ramp to I-80 North. He followed that road across the bay and Treasure Island and then east to I-505 just west of Sacramento, where he turned onto I-5 North. He continued the long drive on that highway toward Salem, Oregon, where he stopped at a Shell gasoline station and filled the fuel tank with unleaded gasoline. He went into the store to pay for the fuel with cash and then went to the men's room. After relieving himself, he washed his hands excessively for a full minute. Then he dried his hands under a loud and forceful Xlerator hand dryer for more than a minute and then left the men's room. He returned to his truck, started the engine with an unnecessary roar, left the station, and turned onto Route 99 East toward Oregon City. After driving for more than nine and a half hours and 633 miles without speaking to anyone but the night clerk, he spent the night in the Canby Country Inn on Route 99 East, which advertised free HBO and a continental breakfast. He watched an X-rated film titled 'Tell Me You Love Me' on HBO until he fell asleep. The next morning, he drove through the Oregon City area and made a mental note of MacDonald's Place, which was only slightly longer than a quarter of a mile, but wider than a typical town street in a quiet and almost rural suburban area with multi-acre single-family residential properties on each side. He drove the length of the street from the cul-de-sac at the western end, to the other end that terminated adjacent to a farm field. Then he jotted down some notes with a pencil on a small lined yellow notepad. Within several minutes, he turned the truck around, left the area, and drove back to his motel for the night. He watched another pornographic film before succumbing to deep sleep.

**** MOSCOW, RUSSIA ****

Karina had been practicing diligently for three months in preparation for her audition. Butterflies swarmed throughout her lithe and toned 24-year-old body as she stepped to the center of the stage within the spotlights, just as she had rehearsed it in her mind, day after day for weeks. Although she could not see them clearly beyond the glare of the stage lights, a dozen people occupied seats about 20 yards from the stage in the center section. They had the power to influence and shape, if not actually determine her future in a significant manner. All but a few people on this planet spend most of their lives constrained at least to some extent by the desires, beliefs, and demands of other people–including employers–and the basic needs of securing food and shelter. She intended to rise above that common life and express herself completely in her own way. She wanted to feel the exhilaration of achieving what her imagination had foretold, and of basking in her father's ultimate and complete pride.

He had always told her she could do anything she put her mind to. He had given her important building blocks of life–the self-respect necessary to respect others, the self-motivation required for achievement and happiness, and true appreciation for the difference between right and wrong. Her elementary teachers had told him that she was indeed special. His love for her was not just of natural paternal origin but was also part of the greater human soul throughout the world.

What do you do when the light of your life is 'special?' You protect and encourage her as priority number one. You clear and pave the way to opportunities that will nourish and sustain her talent. You sacrifice whatever you can from your own life, which is worn and limited, to contribute to the fresh fullness of her life, which is unlimited, indeterminate, and therefore a source of hope, rewarding imagination, and beneficial excitement for all. You do the impossible, the merely difficult, and the necessary. You never turn your back on her. Her life is a source of wonder, promise, and excitement, not just for you, but also for all who enter her world.

He was not responsible for her talent. He was responsible only for having contributed to her birth. About 24 years ago in a small Moscow apartment, one private, simple, innocent natural act of selfish natural desire between two truly loving young people had created this miracle. He watched her in silent hope from within the distant shadows at the back of the main floor of the elegant 2,200-seat, 160-year-old Bolshoi Theatre, far beyond the glare of the stage lights. He had to give her as much distance from him as possible during this uniquely personal challenge, as was her wish. Yet he himself had to know her trial. She was, after all, *his* flesh and blood. He understood her anxiety. He wondered who these people were, sitting in the center forward seats–these people who would decide whether she was good enough, whether she had 'the right stuff.'

What gave them the right to decide her future?

'The system'–the weight and momentum of tradition, the rules of social behavior, precedent, the history of Russia, and the extremely competitive specific culture of the Bolshoi gave them that right. They were judges without consequence to themselves–keepers of the tradition of the 240-year-old world-famous Bolshoi Ballet Company. They took their mission in life very seriously.

**** DUBLIN, IRELAND ****

Two men on different earthly paths were in the same airport during the same layover period among hundreds of other people, but for other than serendipitous reasons. One was a Pakistani citizen, who had deplaned from Etihad Airways Flight 45 after having occupied business class seat 5A next to the port side window of the Boeing 777-300ER aircraft. He had boarded that plane in Abu Dhabi after a five-hour layover. It was during the current layover of three hours and 50 minutes in Dublin that the Russian photographed Shamir with his smartphone camera. The Russian had received his orders from Moscow after police had captured a suspected Chechen radical and applied interrogation techniques designed to elicit truthful information originally intended or sworn to remain secret. A male voice in the earplug in his right ear guided him:

> *"About 14 meters farther... on your left side of the walkway, near the white vertical post in the departure lounge... dark blue business suit... carrying a black briefcase.... No, the other one farther down... yes... on your left.... Wait until you can see his face.... No..., do not leave yet.... Take more pictures..., just to be sure."*

The nearby young woman with wavy dark hair carefully observed the Russian with the camera, and correctly deduced the focus of his photographic interest. Photography in airports is extremely rare because they are places of urgent or impatient activity incompatible with typical photographic interests. She noted the flight designation and its destination, as well as the departure time of the flight at the nearest gate where he had been waiting. Within the next 20 minutes, she watched Shamir board an Airbus A330, operated by Aer Lingus bound for Logan International Airport in Boston on Etihad Airways 7977. Again, he sat in Business class—this time in seat 8H next to a starboard window. During that time, the Russian transmitted those images through the internet to GRU (Glavnoye Razvedyvatel'noye Upravleniye) headquarters in Moscow. Colonel Vasily Koshelev received them within the next hour. He was the deputy to the second in command of the GRU, the Main Intelligence Directorate of the General Staff of the Armed Forces of the Russian Federation, Russia's largest foreign intelligence agency.

CHAPTER 10
Thursday, June 18, 2015

BEGINNING OF RAMADAN

**** *OREGON AND IDAHO* ****

Karim awoke early and ate his free continental breakfast of almost stiff, cool, scrambled eggs, bland orange juice, and a stale cherry pastry. He then drove north on I-205 toward the east side of Portland, where he turned onto I-84 and then continued southeast into Idaho. He crossed the Snake River and exited I-84 onto I-86 North toward Pocatello, where he took another break at a service station. He refueled the truck, bought some snack foods in the nearby convenience store, and then returned to the truck. He followed I-15 North to Idaho Falls and then turned onto Route 20 North to Ashton, where he found the Teton Mountain Inn on North Main Street. After about 10 hours of driving, he stopped there for overdue rest. After checking in, he settled into one of the rustic rooms, which had pine wood furniture and matching wood plank walls and floors. The price was higher than usual, probably because of the dearth of lodging in that greater beautiful geographic setting. However, his concern was not with money or beauty. His boss was wealthy, and his task was necessary. With minimal preparation, he got on the bed and fell into a deep sleep within minutes without checking for the availability of pornographic movies on the television.

**** *MARYLAND* ****

The reclusive American multi-billionaire, Duke Chancellor, owner of the private and super-secret Chancellor Organization was in his office on the top floor of the Plymouth Building–one of his dozens of commercial structures. The modern glass and steel seven-story building was hidden in a wooded area just a few miles west of the I-95 highway and northwest of Laurel, Maryland. Information from one of his worldwide networks of informants, business contacts, and various clandestine agents had recently piqued his interest. The CIA station chief in Moscow, Andrea Sokolov, had established a useful and trustworthy reputation among the political elite in Moscow and had received an invitation to a ballet performance at the Bolshoi Theater last evening by the United States ambassador to Russia, Stephen J. Hartworth. The Russian Minister of Culture, Anatoly N. Medinsky had given him the tickets in a typical political gesture of maintaining at least the official public appearance of friendly relations, if not accumulating points of social obligation that might acquire political usefulness later.

A young Russian ballerina with a growing reputation of being one of the most talented dancers to come along in a great many years–even several generations–caught Andrea's attention through her contacts in the social circles of Moscow. No one else had pushed her into dancing. No one had arbitrarily singled her out to be special. She was neither socially, nor politically engineered. For lack of a better explanation, she was simply blessed with unusual natural grace, physical talent, and beauty. That special talent emerged, blossomed, and developed with remarkable personal drive and care, and constant encouragement from her father. Various influential Russians who valued the arts and possessed the social keys to visibility and success also recognized her unusual talent and encouraged her. She seemed destined to join the world-famous Bolshoi Ballet. However, the Bolshoi selection committee eventually rejected her first audition. They said she had not yet matured as a dancer–was not yet 'ripe' enough for the special prestige of the Bolshoi.

This information from the American embassy in Moscow normally would not have attracted any special interest from within the official world of diplomacy and international intrigue inside Russia, the United States, or anywhere else. Ballet in Russia is close to a national obsession, and the Bolshoi is among the most competitive organizations anywhere, but it has little to do with the international power structure. No doubt, many young ballerinas in Russia strive for the Bolshoi but fail to achieve their dreams. Andrea Sokolov recognized the incredible unfairness or stupidity of denying this young woman the prestigious Bolshoi opportunity to reveal her talents as soon as possible to the rest of Russia, if not the world, and to achieve this personal goal. She was aware that Karina was exceptional in many ways because she had seen her perform in person several times during her recently advancing and most promising career. Andrea had gaged the audience's reactions as well, confirming her own assessment. She had experienced the overwhelming, spontaneous, and thrilling audience admiration herself. Surely, the unanimous joyful response to her performance was not contrived or orchestrated. Nothing other than her natural talent and beauty could explain the irrepressible smiles of approval. She possessed a genuinely rare ability to ignite that universal internal fire of joy, excitement, and appreciation in others. A true, real, and unusual source of human wonder and marvel had to exist within her.

Duke Chancellor had told his people that they were to inform him of opportunities to use some of his vast wealth and influence to create a brighter future by seeking out and enhancing the good and eliminating or at least diminishing the evil, in both the individual and the social or institutional levels. Although many people throughout the world would want to do the same thing, only a few had the financial resources, the contacts, the organization, and the determination to help make certain things happen for the greater good of most people on this planet. No doubt, like-minded individuals throughout the world shared his drive to overcome the inadequacies of traditional forms of government and their often self-serving or shortsighted quests to lead humanity into a better society with the self-righteous laws of unintended consequences. This young ballerina represented another opportunity for Duke to use his considerable financial resources and influence to enhance the life experience of someone with unusual promise and talent. It was a welcome departure from the energy he usually exerted in trying to level the playing field for some of those who were innocent victims of the dark side of humanity and its governmental institutions or simply could not afford opportunities on their own to explore their full potential.

**** MOSCOW, RUSSIA ****

Colonel Vasily Koshelev was dressed in casual business attire as he entered the beautiful Sokolniki Park at its eastern entrance and strolled down one of the many clean tree-lined walkways with occasional use of his cane for a few minutes as if he were any common innocent visitor. The carefully manicured pathways and lawns were remarkably free of litter and debris. After concluding that no one had followed or recognized him, he sat down on a sturdy wooden bench next to a fit younger man in light gray civilian jogging attire who was reading a recent copy of the newspaper, Kommersant.

Then, without facing the younger man, he said quietly, "Major Zhukov, I have another mission that requires your expertise. A certain young woman from Moscow will be traveling to the United States of America this coming Monday from Sheremetyevo International Airport. You will travel with her, remain anonymous, and ensure her personal safety until I have need of your services elsewhere. She is the daughter of a close and dear friend. I cannot go into further details at this time. This is a *personal* request, Major, so make sure you are invisible. I do not want anyone else to discover your activities in either the United States or here in Russia. Possible unfortunate national or international implications could arise that would be premature for me to disclose. This envelope contains your airline ticket and instructions, which, of course, you will destroy after you have committed them to memory."

Boris was a 33-year-old former Spetznaz officer, proficient in close quarters combat, as well as taekwondo, judo, and karate. He was qualified as an expert shooter with pistols as well as rifles, including the specialized Dragunov sniper rifles. Part of his effectiveness in accomplishing occasional tasks of unofficial and deniable origin was due to his mastery of impersonation, camouflage, and disguise. He held the rank of major in the Russian Army, although he was not officially a member of any specific unit of combat, command, or operation, and usually did not wear a military uniform. Unofficially, however, his loyalties were exclusively bound to a certain high-level GRU colonel, Vasily Koshelev. Some of his assignments required his expert use of costumes and makeup. Occasionally he impersonated older women in the accomplishment of his assignments. He held the equivalent of a doctorate in American Studies from the prestigious Lomonosov Moscow State University, established in 1755. Despite his high academic performance, he maintained a low profile among the university population of about 40,000 graduate and post-graduate students, about 7,000 undergraduates, and a faculty of over 6,000 professors and lecturers, as well as about 5,000 researchers. He spoke English fluently, including both the King's English and a delinquent's 'street English' somewhat typical of American youth close to the limits of habitual uncivilized behavior. He had acquired that ability during several postings in large United States cities, including New York, Chicago, Los Angeles, San Francisco, Boston, Washington, D.C., and Atlanta during his years of espionage field training. He was also fluent in French, German, Farsi, and Mandarin, or Standard Chinese, which is the official language of the People's Republic of China. Colonel Koshelev valued the younger man's service because he represented a rare combination of broad-based natural talent, physical strength, ability, intelligence, and loyalty, much like the younger version of Vasily Koshelev before he suffered a leg injury in an automobile accident while on leave in Saint Petersburg 10 years ago.

Boris looked out into the distance, surreptitiously accepted the envelope, and quickly slipped it between the folds of his newspaper. After a brief period without further conversation, thereby confirming his understanding, he stood slowly and walked away toward a northern exit from the park.

CHAPTER 11
Monday, June 22, 2015

**** *IDAHO* ****

Karim continued to drive about 769 miles from Oregon City into the foothills of the rugged mountains of southeastern Idaho. He was searching for certain abandoned gold or silver mines that might still be accessible. Within four hours, he was following the scarcely visible remains of old parallel tire ruts in a desolate area through dry grass, knee-high sagebrush, sand, and stone leading to what looked like the remains of an old mine shaft entrance in a distant hillside. The sun peeked through a partly cloud-covered pure blue sky. No evidence of the modern world was within sight. No telephone poles, electric transmission towers, roads, buildings, billboards, or litter blemished the natural landscape. He was completely alone. The sky had been devoid of aircraft for the last 22 minutes. In the quiet windswept rugged terrain, the only evidence of the modern world was the red truck. He slowed to a stop, turned the engine off, got out into the warm air, and looked around the immediate area for about a minute. The place appeared lifeless. No movements or sounds other than those associated with the occasional wind caught his attention. The local wildlife was silent and invisible to him. He walked about 120 yards up a slight rise toward the mine entrance. After he peered briefly into the mine, he removed the heavy old, rotted oak beam leaning diagonally across the entrance, tossed it aside with effort, and then walked carefully inside. The damp and cool silence of the mine unnerved him for the first 50 yards. After a final chill of uncertainty, he turned around and walked carefully through the dim tunnel back to the entrance. Without hesitating, he walked briskly back to his truck, satisfied that he had found the perfect place for Shamir's plan. He entered the truck, quietly mumbled a prayer for several moments, and then started the engine and returned to the paved macadam country road. From there, he retraced his route back to the highway toward Oregon City and returned to the same motel he had stayed in before. He went to his room and sat restlessly on the bed, suspended in anxiety. Then he turned the television on in a subconscious effort to find peace or just a distraction. After viewing another XXX-rated HBO movie, he composed a text message to his 'uncle:'

> *'To my favorite uncle–I have found a place according to your wishes. I shall remain in place until you need me elsewhere. Praise be to Allah!'*

He sent that message on his smartphone to 963-42-128-3577, Shamir's cellphone number. The electronic intercept capabilities of the National Security Agency snagged that message along with several million other bits and bytes and stored it somewhere in the vast computer storage facilities in the NSA headquarters building at Fort Meade, Maryland.

**** MOSCOW, RUSSIA ****

They sat quietly next to each other in adjoining single light brown vinyl-covered cushioned seats in the departure lounge at Gate 30 in Terminal D for Aeroflot Russian Airlines Flight 100 at Sheremetyevo International Airport. Each of them was postponing their final farewell. He was six feet tall, stocky, powerfully built, and unusually fit for a man in his forty-eighth year of life. He was out of uniform, neatly dressed in light gray slacks, black loafers, and a dark gray sport coat over a pullover light blue sweater. His face bore the lines and creases of the tensions and anxieties of adulthood, the loss of his wife, the last nine years of single and often absent parenthood, and a demanding military intelligence profession. His hair was full, only slightly wavy, and peppered with just the smallest evidence of gray. Her hair was a luxurious and radiantly pure blonde color like her mother's, tied back in a naturally wavy ponytail held in place with a light blue ruffled elastic band. She had the smooth clear face of a classic fashion model–unmarred by blemishes, makeup, crass ornamental jewelry, concerns about an increasingly threatening world, heavy responsibility, or the aging process. Her dominant, intelligent, and captivating glacial blue eyes and firm athletic build of 127 pounds on a five-foot six-inch frame obviously came from her mother. She was wearing a subdued light-blue dress with matching flats and a white sweater with white buttons down the front, and a pocket on each side. He had watched her over the years when he could, seeing her grow and develop from a normal frisky young child into the skinny and independent teenage tomboy who liked to dance. Fate or perhaps a supreme being transformed her over time into a stunningly beautiful, self-assured young woman. She was finally heading toward the realization of her dreams, thanks to the rare and truly altruistic generosity and influence of a reclusive and wealthy American business executive. Throughout her life, she took her mandatory schooling seriously and usually achieved top grades. She had recently suffered the disappointment and deep pain of rejection by the extraordinarily competitive Bolshoi Ballet Company after having been encouraged and almost assured of a position by her intensely wishful, proud, and maternally protective teacher during the last decade. However, she was determined to rise to the top of her profession in the United States. She would focus on showing them, her teachers, and everyone else, that with the freedom to perform truly from her heart, she really was the best. She reveled in their adulation and praise that confirmed to her that she had indeed pleased them beyond compare with her talent. She had sufficient command of the English language through her required education that would make her new and exciting adventure in life slightly less difficult than it might otherwise have been.

He looked at his pocket watch out of habit, even though he had a modern Japanese 'smart' cellphone with many of the current typical practical tools, including a clock and a camera, as well as various factory-installed applications and features for which he currently had little use. He bought it primarily because it was a convenient and almost necessary means of modern communication. He would learn the other applications in time. In about 15 minutes, she would walk away from him forever, or so it appeared to him, down the Jetway and into the Airbus A-333 aircraft. It was scheduled to leave at 9:50 A.M. and take her non-stop across the north pole during the 10-hour and 40-minute flight to John F. Kennedy International Airport, just over 4,645 miles from where she sat. He could almost feel the passing of each second until she would leave. He was fighting the lump in his throat with difficulty, but then suddenly arose from his seat and briskly walked a few steps out in front of her with a contrived air of light-hearted urgency so she could not see his first tears developing. He removed his cellphone from his pants pocket, found the camera icon with some clumsy efforts, and then quickly turned around to face her. He concentrated on holding the device vertically at arm's length to fill the frame as much as possible with her image, effectively hiding most of his face from her view for a few moments. He finally touched the icon for the camera to register her image in its memory with an electronic 'camera shutter' sound, so he could look at it later and refresh her image in *his* memory. She turned her head ever so slightly and tilted toward the camera in a most subtly tempting invitation, and then flashed her brilliant, white-toothed natural smile—the one that made everyone in her audiences, and indeed the entire world smile in return. Then, for just a moment, she saw his tears, and within seconds shed a few of her own. She could not stop them and made no effort to do so. That was their last communication before she stood and went to him. They embraced for what could have been the last time. She was small, delicate, and precious in his strong arms. To Karina, he was massive and solid, but warm and reassuring. He was her father—her first and most genuine protector. He had insisted upon the name 'Karina,' the Russian equivalent of the English 'Karen,' because it means 'chaste' or 'pure,' the way he perceived her. The last call to board Flight 100 drifted out of the nearby low-fidelity public address speakers in the ceiling with an official implicit warning. Then they parted. She picked up her large colorful flight bag with overlapping squares of red, yellow, white, blue, and green from the floor near her seat, and looked back at him one more time before disappearing down the long red-carpeted Jetway.

He called out to her for the last time, "Call me as soon as your flight lands!"

She looked back at him briefly and smiled.

Then the chill of reality invaded her consciousness as she walked purposefully into the cabin to find seat 45E. She was traveling a great distance to a place where she had never been before. Without her special talent and drive, that would have been a truly frightening future indeed. She had to wait patiently for dozens of the other 309 passengers to stow their carry-on belongings in the overhead bins, and then squeeze into their assigned seats with varying degrees of strain, flexibility, or ease. For another five minutes, she worked her way down the starboard aisle, waiting for some and moving carefully around others, to the last row of seats in the airplane, just in front of the rear lavatories. Her seat was the middle one of three abreast in the center seating section of the aircraft. She settled into her slightly more than 31-inch-wide seat with greater agility than would the taller older woman struggling down the aisle behind her. She had gray hair coiffed a little too carefully for someone of average means and forced a smile through her stern and generously made-up face self-consciously, revealing slightly coffee-stained teeth. Then she tugged at her medium-gray suit jacket in the aisle just before she squeezed her mature and abundant form into the seat next to Karina. Seats D, E, and G moved slightly as the woman dropped her weight into seat G on the starboard aisle side of the center seating section.

Within 14 minutes, the Jetway finally moved away from the aircraft, assuring everyone that no one would enter or leave the aircraft until after it landed in New York. Several seconds later, a well-used dark gray aviation tug latched onto the front wheel assembly of the aircraft and started to push the large airliner away from the terminal at the pace of a geriatric stroll. She was finally on her way. Her father stayed in the terminal waiting area for a few more minutes, just staring at the aircraft through one of the recently washed large terminal windows, slowly coming to terms with the realization that his little girl was really leaving, but that she was also entering the most exciting experience of her life. She would also undoubtedly become the focus of men—men whom he could not meet, examine, and evaluate for the quality of their substance, character, and purity of intention and purpose. However, it was the immutable way of nature. Her departure from his world was inevitable. She was a grown woman entitled to her own life. Because she was beautiful, men would gravitate toward her, and he would not be there to protect her if necessary. At least he would know she arrived safely. He could not bear the thought of a flight malfunction, hijacking, or destruction from a terrorist missile or suicide bomber. Nevertheless, he knew that such frightening horror was part of the new world reality, and he was doing his part to keep such threats as small as possible.

Colonel Viktor Alexander Kovalenko was a 47-year-old intelligence officer in the Russian Army. He retrieved the copy of the note upon which she had printed her address in the United States and committed it to his well-trained memory. He was intimately acquainted with the ways of the world and the threats that had developed throughout history as those who would impose their selfish and misguided wills and beliefs upon others eventually brought pain and suffering to innocent human beings guilty of nothing more than following their innate searches for meaning, happiness, and everyday purpose in their earthly existence.

She is her own person. I must let her go. I have done my best and can do no more. Good luck, and be safe, Karina. I shall miss you with all my heart. My greatest love and hopes go with you, and I will always be here for you when you need me.

Aeroflot Flight 100 raced toward the United States across the frigid northern latitudes at slightly less than 600 miles per hour about six miles above the surface of the earth. During the flight, a disproportionately significant percentage of male passengers periodically found it necessary to use the aft lavatories instead of the others positioned at more convenient wing or forward locations, occasionally clogging both aisles while they waited. After the first male passengers had used the aft lavatories, word quickly spread within the aircraft that a visual feast of beauty existed in the last row. Some looked at Karina with deliberately lascivious, or even just friendly smiles, and others with amateurish or immature efforts to hide their obvious innate interest with self-conscious or furtive glances. However, she was naturally comfortable enough with her appearance not to try to hide it. Ironically, the only conceivable way she *could* hide it was with makeup. Most women put at least some effort into *enhancing* their appearance with makeup. One of the fundamental facts of her life was that most men simply could not resist staring at her, and she therefore gradually learned to accept that behavior as part of her normal life. The person in seat 45G was already smitten beyond repair by the young Russian beauty immediately to his left, and yet he could not dare to speak. He could not reveal his heart to her. His orders were to protect her at all costs until she reached her new apartment. He had given his word. His superior officer, Colonel Vasily Koshelev must have known that no one else would be better motivated for this assignment.

He must have known I would fall for her! Was he so utterly cruel as to force me to look into her beautiful eyes, and yet simultaneously suppress my inevitable reaction? Somehow, in some way, I shall break this noble curse!

****** ISTANBUL, TURKEY ******

The tall handsome man with wavy black hair, wearing a black suit and black collared shirt with no tie innocently followed the orderly line of people into the Airbus A-330 aircraft parked at Gate 203 at Ataturk International Airport. Inside the cabin, he proceeded to the starboard side of the plane to find seat 4K in business class next to the window. The non-stop flight would arrive at Terminal 1 at JFK International Airport at 11:45–11 hours and 20 minutes later. His first name was Umar, meaning 'one who is attractive, sexy, cool, funny, popular, smart, manly.' Umar Kasana was indeed all those, and dangerously more. He was Turkish by birth to Rauf and Nisan Kasana in the city of Tatvan, home to about 97,000 residents on the western shore of the largest lake in Turkey, covering about 1,450 square miles. Lake Van is in Bitlis Province, roughly 5,542 feet above sea level in the eastern sixth of the country within sight of the snow-covered dormant compound volcano called Mount Ararat to the northeast. It is also about 10 miles slightly southeast of the dormant Nemrut volcano and 157 miles due north of the town of Cizre immediately north of the Turkish-Syrian border. After leaving his home as a young man, he eventually lived in Lebanon, Syria, Libya, Tehran, London, Saint Petersburg, Prague, Rio De Janeiro, New York City, Tokyo, Hong Kong, and Johannesburg, depending upon who wanted what. He provided Kalashnikovs, Berettas, Lugers, M-16s, Chinese hand grenades, lasers, drones, portable rocket launchers, C4, dynamite, radio detonators, mustard gas, ricin, and other materials even more deadly than these to his clients. He spent most of the last two decades of his 36 years in some of the world's darkest and most threatening back alleys, both literally and figuratively, but also in some of the finest restaurants and clubs in Las Vegas, London, Moscow, Beijing, Tokyo, Rome, New York City, Johannesburg, Istanbul, and the French Riviera. His network usually had contacts with people of malleable morals particularly motivated by cash who had peculiar access to new or used equipment for the right price. Although he had no college or equivalent formal educational degrees, he possessed natural mathematical quickness and fluency in several foreign languages, including English, French, Farsi, German, Arabic, Russian, Chinese, and Japanese. He also had acquired the subtle art of 'social chameleons' through association with people of public influence, popularity, or power on either side of the law as well as through the practice of talented imitation. He was indeed a naturally serious student of human behavior, a social scientist of the street and the shadowy dark alleys of the world, an accomplished liar, and an effective actor. He was the killer shark of the human lot, easily ignoring or dodging rules and regulations where they presented impediments to achieving his personal or professional goals. He could fall back upon several acquired reputations or different well-practiced persona with ease, as if he were possessed of multiple personalities, depending upon his quick and reliable intuition, the immediate situation, and the people with whom he needed to interact to accomplish his goals. He was a dependable businessman, regardless of the transaction and its consequences. His rules were simple: If he agreed to deliver, then he would deliver on time at the specified location for the agreed-upon price. If his counterparty failed to deliver the expected compensation, his life would most likely become at least quite difficult. He never entered a contractual situation from which he had not already engineered at least two well-practiced escape routines. The 'University of Street-Life' granted him its highest degree: license to steal, manipulate, deceive, distract, dodge, cajole, persuade, and psychologically or physically conquer or abuse almost any other human being. The various legal systems around the world were merely occupational nuisances that he could manage whenever necessary with sufficient favors, persuasive pugilistic bodily harm, psychological leverage, lies, or very tempting bribes. He loved the pursuit of wealth, not as an ultimate accomplishment, but for the power that money gave him. Wealth facilitated the greatest exercise of his natural talents and imagination and provided the pathways to satisfaction of his desires and fantasies as well as the framework for his own unique and sometimes variable ethical values. Money gave him *choices*–choices from an active imagination usually not available to most of humanity. It fed as a powerful addiction the unlimited appetite of his already disproportionately strong ego. With sufficient financial means to satisfy all his earthly human needs and desires, his imagination flourished, became insatiable, and drove him to approach the fringes of danger and unique personal excitement. While doing business, he had also assembled over time an international network of reliable 'associates' to help execute each job, and thereby also helped to solidify his secret professional international reputation. His identical twin brother, Umair, had the same character and often facilitated false identification.

**** JAMAICA, NEW YORK ****

While he was waiting for his luggage just after noon, he continued to walk around inside the international arrivals building at JFK International Airport, watching other passengers with a curious but practiced eye. He wondered about their departure locations, where they were going or had come from, and imagined what their plans and intentions were. He was also looking for anyone who might show any unusual interest in *him* because the nature of his business occasionally invited unwanted attention from law enforcement officials. Within the hour, he recognized the striking young blond-haired woman waiting at the arriving Aeroflot Flight 100 luggage carousel. She had just disconnected her phone conversation with her father, satisfying him that she had indeed arrived safely. After Umar involuntarily caught his breath, he was compelled to approach her. His male animal nature left him no choice.

"Miss? Please excuse me, but I have been waiting for you for my entire life, and now I have found you! My name is Umar Kasana, and I would be simply delighted to enjoy your companionship for dinner at a restaurant of your choice this evening!"

She was completely ignorant of restaurants in New York City or anywhere else in the United States. She turned casually toward him with the unintended effect of daring him to keep his gaze upon her beautiful eyes.

She responded flatly in only slightly Russian-accented English, "I am sorry, Mr. Kasana, but I am already spoken for by a handsome Russian colonel."

Unfazed, he responded, "But, surely this honorable Russian colonel could not be so possessive as to deny his chosen one her complete freedom to explore life and companionship as she chooses!"

Just then, the matronly 'woman' who was sitting next to Karina in the airplane walked purposefully and slightly awkwardly toward the two, leveling an unusually penetrating glare at Umar. She did not speak as she arrived within three feet of Umar, looking only slightly up into his eyes. Umar lost some of his bravado, suffered an immediate loss of libido as well as his smile for just a second, but recovered quickly without apparent betrayal of his thoughts. The older woman's body language stated clearly, *'butt out buster!'* Despite his own considerable social talents and physical abilities, something about the older woman triggered his worldly self-preservation instincts. The stance, daring confidence, wary eyes, and large strong-looking hands betrayed the aura of someone proficient in close-quarters combat and quite experienced with dangerous behavior.

This is not a woman, nor is 'she' harmless.... Why the disguise? The odds favor withdrawal... for now....

Umar looked back at Karina and continued smoothly, "Please forgive me, Miss.... I did not mean to be too forward. Perhaps we shall have another opportunity to speak, or to enjoy dinner together at another time..., yes?"

Karina did not answer. Her introduction to the United States of America was starting a little too fast for her complete comfort. The older 'woman' smiled briefly at Karina, conveying a small dose of reassurance, but said nothing. 'She' watched as Karina turned to fetch her luggage. Then 'she' visually followed the man in black as he innocently wandered off into a non-threatening location within the baggage claim area.

Karina had packed two matching light blue heavy-duty hard suitcases full of her clothing and various personal keepsakes to help provide or maintain some familiarity during the hopeful beginnings of a comfortable foundation for her new life in the United States. English was a required subject during her secondary schooling in Russia, so she spoke the language well enough to get by easily in most situations, even though her pronunciation occasionally delightfully betrayed her Russian heritage. She tended to smile and blush slightly with mild, but controlled embarrassment during those rare occasions when she knew she was having some difficulty putting her thoughts into perfect English, let alone the constantly shifting idiomatic 'American' English. However, that effort usually had the irreversible effect of merely endearing her to the person with whom she was speaking–airline personnel, airport workers, strangers, store clerks, or anyone else who had the good fortune to be within speaking distance. She was indeed a memorable sight from any cultural perspective. She usually kept her hair tied back in a neat wavy ponytail that hung halfway down her back, which tended to accentuate her perfectly shaped head, flawless complexion, delicate neck and ears, and finely sculpted facial features. Her divinely proportional figure pleasantly betrayed her profession with toned, muscular legs, shapely and solid derriere, flat stomach, and not even an ounce of unwelcome fat evident anywhere. One might easily imagine that she could unlock a secure Swiss bank vault simply by smiling at it. She had more than enough eager assistance from willing young men in casual attire, businessmen in traditional dark suits, and even older or retired men. In addition to those who shared the enviable task of carrying one of her suitcases, other men with compromised amorous daring or some other kind of undoubtedly contrived excuse would walk along well out of their way farther to the side or behind her. In that manner, they could not only admire the view but also be within helping distance if needed, as if in a spontaneously organized protective 'secret service' just for her. One adventurous, and awkward-looking, rather pudgy, curly-haired, and bespectacled young man from another arriving international flight bravely helped get her remaining suitcase from the baggage claim area to the customs area, and eventually outside to the street and into a taxi.

Before she entered the characteristically yellow 1982-model restored Checker cab, she rewarded those who helped her that far with an ever-so-slight facial blush, her smiling deep ice-blue eyes, and a mildly Russian-tinged, "Thank you, gentlemen! You have been so very kind and helpful to me!"

Merely hearing her speak propelled a few of them directly into a rare ecstatic experience. She handed the dark-skinned middle-aged cabbie a folded slip of white paper, on which she had clearly printed in dark-blue ink the exact address of her destination.

Joe Czarzhynensky, Duke Chancellor's right-hand man, briefly observed Karina, easily recognizing her from the photographs Duke had e-mailed to him from one of his sources in Moscow. He observed the transfer of the note Duke had his Russian contact deliver to her Moscow residence before her trip. The man in black and the matronly woman with gray hair were near the exit from the arrival terminal and within Joe's field of vision. These observations were merely normal background information for an intelligent and observant man. Duke wanted to protect his 'investment' and carefully preserve as much of his anonymity as he could, and that included keeping Joe anonymous as well at this stage of the project. Joe's instructions were to observe from a distance, but not physically greet or speak to Karina unless she was in obvious trouble, and to make sure she arrived at her apartment safely. Joe entered the nearby well-used 2002 Chevrolet yellow cab with obvious scrape marks on the front fender parked behind the taxi Karina had taken. He then slipped a $50 bill to the corpulent middle-aged driver through the cabin partition window. The cabbie's name was on a plastic card clipped to the dashboard.

"Follow that old Checker cab in front of you, Dominic! Do *not* lose sight of it! I don't care if it goes to Boston or Montauk! You follow it! If it goes through a red light, then you go through the same red light! If the police stop you, I will handle that. If it enters a one-way street the wrong way, you follow it! I am serious, and this is not a Hollywood movie scene! After I see the passenger get out of that cab and retrieve her luggage at her destination, then I will give you these for the return trip. If you fail, you get nothing more and I report you to the New York City Taxi Commission and the United States immigration authorities!"

With obvious effort and a wide-eyed expression of surprise, Dominic turned more toward Joe in the back seat.

You shittin' me man? Who'n the hell are you?

After immediate recognition of the two Franklins Joe waved in front of his face, his expression changed instantly, and he said, "*Yessss, sir!*"

While they waited for the other cabbie to finish putting Karina's luggage in the trunk and on the back seat, Joe studied the other driver's appearance. The bearded, hairy, and pudgy middle-aged cabbie in front of them wore black sandals with no socks, and an open-collared white, blue, green, and red plaid shirt unevenly tucked into a well-worn, but clean pair of blue jeans. When the other cabbie was obviously ready to pull out into traffic, Dominic immediately checked his side-view mirror and pulled out into traffic behind him. The two cabbies successfully battled a little less than an hour's worth of metropolitan New York traffic including often maneuvering within a fingernail's thickness of other cars while squeezing through and around various New York vehicular challenges. Eventually, the first cabbie finally safely dropped his beautiful passenger off at the corner of Neptune Avenue and Brighton Fifth Street, near Little Odessa, a popular and primarily Russian enclave of about 33,000 households in southern Brooklyn near Brighton Beach. The neighborhood provided a mild atmosphere of 'home away from home.' She would never know how the cabbie had lengthened the trip slightly just to enjoy her image periodically in his rear-view mirror for as long as he could without provoking too much suspicion. Joe watched as Karina exited the cab and collected all her luggage on the sidewalk. The other cabbie obviously was not going to help her, and no one else was available to help her get her things into her apartment, so he told Dominic to wait while he helped her take her luggage to her apartment.

During the process of moving into her new apartment, she met one of her neighbors, Larisa, a slightly shorter, but moderately attractive single woman also of Russian heritage–in her early thirties–who lived on the floor below hers. The two became instant friends, and Larisa took Karina under her wing, showed her around the neighborhood, and helped her find a grocery store where she bought enough food for her convenience during the next several days.

**** CAMBRIDGE, MASSACHUSETTS ****

Rahim (meaning 'to be kind or show mercy') Nazari, an Iranian geophysics student from the city of Shiraz received a visitor in his modest studio apartment on the fifth floor of 39 Essex Street. His living space included one bathroom and another room used as a combination bedroom, living room, den, and study. A small kitchen area with simple, basic appliances occupied much of one enclosed corner. The rent included heat and hot water, but no air-conditioning. Signs on the walls clearly prohibited dogs. He furnished the place with a used single bed frame with an adequate second or third hand slightly discolored Sealy Posturepedic mattress, one dark-stained old wooden chair, and one even older leather recliner with sun-faded brown leather marred on the back by a few thousand old cat-claw rips and punctures. A faded and heavily worn gray and green carpet rescued from a graduating senior during its attempted disposal at a nearby dumpster covered half of the old wooden plank floor. His benefactor could have arranged for a roommate to help lower his costs, but a roommate would only increase the chances that someone else could discover his secret. Roommates would be unpredictable and uncontrollable. They would talk, and eventually, certain words would slip out in an unretractable fashion, and without clarification, thereby prompting, if not inflaming even the most innocent natural curiosity, questions, suspicion, misinterpretation, and further risk. The $1,750 in rent, plus the cost of books and $44,720 in annual tuition, as well as an allowance for food, was a bargain for what they wanted from him since their resources were virtually unlimited. The visitor from Tehran was the same man who was supporting his studies. Rahim Nazari was a bright young man identified as potentially very useful by certain powerful people in the Middle East with uncertain and transitory bases of operation. They had both money and patience in abundance and the disciplined will to use them as necessary for their purposes. Both the completion of his education at the Massachusetts Institute of Technology and what he was led to believe was the safety of his family in Shiraz were dependent upon his keeping a certain secret. Rahim wanted his degree from MIT. Nothing else would do, now that he had the unexpected and rare opportunity to complete an education worthy of his dreams and talents. He would keep the secret, and he would dissemble as necessary and control his conversations. He would protect his benefactor's identity with all manner of devious self-preservation and subterfuge. That was his most obvious avenue to self-realization and success, if not a life of independent freedom in the United States, once he gave them what they wanted. He did not dare to disappoint his supporters. He was a fearful genius. He told university officials, friends, and acquaintances that he was preparing for a career in the oil-exploration business after his graduate work and that he intended to sell his services and expertise to the highest bidder. After several repetitions of that plausible story, he began to believe it himself. He also had no realistic concept of the severe psychological burden he might have to bear eventually because of the implications of certain secrets, and his unwitting participation in Shamir's nebulous plan. In many ways, he was a typical young man with a normal mind-numbing dose of testosterone. His future was at his command. He was naïve.

Shamir announced calmly, "The time has come for you to earn your tuition, my young friend."

He carefully studied the student's face for several seconds, looking for evidence of his potential commitment to true Jihad as if it were visible in his eyes, the portals to his entire being.

Had he wavered in his faith after more than six years of university life in the land of the infidels? Could he resist even one of the many estrogen-charged female college students attending more than 55 institutions of higher learning throughout the greater metropolitan Boston area?

After more than half a minute of silence, while the two men stared intently at each other, Shamir smiled slightly, and then his eyes softened and his brow relaxed.

"Your commitment is quite admirable, Rahim. Your father will certainly be proud of you! If you need to contact me, here is my cellphone number: 963-42-128-3577."

He handed the younger man a small blank card with the clearly legible phone number hand-written on one side. Rahim put the card in his pocket. Shamir encouraged a parting handshake, but the result was more his grasp of Rahim's sweaty limp hand than Rahim's grasp of Shamir's firm and controlling hand. Silent, uncertain eye contact weighed upon each, but more clearly in the younger man as the wealthy one turned and left the small messy apartment and walked down the stairs to return to other details of his urgent and necessary mission.

Rahim Nazari was a conflicted young man. Six years ago, he had dared to apply for acceptance at the Massachusetts Institute of Technology in Cambridge, Massachusetts. A little-known Iranian commercial trading company selected him from among promising secondary school students in Iran as the only recipient of a full four-year scholarship to the school of his choice, representing the opportunity of a lifetime for a bright and promising student. Moreover, depending upon his grades, would further support his pursuit of a Ph.D. degree in his field of study. His interest was in geophysics and geology in preparation for what he believed would be a secure career in the oil exploration and energy production industry. He had finished his undergraduate degree at MIT two years ago with a class rank in the top five percent and was a little over two years into his graduate program toward a Ph.D. degree. He worked 20 hours a week in the university library system so he could pay for his minor miscellaneous necessities, and an occasional small student luxury, like dinner at a restaurant with his girlfriend, Fantasia. His tuition, room, and board were paid anonymously every year on August 1, when a wire transfer in the amount of US $44,720 was deposited at the Bank of America, NA, at 100 Federal Street in Boston, Massachusetts, with the routing number of 026009593, and referencing his nine-digit student identification number, 688457338. Rahim received a confirmation letter of each deposit. The wire transfer came from HSBC headquarters at Canary Wharf in London, England, the world's second-largest bank. Upon notification of every deposit, Rahim dutifully reported the deposit according to MIT regulations. That report went to his student account counselor at the International Students Office at 77

Massachusetts Avenue, Room 5-133, in Cambridge as confirmation that his bill was paid, and included the date of origin, the name of the sending organ-ization–the Iranian Ministry of Education–and the academic term for which it was paid.

Shamir Rahmani was a wealthy 'free-lance' Islamic Sunni radical who 'in-vested' part of his inheritance of a huge Iraqi oil fortune through complex business interests involving drug supplies in Kazakhstan and Afghanistan. With all his earthly wants and needs amply endowed, he devoted the rest of his life to planning for the establishment of Islamic world domination, as he believed the Prophet Muhammed had intended. Although he was a Pakistani citizen, he was born in Iraq 39 years ago on Sunday, July 4, 1976–one of about 320,000 births worldwide on that date, the bicentennial celebration date of the Declaration of Independence of the original 13 American colonies. No one could have known how he would develop as a child, through his teenage years, and into a young man. No one could have predicted how he would come to believe that he had a personal obligation to subdue an entire nation. After having attended the best schools in London, he applied to and was ac-cepted at Harvard College, and graduated with the class of 1997, the same year that the Hale-Bopp Comet captured the world's attention as the largest and brightest comet since the Great Comet of 1811, which was visible to the unaided eye for 260 days. It was a unique reminder of the greater universe and the mysterious forces of nature, about which most people were com-pletely, if not willfully ignorant.

Shamir was naturally charismatic enough to prompt one to imagine that he could charm the teeth out of an alligator. However, every smile and every contact was a partial promotion of the establishment of his version of Islamic world domination, and with it the ultimate caliphate. To him, that result was an inevitable and necessary consequence of Islamic history taken on as a per-sonal obligation. His purpose in life was as obvious to him as the sum of two plus two, and the unending regular sequence of night and day. His family up-bringing and religious education forbade his sincere examination of possible gray areas between belief and truth and deflected all intellectual efforts to do so. To him, the truth had no gray areas. Not even intellectual debate with the students and scholars at Harvard could convince him otherwise, nor even open the realm of other possibilities or avenues of thought. Within the timeless flow of life, his existence and beliefs were but a molecule of water in the Pacific Ocean, and yet they would eventually affect many tens of millions of lives in his 40th year of life.

CHAPTER 12
Tuesday, June 23, 2015

The little girl in Karina needed a soft and friendly companion, so she asked her new neighbor where she might be able to find a cat that needed a home. After further neighborly conversation, Larisa gave her directions to an official animal care center, along with a street map. Karina wasted little time testing her map-reading skills, and eventually found the New York Animal Care and Control facility located at 2336 Linden Boulevard in Brooklyn. She hailed a cab for the 9.2-mile, 40-minute trip from her apartment to the animal shelter. When she arrived, she was a little frightened by the razor-barbed wire coiling through the top of the chain-link fence surrounding the scarred and amply patched macadam parking lot bordering the Linden Boulevard side of the building. She wondered briefly whether that was to keep the animals inside or to keep people outside. Then she dismissed the thought with mild effort, a brief shiver, and entered the building. After a 23-minute survey of available animals and a conversation with the manager, she adopted a six-month-old light gray Devon Rex hypoallergenic cat and named her Mushka. Satisfied that her choice was just right, she also purchased a cat carrier and then coaxed Mushka into it with smiles, gentle hands, and a few Russian phrases of endearment. She then left the facility and waited at the street corner for another taxi to take her back to her apartment. By the time she arrived about an hour later, she was slightly more confident and 'at home' with her small new friend in her new living environment.

CHAPTER 13
Friday, June 26, 2015

Karina arose at 5:32 A.M. after a satisfying night's sleep under clear skies. She showered and dressed in a casual light blue denim skirt and unremarkable sleeveless white top and sandals. Once again, she brushed the kinks out of her glowing blonde mane and expertly gathered it into a simple, naturally wavy ponytail, fixing it in place with a bright red elastic band. She prepared a modest breakfast of an English muffin, a ripe banana, and organic orange juice. After she finished eating, she put her dishes in the small sink in her tiny kitchen, washed and rinsed them thoroughly, and then put them away in the small cupboard above the sink. Then she went to her equally small bathroom to brush her teeth and finish her morning routine. After she came out of the bathroom, she picked up Mushka and hugged her, inquired a few times in Russian about her plans for the day without waiting for an answer, and then gently put her back down on the floor with an encouraging smile. The cat looked up at Karina with a typically disinterested feline stare as she left her apartment with more than her share of innate youthful optimism, locked her apartment door at 6:30 A.M., left her building, and began a brisk walk toward the Metro Q station. A few morning joggers along the way acknowledged her as a 'regular' in that part of the community, and usually smiled or waved to her. She always smiled back, thereby simply making the day complete for each one of them.

She would never know the wealthy American executive who anonymously paid her security deposit and $375 per month in rent in advance for the next 12 months. Duke easily could have supported her in a more elegant or larger residence, but he did not want to call any unwanted attention to his arrangement. A single, struggling, and beautiful young foreign ballerina residing in a high-rent district anywhere in the Big Apple would eventually attract someone's unwanted attention, and prompt at least time-wasting questions, threatening curiosity, or other annoying intrusions into his well-concealed private organization, if not his personal life. In Brighton Beach, she would attract only her normal dose of considerable attention among others mostly of Russian heritage. This was simply another one of Duke Chancellor's many business deals, but with a sincere altruistic twist. With her meager savings and a small gift from her father that she brought with her, she would still carefully manage her financial life while building what could develop into a very promising dancing career. Her two-bedroom apartment was on the fourth floor of the seven-story Erynn Fifth Apartments at 2911 Brighton Fifth Street, from which she could walk to Coney Island and several other beaches along the Atlantic Ocean. Occasionally she would deliberately take the stairs to and from her apartment as a simple regimen to help maintain her self-concept of staying fit and healthy with regular exercise. She would walk about two blocks to the nearest Metro station, and then take the Q train into Manhattan to Times Square. From there, she would transfer to the Number 1, 2, or 3 train, continuing north to The Lincoln Center for the Performing Arts just north of Columbus Circle. There she would hone her natural dancing talent and sharpen her skills day by day, exercise by exercise, muscle by muscle to marvelous levels of perfection not seen in decades in this country. She would soon become the pride of the 67-year-old New York City Ballet, instead of the Russian Bolshoi.

After a semi-conscious and uneventful ride on the Q train, she arrived at the Times Square station at 7:23 A.M. Then she transferred to the Number 1 train going north toward 20 Lincoln Center Plaza, where she would continue her training with the New York City Ballet Company, founded in 1948 by George Balanchine and Lincoln Kirstein. She sat upright in her seat with perfect natural posture, still absorbed in her new experience, the excitement, and the hustle and bustle of a metropolitan population almost 30 percent larger than that of her hometown of Moscow. However, she was disappointed and saddened by the dirty and graffiti-scarred Metropolitan Transit Authority facilities in distinct contrast to the predominantly rather clean, politically artistic, and well-maintained Moscow subway system, which was started in the Stalin era. She tucked that displeasure into a compartment of her mind that would not interfere with her dreams.

At the 50th Street station, about three and a half minutes after the train left the Times Square station, a tall, handsome, dark-haired man in a light-weight black suit with an open black shirt and no tie entered that subway car. Over three dozen other busy and anonymous men and women reflecting some of the multi-cultural composition of the Big Apple also boarded that car. He stood in the typical commuter posture indicative of an experienced subterra-nean rail traveler–legs spread slightly at a 45-degree angle to the direction of the train, and with one arm perpendicular to the horizontal line through the feet with that hand firmly grasping a nearby overhead metal strap, and knees not locked. After having acquired the practical ability to maintain his balance in any of the world's mass transit systems, Umar Kasana easily anticipated and counter-balanced his weight against the constantly changing, and occasionally unanticipated jerky movements of the subway train as it approached and then stopped at the 59th Street Columbus Circle station platform a little over three minutes later. During the exit of about two dozen passengers, he caught a glimpse of the beautiful Karina Kovalenko, still quietly sitting on a blue fiber-glass seat in the middle of the railcar. Attributing his good fortune to the de-mands of destiny, he smiled to himself, vowing not to let her out of his sight again, as he had at the JFK airport. The old 'woman' was not there to distract him or interfere. What Karina may have lacked in buxom fleshy female attrib-utes from the perspective of generic pure male lust, she more than compen-sated for in mesmerizing facial beauty and exquisite bodily proportion, shape, and form. He changed his prior plans immediately. After all, his plans were always at his command, and other people usually had to adjust theirs to his. He stepped firmly toward her, using his superior weight, height, and solid muscular body to nudge other passengers subtly to the side. A young and fit black man with long, unkempt, partially gold-died braided hair, an abundance of amateur tattoos, and facial scars implying an ingrained belligerent attitude glared up at Kasana after one of those subtle nudges. Kasana glared back down at him with greater depth and intensity foreign to the young man, which gave him serious pause before escalating the minor confrontation. He immediately concluded that he should move to another part of the train–at least to the next car back. Karina noticed the subtle visual exchange, and sudden exit of the young black man, and immediately thought of her father–strong and powerful, with his natural commanding presence. Without looking up at the man in black, she smiled to herself, but then the smile came to the surface.

As if completely oblivious to a train full of other passengers, Kasana looked directly into those ice-blue marvels and said, "So…! We meet again! I am therefore convinced it is indeed our fate to be together! I am sure you have a beautiful name…. What is it?"

She looked up at him, unable to deny some small attraction, and the corners of her mouth turned up ever so slightly.

She said simply, with only the slightest intuitive reluctance, "Karina."

"Ahhh! I was right! Such a *beautiful* name!"

She froze in uncertainty, unwittingly inviting him to change his plans for the day.

Then he inquired with an irrepressible smile and almost juvenile curiosity, "May I ask where you are going?"

She answered carefully with deliberate brevity, "I am going to The Lincoln Center for Performing Arts."

He lied in his classiest manner as he smiled more broadly at her, "Oh! What a coincidence! I was going to a place nearby anyway! I will walk with you!"

He would have walked up the outside of the Empire State Building if that were where she was going. Less than three minutes later, they both left the train at the 66th Street Station. He followed her up the dirty cement subway steps to the street. Once outside in the daily hustle and bustle of Manhattan, she experienced her first view of the skyline from her closest vantage point so far. She smiled as she looked around, mostly up toward the tallest nearby buildings, and then farther south to the *real* skyscrapers. Then she looked up into the clear bright blue sky, absorbing the excitement of the city. He did not react at all. He had been in Manhattan many times before and was already well past the point of a new visitor's awe. Suddenly, she could feel his intense eyes upon her from behind, and she was uneasy, as if naked before an unwelcome stranger.

"I must go to work," she said with a small note of urgency as her smile disappeared.

Her demeanor stiffened, but he continued with his best amorous pleading voice, "Will you have dinner with me this evening? I promise to take you to the very best place, where you will most certainly enjoy yourself!"

By this time, the gray-bearded old man leaning against a nearby streetlamp pole holding an unusually well-polished black cane in distinct contrast to his shabby attire had heard enough. The sun disappeared behind a large cumulus cloud with a dark gray base just forming in the eastern sky, and the cool early morning air reclaimed much of Manhattan with a slight breeze. He walked casually toward Karina with slow deliberation, but without leaning on his cane. Umar intuitively became more alert, sensing the approaching presence of something ominously and vaguely familiar, but he could not identify it precisely. He turned slowly toward the apparent source of his discomfort, looked immediately at the cane, and then into the man's eyes as he approached to within 15 feet and stopped, but did not lean upon his cane. The focus of his attention was obvious.

The 'old woman' at the airport! Same general height... same aura... same... something....

As if suddenly returning from an unknown suspension of time, Umar turned to look at Karina, but she was no longer standing where he remembered her to be. She had just gone into the building, and the door was closing behind her. Without a confident viable plan at this point, Umar turned toward the nearest subway station entrance with complete disciplined composure, and casually walked toward it, continued down the middle of the stairs to the train platform, and boarded the waiting southbound train as the doors closed immediately behind him. He became uncharacteristically uneasy.

Who is he?

****** BALKH, AFGHANISTAN ******

Valentin Murat, a single and little-known free-lance journalist, was drafting an article for the Ak Khaik News Agency in Kazakhstan. The 29-year-old 2007 graduate of Princeton University had majored in Economics and Journalism. His research during the last six years focused on events in Syria and Iraq, where he had traveled periodically. He was pursuing his interest in what he had discovered as a hidden, but potentially dangerous group of people intent upon establishing a caliphate, somewhere in the Middle East or the Muslim world of Central Asia as a seed to promote the spread of radical Islam worldwide under Sharia law. The potential danger was evident to him only because he had the good fortune to have been born into a professional family and received a first-rate education. He knew that such a caliphate was incompatible with democracy and that despite its faults, democracy was the least destructive form of peaceful living and individual opportunity for the greatest number of people. He also knew that Islamic culture was spreading throughout Europe at least partially because of increased immigration from primarily Islamic countries, augmented by one of the world's highest birth rates. His parents had not indoctrinated him with specific religious perspectives but allowed him to discover for himself whether he would have such beliefs. His father was a physician and encouraged his intelligent and only child to seek opportunities to travel outside of his homeland to experience for himself as much of the rest of the world and other ways of living as he could, and eventually to pursue further education in the United States of America. These and ancillary experiences contributed to an unbiased perspective of the international community and the United States in particular, foreign to many of his fellow Kazakh citizens. One of the names that he had encountered frequently in his travels and research during the last two years was Fatih (meaning 'conqueror') Abdul-Kaliq (meaning 'servant of God'), Syrian by birth, middle-aged, charismatic, persuasive, and extremely ambitious.

Valentin drove his dusty black 2009 Fiat west of the city of Mazar-i-Sharif without incident on the A-76 highway under a clear blue sky to the ancient city of Balkh—reputed to be the oldest city on Earth—just north of the highway and not far south of the Kazakhstan border. The city was marred by at least 2,000 years of battle and plunder by Arabs and Mongols. It was not until the ninth century A.D. that Islam became more firmly rooted in the area. Five rather curiously concentric streets near the city center, with other only partially concentric or arc-like equidistant adjacent roads farther away, suggest remnants of ancient defensive fortifications. These concentric roads intersect with eight straight main streets radiating outward like the spokes of a wheel from the innermost circle to at least the fifth circle from the center in perfect 45-degree adjacent geometric relation. Some of those streets extend farther out into the city and beyond. He drove toward the western side of the innermost circular road and left his car parked next to a dark tan mud-walled residential structure adjacent to the narrow unpaved street scarcely wide enough for two small passing vehicles. He exited his car and walked the rest of the way to the Green Mosque for his meeting with the mullah known as Fatih Abdul-Kaliq, who had taken advantage of the opportunity to grant him an interview. However, unknown to Valentin, the cleric had the ulterior motive of sending a message to the rest of the world.

Valentin glanced at the tall trees surrounding the building as he entered the obvious front of the four-story-high Masjid-i-Sabs Mosque, still defaced with bullet pockmarks and other evidence of military conflict on several of the exterior walls. Some of the ornate light blue tiles below its intact radiating 36-ridge 'corrugated' blue-green dome were missing. He could not avoid betraying his status as a first-time visitor to the city, let alone someone unfamiliar with Islamic custom, particularly inside a Mosque. He walked slowly across the ancient light-colored well-worn marble floor that contained randomly spaced natural dark gray colored streaks of equally random shape and size. Suddenly, he heard a male voice speak his name. The slightly questioning male voice from the far side of the room about 50 feet in front of him competing with its own slight echo called out again with only adequate volume.

A disembodied voice echoed toward him, "Valentin Murat?"

Valentin turned to face in the general direction from which he had detected the voice. He obviously appeared different from the other dozen or so people in the large main room, and he must have been the only one looking like he was slightly disoriented or unfamiliar with his surroundings. He was dressed in tan western slacks and a light blue casual shirt–quite different from every other man in the room wearing the traditional shalwar kameez or Perahan Tunban. A man was standing next to a dark wooden doorway at the rear perimeter of the central room, beckoning with his right hand and a slight declination of his head for Valentin to approach. After exchanging minimal polite generic cross-cultural greetings as total strangers, they entered the nearby small, sparsely furnished room with a well-worn plain wooden table and two matching old chairs in the middle. Another bearded man wearing a light gray traditional shalwar sat in a wheelchair at the table with a stolid facial expression and unmoving, dark penetrating brown eyes beneath equally dark thick eyebrows focused upon Valentin.

The first man said to the seated man who was still steadily staring at Valentin, "This is Mr. Murat, from the Kazecon News Agency in Kazakhstan."

The seated man announced with a subtle hand gesture but without an informative facial expression, "I am Fatih Abdul-Kaliq. You may sit."

Valentin attempted to ease the rough and uncomfortable beginning of his interview with a smile inviting reciprocation but was unsuccessful. He took his seat slowly during a temporary dearth of useful intuition, while rapidly trying to think of a way to soften this man up, but the other man continued to dominate the meeting with a strict and dour attitude.

"My people informed me that you wish to know about me. I will tell you only certain things, and then you will leave. I have only limited time here."

Again, with a slightly different but still ineffective smile, Valentin responded, "Thank you for seeing me, Mr. Abdul-Kaliq."

Valentin reached into his pocket to retrieve a small Sony ICD SX-1000 digital recorder, capable of storing more than several dozen world-record filibusters. Then he held it up so the cleric could see what it was and offered a facial expression requesting permission to record their conversation. Fatih Abdul-Kaliq slowly closed his eyes once with a slight nod of his head in tacit permission but hid his great satisfaction in knowing that the recorder would retain his words precisely as he would express them. He waited only so long as it took Valentin to activate the recorder and place it strategically on the table between them so each of their voices projected toward opposite-facing small directional stereo microphones at the top of the recorder. The mullah assumed command of the meeting, as he began to speak in English in a surprisingly educated manner.

"We are seated in the middle of an ancient city that still bears the residual evidence of man's historical struggle for truth and peace. I will soon be the new leader of the Islamic State, which will eventually prevail in its quest for a caliphate, governed by the true believers in Allah, peace be upon Him. We strongly object to the interference of the United States of America against our struggle for self-determination. We, therefore, have developed plans to eliminate the United States from its current dominant world position with the help of Allah, peace be upon Him. It is inevitable! God willing, we will put our plans into motion this year to punish the American infidels and eliminate their interference."

Valentin did not receive that information with the personal degree of credible fear one might expect from a United States citizen but from an intellectual and a world citizen. This man was threatening the existence of the last best hope for most of humanity on this planet. Although the threat appeared impossible to execute, it was nevertheless a threat, and given the statements of people like Osama Bin Laden before 9/11/2001, deserved at least some deliberate consideration.

Is this man an outright lunatic? How is an upstart group of ragtag revolutionaries, jihadists, terrorists, or whatever they are, going to take down the largest economic and military power in the world?

After regaining his mental balance, Valentin asked deliberately, "Is there anything else you can tell me about your plans, Mr. Abdul-Kaliq?"

"God willing, the United States will experience devastation unlike any other in its history. It will be crippled forever!"

The sudden internal heat of unfamiliar fear gripped Valentin. However, he did his best to appear normal despite his elevated heart rate.

Maybe he is exaggerating....

His imagination interrupted his discomfort with flashbacks of the beautiful blue skies and vivid colors of October, which saturated the vibrant and picturesque Princeton University campus where he had studied and made some valuable and lasting friendships. He also recalled the bustling cities of Philadelphia and New York–busy nearby historically rich urban cultural centers of the United States where he had visited a few times during his undergraduate years and had learned to appreciate some of the history of the country. Furthermore, he did not believe that the god this man referred to was the same god most people he knew recognized.

Would these places be changed, or damaged? Would any of their residents or my valued friends die? What about the young brunette woman I met that one time at the Philadelphia Museum of Art just before it closed for the day... the one who excited me so intensely... What was her name...? Ariel? Yes..., Ariel! Will she be only a brief memory forever? What an unbelievably exciting life we could have shared! Will I never see her again? Whatever happened to the concept of only one beneficent god?

Then a frightening thought arose connecting his current interview with other research he had been doing about the disappearance of a Russian general during the second Chechen War.

Suddenly back in the present reality, but with veiled urgency, he said, "I see.... And exactly what is this devastation, and how is it going occur?"

As if sensing that Valentin would have many more critical questions, the mullah ended the interview before the young man might piece together more of the conspiracy than he had intended to reveal.

He said with accustomed authority, "You would be a very foolish young man indeed if you expect me to answer that question. That is my message to the world. Now, our time together is over."

The Sony recorder had just acquired new value harboring evidence of a conversation well beyond its cost as if it had suddenly transformed itself into a precious historic relic that should never be lost or damaged. Mullah Abdul-Kaliq was not a pure enough Muslim to avoid or refrain from evil or even negative thoughts during the current Ramadan. He considered his plans not to be evil or negative at all, but entirely good and positive from a true believer's proper perspective. Valentin was unsettled.

Why does anyone endeavor to inform the entire world of anything? That effort seems indicative of mental instability… or… he really is potentially very dangerous! He just issued a threat…, assuming I would be complicit in publishing his words. The future of humanity could indeed be contingent upon one's interpretation of a presumed source of all universal truth. How can his reality be different from mine? He must know others who have power or influence since he is apparently physically unable to move around much. He did say 'we will put our plans into action!'

CHAPTER 14
Saturday, June 27, 2015

Karina finished another day of practicing dance routines and various rigorous exercises with the constant but encouraging constructive criticism of her mentor. She could turn her body and even spin on her toes–a movement called 'chaine'–at unusually great speed while gracefully holding one finger of either or both hands at an imaginary fixed point above her head. She executed these routines without becoming dizzy or disoriented. She practiced movements like pique, pirouette, plie, and entrechat in various sequences. She also performed static exercises like elevating each foot to a point above her head and holding it there for 30 seconds at a time and longer, frequently without supporting herself against the exercise bar or a wall. After such periods of demanding ultimate performance from her body, she would relax for a few minutes while controlling her breathing and sipping from a bottle of chilled spring water. She executed these and other equally demanding exercise routines several times in varying sequences during hours of practice and instruction. She was spending most of her time as an understudy preparing for the role of Titania in Shakespeare's 'A Midsummer Night's Dream,' which was normally filled by a principal dancer, and featured various solo episodes during the first act of one hour and eight minutes, as well as appearances in the 32-minute second of the two acts. Adaptations of some of Mendelssohn's musical compositions complemented the entire play. As the newest member of the ballet, she graciously accepted the lowest rank among 55 others in the corps de ballet. The entire cast of dancers included 22 principals and 16 soloists in addition to the corps.

Her natural talent and superior energy level easily attracted the attention of Russell Martane II. Despite his professionalism and noteworthy accomplishments during his 25-year international experience as a dancer and most recently as the Ballet Master in Chief, the young Russian beauty undeniably stole at least a portion of his heart. She exuded obvious rare sensitivity and response to the music accompanying her dance. She moved with unique and smooth grace, strength, endurance, and apparent ability to defy gravity on occasion. Her movements were swift when necessary but under constantly marvelous control. She was remarkably steady and disciplined during slower movements as well. Her obvious balance, flexibility, and endurance were amazingly consistent, regardless of her position, transition, or movement. By the end of her third day of practice, he was undeniably convinced of her unusually exciting potential.

With my guidance, she will indeed become the brightest star that this country has not enjoyed for far, far too long!

CHAPTER 15
Tuesday, June 30, 2015

Susan Wong was officially a freelance reporter most recently working for the Washington Post News organization. Unofficially, however, she was also a member of the super-secret Chancellor Organization, one of the many pairs of roving eyes and ears of the reclusive multi-billionaire, Duke Chancellor. She took Professor Teodor Michalik's course at Harvard in 2007. The Chancellor Organization offered employment opportunities to this select source of bright and capable young men and women after they graduated. She was working on an article about the underground international arms trade, and a suspected Turkish arms dealer known as Kasana. Among her notes, she wrote the following:

> *Disturbing reports from the Kazecon News Agency in Kazakhstan point toward increasing contact between certain radical Islamic splinter groups from the Bin Laden era, and the recently organized leaders of the ISIS movement in Syria and Iraq, as well as some of the more radical middle-to high-level political thinkers in Iran. Thorough and timely investigation of every report is not possible currently because of the secretive locations and identities of several of the principal individuals as well as the frequent and sometimes sudden deadly attacks upon unsuspecting innocent citizens, but that does not entirely excuse or minimize the implications of the possible truth of these reports. We may be dealing with a 'where there's smoke, there's fire' phenomenon.*

She sent copies of her initial draft, along with that cover note to her superiors in Washington, as well as to Duke Chancellor. She knew he would respect her ideas and their significance more readily than would the employees in the upper echelons of The Washington Post. Duke's primary interest was the unadorned truth. He had no commercial, financial, or egotistical obligation to share his ideas with the world. He was not in the business of selling newspapers. His consultation business was based upon the truth, and he had worked very hard for decades to achieve a lucrative reputation among corporations and governments around the globe as a trusted source and verification of information. With the proliferation of questionable information–or disinformation–especially throughout the internet, Duke had filled a need among international corporations and various governmental organizations to verify and discover information, and eliminate falsehoods, rumors, false 'news stories,' and propaganda. He could do that primarily because he had no governmental obligation, regulation, or public requirement for burdensome transparency and protocol. He ran a *confidential business* with dedicated, highly intelligent individuals who shared his sense of human perspective and fairness. He had the wealth and influence that facilitated access to information otherwise unavailable to the average person or, many times, even to government agencies.

CHAPTER 16
Monday, July 13, 2015

On this partly cloudy 68-degree day, Colonel Viktor Kovalenko arrived quietly at the headquarters building of the Chelyabinsk military installation at precisely 10 A.M. to assume command. Major Leonid Logonovsky, the prior interim commander, soon to be executive officer, greeted him with an obligatory salute without enthusiasm or a smile and showed him to his office. Major Logonovsky was about six feet, one inch tall, and weighed close to 195 pounds. He had a persistent, but misleading blank facial expression, contrasting intelligent blue eyes, light brown short hair, and a high forehead. A small V-shaped scar pointed downward next to the outside of his right eye. One might imagine that it was an injury from a fight many years ago, but he never offered a detailed explanation to those who inquired. He executed his military duties efficiently, but without humor or even a smile. Perhaps the lack of a woman in his life contributed to his dour appearance and attitude. Maybe his uninspiring appearance contributed to the lack of a woman in his life.

CHAPTER 17
Tuesday, July 14, 2015

Among the many millions of meetings between and among people around the world at any given time, one particularly fateful meeting occurred at noon on this warm day in the city of Balkh, Afghanistan under partly sunny skies. Inside the Green Mosque near the center of the city were three men who wanted the United States out of the Middle East entirely. One primarily wanted revenge for the killing of Osama bin Laden, and another wanted a final solution to the United States' interference with his plans for an Islamic State. The third man, Shamir, was sympathetic to both men because he wanted to see the long-awaited return of Islam to greater world dominance, regardless of the method. He did not have a military organization, nor was he a fighter or an insurgent leader. He was simply a wealthy true believer. He could help bankroll the other two. The three men agreed upon a mutually convenient alliance to achieve world domination. Each agreed to pool their combined resources in intelligence, influence, money, organization, and manpower toward the accomplishment of their common goal–eliminating the United States of America as the primary obstacle to establishing their caliphate to rule the world. Obviously, contemplating or planning world domination was not an evil thought during Ramadan. The Mujahideen 'victory' over the Soviet Union inspired many Islamic extremists to join the Al Qaeda movement and enabled them to believe their greater cause was achievable. Fatih Abdul-Kaliq survived the battle against the Russians under Osama Bin Laden in Afghanistan and proudly bore a sign of his commitment–a 2-inch scar over his left eye allegedly caused by shrapnel.

Ayman Mohammed Rabie al-Zawahiri was born on June 19, 1951, in Maadi, Egypt. He engaged in political Islam while still at school and was arrested at the age of 15 for being a member of the outlawed Muslim Brotherhood, Egypt's oldest and largest Islamist organization. He graduated from Cairo University Medical School in 1974 and received a master's degree in surgery in 1978. He functioned as Osama bin Laden's personal physician. His father, Rabie al-Zawahiri was a professor of pharmacology and died in 1995. The United States State Department still offers a $25 million reward for information leading directly to Ayman's capture. He is a former member of Islamist organizations, which have orchestrated and implemented attacks in North America, Asia, Africa, and the Middle East. He recently had called upon all true believers around the world to unite. Some of those true believers were in Afghanistan and Chechnya and had underground connections with some of the old KGB elements recently participating in the drug trade in Kazakhstan. Fatih Abdul-Kaliq was an ambitious Syrian member of the Islamic State of Iraq and Syria, also known as ISIS, which is composed entirely of Sunni Muslims as opposed to Shia Muslims, who are the minority of all Muslims but are more dominant in Iran and Iraq. His name means 'conqueror, servant of the creator.' Born on September 28, 1972, in Al-Qamishli, Syria, just south of the Turkish border, he had always shown unusual intelligence and imagination in school but studied as little as possible just to get by. His parents taught him to pray five times each day according to Islamic tradition. He subsequently supported himself as a teacher, but also developed expertise in constructing roadside improvised explosive devices-IEDs. Some speculated that those explosives, or the designs for their construction, found their way into Iraq, contributing to the injuries and deaths of many American military service members, as well as many innocent Iraqi citizens.

Shamir became a wealthy 'free-lance' Islamic radical, a true believer who acquired some of his wealth from drug activities in Afghanistan and Kazakhstan. He had been contributing to radical Islamic organizations with money, underground political influence, and old-fashioned arm-twisting during most of the last six years. He was at least as deeply committed to radical Islamic ideals as the Pope was to ideal Catholicism. He was educated, determined, and unknown in the western world. He deliberately maintained as low a profile as possible. He had a grand plan for developing Islamic superiority in the world that would relegate the events of September 11, 2001, to a minor footnote in the history books. He wanted to destroy the United States.

Shamir recognized in Fatih Abdul-Kaliq the kind of determination he wanted to help execute his plan. With Shamir's wealth and influence, he would assure Fatih of a position of power in the new world order he was intent on creating. He would feed the man's imagination with suggestions of the inevitability of Islamic world domination, accelerated by his own plans. He knew about the forces of nature as well as the desires and fears of all men—what moves individuals, and how to influence the masses. He could not escape his own personal charm, daring, brilliance, and intellectual breadth and depth. Harvard was just a waystation—a place to test his emerging ideas and beliefs with debate among the faculty and his classmates. He graduated with honors but was ideologically unscathed and maintained all his true religious beliefs. The freedoms and carefree lifestyles of western cultures dominant among his classmates could not break through his single-minded dedication to extremist Islamic principles or his dream of world domination.

Shamir spoke to the other two, "We will execute several high-profile United States citizens in one day. We have internet access to information about their locations, schedules, and travels. After the executions, we will initiate the rest of the plan. The international and American media will help us by headlining the initial activity, so you will know whether the executions have occurred by watching the news coverage over the internet. Most media attention will focus on those events, so your people should have some freedom of operation to the extent that security measures will concentrate upon individuals instead of what I am planning. Although increased vigilance and security measures are likely throughout the country, it is unlikely that our plan will fail. We believe the manpower available for that degree of security will be stretched to the limits, and many untrained or inexperienced people will be sent to presumed possible, but false targets in dense population areas, including sports arenas, government buildings, airports, seaports, and other border entry points. Electronic surveillance will be intense, so you will limit using any electronic devices because we obviously do not want your locations and movements traced. Is that clear?"

Abdul-Kaliq responded with a facial expression of concentration and finally said, "Yes."

"It is likely that people will conclude that the executions are one complete event. We will give them a week or two to accept that notion, and then we will execute the next phase."

"And what is the next phase?"

Shamir responded with guarded caution, "You will learn that in due time."

"I suspected as much, but I need to have some idea…, a focus…, a guiding light…."

Shamir considered the other man's question without evident emotion for several seconds and then concluded that he should indeed infect the other man's mind with a motivational seed to encourage and sustain his efforts.

"What does every human being fear, my friend…, regardless of his beliefs, wealth, or power?"

"I… I am not… sure what you mean, Shamir."

"Think, my friend…. *Think!*"

After a longer pause than he had sustained up to this point, he finally said, "I would say… death… is what everyone fears."

"You surprise me, Fatih! You did not think thoroughly enough! Those with the proper faith–the best Muslims–do not fear death!"

"What do you mean?"

"I asked, what does every human being fear…. That includes the foolish and the wise, the young and the old, the rich and the poor, the strong and the weak, the learned and the ignorant, men and women alike…, particularly the infidels!"

Fatih was frozen in thoughtless confusion and genuine ignorance of the intent of Shamir's provocation.

"Fear exists in life, not in death! The ultimate fear is *unexpectedly believing* while one is still alive that one's death–the end of everything in life–is realistically imminent and certain…, and that escape from it is *impossible!*"

Fatih continued to stare quizzically into Shamir's shining dark eyes without a clue, but offered, "Well, I know I will die someday…, but in thinking it, knowing it is true, I do not fear it."

Shamir continued, "That is different from looking into the barrel of a loaded gun pointed at your eyes while you are shackled to the floor and seeing the trigger move! Unless you are in *that* kind of position, you do not know real fear!"

After several seconds of silence, Shamir inclined his head and continued, "Look over there near the pulpit…. What do you see?"

Fatih squinted in lack of immediate comprehension as he turned to look, and said, "A candle."

"Yes, my friend…. A candle. A lighted candle. Its flame is but a *grain of sand* in the Sahara of my plan!"

CHAPTER 18
Wednesday, July 15, 2015

After his breakfast, Colonel Kovalenko started to familiarize himself with his new command by visiting every facility and building within the base without advance notice. By late afternoon, he had arrived at the secure concrete vault near the center of the base in a building used for underground storage of nuclear explosive devices. A sergeant guarding the entrance verified his identity, opened the gate for the new base commander to enter the vault, and turned on the overhead lights. Colonel Kovalenko walked down the steel stairs to the lower level of the building and then walked through every aisle in the vault, carefully observing what was on each dark gray steel rack and counting as he went. By the time he returned to the gate, he had noted 91 gray MK-4 series 'suitcase nukes' stored in the facility, each with an explosive yield range between two and eight kilotons. However, one was of a slightly different shape, and darker gray color, as if it had been painted somewhere other than where the others were painted, or presumably manufactured. It was also larger than the others and had no identifying serial number. His original official written inventory indicated only 90 units. Without betraying a hint of his growing concern, he returned to the main level, passed by the sergeant on duty without comment, and left the building under cloudy skies to return to his headquarters office to gather his thoughts.

CHAPTER 19
Thursday, July 16, 2015

**** CHELYABINSK, RUSSIA ****

He picked up the red secure phone receiver on his desk and carefully dialed the number he did not want to dial.

"This is Colonel Viktor A. Kovalenko at Chelyabinsk. Put me through to General Alexi Rusanov at the Nuclear Arms Verification Command."

"One moment, please, Colonel"

After almost two minutes of silence, a firm deep base voice resonated, *"Viktor! How are you?"*

"My health is good, thank you. And yours?"

"I am well, thank you... and looking forward to my retirement next year!"

"Congratulations, General!"

"Thank you! Now, what's on your mind, Viktor?"

"General..., I must be direct. I have great concerns at this base."

"What seems to be the problem, Viktor?"

After a few seconds of mental preparation, the words just escaped as if he had no control over them: "General, I have personally verified an inventory anomaly at Chelyabinsk nuclear storage."

With evident suspicion, the general said, *"What kind of anomaly?"*

"One extra MK-4-like device, unaccounted for on the official inventory I received when I assumed command. It has no identification serial number, and it looks slightly different from, and a little larger than the others."

"You must be mistaken....! Our records are accurate, Colonel! I suggest that you count again!"

"But…"

His voice was cooler, less friendly, and more authoritative as he continued, *"It is simply impossible for Russia to violate its international obligations in this arena, Colonel, so the inventory tomorrow will be the same as the inventory in our records today. Do you understand, Colonel?"*

"Yes, but with all due respect, General…"

"Colonel, you have both the authority and the responsibility to correct your so-called 'anomaly,' so I do not expect to hear anything further about it. Is that clear?"

"Sir, I would like…"

"Goodbye, Colonel!"

Something incomprehensibly mysterious is going on… and I am not sure about what or who is still trustworthy!

By late evening, the peaceful traditional period known as Ramadan in certain specific areas of the world had ended.

CHAPTER 20
Friday, July 17, 2015

THE END OF RAMADAN

**** *ISTANBUL, TURKEY* ****

The Zen Diamond headquarters is located at number 35 Cagaloglu Street, Istanbul, Turkey, which straddles the entrance to the Bosporus connecting the Sea of Marmara west of Istanbul to the Black Sea to the east. The 125-year-old Zen family business had expanded during the most recent several generations to include stores in Antwerp, New York, Dubai, and Moscow. The company's original designers produce over 300,200 pieces of jewelry a year in their own manufacturing facilities for more than 3,010 jewelry stores throughout the world, in addition to about 153 worldwide small stores or kiosks known as 'Zen Corners.'

On this overcast mild day, a man wearing a dark blue business suit with narrow subtle light gray pinstripes, black dress shoes obviously not recently polished, and a white dress shirt with no tie left the main street entrance of the store with a dark burgundy briefcase and walked to the lone yellow 2008 Hyundai taxi waiting at the curb nearest the store. He entered the back of the cab and told the driver in Kazakh-accented Turkish to take him to the Ataturk International airport. The look in the passenger's eye and tone of his rough bass voice told the taxi driver there would be no haggling, and he would be wise not to try to pad either the trip length or the fare. The passenger was obviously not American and exuded a threatening manner. At the end of the first block, the driver stopped at a traffic light. As if on cue, two men rushed from the closest street corner to the cab just as the traffic light changed to green in the taxi's traffic lane direction, and swiftly entered the back passenger area simultaneously, one from each side. The one entering from the driver's side overpowered the original passenger with two powerful blows to his head with a heavy steel chisel, rendering him unconscious. Then the two men emptied the buyer's attaché case containing 93 freestanding finished diamonds into a small jet-black felt pouch with a round blood-red shoelace-sized drawcord. The nervous complicit driver immediately followed the directions coming from the back passenger area, accelerated through the intersection, and continued east toward the Black Sea and away from the airport. At an inconspicuous dirty section of a small fishing pier on the Bosporus, the two perpetrators dragged the unconscious man aboard The East Wind, already moored at the pier. Within 15 minutes, two deckhands cast the mooring ropes onto the pier, and the two-masted schooner silently set sail slightly to the northeast through the Bosporus, and then into the Black Sea to the east for approximately 515 miles.

About halfway through their voyage to the Russian city of Novorossiysk on the northeastern shore, two of the taxi goons anchored the comatose buyer with grade 40 anchor chains to the steel eyelet fixtures of a well-worn 300-pound cement wrecking ball. With the aid of three other deckhands, they tossed both the dealer and the wrecking ball over the side into the water. The cement ball eventually came to rest upon the floor of the Black Sea more than 4,500 feet below the surface. After arriving at the Russian city of Novorossiysk slightly more than 40 hours after leaving Istanbul, they boarded a single-engine Russian-made RA-1005-G propeller plane for the six-hour and 50-minute flight to Chelyabinsk, about 1,540 miles farther to the east. Such small private aircraft are often necessary for basic transportation in some areas of Russia, because the world's largest country, spanning 11 time zones still has thousands of villages and settlements not accessible by good, surfaced roads.

Eventually, Lloyd's of London would be obligated to compensate the Zen organization for its loss. However, one of their senior investigators, Lawrence Thompson would not take that insurance loss lightly and started to conduct his investigation as if it were his only full-time occupation. The average weight of the stolen round cut diamonds was around 3.83 karats. Each held the highest clarity rating of VVS1, with flawless 'D' color, and an average value of $261,660 in United States dollars. The heist had an approximate total wholesale street value of $24,853,320. This group of diamonds, however, also contained several stones specifically registered with a secret unique laser light-dispersion technology by the world's primary wholesaler, DeBeers Diamond Company. That identification system included placing a finished cut diamond in a proprietary manner in clay at the precise center of a hollow globe, three feet in diameter. Over 20 million tiny light sensors affixed to the inside surface of the globe registered the refracted light of a specific laser beam of known frequency and intensity aimed at a specific location on the surface of the stone at a specific angle. The resulting measurable array of reflected colors, intensities, and angles of reflection upon the inside of the globe was electronically documented with a code identifying that specific diamond. The probability of two diamonds having the same 'laser-reflection/dispersion fingerprint' is approximately one per 20 million stones.

The criminal world has used diamonds as currency for as long as diamonds have been the subject of human desire, primarily because they occupy space and storage much more efficiently than equivalent values of cash. They are lightweight and therefore can be transported much more easily than any equivalent world currency or gold, but their liquidity is more problematic. Their liquidity is usually more of a problem for the seller of merchandise taking diamonds as payment than for the buyer using diamonds as currency in a purchase. The seller usually desires to convert the value of the gems eventually into a major world currency, and that can be difficult for those without patience.

**** NSA HEADQUARTERS, FORT MEADE, MARYLAND ****

James Levin was a graduate of the Defense Language Institute at 1759 Lewis Road in Monterey, California early in his United States military obligation in what was known at the time as the Army Security Agency during the early 1970s. After his discharge in 1974, he resumed his college education at the University of Virginia and graduated with a major in Middle Eastern Studies.

The 62-year-old analyst was listening through high-quality headphones to an electronic intercept of a specific cellphone conversation from an unknown location in Syria.

> *"I have a cli (garbled)... who would (garbled)... a small purch (garbled)... What (garbled)... you offer me?"*

"... yes. (garbled)... said (garbled)..."

"... I want (garbled)... with the greatest (garbled)... you can find."

".... (garbled)... will b (garbled)... expen (garbled)... how..."

"That will not be..." (garbled)...

"What?"

"I said (garbled)... million will not (garbled)... problem."

"When (garbled)... where?"

"... details tomorrow... Same (garbled)... differ (garbled)... will call..."

"Praise be (garbled) lah..."

The intercept faded into a dull background steady hissing sound. James leaned forward over his workstation and stared straight ahead at his monitor with his jaw hanging down. His eyes were wide open, scanning from left to right across his monitor, looking for the visual electronic signature of the signal again. The prior densely jagged voice pattern window in the upper-left portion of his computer monitor became a flat green line with occasional random low amplitude spikes. He waited quietly, suspended in anxiety and apprehension. Suddenly his body demanded another breath. A small, but intriguing series of bits and bytes among the trillions of batches of digital information racing throughout cyberspace had just briefly visited his infinitesimally small place in the universe, and then it was gone.

Then a familiar voice crashed through the walls of his intense concentration, "Hey, Jimmy! Do you want some popcorn? I'm goin' to the snack bar."

He ignored her.

"Hey, Jimmy!"

"NOT NOW!"

"Geez! I only asked whether you wanted some *popcorn*!"

"Sorry, Jill. Get superman in here, right now...!"

One of Jill Smith's 'boys'–the four male analysts for whom she provided secretarial and technical assistance in the analysis group–had just stumbled upon something extremely important, forgot about her popcorn, and rushed to their supervisor's office.

"Levin's found something important.... He wants you to see it right now!"

James Levin was still concentrating upon the bright green comatose electronic squiggles flowing across his monitor, adjusting a few switches and knobs on his receiver, turning up the volume, but the voices were gone when William Hickey, his supervisor, got to his workstation.

"Okay, Levin, what d'ya have?"

"I think someone in Syria is trying to make arrangements to buy a nuclear bomb! Here's my transcription."

After a minute of silent concentration as he read and then pondered the transcription, Hickey uttered solemnly, "Holy shit! This is not good! You *did check* to see that it was being recorded, right? Did you get the phone number?"

"Yeah, recorders were on, and yeah, it's on the other side… 963-42-128-3577… in the Hadar, Syria exchange. I already checked."

"Where was the other end of the conversation?"

"I don't know that yet, sir. It'll probably take a little time to figure that out."

William Hickey was a dedicated career government service employee. The only job he ever had was at the National Security Agency after he graduated first in his class from the City College of New York in 1976 with a bachelor's degree in Philosophy. His native intelligence and unique education from growing up in the Big Apple qualified him for an interview for employment at the agency shortly after he graduated. With the personality of a respectful 'wise guy,' he gradually worked his way up through the ranks of the NSA while mellowing every few years with a renewed appreciation of how dangerous the world really was becoming. He still had remnants of his former youthful physique and handsome face, but his obviously retouched dark hair was thinning, and his gut was not. He proudly wore a red bow tie every day to work, and always wore suspenders and colorful shirts that may or may not have clashed with his tie or his suspenders, depending upon the day of the week. However, he naturally commanded enough respect during conversation to squelch any premature comments about his attire or his intellect.

"Okay…. Listen up, everybody! We're gonna monitor this number 24-7. No snack break, no lapse in coverage. Not one second! Jill, make sure food breaks are staggered for each shift, and that every shift operates by the same rules–recorders always on, and someone always listening to that channel 24-7. We need to find out who these guys are… *both of them!* I'm gonna pass this up the line right now as is."

CHAPTER 21
Saturday, July 18, 2015

A message from Valentin Murat arrived through System 15, one of Duke Chancellor's several impenetrable communications systems, on the top floor of The Plymouth Building, situated in the woods just west of I-95 in Maryland. That building was coincidentally only several miles north of the National Security Agency Headquarters Building at Fort Meade on the other side of the interstate highway. Valentin did not have any credible connections with any state security organizations, so he sent his information to the only person he knew who would know how to assess and handle it properly and get it to the people who needed to know about it with the degree of importance it deserved.

'You will recall that a substantial number of diamonds were stolen at the Hong Kong international gem show exactly one year ago, on Friday, July 18, 2014. It is my unsubstantiated theory that an international arms dealer stole these diamonds. My hunch is bolstered only by the recent diamond robbery in Istanbul. A certain wholesaler from the De Beers Company has disappeared, and my sources in the Turkish State Police indicated to me that there is absolutely no trace of the stolen merchandise, although I suspect that is the typical result. The dealer's last known location was Istanbul, most likely at the Zen store on Cagaloglu Street. I understand that the company has instituted a new and unique process of identifying certain diamonds. Therefore, I would suggest that some new method be established to monitor diamond shipments or transactions at known retail or wholesale outlets, particularly if they do not have

the usual legitimate certificates of authenticity. In that way, we might locate some of the diamonds from the Istanbul heist and shed some light upon whoever might attempt to move or liquidate some diamonds, possibly in a transaction for armaments, leading to the identification of principals related to these transactions. Official commercial armament companies and their international sovereign buyers do not, as a rule, deal in diamonds, so I suspect someone under the radar with dangerous motives might be at work somewhere. This is just a thought for your consideration because I have no way of reaching high enough in the international law enforcement community in a credible manner with this kind of thinking. V.M.'

Duke replied:

'Point noted and thank you for your thoughts. I'm very glad to have you onboard!'

****** FORT MEADE, MARYLAND ******

James Levin, Jill Smith and her boys, and William Hickey had an uneventful day. The elusive cellphone signal did not return. Unknown to them, the telephone conversation they intercepted yesterday came from a cellphone that no longer exists. However, James Levin continued to search through the millions of conversations and 'clips' of conversations stored in the vast NSA computer memory capacity as part of the MYSTIC program that started in 2009, which enabled 'retrospective retrieval,' and reached full capacity in 2011. He was not scheduled to work on Sunday, but his other interests and his personal life would have to wait. He simply had to follow up. After more than 10 hours of intense searching, insatiable curiosity, and a minor peppering of fear, he found the recording of that same conversation from the other cellphone. Satellite triangulation determined the coordinates of that other cellphone at 39.043889 degrees latitude, and 125.758477 degrees longitude, which appeared in the intercept summary at the end of the recording. It was after 10 P.M. His exhaustion finally eclipsed his curiosity, and he had not had supper. He turned the lights off in his office and walked unevenly out into the hallway. The door closed automatically behind him, triggering the silent automatic locking mechanism with a distinct 'click.' He walked down the lighted empty hall to the nearest exit. The information would have to wait until tomorrow. He continued out into the huge and generously illuminated parking lot, walking through the typical nighttime number of unoccupied parking spaces directly toward his now isolated bright red 2013 Mini Cooper. Its location was more obvious than it had been during the massive morning flow of workers searching for the most convenient, and eventually the least inconvenient parking spaces. He opened the car door and immediately slipped into his subconscious 'home commute' behavior routine–close door, foot on brake, ignition, seatbelt, headlights, radio, transmission in gear, foot off the brake–and headed for the exit. His intellectual concentration briefly interrupted his habitual driving concentration.

Where the hell is 39 and change by 125 and change? Somewhere on the far side of the Pacific Ocean?

**** *JFK International Airport* ****

Umar left JFK International Airport at 7:20 P.M. on Aeroflot Flight SU103, which was due to land at Sheremetyevo nine hours and 25 minutes later.

CHAPTER 22
Sunday, July 19, 2015

**** CHELYABINSK, RUSSIA ****

Colonel Kovalenko arrived unannounced at the nuclear storage building within the Chelyabinsk Army Base, walked toward the sentry at the main entrance, and returned the obligatory salute without betraying his concern. He continued within the facility, following normal procedure, again showing his identification badge at the next sentry post.

"Unlock the gate, Sergeant Voloshin!"

"Yes, sir."

"I will not need your assistance, Sergeant. Remain at your post."

"Yes, sir."

Colonel Kovalenko turned away from the sergeant with focused intent evident upon his face, and a slightly elevated heart rate. He went through the heavily painted gray steel gateway, closed the gate behind him until it clearly latched in the locked position, turned all the main lights on, and walked purposefully into the vault. He took out his pad and pen and started checking off serial numbers, comparing each one on his pad with the white stenciled numbers on each physical device on the chest-level gray steel rack in front of him. Step, by step he followed the same procedure down the aisle, right to left, checking off every device against his list. Every one of the MK series devices had to have an official serial number by military regulation. Perplexed, he returned to the steel gate, motioned to the sergeant to open it, and walked impassively back through to the entry station. The gate slammed shut behind him into the automatically locked position.

"Thank you, Sergeant."

Somewhat less perplexed, but with growing suspicion and fear, Colonel Kovalenko returned to his office with a ledger in his own handwriting, accounting for all 90 nuclear devices, and confirming that *only* 90 were there.

Something is seriously amiss, and I am going to get to the bottom of it!

****** ISTANBUL, TURKEY ******

Umair Kasana left Ataturk International Airport at 1:30 A.M. into an overcast sky on Moscow-based Transaero Airlines, Flight 802 bound for Vnukovo International Airport, scheduled to arrive at 5:30 A.M. After landing, he would have an 18-hour and five-minute layover to review his plans before continuing to Chelyabinsk.

****** LONDON, ENGLAND ******

Lawrence Thompson left Heathrow International Airport at 7:55 A.M. on Turkish Airlines Flight 1988 and arrived at Ataturk International Airport in western Istanbul at 1:45 P.M. After minimal customs procedures, he hailed one of the ubiquitous late model Hyundai taxis outside the airport arrival terminal and told the driver to take him to 35 Cagaloglu Street. After an hour and 14 minutes, mostly spent in hectic, random, and chaotic vehicular traffic, he paid his fare, exited the taxi, and walked through the entrance to the Zen Diamond store. He calmly introduced himself to the clerk behind a jewelry display case to his right and asked to see the manager.

The thin young dark-haired Turkish woman with minimal makeup responded, "Ah, yes! We have been expecting you, Mr. Thompson! If you wait just a few moments, I will get Mr. Erkan for you."

Tisha (meaning happy and joyous woman) came around to the main floor from behind a row of display cases, walked toward the back of the store, and disappeared. Just 30 seconds later, she reappeared, walking ahead of a distinguished-looking white-haired trim man wearing a dark blue pinstripe business suit, white shirt, and dark blue tie. His appearance betrayed a modest success in denying his sixth decade of life but not his fourth decade in the jewelry business. The two walked toward the current visitor.

"I am Lawrence Thompson, representing Lloyd's of London. Thank you for seeing me, Mr. Erkan. I have been obliged to investigate this matter, so please do forgive my urgent manner. I understand that you have some recorded surveillance camera coverage of your building. Is that correct?"

"Thank you for coming, Mr. Thompson! Yes, we have such video equipment. The police have already reviewed the recordings but have not been very informative about their findings. However, I understand your interest as well."

"I would like to review the information from the day of the recent robbery on Friday, July 17–all 24 hours of that day, please."

"I understand. I had been expecting you would want to do that, so I have prepared a room for you with everything you might need. Come with me–right this way, please!"

The two men walked to the back of the store and entered a small meeting room next to the manager's office. For much of the next three hours, Lawrence studied the digital recordings from four separate cameras, two outside, and two inside the store on a 17-inch Dell Latitude laptop computer, fast-forwarding through obviously uninformative sections. Out of the total of 96 hours of recordings, he isolated a total of fewer than 90 seconds of an unusual series of events. The first image of a man with a dark burgundy briefcase, presumed to be the diamond dealer, was leaving the store and getting into a cab. The cab moved left to right down the street to the first intersection, just barely visible at the right-most border of the wide-angle view. The other outside camera had an even wider-angle lens covering much of the street in both directions in front of the store. Near the right side of the somewhat distorted wide-angle view, two men in dark clothing who might have been at least partially responsible for the robbery rushed to that same cab, opened both rear doors simultaneously, jumped into the back seat, closed the doors, and then the cab moved forward as the traffic light changed to green.

Thompson said dryly, "Someone obviously knew that person with a briefcase full of diamonds was going to be at that location, and in that particular cab. Who?"

"Honestly, I do not know. However, you should know that De Beers officials informed me that several uniquely identified gems were included with the batch that was stolen, so it is possible to identify them in the future, contrary to common belief. That possibility could contribute to identifying other people, depending upon whether someone tries to get an appraisal or show the diamond to a dealer or convert the value of at least one diamond to cash somewhere. We may never know that, but there is some hope, anyway. Most people just want to have a diamond to look at or keep because of its personal significance and not sell it. Therefore, when we see a sale or even an *attempted* sale, it should be worth looking into. They have apparently alerted all their retail outlets to be extra vigilant and to report any new suspicious transactions immediately."

"All right…, that's certainly a step in the right direction, but I shall have to conduct my own investigation as well. If you have nothing further to tell me at this time, then I must be on my way."

"No…, nothing else that I am aware of right now, but I will let you know if something else develops."

"Here is my card, Mr. Erkan. Thank you very much for your time. Good day."

****** Moscow, Russia ******

The man in black left Vnukovo International Airport at 11:30 P.M. on UTAir Flight 555, a domestic Russian carrier bound for Chelyabinsk, due to arrive at 4:15 A.M. the next morning.

****** Fort Meade, Maryland ******

Howard Horwitz was on break, so he pursued his uninvited theories about terrorism with James Levin and sauntered into his personal space.

"Just humor me for a minute, will you? Suppose that someone we don't know about is still really pissed off about our raid in Abbottabad in May 2011. I mean angry enough to be obsessed with retribution at any cost, and at an unimaginably excessive level. Do you really believe Bin Laden's death is the end of terrorism? I'm not so sure, Jim. Do you think the Pakistanis are proud of our waltzing into their country and killing Osama Bin Laden? Why do you suppose the president didn't tell them we were coming? Because he obviously didn't trust them, *that's why!* And why didn't he trust them? Because our military units or unmanned strikes had always arrived at least several minutes too late in every previous attempt to nail him in the last decade! That tells me at least one person is 'in the know' in Pakistan, Afghanistan, or some other 'stan' somewhere, who was connected to Osama or someone in his organization and got the word out about our coming for him! And we trusted the Afghans at Tora Bora? Give me a break! Maybe it was the Taliban. Maybe the informer was someone in the ISI. And by the way, whatever happened to all his wives after that Abbottabad raid? I, for one, don't believe that all the troublemakers are at Guantanamo, nor do I believe that al-Qaeda is as debilitated as the president says. Ayman al-Zawahiri is still alive, and he is apparently the new number one guy. Someone in our State Department is willing to pay a $25 million reward for information leading to his capture. Didn't Zawahiri call on fellow Muslims to kidnap Western tourists in Muslim countries in 2012? Those worldwide United Nations sanctions against him for being a member of al-Qaeda apparently have not had any effect. The philosophy of terrorism still lives, and I would not be surprised if the al-Qaeda organization has spawned other groups or has a new name–like ISIS. These people used to wage war over *stealing camels* in the seventh century, for God's sake, and they want the entire world to go back to the seventh century! How screwed up is that? They're big on revenge, and that's at least one reason why the story is not over! And by the way, exactly how does an Egyptian physician–theoretically a man of life science and dedicated to saving lives–become a terrorist? That guy is getting up in his years, (Born June 19, 1951) so I wouldn't be surprised if some yet unknown name is elbowing his way to the head job even as we speak–someone we don't know anything about! *Hey!* Are you listening to me?"

James Levin was just finishing a strawberry jelly-filled doughnut, quietly trying to absorb Howard's tirade without offending him.

Then Levin said idly, "One of his wives apparently lives in Jeddah."

"How do you know that?"

"I *read*."

"So... do you believe everything you read?"

"We're both in the intelligence business. Where I do not have personal knowledge or research, yes..., I tend to believe what appears credible."

Howard finished his part of the conversation in frustration, "You're exasperating sometimes!"

Levin looked askance at him with a facial equivalent of '*REALLY?*' Then he returned to his work concentration and moved his mouse next to a few crumbs on his desk, easing the arrow cursor across his computer monitor, while carefully watching the coordinate numbers change in the small white window moving with the cursor. He was trying to find the visual map location of the signal transmission from that last cellphone conversation.

Suddenly he choked on a mouthful of doughnut and then exclaimed, "HOLY SHIT!"

Jill Smith called over to him, "What's going on, Levin?"

"I need superman, right now!"

Howard drifted away from Levin, and said, "Okay, Jimmy.... I know you're busy. See you later...."

She lurched out of her chair and raced into the supervisor's office, but he was not there. Then she hurried back to Levin's station and said, "He's not in his office! Do you need me to go find him?"

"YES! I mean NO! Ping his pager!"

She hurried back to her desk and pressed a button on her desk phone, just as William Hickey, the section supervisor opened the door and walked in.

Levin shouted to him, "It's Moranbong Park!"

Hickey looked over at him blankly, and responded, "*What's* Moranbong Park?"

"The location of the other end of that ominous telephone intercept on Friday!"

Hickey still looked at him with a blank facial expression. He had not immersed himself in the search as intensely as Levin had, so he could not immediately make the association that was so readily evident to Levin.

After noting the implicit lack of comprehension in Hickey's face, Levin said with emphasis, "That's in *Pyongyang*, Mr. Hickey!"

"Holy Shit!"

"Yeah.... That's what I said, too!"

"Why didn't you just say Pyongyang in the first place?"

"Well, sir, I thought it was odd that the call was from a cellphone in a public place–Moranbong Park–and not some kind of government office building or any other kind of building. If a government person of some sort was on the line, then why was he going to all the trouble of not having this conversation from his office? Maybe someone we may not know about over there is flying solo… without official sanction. Or…, maybe the government has nothing to do with it, and the guy was not a government type in the first place, but…"

"Not likely at all…"

"Pretty scary either way, don't you think?"

Hickey said thoughtfully, "Yeah…. It is…. I've got to send this upstairs right away. Stick around in case I need you to provide the details."

CHAPTER 23
Monday, July 20, 2015

About 1.3 million people live in the industrial city of Chelyabinsk, Russia, located approximately 1,106.3 miles east of Moscow, and about 82 miles north of the Kazakhstan border. It is the sister city to Columbia, South Carolina. On February 14, 2013, a meteor sliced through the upper atmosphere, clearly visible from the entire metropolitan area, and created a shock wave responsible for about 1,500 deaths in the area. Few people in that region or in the rest of the world knew what was stored within the Chelyabinsk military installation just slightly northeast of the city proper. No one would ever know the utter devastation that undoubtedly would have occurred if that meteor had traveled closer to or hit the storage facility inside the army base. Most people had enough to think about with the daily business of earning a living and taking care of their families without contemplating Armageddon.

The cloudless, moonless night of July 21, 2015, brought Fahrenheit temperatures down to the low 60s at 2 A.M. A common IVECO C-50 van, obviously unprofessionally spray-painted dark gray with several splotches of dark green and medium milk-chocolate brown, turned north and away from Pobedy Street and parked behind a small grove of trees between the street and the old, barbed wire exterior perimeter of the military base. The moon would not rise until 9:44 A.M. the following day. A very fit man wearing black clothing and a black ski mask was in the driver's seat, and another man wearing identical clothing exited from the passenger side of the cab with an eight-inch hunting knife strapped to his leg, a bolt cutter strapped to his back, and carried an AK-

47 type 2 automatic rifle. In his ammunition pockets, he had four extra curved clips with the standard 30 rounds of 7.62 x 39mm ammunition in each. He walked carefully to the exterior barbed wire fence about 90 feet outside the main 16-foot-high gray concrete wall of the interior base perimeter. The driver waited in nervous silence. He would drive away in exactly one hour, whether his disposable comrade had returned with the merchandise or not.

At precisely 2:15 A.M., the electrical power to the base stopped. Three minutes later, a man dressed in civilian clothing approached the area from farther north between the western wall to his left and the barbed wire perimeter to his right. He walked deliberately with the obvious effort necessary to drag the heavy duffle bag, just as the man in black started cutting the chain-link fence and coil of barbed wire laced through the bottom of the fence all the way to the ground. The base was curiously quiet. The German Shepard dogs were not on patrol in the open weed-infested dirt corridor between the barbed wire perimeter and the main 16-foot high outside perimeter cement wall surrounding the compound. Within 45 seconds, the man with the duffle bag was on the civilian side of the barbed wire fence outside the compound. The two men hurried to the waiting van as quickly as they could within the limits imposed by grasping opposite ends of the bulky duffle bag. At 2:51 in the morning, the driver was at the rear cargo door of the van and opened it as soon as he heard the others approaching through the small grove of trees. The nervous man in black helped the man from the compound place the duffle bag in the cargo area next to several boxes of bottled water, piroshki, two loaves of black bread, one large loaf of rye bread, and a small cardboard carton containing a few paper packages of non-perishable foods and various snacks. Another man in black mended the fence with wire sufficiently to hide the break for a while—maybe a long time. By 3:28 A.M., the driver closed and locked the cargo doors, and all three men entered the van. Local uniformed police were curiously absent from that area. The van slowly moved out onto Pobedy Street heading west, and within 13 minutes turned onto the M-5 highway heading south.

At precisely 3:50 A.M., the electrical power in the military installation mysteriously returned, and a series of dissonant alarms and wailing sirens started blaring repeatedly throughout the compound and most of the city of Chelyabinsk. Among Russia's roughly 59,870,000 internet users, a few Chelyabinsk residents started to log onto the internet social websites with comments and questions about the alarm, much like the local residents in Abbottabad did as the United States helicopters carrying SEAL Team Six hovered over Osama Bin Laden's compound during the night of May 2, 2011. Shortly thereafter, Alan Woodward, an NSA communications analyst at Fort Meade logged the increased communications traffic originating from the Chelyabinsk area via a United States VORTEX satellite positioned about 200 miles above Earth.

The van continued south out of Chelyabinsk on the M-36 highway, also known as the Ural Highway, through the lake district toward the small farming town of Voroshilovka, about 386 miles from Chelyabinsk. Almost eight and a half hours after leaving the military installation, the van arrived just outside the town along the side of the road near an intersection with a nameless narrow dirt road through a large flat field of lush mature green corn stalks stretching as far as the eye could see toward the east. The three men left the cab, quickly went to the rear of the van, and opened the door to verify the contents of the duffle bag. Satisfied that the device was indeed what they had expected, the man in black handed the Russian a small tan leather pouch slightly larger than a grapefruit. The Russian opened it and carefully emptied it upon a clear area of the floor of the cargo area and counted the 60 sparking D-clarity clear carbon gems, ranging in weight from 2.5 to about 3.5 karats, with a presumed total value of approximately $30 million in United States currency.

The military officer said, "You will recall that if I find that these are not worth what we agreed upon, then my KGB comrades and their international underground friends will be looking for you. Do we understand each other, gentlemen?"

The man in black responded firmly, "We do not disappoint our customers, Major! We have a reputation to maintain!"

Major Leonid Logonovsky did not mention that he had an ace in the hole–the real operational codes–a source of future revenue, bargaining advantage, and security, neatly printed so anyone could read and understand them. Within three minutes, an identical van, but with a slightly different spray-painted color pulled up behind the first van from the intersecting dirt road through the cornfields to the east and stopped, leaving the engine running. The accomplice from the military base got out of the first van and entered the other one. Major Logonovsky stared at the obscure dark forms of the three men behind the windshield for a few seconds and then turned slowly toward the man in black and his accomplice.

"We will follow you for most of our journey–to 'confuse' any possibly interested third parties... gentlemen. These men are experts in special tactics."

The man in black and his accomplice entered the first van, and Major Logonovsky got in the second van. Within a minute, the two vehicles continued south. Approximately 20 minutes later, a dirty white Mercedes automobile turned onto the highway and moved advantageously through traffic to within four vehicles behind the two vans, and then maintained that position, give or take a few vehicles more or less as traffic allowed.

****** *TEL AVIV, ISRAEL* ******

David Rosenberg graduated from Tel Aviv University in 1993 with a degree in Business Management and earned an MBA degree from Harvard in 1996 before returning to Israel, where Mossad recruited him. He eventually rose through the ranks to become Director of Operations. He had become acquainted with Professor Teodor Michalik while he was at Harvard during several faculty-student social occasions, and the professor became favorably impressed with the young man's intellectual breadth and stubborn pursuit of the truth. His mind resembled a steel trap and contributed to his reputation as a formidable debate opponent and potential investigator. Although he did not take professor Michalik's course, the professor mentioned his name to Duke Chancellor as someone he might want to have in his organization. Professor Michalik was one of the few people from whom Duke was inclined to take any advice. He sent his trusted lieutenant Joe Czarzhynensky to Tel Aviv with the task of interviewing David Rosenberg and forming an opinion about whether he would be a good fit in The Chancellor Organization. Joe again left his restaurant in Reading, Pennsylvania in the hands of his close friend and manager of the restaurant, Bart Lupold. He drove to the Philadelphia International Airport southeast of Reading and proceeded to Terminal A, Gate 19. US Airways Flight 796 was not scheduled to leave until 9:34 P.M.–another 53 minutes–so he took the time to relax and soon succumbed to a light snooze in his seat in the departure lounge.

Everything was unfamiliar. The sky was overcast. He did not recognize any of the few buildings or the roads, and he did not know how he got there. He was alone... alone like he had never experienced before. Not another soul was within sight. The only sound was from the steady mild wind. It was terribly frightening. The only cars he could see were in disarray, empty and not moving. He was hungry and started to look for a grocery store or a restaurant. None were nearby, so he walked. He kept walking... and walked some more even though he was extremely tired. The sky was darkening from the west. At least he believed that was west... Why would it be dark in the west? A group of buildings was down in the valley about a mile ahead, so he walked toward them. When he got there, he saw a grocery store, but it was closed. The sign on the front door said, 'NO FOOD.'

The airport public address system suddenly announced that his flight was boarding, and he lurched back into reality as his hand flew involuntarily to the side and the back of it smacked the armrest, spreading rare, but momentary pain over his hand and slightly up his arm. He winced with nature's evidence that he was certainly awake. He grasped his carry-on bag with his other hand and forced himself to hurry to the Jetway.

**** ISTANBUL, TURKEY ****

In the unexamined course of human history, people disappear every so often without much explanation or apparent reason, and sometimes without a trace of meaningful evidence. Most others tend not to notice, unless the one who disappeared had a recognizable name or a special position in the social, political, or economic machinery of the world, or was a concerned friend or acquaintance of such a person. Most often, however, those who disappear do not have even a remote connection to the fate of the entire world. A farmer in Iowa could not be expected to know, let alone care whether someone was killed half a world away in Istanbul, Turkey, a city with over 13.8 million people, and then unceremoniously dumped into the Black Sea with a 300-pound cement pendant. A business executive or homeless person in Chicago or a lawyer in London could not be bothered with such information, either. That disappearance could have been an isolated event, a result of revenge or simple madness—but it was not. It was a small but necessary consequence of deliberate activity within someone's grand plan for the future of us all.

Security officials of the De Beers Diamond Company inevitably learned that one of their salespeople had no activity within the organization, or within their computers. Someone was not where he was expected within a reasonable period. Someone did not meet someone else at the appointed time and place. Someone did not show up for work, did not answer a string of phone calls, did not move his parked car for days, and did not leave even a trace of his existence. Then the official machinery of inquiry began. People started to notice. The Istanbul police started to notice. They had the license number of the taxi from the video surveillance tapes at the Zen store on Cagaloglu Street. Lawrence Thompson had the $585,000 license number from the taxi as well.

That price is a 10 percent increase over the past year. Art, stamps, and baseball cards are not the only examples of 'unofficial' investments in the world. Operating a taxi in Istanbul is big business, with partial ownership in a license trading on several private unregulated bourses within remote working-class sections of the city, because the city government had not increased the number of permits issued for taxis, and only Turkish citizens could buy a license. Turkish banks finance the purchase of about 1,000 taxi licenses a year, representing annual total lending of over $9,400,000. Not surprisingly, a growing business in as many as 40,000 unmarked, unlicensed cabs has developed. The headquarters of that business is in the back streets of the Gungoren district, close to the Oto Center in the Bagcilar neighborhood below the road that links Europe to Asia. The number of authorized licenses remained at 17,353 while the population growth increased from 9.2 million in 1997 to more than 13.8 million recently. It is in effect a monopolistic market, complete with its own terminology and practices. Istanbul has about one taxi per 805 people, compared with 662 in New York City, and 363 in London. Since the price of a license is so high, slices of permits also called 'plates,' trade as 'wheels,' representing quarters of a 'plate.' At the Oto Center, a quarter of a 'wheel' is called a 'nut' and sells for about $24,580. Despite the price, as many as 20 license plates a day change hands. Registered taxi drivers, who often work 12 hours a day, must pay as much as the equivalent of $1,731.23 per month, or more than $67 per working day to rent a license plate, thereby placing a severe burden upon their ability to make a profit. However, the license plate owner is not necessarily the person who drives the car. It is therefore understandable how a certain taxi driver could be persuaded by the equivalent of $50,000 to be at a particular location, at a certain time, on a specific date, ignore certain varieties of uncivilized behavior, and then drive his passengers in any condition to a specific location near a remote pier. Furthermore, it is equally understandable that he could conveniently forget the whole episode and then hustle back to high-traffic areas to try to snag the next fare. He needed to feed his family, just like every other head of household. He had expenses, just like every other small business operator. What harm could arise from being paid to be at the appointed location at the appointed time? Is it always necessary to investigate the source and purpose of a request to justify receiving payment? The offer of cash usually comes from someone either unable or unwilling to act on his own, to take responsibility for what he wants to have or do, to accomplish certain purposes hidden in his own mind and in his own philosophy of the world. Many times, it is also unwise even to talk about such occurrences, particularly to the police.

CHAPTER 24
Tuesday, July 21, 2015

About 133 miles northwest of Tajikistan's capital of Dushanbe, the two southbound vans entered the notorious Anzob Tunnel as the temperature hovered
around 82 degrees. By that time, the dirty white Mercedes was immediately
behind the second van. The village that originally had a popular market on
Mondays grew to become Dushanbe, which means 'Monday' in the Persian
language. Until 1929, the city was known in Russian as Dyushambe, and from
1929 to 1961 as Stalinabad. At 11,056 feet above sea level, the tunnel connects
the Tajik capital to the country's second-largest city, Khujand to the north.
Prior to the completion of the tunnel in March of 2006 at a cost of about $110
million in United States currency, travelers had to cross the border into Uzbekistan to the west to travel between the two cities. Before the tunnel was
completed, the threat of avalanches throughout the year led to periodic dis-
ruptions of commerce. The tunnel is also a transit route between Dushanbe
and Uzbekistan's capital Tashkent. The Anzob tunnel soon became a symbol
of goodwill between the peoples of Iran and Tajikistan, who share a common
history, language, and culture. Construction was started in 2003 by the Iranian
Saber International consortium. Its completion put an end to Uzbekistan's
ability to halt traffic between Tajikistan's two largest cities. Due to the significance of the tunnel, limited traffic flow was permitted after a driver signed a
waiver form specifying potential hazards like flooding, noxious exhaust, and
consequent smog from construction equipment still operating periodically inside the tunnel. The final construction phase included the installation of ven-

tilation and drainage infrastructure. The entire journey through the tunnel could take as little as 15 minutes in extraordinarily light traffic with little water on the pavement, to almost an hour in heavy traffic with flooding from water seeping through the ceiling of the tunnel from the mountain overhead. However, it reduced the pre-tunnel travel time between Dushanbe and Khujand by about five hours. The tunnel was usually dark because the few electric lights near the ceiling that were functioning emitted inadequate light, and the dirty vehicle headlights could not penetrate much of the automotive exhaust-laden stale wet air. Although large fans rotated near the middle of the tunnel, they were ineffective in maintaining a constant flow of fresh air against the airflow caused by traffic. Therefore, the concentration of automotive exhaust in the tunnel tended to remain constant and high. One and a half traffic lanes were available to permit the culturally chaotic traffic to move in both directions without any coordinated or organized human or automatic traffic controls. The three-vehicle caravan moved well into the stifling exhaust-filled tunnel along with other traffic at a pace consistent with driver expectations of large potholes, both visible and submerged with an unknown depth. The trucks ahead of them provided a 'road litmus test' with their larger wheels and higher ground clearance. The somewhat compensating benefit of being behind one of those trucks enabled an observant driver to navigate through and around most of the underwater hazards to some extent by watching the behavior of the truck ahead and following, or not following, carefully in its tire paths.

After traffic eventually slowed to another halt, the two men exited the first van, and then casually removed the 150-pound duffle bag from the rear cargo area. They carried it between them while stepping through the water on the pavement in the darker space between the west wall of the tunnel and the uneven line of traffic. They passed the second van and continued to the trailing dirty white 2004 Mercedes E-Class automobile. The driver of that car had already released the trunk lid latch as the men approached. They went to the rear of the car, lifted the trunk lid, placed the duffle bag inside the trunk in less than 15 seconds, closed the trunk lid, and returned to the forward van without attracting unwanted attention in the poorly lighted and murky tunnel. More importantly, the mountain above the tunnel hid the transfer from the prying eyes of drones or satellites orbiting far above Earth. However, in the small black Fiat behind the Mercedes, a male journalist from the Kazecon

News Agency watched the unusual activity. Valentin Murat was a reporter specializing in news and information about the securities markets, legislation, industries, and companies doing business in Kazakhstan. One of the men looked his way with a brief dark stare before returning to the truck. After another four minutes, traffic eased forward again. The cargo transfer was just another unplanned innocent inconvenience in the Tunnel of Death, so named because asphyxiation from automotive exhaust inside it was a real danger.

When the snow melts in spring, the tunnel is at its most treacherous. Every year several people die inside it from carbon monoxide poisoning. Apparently, no one else had paid much attention to two men carrying a duffle bag from a truck to a car, except the reporter in the black Fiat. It was part of the nature of the culture. Maybe it was another shipment of drugs. No one cared, because so much of the economic structure of Tajikistan was dependent upon, if not controlled by the drug trade of about 90 tons of heroin per year. To show too much interest in someone else's 'business' could be an invitation to eventual personal, or family harm, or even death. The unusual wealth evident in expensive foreign automobiles and palatial houses in attractive residential settings on both sides of the Varzob River north of Dushanbe in a civil war-torn country like Tajikistan suggested an underlying economic system based upon collusion between 'business' and 'government' in the drug trade. The occasional law enforcement was symbolic and superficial, but never effective in the end, and confirmed the relative value of social and individual integrity trumped by sufficient sums of money.

Farther downhill on the M-34 highway closer to Dushanbe, the largest city in Tajikistan, they drove through the Varzob district, containing luxury villas of the rich and powerful. No doubt, drug trade profits paid for many of those houses that line both banks of the Varzob River, which roils and roars down into the valley below.

**** *TEL AVIV, ISRAEL* ****

Joe arrived at 2:33 P.M. at Tel Aviv International Airport, Terminal 3. He rented a small dark blue 2015 Ford Focus sedan from Hertz in the airport terminal south of the city and drove for a little more than an hour to Tel Aviv, continued north through the city, and then slightly farther north to the distinctive Mossad headquarters building.

Mossad was formed on December 13, 1949, as the Central Institute for Coordination at the recommendation of Prime Minister David Ben-Gurion to Reuven Shiloah, who created Mossad. Ben-Gurion wanted a central body to coordinate and improve cooperation between the existing security services—the army's intelligence department (AMAN), the Internal Security Service (Shin Bet), and the foreign office's 'political department.' In March 1951, Mossad was reorganized and made a part of the prime minister's office, reporting directly to the prime minister. It is responsible for intelligence collection, covert operations, and counterterrorism, protecting Jewish communities as well as bringing Jews to Israel from countries where official Aliyah agencies are forbidden. Its director reports directly to the Prime Minister.

Mossad informed the FBI and CIA in August 2001 that based on its intelligence, as many as 200 terrorists were slipping into the United States and planning 'a major assault on the United States.' The Israeli intelligence agency cautioned the FBI that it had picked up indications of a 'large-scale target' in the United States and that Americans would be 'very vulnerable.' However, it is not known whether United States authorities thought the warning was credible, or whether it contained enough details to allow counter-terrorism teams to create an effective response. A month later, terrorists struck at the World Trade Center and the Pentagon.

Joe entered the northeast larger building and registered at the reception desk, indicating he was an expected visitor of David Rosenberg.

The young, dark-haired female receptionist smiled slightly and said, "Good afternoon, Mr. Czarzhynensky. We have been expecting you! Mr. Chancellor sent word down from the top to expect you about now. Please have a seat. David will be down here shortly."

Joe responded genuinely, "Thank you!"

Within four minutes, the 43-year-old trim, athletic and bespectacled David Rosenberg strode jauntily across the bright reception area to where Joe sat in a modern blue cushioned armchair. Joe was dressed in 'casual blue' American business style, but without the tie. The curly-haired, slightly tanned David was dressed in similarly 'casual Mossad civilian attire'–plain tan khakis, colorful sport shirt and brown loafers. Joe arose from his seat and the two men greeted each other.

"Thank you for seeing me, David."

"Oh, no! Thank you for coming all the way over here to see me!"

"Are you free for lunch?"

"Of course! I blocked out an unlimited period for you today. Let's go! I'll drive!"

After a moderate walk to the parking lot north of the installation peppered with basic introductory exchanges of inconsequential personal information, they entered David's 2011 Honda Civic, and he turned on the radio to help obscure detection of any conversation until they reached the restaurant. Big Mama's on HaHashmona'im Street in downtown Tel Aviv provided popular Italian dishes of international appeal in a casual and noisy dinner-hour atmosphere, where the two men could exchange further unofficial exploratory conversation.

After they arrived at the restaurant about a half hour later, David parked in the only parking space available along the crowded street near the restaurant. They left the car and entered the restaurant, which had ample seating hours ahead of the busiest time of the day. They found a secluded table and sat down to look over the menu. David wanted to take advantage of this opportunity to teach Joe about how they might convey information in an unsecure location in the future in a way that minimizes discovery or understanding by the wrong people.

After deciding upon the lasagna dinner, David said, "I am going to mention a name within a sentence about the weather. In Arabic, that name means 'servant of God.'"

He then looked subtly around the dining room before continuing. A tall woman with large circular earrings and long silky dark hair sitting alone at a corner table, apparently reading the menu.

Without any evidence of recognition, he wiped his mouth with his napkin, effectively hiding his lips for a brief period, and then continued, "As I continue discussing meteorology, you will hear another name, which means 'pure' or 'chosen.' Sometimes it is not wise to put two words next to each other in conversation, because it can convey to adversaries who might be listening that we are aware of people or events that it would be to our advantage to keep extremely secret. We believe that this person is a new and advancing individual in Al Queda, the organization we believe is now headed by Ayman al-Zawahiri."

He looked over at Joe for an indication of his understanding. Joe simply returned his gaze and nodded subtly in the affirmative without saying anything.

David continued softly, "Good. We both know how hot it can get in this country, but we do not make excessive use of *Fatih* air conditioning equipment in many places. Although we do not get much rain, we do use *Abdul-Kaliq* irrigation supplies to improve our agricultural efforts. We have some reason to believe that these circumstances resemble efforts to plan 'nekome' (Hebrew for revenge) for the fatal behavior of certain seals near OBL."

Joe immediately grasped David's intent to communicate the two names, Fatih and Abdul-Kaliq. He also knew that OBL referred to Osama Bin Laden, and he caught the reference to 'seals,' indicating 'Seal Team 6.'

David continued subtly between minor deliberate chewing of his food without mentioning officially sensitive methods and sources: "We believe this person is angling for leadership, replacing Z-man, because he believes strongly in revenge. The true Islamic revolution is too slow for him, so we think he could be operating independently. We believe he has Chechen rebel underground contacts and access to money. We also believe that for the first time, the Islamic State and former Al Queda splinter groups of AQP (Al Queda Prime) appear to be talking with each other more than had been the case during the prior six to eight months or so. We also suspect that the Iranians are 'within listening distance.' AQP communications were usually by courier or other non-electronic means since the United States had become quite proficient at intercepting their electronic communications after 9/11/2001."

Then he looked up and around the restaurant briefly. Another young woman with dark wavy hair was sitting at the same table as the other woman with silky dark hair and large circular earrings. The two men finished their food with only minor inconsequential further discussion. The sun was low over the Mediterranean Sea, and the temperature was falling only slightly as they left the restaurant. Joe enjoyed the food, but still preferred his own restaurant. The two returned to David's car and took the scenic route through and around Tel Aviv on the way back to the Mossad complex to the north, again with the radio on. During the trip, David offered his thoughts in cryptic, but nevertheless sufficiently clear oblique references and analogies to Joe, about 'something brewing' in the Islamic world. Joe spoke in general terms about the Chancellor Organization, and how they occasionally work with official clandestine organizations to accomplish certain goals that often cannot be achieved through official or traditional means. David left his automobile in the parking lot and the two returned to David's office. Joe then focused upon getting an answer to the question of David's cooperation with The Chancellor Organization.

Joe said, "Now, given what you know about our private organization, and what I have told you today, will you work with us, basically by being our eyes and ears on an unofficial, but reciprocal and mutually deniable basis? We do not want you to lose your job!"

"You forget, Joe.... This is *Mossad*. The man upstairs and I are the only two people in this organization who know who you are and what you do, and he is willing to extend certain 'courtesies' to your organization in a reciprocal deniable manner in the interests of mutual benefit. The answer is yes, I will work with you!"

"I stand corrected, and I am delighted with your answer! Duke will forward a secure communications protocol within the week."

Joe headed back to the airport for another tiring flight back to Philadelphia, unsettled about David's reference to the Islamic State and Al-Queda, let alone the peculiar reference to Iran.

**** KARACHI, PAKISTAN ****

The 76-foot-long Marlow Voyager yacht left the fuel dock near Karachi after taking in 2,250 gallons of diesel fuel, paid for in cash. Now loaded to the brim with 4,522 gallons of fuel–slightly more than its official specified capacity–she headed out to sea under overcast skies. Oddly enough, across her American-built stern was the name Destiny, written in Arabic. Three and a half miles out, her skipper cut fuel to the engines and dropped anchor. She was registered in Cypress to a trust, so public evidence of the true owner was obscured behind legal 'language putty,' smoke, and mirrors at best. The owner obviously favored privacy in a very determined manner and had the means to achieve it. The yacht was made of e-glass, Kevlar, and carbon fibers, along with lightweight core materials. Her centerline was 78 feet, 11 inches, with overall length of 82 feet, seven inches. She displaced 115,000 pounds, had a five-foot draft and a stated fuel capacity of 4,500 gallons, which theoretically would take her about 5,000 miles without refueling, depending upon speed and weather conditions. Drinking water capacity was 100 gallons, and water capacity for domestic use was full at 400 gallons. Her bulkheads, decks, and teak coamings were of sandwich construction, with fine Burmese teak weather decks, and teak taffrails. Her power plant consisted of two Caterpillar C-15 776-horsepower diesel engines capable of delivering a top speed of 30 knots, equivalent to about 34.5 miles per hour–possibly more with tender loving care.

**** McLean, Virginia ****

CIA agent Leah Cummings left her home in McLean, Virginia and drove to Ronald Reagan International Airport for her one-hour and 20-minute US Airways flight to JFK International Airport in New York, where she had a two-hour and 35-minute layover before resuming her nine-hour and 50-minute trip to Istanbul. She spent some of that time reading an old article published in The Economist in 2012 that she had acquired in general preparation for her mission:

> 'Tajikistan is the poorest republic of the former Soviet Union, yet its capital, Dushanbe, population 778,500, is awash with cash, construction, and flashy cars. It is easy to guess where the money comes from. Tajikistan has little industry but, with a porous 1,300-km (800-mile) border with northern Afghanistan, it is at the heart of a multi-billion-dollar heroin-smuggling network. Bizarrely though, unlike other transit countries such as Mexico, Tajikistan sees little drug-related violence. The heroin, instead, seems to help stabilize the place. The UN Office on Drugs and Crime estimates that about 30 percent of Afghan opiates–including 90 tons of heroin a year (worth between $5.5 billion and $6.2 billion)–pass through Central Asia on their way to Russia, mostly through Tajikistan. The trafficking route is the country's most valuable resource, and its anemic economy is hooked. Researchers believe the industry is equivalent to 30 percent to 50 percent of Tajikistan's GDP. But officials from NATO, which is trying to extract itself from the region, say they have no intention of upsetting the status quo.
> 'For most Tajiks, the alternative is so frightening that they are

happy to look the other way. If senior officials clamped down on the trafficking of heroin, they would have to arrest powerful political figures, which could spark serious violence and re-ignite civil war. Figures from Tajikistan's Drug Control Agency show an 80 percent drop in opiate seizures since 2001. During the same period, the United Nations drugs office says production in Afghanistan almost doubled. This means authorities stop only a tiny fraction of the heroin slipping through the region. Although the police conduct regular busts, they usually involve low-level upstarts with no connections to the main operators. In this way, diplomats say, officials protect their own trafficking networks, allowing no footholds for smaller players.

'Foreign officials admit to having little incentive to challenge the authorities' hold on drug smuggling. Besides, taking a large amount of cash out of the economy could plunge the country into chaos. The real mission, says an anonymous Western diplomat, is keeping the government happy to assist the NATO war effort in Afghanistan. Every American soldier deploying to Afghanistan flies over Tajikistan, he says. 'Are we going to jeopardize that? No way.' A European official says the people doing the trafficking are the same counter-narcotics people that Western countries are training. 'We give them cars, and they use them to transit drugs–look at their houses,' he says of the mansions cropping up around town. With the economy so addicted to heroin, little incentive arises to build or produce other things. Meanwhile, Porsches continue to cruise around Dushanbe, often stolen in Europe and traded for drugs along the Silk Road.'

This is part of the world in which Shamir conducted most of his operations–a world far removed from middle-class America, and unimaginable to a young Russian ballerina. It was a world fostering traditional hate, and planning revenge, but occasionally executing it poorly. Throughout history stories of perceived injustices and injuries passed on from generation to generation in a store of justification to be used at any time to retaliate at the slightest excuse or provocation. Such injustices eventually became 'legitimate' subliminal components of the culture. Young people internalized historical grievances acquired generations, if not centuries before their births by people whom they could not know, and then applied them to their contemporaries who had absolutely no responsibility for, or even any understanding of the original per-ceived injustice or injury. It was a world where money spoke the loudest and most forcefully, and where men often dispensed 'justice' personally, privately, and quickly. It was a world in which certain people were connected in unex-pected or circuitous ways with other people who might desire to engage the services of people like the Kasana twins.

**** TAJIKISTAN ****

The two vans continued south on the A-384 highway out of Dushanbe across the Vakhsh River to Kunduz, Afghanistan, and then Kabul, and on to Ghanzi and Kandahar without significant unwanted attention. The second van left the highway and drove onto a small road south of the town of Spin Buldak, several miles north of the Pakistan border, and disappeared. The remaining van and the Mercedes behind it continued to the Spin Buldak border crossing on the A-75 highway into Pakistan.

Two heavy-duty German Unimog military utility trucks bearing the in-ternationally recognized Mercedes emblem on the front grille blocked the road at an angle facing slightly north toward traffic entering Pakistan. Each truck parked with its front tires straddling the center of the pavement, one slightly behind the other, effectively blocking the entire two-lane road. An armed Pakistan Army corporal approached the truck coming from the north, holding one hand up, palm away from him in the universal indication to stop, as he grasped his German-made Heckler & Koch G3 rifle firmly across his chest with his other hand. The driver slowed the truck to a halt and carefully rolled down his window as he watched the approaching Pakistani corporal. The small black Fiat arrived behind the short line of vehicles and slowed to a stop about 20 yards behind the dirty white Mercedes.

The corporal's strident official voice pierced the background diesel engine noise from the Unimogs, "Papers, please!"

The man in black showed the required, but counterfeit papers of vehicle registration, the appropriate passport, and just the right international look of civilized innocence.

After briefly scrutinizing the paperwork and then handing it back to the driver, the corporal asked, "What is your cargo?"

The driver had not expected a thorough official search of his van. This was an unexpected inconvenience, and a critical interruption of the plan, since it implied that they would probably also search the Mercedes. He tapped his brake pedal three times, signaling the driver of the Mercedes behind him to expect the unexpected, including a search. They had discussed bribery as the most viable solution to interference. Armed conflict was too dangerous and prone to attracting reinforcements with superior forces.

"I have nothing. I am returning empty to Quetta," the driver said, trying to keep verbal exchange as simple and uninformative as possible.

He carefully tapped his brake pedal three times again, which activated the rear brake lights.

The sentry said, "Open it!"

The driver slowly opened the driver's door as the sentry moved away, stepped out onto the road, and walked back to the rear doors. He opened them with the sentry standing between him and the Mercedes 10 yards behind him. He glanced ever so subtly at the Mercedes driver, and then turned back to face the corporal, watching his eyes intently while rubbing his fingers together against his thumb slightly behind him in the universal sign language of 'money,' hoping that the Mercedes driver would get the message.

"See? Nothing here but some food for us to eat."

The sentry looked slowly around the inside of the cargo area, nodded, and started to walk back to the two trucks blocking the road and motioned one Unimog truck with his hand to back up and allow passage. The rear axle of the Unimog cleanly backed over a rock large enough to stop or damage the underside of the Mercedes. While the sentry was facing the Unimog, the man in black turned surreptitiously toward the Mercedes, and briefly mimed the counting of money with his hands, and then immediately turned toward the van. He stepped back up into the driver's seat, closed the door and drove his van past the remaining blocking truck with a sigh of only partial relief, and continued along the renamed M-25 road into Pakistan toward Chaman. The Mercedes was still at the roadblock, but the man in black could not slow down, because it might imply a relationship with the Mercedes driver. He had to keep moving at an acceptable speed without knowing how long the border guard would detain the automobile, or even whether he would thoroughly search it. He considered whether the sentry might arrest the driver, or possibly, injure, or even kill him. *Was the sentry unusually suspicious, or too eager to exercise his small measure of authority out of boredom or unfulfilled ego?* The other Unimog moved back across the southbound lane. The man in black was more than a half mile down the road when the Mercedes stopped near the sentry. He could no longer see the car in his side view mirror.

Again, the sentry's strident voice pierced the sound of the Unimogs, "Papers, please!"

The driver handed the counterfeit required registration and passport to the sentry with 20 crisp mustard-colored 5,000-rupee bills–equivalent to about US $983.18, or more than 3.8 times the monthly average wage in Pakistan–tucked inside the front cover of the passport. From the Fiat behind the Mercedes, Valentin could see the sentry's unusual, time-consuming, and undoubtedly unofficial double take and concluded wisely that the driver had just offered a bribe. For half a minute the sentry slowly walked around the Mercedes, scrutinized the tires, slowly looked underneath the car two times from differed angles, went to the front and examined the grille, and then slowly returned to the driver's window in deep thought. He was still weighing personal temptation against his official duty for a few moments before he finally handed only the papers back to the driver.

He stalled several seconds, stared at the driver, and then said with imagined authority, "Your car is dirty. You should wash it."

He then turned away after having smoothly pocketed the money and motioned with his hand to the same Unimog driver to back up and allow the Mercedes to pass through. Although the driver had to make up the time since the truck left, he could not immediately accelerate and thereby possibly arouse the sentry's curiosity. The sentry might reconsider and make a radio call to police or other military units farther down the road and nullify the bribe with some unwelcome action. Northbound traffic that could have distracted the sentry had ceased four minutes ago. Then Valentin approached the sentry and stopped, while the Unimog again blocked the southbound side of the road. He was trying to control his anxiety as well as his intense curiosity about what he had just seen.

The mechanical military voice repeated, "Papers, please!"

Valentin handed his authentic papers to the sentry.

"What is your business in Pakistan, Mr. Murat?"

I'm going to report what I just saw to people who will believe me and do not take bribes!

"Mr. Murat?"

"Oh... Sorry. I'm a reporter on assignment. Free-lance, general human-interest articles, mostly."

The sentry looked steadily at him for another 10 seconds, glanced through the open window around the interior of the empty car, stared into Valentin's eyes for another unnecessary period of several seconds, and then slowly turned around and waved the Unimog off the road one more time. Valentin continued driving farther into Pakistan without incident on the N-25 Road to Qilla Abdullah. He drove parallel to the railroad to Kuchlack, past the Quetta International Airport, and then toward Mastung. Without any idea of how long his journey would last, he continued to follow the other car past Kalat, Khuadar, Wad, Bela, east of Uthal, and then east of Sonmiani. Unaware of how dangerous his unplanned quest was, he still carefully followed the white car, sometimes allowing two, three or even four cars to get between his car and the Mercedes at various distances. He took each passing minute as successful validation of his stealthy but amateur clandestine driving skills. Gradually, he measured his success by the half hour, as he continued without adverse incident or losing his quarry. He checked his fuel gage and assumed that he could keep following the truck without fear of running out of fuel. They apparently did not know anyone was following them. Pakistan does not have many main roads, so many cars on any particular stretch of road could normally appear to be following other cars unintentionally at any time. Determination of whether one was deliberately or coincidentally following another was impossible.

**** ANKARA, TURKEY ****

Lawrence Thompson left Heathrow at 7:05 A.M. in a light drizzle on British Airways Flight 678, bound for Istanbul, and arrived at Ataturk International Airport on schedule at 12:55 P.M. After a brief layover, he then boarded Turkish Airlines Flight TK2154 leaving Istanbul at 2 P.M. After an uneventful flight, the plane landed close to schedule in Ankara at 3:05 P.M. He left the airplane among other passengers and went to the luggage carousel to wait for his checked luggage. About 10 minutes later, he took his bag and went to the

Hertz desk in the rental area at the Ankara Airport, rented a late model white Ford Fusion, and then left the building to go to the rental car parking lot. Within five minutes, he identified his car, got in, and drove to the National Records building with the help of his portable Garmin Nuvi 42LM GPS unit.

The MERNIS project of 1971 created a national system of identification to organize and simplify institutional public life conceptualized in 1976 by the Turkish State Planning Organization, which was implemented by the Middle East Technical University. The purpose of introducing identification numbers was to resolve the problems that arise from identical names of different citizens and to speed up the information transfer among public institutions and reduce errors. It was in effect an admission that Turkey's, if not the world's population had increased to a level requiring efficiency of standardized social manage-ment, in effect giving every Turkish citizen a 'numerical name' in addition to his traditional given name. It was also an implicit admission that relative ano-nymity within a growing population would tend to encourage undesirable in-dividual behavior incompatible with the officially desired larger social harmony. With the identification number, services like voting, taxation, secu-rity, education, health care, social security, military recruitment, banking, and many others can be carried out more quickly, rationally, and reliably. Civil reg-istration software was prepared by establishing the first population database in 1990 in a central structure capable of working online on the internet. As of 2000, everyone in Turkey received an 11-digit Turkish Republic Identity Number. The first number was given to Ataturk, the first president of Tur-key–10000000146. By 2007, the central architecture was adopted and all 923 local servers in the provinces were abolished and migrated to a single central database.

Lawrence parked in a nearby designated visitor parking lot, left his car, and walked about 50 feet to the main entrance of the building. After consulting with a clerk at the front reception desk and informing her that he needed to research the identity and background of a particular individual involved with an international insurance claim, she directed him to an area of computer ter-minals where he could conduct his research. Within 25 minutes, he discovered that Nisan and Rauf Kasana had only two sons–Umar and Umair–with inter-esting identification numbers. Umar's was 23155068197, and Umair's was 23155068266. According to the official algorithm establishing Turkish identity numbers, the last two digits of each number served as a checksum to help re-duce errors in use of the number and help to verify the authenticity of the en-tire number. With that in mind, he concluded that the two sons had sequential identity numbers if the checksum were ignored in each case. That in turn im-plied that the identity numbers were issued at the same time, which in turn suggested that the two were born within a brief period, obviously implying that they were twins! *What kind of twins? Identical or fraternal?* He also noted with interest that their first names were remarkably similar, differing by only one letter. Not only that, but their current age was consistent with the pre-sumed age of the men identified as Kasana in each of various other reports he had seen of their activities. Each of them could often enough use his own or his brother's name, or even just the first initial and last name, which could ob-scure any firm official determination of when and where either of them trav-eled by air. He wrote in his notebook:

> *Have reason to believe that Turkish arms dealer is a twin–possibly an identical twin! Names are Umar and Umair–similar enough to complicate our task even more! Birthdate is September 10, 1983.*

CHAPTER 25
Wednesday, July 22, 2015

The Mercedes stopped under a large tree near a small dirty white house at the outskirts of the village of Nakka Kiri under cloudy skies, and the driver got out of the car and went inside the house. The original greenish-brownish van that started from Chelyabinsk was behind the house, but Valentin could not see it from his location. He carefully noted the location of the car but continued to drive down the road about a mile to a Pakistan Burma Shell gasoline station and filled his gas tank with unleaded gasoline. After that transaction, he turned his car around to return to a closer, but still obscure and safe location near an abandoned building from which he could keep an eye on the Mercedes as well as the van behind the house. He slept in his car about a quarter of a mile down the road and managed to get several unsatisfying 15- to 30-minute naps in uncomfortable positions while periodically trying to keep an eye on the two vehicles. Neither one moved during the entire night.

**** *DUSHANBE, KAZAKHSTAN* ****

At the instruction of his customer, a clerk at the National Bank of Kazakhstan with the SWIFT code NBRKKZKX sent a wire transfer in the amount of 8,391,928.59 Kazakh tenge (KZT) to the Dolati Branch of Bank Keshavarzi, with the SWIFT code KESHIRTH340 in Tehran, Iran. A clerk in that branch converted that amount into 1,328,586,480 rial for deposit in a private business

108

account. That amount was then withdrawn and converted into USD $44,720 and wired to the HSBC bank at Canary Wharf in London.

**** *LANGLEY, VIRGINIA* ****

Leah Cummings accepted her assignment to investigate known international arms dealers and those who associated with them. She had traded her prior frustration and unrewarding series of pseudo-professional clerical jobs for an intellectually and morally challenging career in the Central Intelligence Agency. Leah was a confident 32-year-old woman, now earning over $67,000 per year and feeling much closer to the glass ceiling in a responsible and mean-ingful position.

CHAPTER 26
Thursday, July 23, 2015

Valentin awoke just as the sunrise glare announced another new day and started to warm the air once again. He got out of his car to stretch and looked casually back down the road to see that the Mercedes was still parked in front of the small house. Within 12 minutes, a dark blue 2006 Toyota Camry with a generous number of slight cosmetic blemishes, rust marks, and a noisy muffler arrived from the south. The driver decelerated near the Mercedes, crossed the road, and pulled into the open dirt area behind the Mercedes facing the opposite direction, and then backed up so the trunks of the two automobiles were within four feet of each other. The man in black came out of the house, and the driver of the Toyota emerged from his car and joined the other man between the two cars. He was dressed for the weather slightly less uncomfortably in khakis, an open-collared white short-sleeved shirt, and tan sandals. The man in black opened the trunk of the Mercedes, while the other man opened the trunk of the Toyota. Then both men simultaneously reached into the trunk of the Mercedes and lifted the heavy canvas package out of the Mercedes with obvious effort, placed it in the Toyota trunk, and quickly closed both trunk lids. The man in black entered the Toyota and started the engine. The other man entered the Mercedes and drove north. The rumbling Toyota turned around and continued south.

Now Valentin had to decide to follow the merchandise, follow the Mercedes, or eat. He was ravenously hungry, but the mysterious package was the most critical issue, so he started his car to follow the Toyota. He did not recognize either of the men, but he also did not know whether the new driver would be as ignorant of his presence as the man in black apparently was. Either way, he could not abandon what he had already invested so much time and mental energy in pursuing. His suspicions were increasing with his curiosity.

It is not every day that one sees two unrelated automobiles appear at sunrise in a small obscure Pakistani village, and two men transfer something heavy enough to require both to lift from one car trunk to the other. It was also suspicious that they did not spend much time, nor talk during the process, which implied that they were executing coordinated plans made some time ago. It was further suspicious that each automobile left in the direction opposite from which each had arrived. Such a sequence of events had to be evidence of careful planning beforehand, and careful planning required communication, which implied organization and purpose.

With increasing adrenalin, Valentin carefully followed the Toyota down the N-25 road because that was one with the mysterious satchel. He followed it several miles east of the coastal town of Gadani, and then through Hub Chowki. The road widened north of the Masroor Pakistani Air Force Base near Karachi and continued into the northern outskirts of the city. He drove well behind the Toyota as it turned right onto Estate Avenue, and then continued south to Mauripur Road South, and then to Moulvi Tamizuddin Khan Road. He followed it across Queen's Bridge, where the road became Club Road. His mind churned unproductively but sustained his daring motivation to continue what he started.

The two automobiles continued to Abdullah Haroon Road, where the Toyota turned left for one block to the next right turn onto the N-5, a divided roadway called Shahrahe Faisal National Highway, and within a few miles, drove through the Karachi suburb of Malir. The cars then went south on the N-5 road by the railroad yard to where the road ended near the pier. Moored nearby at the pier was a luxurious yacht with Arabic script across the stern. The entire 1,651-mile trip from Anzob to the Karachi pier took over 36 hours. He was tired but forced himself to concentrate upon the Toyota and the behavior of the driver. He steered his Fiat to an inconspicuous location next to a large, corrugated metal warehouse and out of sight from the Toyota. He turned off the ignition and activated the laptop computer that he always carried with him for occasionally recording his thoughts and writing news stories. He was convinced that what he had experienced in following the cars was unusual enough that he had to report it to someone who could use or forward the information. Otherwise, he would have wasted a small, but meaningful part of his life, or at least a period of extremely engaging curiosity. He activated his end of the secure System 16, a direct super-encrypted internet link to Duke Chancellor. He contacted Duke first, primarily because Duke was the only person he knew who would take his information seriously the first time and could act upon it or forward it if required, with a minimum of bureaucratic interference, doubt, or other unnecessary impediments. After that, and only after that, he would tell the Pakistani State Police in Karachi. He spent only a few minutes with his cellphone on the internet locating the police station on Preedy Street, between Montgomery Street and Ramchandra Temple Road. The dark and still invisible web of Shamir's evil plan had touched yet another innocent human being.

> 'Urgent. Personally witnessed transfer of heavy satchel from a truck to a dirty white Mercedes southbound in the Anzob Tunnel. Followed Mercedes toward Pakistan. Noted apparent bribe paid near Spin Buldak at Pakistan-Afghanistan border Route A-75 by driver of dirty white Mercedes–license tag 7786AB01. Followed Mercedes south to Nakka Kiri, where two men lifted same unknown canvas package out of Mercedes and put in blue Toyota, license plate RIZ-6645. Followed Toyota to current location–pier at Karachi. Mercedes location now unknown. V.M.'

The man in black had rounded the corner of the nearest warehouse and aimed at the figure behind the windshield. The electronic time and date stamp followed the message as Valentin hit 'send' and then slumped in his seat as a single 7.62mm x 51mm bullet from a German Heckler & Koch PSG1 sniper rifle ripped through the windshield and then his skull. Within the next half hour, Destiny left the pier with a curious canvas package, a full load of food and water, and three passengers in addition to the original three-man crew. Among the three passengers was Russian Army Major Leonid Logonovsky sitting on the deck with a $2,200 bottle of 16-year-old Longrow Single Malt Scotch Whiskey. The two remaining passengers were unknown Syrians. The man in black was not aboard Destiny when its engines started.

CHAPTER 27
Friday, July 24, 2015

**** CHELYABINSK, RUSSIA ****

"Vasily, this is Viktor. I would like to speak with you in person. When will you be available?"

"I am very busy for the next two weeks, Viktor, but for you, I will squeeze you in anytime you want!"

"How about this coming Monday? I will meet you at Café Pushkin in civilian attire for a late evening dinner. When I get to Moscow, I will call you with an exact time schedule."

"Fine. I will look forward to your call, Viktor. It's been a long time, hasn't it?"

"Yes. Thank you for being available. I will call you when I land."

**** SAN FRANCISCO, CALIFORNIA ****

Sammy was surfing the internet again and wondered whether he could hack into the Google servers–just for the heck of it. He was not on an urgent assignment for The Chancellor Organization and had nothing better to do other than sharpen his already impressive computer skills. Besides, it was another interesting personal challenge–food for the brain, and something new to help absorb his unlimited curiosity.

All work and no play make Sammy a little rusty. Let's see what… this… does… Hmmmmm.

He hit the 'enter' key and waited. Five hours later, it was dark outside, and he was still typing commands, inserting, and removing instructions in a module of computer code he had been working on for the last three weeks, testing it, revising, and removing code, and retesting. He had not eaten during those five hours. His intellectual curiosity was feeding him.

"Well! That sure didn't work!" he said to the far wall in his bachelor's pad.

His intense concentration helped another hour slip by, as he punctuated the completion of this latest inspiration with a dramatic strike on the 'enter' key.

"THERE…! Take *that!*"

Midnight came and went, but his voracious curiosity and a glass of diet Coke over ice kept him awake. He watched his computer monitor in amused silence as the twin four-gigahertz Intel Xeon processors executed the instructions of his computer code, heating the internal electronic guts of his old desktop unit as well as the air in the room, despite the liquid cooling system inside the tower case.

Whoops! What's this?

In less than a second, page after page of characters started cascading up from the bottom of his 24-inch wide ultra-high-definition monitor across the entire width at unreadable speed like an inverse Niagara Falls. He sat back in his padded desk chair and watched, almost mesmerized, as a large section of stored Google data continued to flow across his monitor.

"WOW!"

After another 15 minutes, he terminated the program and made sure he saved this most recent module of code to a high-capacity external solid-state USB-3 storage drive, as well as a few blank CDs. He also saved the dump of data on a two-terabyte external hard drive for future analysis.

Can't be too careful with this stuff!

CHAPTER 28
Saturday, July 25, 2015

**** *KARACHI, PAKISTAN* ****

The man in black rode in a taxi through a light rain to Karachi International Airport. No non-stop flights were available to Istanbul, so he booked a one-way trip on Etihad Airways, Flight EY222, which was an Airbus A-320, leaving at 5:35 the next morning to Abu Dhabi International Airport, arriving at 1:10 P.M.

**** *SAN FRANCISCO, CALIFORNIA* ****

Sammy was still concentrating on the Google data dump and his decryption programs, searching for the plain underlying information. He was still in his pajamas, but his eagerness to search the database was far stronger than his habit of clothing himself. He put two pieces of whole wheat bread in his little General Electric toaster oven, set the temperature control for 'dark,' and retrieved a dish of butter and a plastic gallon jug of fresh organic orange juice from his refrigerator. He poured the juice into a large glass in the kitchen and carried it to his combination computer desk and dining table. He turned his computer on and went back to the kitchen to wait for his toast while the boot sequence and start-up routines on his computer ran to completion. After another idle minute and a half, he buttered the two pieces of toast, dropped a dollop of mint jelly on each, spread it evenly over the entire surface of each piece of toast, put them on a plate, and returned to his computer with the plate.

He retrieved the file of the data dump from Friday night and started to run some baseline searches for patterns in the data. He knew that certain two, three, and four-letter words have a characteristic statistical frequency in the English language, like 'go,' 'to,' 'of,' 'it,' and 'or' for two-letter words. 'The,' 'but,' 'for,' 'man,' 'and,' and 'hit' as examples of three-letter words, and of course the vast array of commonly used four-letter words, including those like 'this,' 'that,' 'come,' 'have,' and 'with.' Even with typographical errors, run-ons, and misspellings so rampant in internet messaging traffic, he could still search for similarities with 'fuzzy logic' algorithms such as 'sounds like' or 'looks like' or 'includes' such words or letter sequences. He loaded one of his stored search routines which he had previously written for just this kind of search and started its complex analytical processes on the large data dump. Satisfied that the program had started and was running properly, he went back to the kitchen to put the orange juice container back in the refrigerator and retrieve the plate with the two pieces of toast. When he returned to his dining table with his toast, the same display was still on his monitor, but the cursor was still flashing, indicating that the program was still running.

He went back to the kitchen and retrieved a Costco-sized box of Cheerios from a cabinet and set it on the table. Then he got a bowl and another plate from another cabinet, put the bowl on the plate, and poured enough cereal into the bowl to challenge the rim when he added organic whole milk and a medium-sized whole sliced banana. Within a few more seconds, 'finished' appeared on his monitor.

"What do you mean—you're 'finished'?"

Sammy had such an intimate relationship with his computer that when he was alone, he openly conversed with it often enough possibly for a fly on the wall to question his sanity, although he had not yet given it a human name.

"Oh! So, it's encrypted! Of course! Well, we'll fix that little problem…"

He created a copy of about 10 percent of the larger data dump as input to his decryption programs so it would not take too much time to run. He then started another program that would digest that partial copy of the data dump with known decryption algorithms, as well as several that he had invented, and a few experimental routines he had yet to test thoroughly. This run would create output files of each decryption system and take most of the day, or longer, so he turned his attention to other pressing matters—like finishing his breakfast and then going back to bed while his computer worked.

Man created the code, so man can break the code. It's just a matter of time... and ingenuity... and more time... and... a little bit of luck!

**** BEIJING, CHINA ****

With the mature and confident voice of experience, the old man said, "We are going to give you a brief refresher course in Chinese history and economics, Mr. Chang. Please... come this way."

The rain had stopped earlier that morning, but the sky was still overcast, and the humidity remained uncomfortably high as the sun made periodic attempts to break through the dissipating cloud cover. The older man walked toward the waiting dark gray military helicopter in a slow, but strong and confident gait. The younger man followed behind him. Out of respect for the older man, the young pilot engaged the main rotor only *after* his two passengers had boarded the helicopter and closed the door. The strong flow of air from the main rotor could have knocked him over and caused very unpleasant personal consequences. After the two passengers sat behind the pilot and fastened their seatbelts, the older man tapped the pilot on his right shoulder and indicated with his hand that they were ready. They put their white plastic headphones over their ears and adjusted the attached voice microphones closer to their mouths for in-flight communication. The main rotor started to move, gathering momentum and speed rapidly, until it was at take-off velocity. The two passengers could feel the initial minor lift off the ground, and then a stronger push against their seats as the aircraft accelerated and ascended forward with a slight tilt into the smoggy atmosphere to the east. Within 13 minutes, they were circling over the city of Beijing but under the remaining cloud cover. The old man started speaking into his microphone.

"In 2013, China bought from the United States $25.9 billion worth of agricultural products, including soybeans and cotton, hides and skins, and distiller grains. In total, we bought about 7.7 percent of United States exports around the world. This rate has been increasing steadily since China joined the World Trade Organization in 2001. China was the United States' largest supplier of goods in 2013, about $440.4 billion, which was an increase of 3.5 percent from 2012. That trade balance recently favors China, and we expect that trend to continue. Now…, Beijing, the city you see below, has over 22 million residents, a significant portion of whom work in factories that supply the goods that we ship for consumption around the world, including the United States. Currently, 20 urban areas in China with over four million residents each, contribute to the manufacture and production of similar goods sold to world markets, including the United States. About 32 cents of every American debt dollar is owned by the United States in trust funds for social security and other retirement funds. China owns about $1.2 trillion of that debt, which totals approximately $14.3 trillion. The peace, tranquility and hopes for a bright future for China are to a certain extent dependent upon the consumers in the United States who purchase the goods we manufacture. About 17 percent of Chinese exports go to the United States, and 16 percent go to Europe. They are not our only customers, of course, but their absence from our market would become a problem. You see, Mr. Chang, if those people down there lose their jobs because the products made by their employers were not selling in the United States, then many of them would not be able to afford many of life's discretionary purchases, which would likely cause them to become rather unhappy. Furthermore, an increasing number of them would not be able to afford life's necessities–like food and shelter–which would make them even more unhappy, if not angry. If that condition were to become a *trend*, Mr. Chang, then China would have a *very* significant problem! You will recall from your history books that China had endured a few episodes of popular unrest during the last several thousand years at least partly due to a lack of sufficient food for the average citizen. Oppression and natural disasters exacerbated some of those uprisings. Because they did not have enough food, the masses finally rebelled against the Han dynasty in the seventh year of Guanghe, about 2,000 years ago. That rebellion lasted about 21 *years!* Imagine what civil unrest could develop if even 10 percent or 15 percent of those people down there become that desperate or that angry… Mr. Chang. I hope you can appreciate my point in taking you over the city, so you can visualize just how *many* people live and work down there… and elsewhere in China. Our elevated position offers perspectives unavailable at the street level, or in my office."

The older man looked intently into Chang's eyes and concluded that he had indeed made his point. Then the older man tapped the pilot's shoulder twice, indicating that he should take them back to the launch pad. Within the next 30 minutes, they were back in his office. The older man sat heavily upon a deep burgundy upholstered teak chair with gold thread designs of little dragons. It was set apart from his desk and across from a matching chair on the other side of an elegant, polished teak tea table with inlaid squares of every known kind of wood from around the globe. He gestured with his left hand in a manner inviting Mr. Chang to sit across from him in the other chair. After the younger man sat down comfortably, the older man looked intently into his eyes with the experience and wisdom of a certain advanced age, intelligence, and authority. Then he began to speak.

"It has come to my attention that China must become even more vigilant in the larger world arena as our economy expands and we become more influential in world finance and commerce. I have chosen you for a most important, interesting, and potentially exciting assignment, Mr. Chang. Your education, familiarity with the American culture, youth, language facility, military and recent State Security employment experiences, and loyalty, qualify you in the minds of our government officials as the right man for this most difficult job. You will be mostly on your own, following your instincts, and might feel like you are on a vacation from time to time. Your assignment will be to observe and analyze potentially important events and developments in the United States *before* they become widely known, even in their own media— or anywhere else. You will search for, assess, and analyze information, events, and developments that can have an impact upon China—and report them directly to me, immediately! Your official portfolio will be that of a senior agent of the Ministry of Trade, with the mission of improving international trade relationships. This assignment might help take you into some of the circles of political or corporate power and influence in the United States. Your expenses will be covered for the greatest part at my discretion. You will also have whatever support you think is appropriate, including living expenses, along with whatever materials, human, and logistical support you deem necessary. You will be responsible, however, for your own personal matters. We will have an understanding of honor in that regard, and you will file reports to me on a regular basis. You will have a dedicated state-of-the-art secure communications protocol for that purpose. It is called 'Comm-S67.' In addition to all regular telephonic capabilities, it has the capacity to intercept telephone signals. You can tune it to varying distances, frequencies, specific numbers, or signal strengths. Do not mention that phrase at any time after you leave this office–not even to the wind. We have taken the liberty of storing several official Washington area phone numbers in its monitoring memory–including the White House, FBI officials, CIA officials, and Homeland Security officials. I have told you now only because your knowledge of that name will be the only verification of your identity under potentially urgent or adverse circumstances requiring exfiltration. This device has unique and remarkable intercept capabilities that you will master before your departure. Therefore, you shall limit its use, lest either the Russians or the Americans have invented something similar that could detect your use of it. In any event..., hear me correctly, Mr. Chang.... Never..., *never* lose sight of your task, and never forget what can happen..., if the people of China do not have enough food to eat! The United States accounted for over 24 percent of the value of China's agricultural imports during 2012-13, a larger share than any other country. United States agricultural sales to China doubled from 2008 to 2012, reaching about $26 billion in annual sales. China has overtaken Japan, Mexico, and Canada to become the leading export market for United States agricultural products. Now..., do we *understand* each other..., Mr. Chang?"

Lei Chang swallowed subtly once with mild effort, and then responded with a clear and respectful voice, "I understand completely everything you have told me, as well as the implications you have emphasized. I look forward with honor to serving my country to the best of my ability in this critical position."

Lei Chang was a handsome 33-year-old bachelor with a disarming ready smile of almost perfect natural teeth in a strong unblemished face. He was a graduate of the University of California at Los Angeles, where he acquired a natural familiarity with the American way of life and cultural values. He was a former Chinese Olympic high-diving silver medalist, and a master chess player. In addition to several Chinese dialects, he was conversationally proficient in Russian, French, Japanese, English, and Farsi. He had also achieved respectable mastery of Chinese martial arts after 24 years of practice and study. He also held the equivalent of a master's degree in International Political Science from Peking University, *the* premier Chinese University, where both of his parents were full professors. His complement of intangible personal assets, discipline, and character, however, made him a man not to trifle with, either physically or intellectually, and the old man knew that. Lei began his new assignment with a trip to Tokyo, where he intended to spend a few days before continuing the long journey to the United States. He left Beijing at 8:25 A.M. with the diplomatic credentials that would allow him to travel anywhere in the world. His first flight was Japan Air Lines Flight JL860, which was a Boeing 737-800. That plane would arrive at Tokyo Narita International Airport at 1 P.M., three hours and 35 minutes later.

CHAPTER 29
Sunday, July 26, 2015

**** ABU DHABI, UNITED ARAB EMIRATES ****

After a nine-hour layover, the man in black boarded Etihad Flight EY-201 at Abu Dhabi International Airport at 10 P.M. due to arrive at Ataturk International Airport in Istanbul, Turkey at 6:25 the next morning.

**** MOSCOW, RUSSIA ****

"We will meet for dinner at 19:00 hours at Café Pushkin. You will arrive by 18:45 hours, and I will arrive at precisely 18:55 hours. If I see you seated in the library at that time, I will know that you have arrived without detection. If you are anywhere else but the library at that time, I will know that you suspect that you may have been followed for whatever reason, but we will enjoy our dinner anyway. If you order fish, I will know that you are suspicious about your superiors, so in that event we will limit our conversation to inconsequential social matters. You must be completely familiar with the code because we cannot risk any detection whatsoever. Make no assumptions that you cannot personally verify.... You know the possible consequences if we fail. Agreed?"

The other man said, "Agreed."

Colonel Viktor Kovalenko terminated the telephone connection with GRU Colonel Vasily Koshelev and left the phone booth on Stoleshnikov Lane in central Moscow. He walked by the stores offering expensive merchandise, periodically casually looking at reflections of the other side of the street in the store windows to see whether anyone was paying any particular attention to him while he feigned window shopping. He continued with habitual military intelligence caution, making maximum use of his peripheral vision, occasionally stopping to look around, and eventually disappeared below street level into the Moscow Metro. Opened in 1935 with a single 6.8-mile line of track and 13 stations, it was the first underground railway system in the old Soviet Union. The Moscow Metro now has 188 stations, and its route length is about 194 miles. The system is mostly underground, with the deepest section 243 feet below street level at the Park Pobedy station. The Moscow Metro is the world's third most heavily used rapid transit system after the Tokyo Subway and the Seoul Metropolitan Subway in South Korea, and consequently affords a great deal of anonymity, which is precisely what he wanted for the next several hours.

Army Colonel Vasily Koshelev was the 47-year-old deputy to the second in command of the GRU. He wore a plain dark gray civilian business suit, white shirt, and dark tie of unremarkable design. The GRU deployed significantly more agents in foreign countries, including the United States, than did the SVR, the successor to the KGB's foreign operations directorate. It also commanded as many as 25,000 highly trained Spetsnaz troops. Sometimes compared to the United States Defense Intelligence Agency, the GRU's activities encompass those performed by nearly all joint United States military intelligence agencies as well as other national United States organizations combined. The GRU gathers human intelligence through military attaches and foreign agents and manages significant signals and imagery reconnaissance operations. The GRU Space Intelligence Directorate has used more than 130 satellites with significant intelligence-gathering capabilities. At one time, the GRU and KGB signals intelligence network employed about 350,000 specialists.

He rubbed his slightly pock-marked, but otherwise handsome and intelligent face as he contemplated the personal discomfort of making a commitment either way, when each choice could have at least some negative professional, if not personal consequences. He approached a secluded corner table that minimized his visibility from behind. He lowered his still solid six-foot frame into the cushioned chair closest to the corner of the room with habitual moderate dignity and rested his plain black polished cane against the side of the adjacent empty chair to his right as he surveyed the room around him. From his location, he could see into most of the dining area, and would be aware of anyone else who might be watching him. He had been waiting patiently in the library at Café Pushkin for a little over 10 minutes when Colonel Viktor Kovalenko arrived in unremarkable gray civilian business attire precisely at 6:55 P.M. and walked straight to the library. Colonel Koshelev had always admired his friend's decisiveness, punctuality, and other natural leadership qualities, regardless of politics. After minimal and bland social pleasantries while exercising his peripheral vision, Colonel Kovalenko drew the other chestnut brown wooden chair with a red seat cushion away from the table and sat down across from his friend. Within two minutes, a server approached and took their orders for appetizers. They both started with a bowl of sausage solyanka, while each was internally assessing his official life. After five minutes of their small talk and light general observations about the worrisome state of the country and the world, the server returned to take their orders for the main meal. Both men were still adjusting to why they were there, as if an unknown force propelled each to this point in time. They both accepted the future they were about to define for themselves. However, they could no more define the future than they could stop its often-unexpected attack, or even prepare for it sufficiently to maintain their sense of purpose throughout its subsequent path of unknown and unintended consequences. There would be no turning back. The future often invaded the present uninvited, challenging, relentless, disturbing, and inescapable, regardless of one's awareness or preparation. They were both adults, completely purged of any residual innocence or childish yearning for fairness. One had special knowledge, and the other had a dream. Both desired life without the cascade of burdensome regulation, footnotes, disclaimers, caveats, cynicism, and constant corruption. The blessings of obscurity afforded by modern technology facilitated insidious individual mischief, if not outright terrorism–the naïve practice of trying to persuade the rest of the world to recognize, if not completely adopt one's uniquely 'correct' personal life philosophy at any cost.

"I will have the roast beef, please," said Vasily.

Colonel Kovalenko looked up into his friend's benign gray eyes with subtle gratitude for this small note of assurance, and then carefully turned to either side and glanced around the room, casually looking for anyone who might deliberately hold his wary eye for more than an innocent second.

"Viktor, we cannot escape the facts. The Russian Army is but a shadow of itself before the collapse of Communism. We have a stupid policy of requiring only one year of service from new recruits, because everyone knows about the hazing and bullying in the lowest ranks. No one wants to serve! It is a mindless, self-perpetuating disgrace upon the military. In the old days, before the Soviet Union dissolved in 1991, we had five million troops in the armed forces! Now we have less than one million in just Russia–very odd with about half the population of the Soviet Union but most of the territory. Although our armed forces lost over 80 percent of their strength since 1991, a disproportionate number of officers remained. A decade ago, the Russian military had about 1.2 million personnel, 400,000 in the army itself, and the rest in paramilitary units that were mostly uniformed and armed like soldiers. However, about 355,000 officers remain. That's more than one in three! With all that, some 40,000 officer positions were still vacant. The reorganization eliminated over half of them but left many surviving officers bitter and frequently in a bad mood. We need a non-commissioned officer corps like the Americans and British have, to instill proper discipline and pride in serving. It takes almost an entire year to train new recruits to be effective in some capacity, so what sense does it make to train them, and then discharge them just after they have been trained and have gained no real experience? Not only that, but the pool of available recruits has diminished to about half of what it was then. The damned economy fell apart, and, thanks to those political idiots under Communism, too many smart and good people left the country, and nobody wanted to have children! Now we have little but drunkards, dimwits, and drug addicts with bad attitudes to choose from! I understand the hazing is most frequently committed by troops who have been in six months or so against the new recruits. But this extends to a pattern of abuse and brutality by all senior enlisted troops against junior ones. It has long been out of control! The abuse continues to increase because of the growing animosity against troops who are not ethnic Russians. Even the military cannot eradicate prejudice! More senior non-commissioned officers and commissioned officers are becoming discouraged with these conscripts, and good officers are leaving–and truthfully, I can't blame them! What an idiotic military system that is! Especially since the Chinese have over three times our standing army and spend three times what we do on defense! We will never catch up to them! Who is going to win the battle when one of their well-trained marksmen sets his sights on one of our inade-quately trained and unmotivated dimwits? Not only that, but corruption in-vestigators believe that about 20 percent of the military budget is lost to corruption and outright theft. So just spending more money on the military is not an easy fix either. Even worse: many, if not most Russian arms manufac-turers are corrupt and incompetent. This has gotten so bad that many reform-minded generals and admirals prefer to buy foreign weapons. This means paying more but the quality is much better and you get stuff on schedule. Get-ting the corrupt officers out of the military may prove more difficult than elim-inating the young bullies."

"I know, Vasily.... I know. The world is changing far too fast. I too have become discouraged, especially since Kristina died. We had 22 good... no... *very* good years together. My life *meant* something with her to come home to, even though I was away on assignments for many months at a time. She gave our home warmth and comfort, and an aroma of familiarity. It was very special coming back to her, knowing she was there for me. But now, she has been gone for over two years, and all I have is Karina... and the army. It is indeed sad to say that I appreciate Kristina more now that she is gone than perhaps I showed her when she was alive."

He drifted into distant thought momentarily, and then recovered and con-tinued to speak.

"Well..., the image of having been a military officer in the former Soviet Union somehow leaves something to be desired, don't you think? The older I become the more I question what I have been doing with my life–the more I question what life *is*. When I was younger, I was too naïve to seek wisdom, and too smart or too busy to need it. The Army was my life and my exciting future. Every action and assignment had a reason–an understandable higher purpose. Now, I am not so sure. Recently, I have been assigned to the general headquarters command. I am the commanding officer at Chelyabinsk as a home base, but I am supposed to roam about the country checking every nu-clear storage facility for proper inventory and compliance with domestic and international agreements to reduce the number of conventional nuclear war-heads and other nuclear devices. I have become aware through sources I have no reason to doubt, that the last officer to have that position mysteriously disappeared in Kazakhstan. I am asking you as a friend, Vasily. Do I have something to fear from this assignment? Do the wrong people have me in their sights?"

"It would be extremely difficult for me to ask certain questions, Viktor. Elements of the old KGB are still alive and well in several former soviet republics, including Kazakhstan, and possibly Ukraine despite officially having been disbanded after the failed coup against former President Gorbachev. And, as you would guess, they are still here in Moscow. It will not surprise me if they have some kind of residual organized underground structure, perhaps with underworld criminal associates supporting international agents. We cannot know exactly what their intentions are, and whom to trust, but I would bet that they are set upon returning to their old influence and reestablishing the glory days of the old Soviet Union. The leaders are older men, even older than we are, with all due respect, and I imagine they are not inclined to give up the only life they have ever known. One must step lightly, Viktor. Old habits and associations are hard to break—especially lucrative ones with criminal associations, or those that either promise or assure power, security, money and influence, particularly through illegal means, if not simple outright bribery... particularly in the heroin business."

"Well, something is not quite right, now, is it? Not so long ago—In September of 1997 I believe—General Alexander Lebed alleged that about 100 small 'suitcase' nuclear bombs were not under the control of the armed forces of Russia—and he said that to an American news reporter on their '60 Minutes' television program! The official response from our government was that we never had them! Unfortunately, he died in a helicopter crash about five years after that, so we cannot ask him about that. It is odd that he died that way. When our friend, Stanislav Lunev defected to the United States back in 1992, he confirmed that such nuclear devices existed and even speculated that they possibly had already been deployed—perhaps already hidden at various locations within the United States—possibly even in Virginia, near the national capital! He was in the GRU, like you! He should know! How could he deliberately put his career and even his life in danger by lying? He had to be telling the truth! Obviously, someone has not been telling the truth, and when I get too close to people I cannot trust because they do not always tell the truth, I get nervous and even more distrustful. And when I am obligated sometimes to interact with unfamiliar superiors whose loyalties are not clear, I tend not to be reckless. Did Alexander Lebed have nothing better to do with his life than tell lies–especially about such dangerous weapons? I do not think he was a liar! He was a man of substance, and I considered him to be my friend. I believe he had it right when he said, 'Most Russians don't care whether they are ruled by fascists or communists or even Martians as long as they can buy six kinds of sausage and lots of cheap vodka in the store.' Is that not true? What kind of country are we serving? He was honest enough to admit he was not without sins. He said that there cannot be an airborne assault general who has no sins. I suspect that is true of anyone in a position of real power, leadership, and authority. He said, 'I spit on popularity ratings. I live and serve as I see fit.' Putin has said that these stories about missing nuclear weapons are just myths… legends. And now, I am being put in the position of having to verify the truth of what an alleged liar has said! Even if we did not have them then, we certainly have them now, because I have *seen* them at Chelyabinsk! When I was a young child, I did not know the difference between telling a lie and telling the truth, partly because I could not differentiate between fantasy and reality, but my father soon taught me very clearly what the difference is, and I never forgot that! I am too old and too proud to lie, Vasily! I want to live and enjoy Karina's love of life! It is *her* life, not the army, that now gives my life meaning. She has dreams and aspirations while I have too much experience with the dark side of people and politics. I want her to continue to have a *life*, Vasily! You may not know this, but she has become quite an accomplished ballet dancer. The Bolshoi rejected her a while back, but she has since moved to the United States to pursue her dreams there!"

Vasily did not tell his friend that he already knew that and had sent an unusually capable man to accompany Karina to the United States surreptitiously and watch over her during her journey. He had always known how special she was to Viktor, but he could not risk insulting Viktor by telling him that he had assumed a paternal role by sending a man to watch over her. He had just the right official position, influence, and power to do that. Viktor did not. It was the least Vasily could do for his friend. Deep down inside, Vasily knew that we all need the Karinas of this world. Viktor slipped into reminiscence.

How many years ago was it… when I had lain with Christina… in 1991 before I was sent away on a special detachment mission as an intelligence officer with one of those nuclear submarines, those horrid monsters of death? I had come home from hav-

ing been aboard the first Akula Class submarine a year later to find my first-born child–a girl, so pretty with sparking light blue eyes, and a smile–already walking. Oh, those eyes... and that smile! She could have anything she wanted in life with that smile as reward or inducement! Little did I know of her future. I had only the naïve hope of a young father. Every night I was home, I would read to her, and she would unknowingly and so naturally reward me with her pure innocence and her smile of excitement. I would take her to the park and tell her about the world–the only world I knew. I would tell her stories of far-off lands, the stars and the planets and great distances, fueling her wonderful, natural childish fantasies. I would never lie to her, but I would allow her to exercise her imagination. I would not tell her the dark truths as I had learned them, about the ugly deeds men do when they pretend to have power, when they have political meetings, the things they plan in the name of the greater social good and for their own fleeting social greatness, personal comfort and imagined immortality. I would not talk about the selfish laws and regulations they invent to make the impossibly perfect life for everyone–the way they stifle thought and creativity so foreign to their own preconceived notions, standards and principles, the way they fear loss of power and loss of control. No, I would not pollute my little girl's mind with such thoughts. I would not poison her appetite for exploration, discovery, imagination, happiness... and the fullness of life!

"Viktor? Viktor..., are you still here?"

"I'm... sorry.... Yes.... You were saying?"

"Why don't you just resign your commission?"

"You already know why! Because I have been in so long that I cannot do anything else, and I am not yet eligible for my pension! I know nothing else and am too old to learn enough new tricks! I am an officer and a professional soldier! Not only that, but I know too much truth about things that powerful politicians tend to lie about! If I leave immediately after starting this assignment, how will that look to the old KGB or even to your superiors in the GRU? Surely, they know who I am and what I am doing! The subject matter of this new posting is not only military, but it is by its very nature decidedly political, and I am not a politician! If I leave now, they will continue to keep an eye on me for quite some time to come. And some day, when I least expect it, they will make me disappear! I am but a cog on a gear in the machinery of the larger military-political system, and every so often I must for the sake of appearances and my own professional or personal survival mesh with the next gear and other 'cogs' I prefer not to have to deal with. What happens after the machinery expects that cog to be there, and it is no longer there? Surely someone in control will notice the subsequent 'vibration!'"

Vasily started to interject with sincerity, "Viktor…"

As if he were questioning an established fact, Viktor said, "You think I am… *paranoid*, don't you?"

With mild tension in his facial expression, Vasily turned his head slightly and looked over Viktor's left shoulder without specific focus across the crowded room toward the multi-paned street window as if he were deep in unwelcome thought. He rested his gaze upon an attractive young woman–likely in her middle twenties–with mid-length light blonde wavy hair and smooth soft skin, wearing a coal-black dress that assisted the imagination. She could easily have been a fashion model. Sitting across from her was a grizzly old fart with oddly colored unruly hair and no chin, wearing a pink tie, light blue shirt, and a disgusting light brown business suit that obviously did not fit his disproportionately abundant form. Her mild smile looked forced, disinterested, and metallic. *What was she doing with such a… slob? He probably had money, influence, or personal leverage… maybe.* His blubbery smirk looked intentionally and blatantly lascivious. Vasily imagined that he was a political kingpin of some sort, or someone who did 'surface work' for the 'underground.' Then he trashed further thought about him, and briefly imagined resting his face upon her breast, inhaling her scent, feeling her warm, smooth, soft skin. Then he shifted his gaze slightly to his right and stared absently at the ornate gleaming gold pendulum swinging from side to side inside the majestic highly polished deep brown antique Hermle grandfather clock standing in the far corner near the entrance to the library. It was dispensing the extra time he needed with scarcely audible, slightly muffled clicks coming from its intricate inner mechanical heart. After several seconds, he turned his head back to the table, deliberately avoiding Viktor's eyes, still lost in thought, and then looked down briefly at the food on his plate. After a few seconds he reached slowly for his glass of water, brought it carefully to his dry lips and drank several sips slowly, killing more time as he gathered his thoughts. Viktor waited patiently, still looking hopefully into Vasily's diverted gray eyes.

Vasily finally looked directly at him and responded with deliberation, "No…. I don't think you are paranoid."

He finally looked even more intently into Viktor's eyes, giving him the assurance he needed to give out of genuine respect for an old and true friendship, and that he now knew more poignantly that Viktor needed to see. Their mutual respect had grown subtly over the years to form a rare and unbreakable bond.

"At some point, my friend, we all arrive at a position of owning dark secrets–some large, and some small–and of having sinned or violated our formative self-concepts, not because we desired thus, but because many times without intention, preparation or awareness, we encountered the brute unexpected clash between our own political or even natural personal and vital self-interests, and those of others, some of whom were connected to still others, and sometimes even to powerful people unknown to us. It is not the violation of law, nor the disregard of custom, but the excessive denial of the self that truly imprisons us. We are military officers. However, we are first and foremost, simply human. Life is sometimes merely the unanticipated encounter between what or who we think we are and what we ultimately cannot control–between what we *believe*, or want to believe, and the unknown *ultimate reality*. Secrets can poison the soul, and injure the future, Viktor. Surely… you already know that."

He listened to Vasily quietly, taking in his words, but remained unsettled. He tried to postpone the newly imagined momentum of his life with a long sip of water from his glass.

Where will it lead if I do not take control of it, if I do not dare to do what I know is right?

After an uncomfortable several seconds, Viktor spoke as if compelled by some unknown force, "Vasily, please listen to me very carefully…."

Vasily subtly looked around the dining room as several muffled 'clicks' from the giant Hermle clock dominated his hearing before he faced his friend expectantly, and then said quietly, "I'm listening."

Viktor continued only slightly louder than a whisper, "You know what is stored at Chelyabinsk…."

Vasily nodded subtly in silent affirmation.

Viktor continued in scarcely audible words, "My first personal inventory on Thursday, July 17, indicated one more than that stated in the official record given to me upon assuming command. The next day I called the verification command to report the discrepancy and was told in no uncertain terms that the official inventory was correct, and that I was to adjust my thinking to accept that 'reality.' Obviously, I could not get rid of the extra device, so I assumed I was to make changes in the official inventory count and not mention the discrepancy again to anyone."

"Are you telling me that someone made a mistake in counting?"

"No. I am telling you what must be true after I made another visit to the storage vault on Monday, July 20 and counted again, just to make absolutely sure I had not made a mistake in counting the first time."

Viktor stopped speaking abruptly and took a spoonful of his cooled solyanka while he looked carefully around the room.

After satisfying himself once again that no one else in the dining room was paying any attention to him, he said quietly, "My second inventory *matched* the original official orders!"

Another series of muffled clicks from the corner of the room coincidentally dominated an odd and sudden, but momentary pause in all conversation throughout the entire dining room as Vasily reached for his glass of water, raised it to his lips and then took his time swallowing the water.

Vasily stared intently into Viktor's eyes as he said softly, "Viktor… If I have followed your discussion correctly, you are telling me that one extra device was in the vault when you arrived… and then somehow it was removed… and therefore the official count then matched the actual inventory number. Is that what you are saying? One is missing?"

Viktor nodded his head subtly and slowly in affirmation.

The two men then settled into the quiet completion of their dinner, each knowing that some unspoken decision had been reached between them.

**** TEHRAN, IRAN ****

A clerk at the Dolati Branch of Bank Keshavarzi in Tehran sent a wire transfer in the amount of 1,328,586,480 Rial to the HSBC headquarters bank at Canary Wharf in London, England. He did not know its purpose, and he did not care to know. He had absolutely no personal or official element of curiosity. It was just another normal transaction he was paid to process—one minute detail in someone's evil plan—one virtual molecule of water in the vast rushing river of world events.

CHAPTER 30
Monday, July 27, 2015

**** *MOSCOW, RUSSIA* ****

Colonel Kovalenko left his hotel early and took a taxi to the Vnukovo International Airport to board his return flight to Chelyabinsk. He was early enough to spend some thoughtful moments in the departure lounge, looking out without focus into the cloudy sky, weighing the pros and cons of his imagined future.

He arrived at his office just before 8 A.M. He rested his cane against a corner wall in his office and then limped slightly as he went to his desk and carefully scanned the neatly arranged vertical array of pink and white notes in chronological order according to the time of their receipt. The pink ones were the more important ones. One pink note grabbed his attention. He picked it up and read it.

> *'A freelance business journalist from Kazakhstan was killed in his car with a single bullet from a German sniper rifle near the pier in Karachi on July 23. Pakistani authorities have confiscated all evidence. He was allegedly the author of a recent newspaper article about Russian underground elements and possible collusion with former KGB agents related to the recent unconfirmed rumors of a missing Russian nuclear device.'*
>
> *What was a citizen of Kazakhstan doing in Karachi that got him killed? People kill many times to silence another person, and often to exact revenge…, or send a message to discourage others from… doing something. This does not appear to be revenge. He was a re-*

porter. He was being silenced. What did he know? What was he working on? What did he see? What was in his brain? Where are these 'unconfirmed rumors' coming from? What if he knew absolutely… that a Russian nuclear weapon is missing! Oh my God!

**** SAN FRANCISCO, CALIFORNIA ****

"Eureka!"

Plain English rises as a phoenix from the ashes of code!

Sammy finally cracked the Google encryption algorithm, with the exception of several minor formatting irregularities. For at least the last 48 hours, he had been downloading stored Google data, presumably e-mails, general advertising messages, news clips, promotions, blogs and formal documents, reports, or other messages of one sort or another. He could now assess what was on people's minds around the world. He was no more interested in the trivial minutia of other people's personal lives than he was interested in exploring the innards of a worm. What he wanted was an opportunity to study mass communications in a way that revealed large areas of current reference. By counting the frequency of the word 'Madonna,' for example, or a phrase like 'go *** in a lake,' using the asterisks as a wild card that could stand for any characters, during a specific period of time like a week or a month, or two months or 10 months, or even daily, he could learn what interested many people. Then, by calculating the statistical significance of that frequency versus the larger universe of word usage during the same period, he might be able to gage changes in the focus of the internet world's attention. To the extent that people usually communicate on the internet for rather immediate or personal purposes, he could get an unusually current idea of what the 'communicating world,' including the general media, was focusing on almost in real time. Moreover, by calculating the usage during a period of a month, for example, and then looking at the same monthly word frequency four months later, he could get a sense of how public attention may have changed during that period, if at all. Since the only language he was familiar with was English, he would not appreciate such analysis as much using as many languages as were present on the internet. However, since English was the most dominant internet language (about 27 percent), he believed it would still qualify for the statistical assumptions he would be using. Chinese was at 25 percent, and Spanish was at 8 percent, rounding out the top three. Russian was about 3 percent.

How neat is that?

He bit into a Saltine cracker smothered with fresh extra-chunky Skippy peanut-butter, and then gleefully started playing with his analysis programs, plugging in words to see what the usage frequency was and whether it was statistically significant, feeding his voracious intellectual curiosity.

Heeeere we go!

He was in an impish mood and started with 'go **** in a lake,' deliberately using wildcards. After an hour running his series of analysis programs, he found nothing significant in the frequency of that kind of phrase.

Oh well...

Then he tried another word, 'Washington,' instead of the phrase 'go **** in a lake,' and discovered as he expected, that it had a statistically significant frequency.

In a more somber effort, he wanted to see whether expected use of certain words from a common-sense perspective appeared in his analysis programs as significant. He chose the words 'bracket, brackets, bracketology' as a word set that would be interpreted by the program as interchangeable or having much the same meaning or reference. He set the analysis baseline for the month of December and ran the program to search for that word set only during the month of December for as far back in time as the data existed. Then he ran the same program using the month of March, when in the United States at least, one would expect increased focus upon the popular college basketball tournament and the associated use of the term 'bracket.' After running the program in the same manner for March, he discovered a statistically significant increase in the occurrence of that word group in March compared with its usage in December. When he compared the results for March against all other months of the year, he found a similar statistically significant higher frequency of that word usage in March compared with all other months. Still glowing with the intellectual high resulting from his discovery, Sammy was compelled to share his work with Duke, who had a strong interest in computer applications throughout his vast business empire. He sent a message over Duke's super-secret System 16:

> *'Basically, the internet gives us the capacity to 'take the pulse' of the internet world, and by implication the real world in general.*

Assuming that millions of people are on the internet during even any one small period of time, like 15 minutes, we can get a measure of what has their attention during any particular timeframe. Although several search engines do this kind of broad filtering, they probably do not do it with the precision that I have discovered. I have noted baseline measures of the occurrences of certain key words or phrases in any language. Using those, I can then determine whether unusual attention is given to those words by measuring the degree to which occurrences of certain phrases or words deviate from their established long-term or recent typical frequency baselines. English is favored on the internet as suggested by its use in 55 percent of the million most-visited websites, as of April 2013, according to Alexa.com. That estimate may have changed by now, since more languages are being used on the internet, but we should assume that degree of dominance even today for most practical purposes. Other languages which are used at least in two percent of websites are Russian, German, Spanish, Chinese, French, Japanese, Arabic, and Portuguese. Briefly, we know that word usage can be broken down into groups of typical usage, like spoken or conversational word usage, prepared news broadcasts, literary fiction, magazine, and academic articles would be examples. Certain words occur more often within one group than within another. For instance, the phrase 'eight-week' occurs more often in scientific literature than in most fiction, and 'love' and 'braid' occur far more often in fiction than in any of the other four groups. What I have done is capture a large amount of google word usage—primarily emails and blogs I am assuming and analyze it. I was doing this basically out of boredom several months ago, but since then have become quite interested in the applications of certain kinds of analysis of this data. I really don't know whether the FBI, NSA, CIA, or their foreign counterparts are doing this kind of work, but it wouldn't surprise me if they were. Some current search engines already do this kind of thing, but they always seem to come up with rock star names. In any event, I have not seen anything published on the internet or elsewhere indicating that they are doing this kind of analysis, so if they are, they are probably doing it under wraps, and it is likely classified at the highest levels. What I have found is that the word 'mead' has occurred more frequently recently than its baseline frequencies among various word usage groups would imply. It's not a huge increase in frequency in absolute terms, but it is odd that such an innocuous word would show up like that. Mead could refer to paper, school supplies, valve components, wine making, a drink made of water, honey, malt and yeast, or any number of people with a surname of Mead. Also, a spelling of 'meade' might be relevant, implying telescopes or other optical devices It could mean Lake Mead, George Mead, Margaret Mead, or whatever or whoever else might have such a name. Anyway, this analysis might be useful because recent usage of the word 'mead' is about two standard deviations above what it was at least 10 months ago, even though many people do not spell very well on the internet, perhaps because of ignorance, or maybe fat fingers. I find it hard to believe that usage is referring to a person, because related searches in the general news media show no such interest in the word 'mead,' other than references to Lake Mead in Nevada, and it's recent falling water level. So, if common interpersonal conversation includes the word at a greater frequency than what occurs in the public media… what is that saying? Sammy'

Duke responded within minutes:

'That is really interesting! Can you determine the locations which have or produce the highest frequencies?'

Sammy replied:

'Not specifically. Not that I know of without a court order, anyway. It might be possible to make a really good approximation of the location of the internet service provider, however.'

Duke responded:

'Find out where the sources are as closely as you can and let me know what you discover!'

Sammy replied:

'Will do. More later.'

CHAPTER 31
Tuesday, July 28, 2015

One of her duties at the Chancellor Organization was to check all the communications logs to and from every Chancellor computer throughout the world to verify that all channels were functioning properly, and to verify security. Stephanie Paris was just about finished when she discovered that one of the encrypted links had not been accessed for more than a week. That was not a critical issue in and of itself, but it was, nevertheless, unusual. The flow of information throughout the Chancellor Organization was consistent in frequency and volume for each channel, so the absence of contact on even one channel was cause for at least some further investigation. The business was dependent upon information–true, unbiased, recent, and accurate information that is too often a rare commodity in the modern world, particularly on the internet, where too many people spout 'information' of questionable veracity tied to someone's agenda, deliberately or maliciously, truthfully, or otherwise, often with unknown intention and purpose, or without either.

She walked into her boss's office. He was apparently open to interruption, so she said in a tone of mild concern, "Mr. Chancellor, my latest review of the network shows one anomaly. You will see it highlighted on page 28 of the report. The encrypted channel for Valentin Murat has not been accessed at all for more than five days. That's a little long for him."

Duke opened the report on his desktop computer and scrolled to page 28 and sighed.

"Please get Major General Raza Arshad on the phone, Stephanie."

Two and a half hours later, Duke's private phone rang at his desk.

"Thank you for calling back, General Arshad. How is Amir progressing with his schooling and violin lessons?"

"He is doing quite well, thank you! I believe I still owe you and your organization a significant debt of gratitude for restoring my son's sight, Mr. Chancellor. Now, please, tell me… What can I do for you?"

"General…, I do not wish to inconvenience you beyond your personal or professional comfort level, but I am quite concerned about one of my people located in your part of the world where I do not have other reliable sources of information right now. His name is Valentin Murat, and he is a journalist for the Kazecon News Agency in Kazakhstan. We have not heard from him for more than five days, which is quite unusual, and my intuition is causing me increasing concern. His last known location was at a pier in Karachi when we received his most recent communication. I realize that your sphere of influence and official responsibilities do not necessarily extend outside Pakistan into foreign countries, but I wanted to use every possible avenue of inquiry without prematurely elevating the attention of official national governmental agencies or before this matter becomes more of a personal and organizational concern with negative consequences. However, if an unusual problem develops, then I will do what I must do through traditional channels."

"I understand completely, Mr. Chancellor. I am limited in my official ability to inquire outside of Pakistan, but I, too, have some ability to exercise certain privileges and consult certain 'sources' of information within Pakistan who under special conditions of obligation can be persuaded to cooperate. I would be happy to see what I can discover for you during the next week or so. May I contact you at this number?"

"Yes, indeed! It is quite secure. Thank you, General! I appreciate your generosity very much. Please let me know anytime, day or night, if you need anything further from me in this matter. Raj Sampat will also be available to you if you think his services would be useful."

"Thank you, Mr. Chancellor, but I believe I should proceed as inconspicuously as possible without his assistance for the time being."

"Very well, General. I will look forward to your call. Thank you!"

"Goodbye, Mr. Chancellor."

**** LONDON, ENGLAND ****

A young male clerk at HSBC Bank at Canary Wharf in London sent a wire transfer to the general account of MIT, with notice to the Bursar of the Massachusetts Institute of Technology, Cambridge, Massachusetts that it should be credited to the tuition account of Rahim Nazari. The transfer amount of $44,720, a mere pittance relative to the assets of the second largest bank in the world, was just another normal transaction among the hundreds of other transfers he would process that day. He could not know the indirect implications or eventual consequences associated with that transaction.

CHAPTER 32
Wednesday, July 29, 2015

**** KARACHI, PAKISTAN ****

General Arshad took several days of personal leave to fly to Karachi from Quetta knowing that his commanding personal presence in military uniform would be most effective in getting the information he needed without prompting too many unwanted questions. He already knew that the Pakistani bureaucracy at both the official military and local police levels would impede his efforts beyond his level of patience, but if he traveled in civilian attire, then he would not have available his accustomed level of obvious military authority and associated persuasive scripts. He had to honor his secret relationship with Duke Chancellor without revealing any connection between his personal or official status in Pakistan, and the minor, but honor-bound favor he had promised to do for Duke. He boarded Pakistan Airlines Flight 363 at 2:40 P.M. at Quetta for the non-stop one-hour and 20-minute flight to Karachi. After landing and deplaning by 4:25 P.M., the air was still warm as he hailed a cab outside the main airport terminal and told the driver to take him to the Sindh administration building on Fahkrudden Valika Road. By 5:34 P.M., he was inside the Sindh police station asking for the chief of police. Police Chief Jamal Goraya saw the handsome six-foot, two-inch tall General enter his police station, and immediately sensed that something unusual was afoot. The six-foot tall, 41-year-old muscular chief of police arose from behind his desk in his glass-enclosed office at the rear of the station, put on his uniform jacket, smoothed his moderate black mustache, and walked out to greet the general.

"I am the Chief of Police, Jamal Goraya. What can I do for you, General?"

"I am Major General Raza Arshad, commander of the special Services Group. I have need of information regarding the disappearance of a Kazakh-stan citizen named Valentin Murat six days ago in this city down by the pier."

"May I ask why the Special Services Group has an interest in Mr. Murat…, General?"

This was precisely the kind of official curiosity nonsense that the general did not want to entertain.

General Arshad stepped closer to Goraya, looked slightly down into the eyes of the shorter man, and said in quiet, but firm steely words, "Because *I say* it has an interest…, Chief."

The other man responded with apparent polite political resignation, even though he could not shake the curiosity implicit in a major general doing what a lower-ranked officer would be expected to do, "I see."

General Arshad's demeanor did not change as he waited patiently for his intention to register in the policeman's head.

After a brief pause Goraya said, "The reason I asked about your interest, General, is that Mr. Murat is dead. I find it curious that the commanding General of the SSG suddenly shows up in my office asking about an obscure Kazakhstan journalist so soon after he was murdered in an apparently expert manner–a single gunshot through both his car windshield and his head. That's why I asked what your interest is. Is there something I should know regarding this case…, General?"

General Arshad masked his shock effectively and tried one more time to squelch the police chief's growing curiosity with his senior commander's demeanor as he said, "Mr. Murat's disappearance–and now certainly his demise–has potential international implications well above the authority of the Sindh chief of police to manage. I am not at liberty to elaborate upon the matter any further than I already have. It would be in *everyone's* best interest if I could see the evidence you have gathered regarding this incident… as soon as possible…, Chief Goraya."

Goraya carefully considered the clear implication that he was outranked both officially and politically, a position he had not experienced in many years, and reluctantly began to cooperate.

After several seconds, Goraya responded, "Well, if you will have a seat at the empty desk over here, General, I will bring you what we have."

"Thank you!" the general said brightly in feigned politeness, as he returned to his full upright stature, and then walked with only five strides toward the indicated plain gray metal desk, removed his hat, and set it carefully on the desk.

Chief Goraya returned slightly more than four minutes later with two transparent plastic boxes bearing evidence labels on which was typed, 'Murat, Friday, July 24, 2015,' and a list of the contents. He carefully set the boxes containing various materials and papers down on the desk in front of General Arshad, deliberately avoiding his hat.

"This is all we have, General!"

"Thank you, Chief. I will not take any more time than is absolutely necessary."

General Arshad ignored the box obviously containing Valentin's clothing and focused his attention upon the contents of the other box. He carefully picked through the few items in the box and glanced at various identification cards in the wallet, an empty water bottle, a notebook computer, and a Sony digital recorder with twin stereo earpieces, a briefcase containing several handwritten notes, a power cord for the computer, and an old appointment book. He glanced through the appointment book and the hand-written notes, looking for what should be the most recent entries. The last one was dated Friday, June 26, 2015, at the Green Mosque in Balkh, Afghanistan. He made a note of that information in his own notebook, and then picked up the Sony recorder and placed the earpieces in his ears. He turned it on and scrolled through the five electronic folders identified in the recorder's main menu. He assumed the last folder was the most recently used, opened it, and pressed the 'play' button. After just a few seconds of background noise, he heard the contents.

> 'We are seated in the middle of an ancient city that still bears the evidence of man's struggle for truth and peace. I will soon be the new leader of the Islamic State, which will eventually prevail in its quest for a caliphate. We strongly object to the interference of the United States of America against our struggle for self-determination. We have plans to eliminate the United States from its current dominant world position with the help of Allah, peace be upon Him. It is inevitable! God willing, we will put our plans into motion this year.'

'Is there anything else you can tell me about your plans, Mr. Abdul-Kaliq?'

'God willing, the United States will experience devastation unlike any other in its history. It will be crippled forever!'

'I see.... And exactly what is this devastation, and how is it going to come about?'

'You would be a very foolish young man indeed if you expect me to answer that question. That is my message to the world. Our time together is over.'

General Arshad was internally taken aback by what he had just heard, but with habitual discipline, remained impassive on the surface. He casually looked up and around his location for just a few seconds. No one was paying any attention to him, so he returned his focus to the recorder. With slightly elevated heart rate, he retrieved his pen and notebook from his inside jacket pocket, and then replayed the same file... only this time he took meticulous notes. When he was finished with that file, he listened to each of the other four files. Two were blank, and the remaining two contained no useful or valuable information—apparently just some thoughts about academic work Valentin had been doing on the side.

About 45 minutes after he had entered the police station, he placed his notebook carefully in his jacket pocket, picked up his hat and carefully put it back on his head with both hands. Chief Goraya noticed from his office that the general was preparing to leave and walked out to where he was seated.

As Goraya approached, General Arshad stood up and asked in an official routine manner, "Have you listened to any of the recordings in this device?"

"No, not yet. We are short of staff, and have had other, more pressing cases to occupy our time, General."

With well-hidden internal relief, General Arshad responded in a bland official manner, "I see... Well, thank you for your time."

General Arshad smiled innocently for only a moment at the chief, then turned away and left the police station, comforted by evidence that the traditionally slow police procedures had not changed during his career. Outside, he hailed a cab, and returned to the airport. Since he did not have secure communications equipment with him to contact Duke Chancellor with what he had just learned. Since the next flight back to Quetta was early the next morning, he booked a room for the night at the Ramada Plaza Karachi hotel near the airport. He needed to get this information to Duke before Goraya had another opportunity to listen to what was on that recorder.

CHAPTER 33
Thursday, July 30, 2015

After a long night of many short catnaps and little genuine sleep, General Arshad finally awoke completely at 5:22 A.M. under clear skies, showered and dressed in record time. He checked out of the hotel immediately, quickly hailed a waiting taxi, and told the driver to drive him to the airport without delay. During the cab ride, he continued to mull over the words from the digital recorder and slowly allowed himself to sink into an unfamiliar personal concern. He already knew that the world was full of unpredictable events and people who presented serious threats to a peaceful status quo. However, he had not heard of this threat before.

The skinny young male cabbie looked as though he might not be old enough to drive. Nevertheless, he did an expert job of weaving through various traffic challenges and arrived at the main terminal just 24 minutes later. After consuming a cup of coffee and a bland muffin of unfamiliar taste and origin at one of the food kiosks near the airport lounge area, General Arshad boarded Pakistan International Airlines Flight 352 at 7:20 A.M., due to arrive at 8:40 A.M. in Quetta. Within a half hour after landing, he was in his car and dialing the special cell number for Duke Chancellor on his own secure mobile phone. The time was nine hours earlier in Maryland–10 minutes after midnight. The call awakened Duke from only a light sleep.

Duke answered, *"Yes?"*

"Mr. Chancellor, please forgive me for calling at this late hour, but you should know as soon as possible what I have learned. I could not get to my secure phone until just a few moments ago."

Out of habit, Duke switched on the nearby small bedside lamp and said, *"General Arshad! Thank you for calling back so soon! I had not expected to hear from you this quickly!"*

"First of all, I must tell you that according to the Sindh chief of police–a man named Goraya–Mr. Murat was murdered at the pier in Karachi, apparently by someone experienced in such tasks. A single bullet went through both his car windshield and then through his head. I'm so *very* sorry to have to tell you this about your young associate."

"Oh my God! I had no idea he was in danger!"

There must be some connection between his death and the last message he sent!

General Arshad continued, "I do not believe the information I discovered would go very far in the right direction with the proper attention it deserves in Pakistan if I were to send it up the traditional channel of communication with all the required cumbersome bureaucratic documentation. I wanted to get this information to you before it could rise to official governmental levels or the ISI in Pakistan. It is bad enough that the police have it. They can be rather slow most of the time. I discovered what I believe is Mr. Murat's personal voice recorder in an evidence box at the Karachi police station. Fortunately, I persuaded the chief to allow me to examine the evidence, including his modern Sony digital recorder. I listened to all the recordings in it. However, after realizing how important the most recent message was, I listened to it again and took precise notes. Two different voices were recorded–one I believe was Mr. Murat's and the other was someone named Fatih Abdul-Kaliq, who claims to be the new leader of the Islamic State, or soon will be the new leader. I don't know which. Nevertheless, may I quote the relatively short conversation to you, or is this not a good time?"

At this point, Duke was completely awake with an elevated heart rate and said, *"Now is fine! I wish to know everything you have learned, General…. Please do continue!"*

"Very well, Mr. Chancellor. I will identify each speaker, but the rest is exactly what was recorded on Friday, June 26, 2015, at the Green Mosque in Balkh, Afghanistan:

"Fatih Abdul-Kaliq: 'We are seated in the middle of an ancient city that still bears the evidence of man's struggle for truth and peace. I will soon be the new leader of the Islamic State, which will eventually prevail in its quest for a caliphate. We strongly object to the interference of the United States of America against our struggle for self-determination. We have plans to eliminate the United States from its current dominant world position with the help of Allah, peace be upon Him. It is inevitable! God willing, we will put our plans into motion this year.'

"Mr. Murat: 'Is there anything else you can tell me about your plans, Mr. Abdul-Kaliq?'

"Fatih Abdul-Kaliq: 'God willing, the United States will experience devastation unlike any other in its history. It will be crippled forever!'

"Mr. Murat: 'I see. And exactly what is this devastation, and how is it going to come about?'

"Fatih Abdul-Kaliq: 'You would be a very foolish young man indeed if you expect me to answer that question. That is my message to the world. Our time together is over.'

"That was the entire recording, Mr. Chancellor, exactly… word for word!"

"That is absolutely amazing! Is it possible in any way that you can secure that recorder and send it to me?"

"As much as I would want to honor your request, Mr. Chancellor, I'm afraid not. Now that I have already handled the evidence, if it were to disappear, I strongly suspect I would be in a very compromised position, and therefore rather useless to you in the future. Besides, I believe it would prompt too many inconvenient questions regarding my interest in what so far has been a routine police case."

"I understand completely, General, but I had to ask."

"I certainly understand."

"Thank you very much for your efforts. I will treat this with the utmost confidence, trust, and importance it most certainly deserves. Please do not hesitate to call me again if you come across anything else that could be even only remotely related to this information. And, of course, this conversation will remain absolutely confidential! Will you please send me a copy of the notes you just read, General?"

"I will certainly do that, Mr. Chancellor."

"Thank you very much! Good night, General."

"Mr. Chancellor…?"

"Yes, General?"

"I would be *extra vigilant*, if I were you...."

"Thank you, General. I will most certainly keep that in mind."

**** MARYLAND ****

Duke Chancellor terminated the phone call, replaced his phone on his nightstand, reclined on his bed and stared restlessly at the ceiling. He simply could not dismiss the feeling of responsibility for Valentin's death. Guilt crawled over him, coating him as if it were like bitter molasses. He juggled various thoughts as they rapidly invaded his mind, mixed with what General Arshad had quoted, for about an hour before he finally turned his bedside light off and succumbed to overdue sleep, but with sustained effort.

I must find out what Valentin had seen or done that got him killed. I must do at least that much. Was he simply in the wrong place at the wrong time? Why, God? WHY? He was young, strong, intelligent, and full of promise...! WHY? The world needs <u>more</u> people like him—not fewer!

**** MATARA, SRI LANKA ****

Seven days and 2,945 miles after leaving Karachi, the luxury yacht approached Matara, Sri Lanka. The sun was sinking slowly toward the slightly cloudy horizon in one of Mother Nature's most splendid displays of light and color as Destiny approached the pier. Within minutes, deckhands secured her to the pier, and started filling her fuel tanks. During that period, another deckhand brought minor food supplies and fresh water on board as the colors in the western sky faded. After refueling was complete, the crew untied the mooring ropes as the portside thrusters immediately started to push her away from the pier. Half a minute later, the thrusters fell silent. Then the captain pushed both main throttles forward and the big twin Caterpillar engines responded with the smooth muffled roar of their power as Destiny moved out of the harbor. Then he slowly pushed the throttles to their maximum forward positions, as he watched the glowing white tachometer pointers obediently move slowly toward their respective red lines. Those remaining on the pier watched the yacht accelerate with remarkable speed for her size. Her bow lifter higher as she entered the open sea, again heading toward the east, and soon put the fading sunset behind her.

CHAPTER 34
Friday, July 31, 2015

**** *CHELYABINSK, RUSSIA* ****

Shortly before 8 A.M. on a gray day, Colonel Kovalenko once again went to the storage vault and personally verified the weapons count. Satisfied again that the inventory had not changed from his last count, he returned to his office and settled in for another day of routine matters apart from the 'inventory problem.' However, he simply could not force his attention away from it. It was indeed the 'elephant' in his office and the 'stone' in his shoe.

He called out in routine manner to the head of his immediate staff, "Sergeant, please find Major Logonovsky and tell him to come to my office without delay."

The younger man responded with caution, "Sir, Major Logonovsky is no longer here. He was transferred yesterday to the 821st Main Space Intelligence Center, headquarters of the Russian military space surveillance network."

"Oh? And exactly where is *that*, Sergeant?"

"In Noginsk, sir…, about a kilometer southwest of the village of Dubrovo in Moscow Oblast, sir. You signed the orders yourself…, sir."

Colonel Kovalenko glanced over at the sergeant with veiled frustration.

I did no such thing, you dimwit!

He knew that what he had just heard should remain within him without comment for the time being, and calmly responded, "Very well, Sergeant. Return to your duty…, and make sure that I am not disturbed for the next hour."

"Yes sir."

Colonel Kovalenko waited for another three minutes in deep thought before calling his friend Colonel Vasily Koshelev at Khoroshevskoye Road number 76, Khodinka, Moscow–GRU headquarters.

The expected familiar voice answered after only two rings, *"Koshelev…"*

"Vasily, this is Viktor. I just learned that my executive officer, Major Leonid Logonovsky has been reassigned to the 821st Main Space Intelligence Center near Moscow, according to orders that I am told bear my signature. The problem is that I never issued, heard of, nor signed any such order, nor was I consulted! It appears that I cannot trust the officers assigned to this installation, Vasily, so I am calling you. What the *hell* is going on, Vasily?"

"That is very strange indeed, Viktor… Let me look around… make some calls… talk to some people, and then I will get back to you."

With a moderate sigh of relief, Viktor said, "I would really appreciate that, Vasily. Thank you."

"Goodbye, Viktor."

**** CAMBRIDGE, MASSACHUSETTS ****

A clerk in the bursar's office at the Massachusetts Institute of Technology received a wire transfer of $44,720 from HSBC headquarters at Canary Wharf in London, the second largest bank in the world with assets of $2.723 trillion, behind the Industrial and Commercial Bank of China with $3.062 trillion in assets. No one at the bank had any reason to think about the reasons for, or the background of such a small transfer. The clerk also had no reason to investigate that transaction. Then, according to standing written instructions for that account, he credited that wire transfer to the tuition account of Rahim Nazari, just another graduate student in the Department of Geophysics—one of thousands of students at that university. That clerk was just doing his job. Neither he nor the clerk at HSBC could know or wanted to know the ultimate source of that money or how it was acquired. Neither had any concept of what kind of treachery would eventually occur at least partially because they had properly moved that sum of money electronically from one account to another. Shamir had counted upon their human nature—the unquestioned habitual tasks of getting from morning to night with the least discomfort and the least effort possible... and the fewest questions.

CHAPTER 35
Saturday, August 1, 2015

Colonel Kovalenko took a leave of absence–one of the few privileges afforded by his rank, current assignment, and length of service. He needed to ensure his anonymity in the only way that satisfied his personal security and vast experience in covert military operations. He retrieved one of his several old identification packages from the safe in his apartment office just outside Chelyabinsk and mapped out an obscure route to a distant old Catholic Church in Krasnodon, Ukraine. Due to the long-held views of the Russian Orthodox Church, the Russian State does not recognize Catholicism as a legitimately Russian religion, and Catholics have often been considered outsiders, even if they were ethnically Russian. The old Soviet Union, which persecuted many religions periodically throughout its history, also classified Catholicism as a non-Russian allegiance. It was precisely because of that reputation that he chose Catholicism as an avenue through which he could communicate completely honestly with another person who had credible discretion. He wanted advice from someone he could trust immediately, and he wanted to plant a secret seed of persuasive information that could make its way out of Russia without his signature on it. The only avenue he could imagine as adequate for both his needs and fears was through a priest. Not just anyone could be a priest. Only the most habitually sincere, wise, and respectful among men could even remotely qualify as deserving of immediate trust. He did not have the time to develop the necessary trust with a stranger. His future and obligation to himself required responsible unburdening of his suspicions as soon as possible. He had to take that leap of faith in the confessional. He believed that even a *priest* could not keep his information secret and would carefully send it up the line to someone who would eventually carefully inform appropriate authorities outside Russia. He did not travel by air because he did not want to leave any easily visible or documented record of his travels that the GRU, KGB remnants, or others would certainly discover eventually, figure out where he went, and then possibly find him, and question him eventually about his activities and motives. In common civilian attire, he drove a rented automobile under one of his prepared aliases for 11 hours and 46 minutes over 453 miles to the town of Tolyatti, the home of Avtovaz, Russia's largest automobile manufacturer. He stayed at the Patio Hotel in a single room for the equivalent of just over $32 for the night. After settling into his room, he checked his appearance in the bathroom mirror carefully, darkened his hair, shaved, and added a more youthful appearance to his face with some simple makeup. The chances of his behavior or communication becoming known to the GRU or other entities harmful to his career or personal future would be less in Ukraine than what he would expect if he tried to communicate formally, or even secretly within Russia.

CHAPTER 36
Sunday, August 2, 2015

As clouds threatened rain, Viktor awoke early to start his 362-mile drive south-west during the next eight hours and 10 minutes on the P-228 highway next to the Volga River to the small village of Kamyshin on the west bank. He drove without adverse incident to the Opava Hotel on Oktyabrskaya Street and took the only available room, an adequate small efficiency with a moderately com-fortable double-size mattress on an old ornate iron bed. The room also had a Japanese television, a small refrigerator, an orange rug on the light tan wooden plank flooring, and a small but clean bathroom for about $46 per night. After a light 'nutritionally correct' supper at a nearby café, he returned to his room just after 6 P.M., and settled in for the night.

About 1,008 miles southwest of Kamyshin across the Black Sea, a man and a woman were sitting on opposite sides of a dining table obviously designed for no more than two adults, at least one of whom desired privacy. Their table was located within one of the small alcoves along an interior eastern wall of the stylish and urban Mikla Restaurant, designed with chrome accents rem-iniscent of the 1950s. However, the furniture was a 1970s style, and the dark well-polished wooden bar was reputed to have come originally from genuine old railroad sleeping cars. The fading orange light of the sun just now touching the horizon still illuminated the interior of the restaurant here and there, with

155

what might have been warm romantic ambiance or suggestion. Approaching dusk diminished nature's light as thousands of artificial lights gradually appeared across the Bosporus and most of the city of Istanbul immediately below the restaurant. Reflections of the city lights from the surface of the currently calm water added to possibilities of a romantic evening.

Umar Kasana swallowed another fork-full of his salmon-steak dinner and placed the utensil back on his plate while still chewing the last of his fish in a crudely deliberate and lascivious manner as he once again looked up and across the table at the lady of the evening. She was elegantly dressed in fashionable western style, including a bright red sleeveless dress with a suggestive but still only modestly plunging neckline, accented with a bright blue silk scarf around her neck, and an equally attractive white sash around her firm and slim waist. White high-heeled shoes accented the ends of her long, smooth, and shapely legs partially visible under the table. Most of her long natural honey-blonde wavy mane was held in place with a thick bright red ruffled elastic band toward her left side, allowing much of her hair to rest partly on either side of her firm shoulder. Her only slightly made-up cover-girl face and striking, intelligent, emerald eyes presented the challenge of practiced and confident self-awareness sufficient to defeat the interested or otherwise involuntary stares of most men, regardless of age or cultural heritage. The maître' d quietly approached their table with a smile.

"Good evening, Mr. Kasana! I am happy to welcome you and your... *guest*... to my restaurant this evening!"

He shifted his glance with a more deliberate and appreciative smile and a slight bow toward the young woman, as she toyed with the raw grouper artistically dressed in olives and lemon on her plate. Then he turned back to extend his hand to the very fit looking, handsome, and moderately bearded man seated across from her. Umar responded smoothly with his right hand to offer his trademark iron-like rigid handshake without nearly crushing the other man's hand, along with a well-crafted generic smile of only bland but appropriate business proportions.

In just slightly accented English, he responded, "Your cuisine is delicious, as usual, Kemal!"

Then he surreptitiously curved his right hand around the small piece of paper as Kemal released his handshake, and Umar easily secured the small, folded paper, effectively hiding it in his palm with the tip of his ring finger and withdrew his hand to rest it upon the cream-colored linen tablecloth. Then he casually clasped his right hand with his left, still effectively hiding the paper while smiling in a gracious indication that it was time for Kemal to leave. The young woman again politely looked up at Kemal and deliberately rewarded him with an innocently teasing smile that he imagined might mean she was offering something he knew he could never have. Umar covertly slipped the paper into the right-side pocket of his black sport jacket with the smooth effectiveness of an experienced and slick street magician. He faked a minor adjustment to his jacket as he casually returned his empty right hand to the surface of the table with a final brief glance in Kemal's direction as he disappeared into the depths of the restaurant. Umar turned back toward the woman with an amused smile as he subconsciously rolled the corner of his cream-colored linen napkin upon itself with his thumb, index, and middle fingers of his right hand. Without comment, she filed that slightly neurotic habit in her professionally well-trained memory.

"Interesting, isn't it, that we are seated here apparently just as innocently and anonymously as all the others? But, as you surely must know, we all have secrets… do we not? And we secretly desire to know the private lives of others, even sometimes because we wish to gain some advantage over others, or merely a perspective of our own lives by comparing ours to the lives of others. For centuries–even as long ago as the seventh century BC–this city has been one of the world's most intriguing and important historical crossroads between East and West, and North and South. Earth's geological configuration has made it so. And at one time, it was the largest city on the planet! How things have changed! For thousands of years, merchants, businessmen, and traders have passed through here over land and by water, transporting goods up and down the Bosporus out there, eventually to and from the Mediterranean Sea and beyond. They even travelled to and from the Far East, changing money, and not a few of them met to conspire for one purpose or another, or even to spy upon or hide from others! When I visit such fascinating places as this, my admittedly vivid imagination wanders as I look around at other people and easily make up stories about them. Sometimes I even want to engage them in conversation, just to compare my imagination with their real lives, or at least what they *say* about themselves. I marvel at their sheer diversity and number!

Take, for example, that overweight balding man sitting right over there. I imagine him to be a wealthy divorced shipping magnate, waiting for a new potential customer so he can close a business arrangement to help keep up his uncomfortably large alimony payments!"

She joined his impromptu game readily with a natural subtle twinkle in her eye, and whispered across the table, "And he's been screwing his neighbor's beautiful young blonde-haired wife for the last six months!"

For just a moment, Umar lost his customary self-control and then spontaneously burst into raucous laughter for a full 10 seconds at her unexpectedly bawdy elaboration of his imaginary story. He noted her surprisingly salacious mental agility with great interest. A few patrons along the outer windows on the other side of the room from their location partially turned around in their seats, after having heard his sudden outburst of laughter, but with only slightly more than mild interest before turning back toward their tables and prior interests. She smiled easily, still in control of her special self-confidence, and eagerly continued the game.

"Can you see that nicely dressed handsome man with dark hair in the gray suit and ugly green tie over there near the corner, sitting with that hooker in the black dress?"

He turned his head slowly and innocuously, glanced briefly in the direction she indicated and smiled to himself, but then just as slowly turned back toward her with an obscure questioning facial expression as he asked with unexpected amusement, "How do you know she's a hooker?"

She smiled mischievously as she deliberately leaned slightly toward him for just a few seconds, mildly accentuating her modest cleavage and then said pointedly, "Women's intuition! If you don't believe me, then why don't you just walk over there and *ask* her whether she's a hooker?"

The woman in the black dress with long wavy dark hair casually played with a pen on the surface of her table, innocently tapping the end closest to her several times, while pointing it toward Umar using her peripheral vision as she maintained the appearance of an animated conversation with the man in the gray suit sitting at the same table across from her. She was wearing a silver necklace with a silver equilateral triangle hanging from it. On her left wrist was a matching bracelet with an identical silver equilateral triangle charm.

Umar smiled confidently, effectively masking his genuine surprise at her daring challenge and said, "Because she would not tell me the *truth*, and because that's *not* the way *I* play the game! Besides, she is simply not as beautiful as you!"

She chuckled gently with self-assurance and continued playfully without missing a beat, "The guy she's with is actually British… works for MI-6. He's smart as a whip and *deadly* with his hands!"

Umar smiled deliberately and suggestively while mentally trying to keep up with her, looking deep into her eyes with obvious hopeful interest as he continued improvising.

"Do you mean… *in bed*, or…,"

Unfazed and suddenly with a contrived serious facial expression, she again leaned toward him in feigned conspiratorial fashion and whispered urgently, "I mean he can *kill* with his *bare hands… with ease!*"

Then she sat back in her chair and smiled in a well-practiced, confident, and completely disarming manner as he continued the game.

"The other woman sitting at the table behind him is an old American biddy on vacation, a former schoolteacher, taught Latin to a bunch of high-school kids in Las Vegas, started a knitting club in her spare time. Then she met a rich widower at a local casino who owned a large hotel chain, married him, and then later hired an amateur hit man from Los Angeles to do him in so she could inherit all his money! She was never caught! Now she just travels without a care all over the world!"

Leah said, "I do agree that she's American, but she's really an American CIA agent–graduated from Radcliffe College, where she played field hockey, and has friends in some *very* high places! Expert shot with a pistol or a sniper rifle! But she is really disguised just to *look* old! She is actually quite attractive and very much in shape under all that costume and makeup! I would bet she's an expert in self-defense as well!"

They laughed together easily, then eagerly looked inconspicuously around the dining area with residual smiles for another inspiration to make up another story and competed with sometimes wildly fantastic or even more-bizarre scenarios as they continued their game for another 10 minutes before their server returned to collect their dinner plates and offer dessert menus. Later, after finishing her Turkish coffee served with a slice of vanilla, and a small dish of delicious red raspberry sorbet, she gracefully excused herself to visit the ladies' room. Umar briefly studied her retreating attractive figure, and after she was completely out of sight, he retrieved the slip of paper from his pocket and read it.

> '*I trust you are enjoying my choice for your companionship this evening. However, an important person requires your services. Look for a black Maserati Quattroporte automobile outside the restaurant.*'

He internally, but vehemently cursed this unwelcome interruption of his evening plans for another conquest. However, business was business, and he had a very useful and hard-earned professional reputation to maintain. With unusual effort, he rationalized an exit from his conflict by reminding himself that other 'female opportunities' would certainly arise in time. He had already concluded that the admittedly alluring lady was probably a quid pro quo. She returned after an efficient, or contrived visit to the ladies' room, and smiled completely innocently at him. He stood up as she approached the table, and then sat down after she did, and started one of his more eloquent apologetic soliloquies.

"I am so very sorry, my dear, but I have been called away to attend to an unexpected and urgent business matter. However, I shall return within 15 minutes at the most."

Assuming that his most wistful, well-practiced smile and a knowing wink would hold her in eager anticipation until he returned, he stood and left the table, crossed the dining area at a deliberate business pace, and walked directly toward the front entrance. The man in the gray suit placed several currency notes on his table, stood up, and casually followed the man in black at a distance. He surreptitiously pressed a 'quick-dial' button on his cellphone, smoothly brought the small device up to his right ear and spoke softly into it with a British accent.

"Yes. I have him now," said the man wearing the gray suit and ugly green tie.

Michael Winston smoothly continued the motion of his right arm back to his side, effectively masking his brief phone message to all but the most experienced in professional international spy craft and left the restaurant. After a few minutes passed, the 'hooker' in the black dress also stood but walked in the opposite direction toward the ladies' room. She never appeared in the dining area again. The images of Umar Kasana from her 'pen' raced through the internet to a computer at Mossad headquarters just north of Tel Aviv, Israel.

Leah Cummings casually placed her phone back in her purse, retrieved a plastic freezer bag, surreptitiously reached across the table, and grasped the handle end of Umar's fork with her napkin, and placed the fork in the freezer bag, sealed it, and then put it in her purse. She waited patiently for several minutes and slowly looked around the restaurant. Then she calmly stood up, removed her blue scarf and the ruffled red elastic bow holding her hair in place, calmly placed them in her purse, and then briefly shook her hair loose. With no particular visual focus, she walked across the old hardwood floor through the restaurant away from the front entrance and exited through a rear service door. She had successfully impersonated a local 'associate' of a high-class international escort service, orchestrated by the Central Intelligence Agency. She started to work her way back to CIA headquarters.

Umar admired the sleek black luxury sport sedan at the curb in front of the restaurant as soon as he went out through the front exit. The air was still, and the street was silent and almost empty. He could not determine whether the finely engineered engine was running or not because it was so quiet. Melek (meaning 'Angel' in Arabic) noted the man she knew was a Turkish arms dealer exiting the restaurant and approaching the Maserati. She memorized the license number of the expensive car as she drove by it facing the same direction. Umar then walked up to the front passenger door of the Maserati and bent down to look inside as the window suddenly slipped down into the door with scarcely a hum. Neither he nor the driver recognized the woman in the small car that had just passed down the street on the driver's side of the Maserati only several seconds before. A little more than a block away, she pulled over to the side of the street into a vacant parking space and waited.

The driver of the Maserati politely commanded in a confident business tone through the open passenger side window, "Get in."

After looking around casually for any unusual or unexpected people or activity for about 10 seconds, Umar opened the passenger door, eased his agile form into the car, and closed the door. He waited, looking around through the darkened side windows of the car with a practiced eye sharpened through over a dozen years of clandestine and sometimes illegal service for whoever paid the highest price.

Shamir had done his research thoroughly. He said in a practiced business tone, "I am aware of your reputation, and I require your services, for which I am prepared to pay handsomely. If you are carrying a cellphone, I strongly suggest that you take the battery out temporarily and place your phone in this lead-lined bag."

Umar understood that doing so would prevent satellite recognition of his phone, and therefore, by implication, his location. While eyeing Shamir carefully, he calmly reached inside his jacket for his cellphone. He then removed the battery and placed both the phone and the battery in the lead-lined leather bag Shamir offered him, and then put the bag in his jacket side pocket. He sensed that this encounter was beginning to resemble the form of several other meetings he had had in his career with experienced, professional, or otherwise influential or powerful people, some of whom who made most of their living on the dark side of the street, and *never* worked alone.

Umar said, "And I require the satisfaction that I am paid up front. If you know who I am, then you also know the nature of my business and the risks I am likely to encounter…, and my *rules.*"

"I am aware," Shamir responded evenly.

Shamir reached inside his baggy shalwar pocket and pulled out a noticeably large single clear finished round gem of stunning brilliance and placed it in a cup holder in the center console between the two front seats. He knew the language and currency of clandestine international business quite well. He also knew he should not spend much time at this location, or in the city of Istanbul. He started the powerful 523-horesepower engine and drove carefully away from the restaurant and down Balyoz Street toward the Bosporus.

"I have access to many more of these. If you take this stone as an initial retainer, then you are committed, and my international organization will cooperate and provide the assistance you will need. If you fail, then we shall reclaim our investment… and your life. I have taken precautions. A small, but very nasty directional explosive projectile device is under your seat, which I can activate easily from my door window control panel. Do we understand each other, Mr. Kasana?"

Umar swallowed surreptitiously and mentally cursed his uncharacteristic lack of awareness and preparation as he looked over at Shamir, whose smooth hand with manicured fingernails was on the control panel.

He said evenly with a note of potential retribution, but unwilling to doubt the other man, "Yes.... I believe we do."

"We shall continue to drive through the city a little farther. It is a nice evening for a sightseeing tour. Don't you agree?"

Kasana did not respond. Shamir did not expect him to respond.

A rented dark blue late model Fiat 500 Abarth pulled away from the curb about a block behind the Maserati GTS and followed it at an innocent distance. Melek waited until it was past her, then pulled out into the street behind the Abarth, and kept it within her sight, but at a distance from which she could turn down another side street to abandon her effort or restart it with greater assurance of avoiding suspicion. She also kept her eye on the elegant $125,590 Italian luxury sedan as it continued smoothly and quietly into the inner shadows of the city in a deliberately convoluted manner toward the Bosporus. About 17 minutes later, it entered a small, deserted park bordering the water. Shamir stopped his car in a parking slot facing the water, placed the transmission lever into the 'park' position, and turned off the engine. The driver briefly studied his side and rear-view mirrors as Umar briefly admired the interior luxury of the automobile. Then both men stared through the tinted windshield across the Bosporus toward the eastern part of the city for several seconds. The smaller blue car with its headlights off silently and slowly coasted into a parking space unnoticed about 110 yards away in the tree shadows near the far south end of the same parking lot. Melek did not enter the parking lot but found sufficient space to park on the nearest street from which she could still observe the parking lot below. She waited patiently, aware of both cars and the curious coincidence of their relative locations after she observed the Abarth following the Maserati to the same general location. She sent an encrypted text to her superior officer:

> 'Kasana is now meeting near the Bosporus with someone in a late model Maserati, license plate 66-EH-1477. Someone else in another car appears to be interested in at least one of them, but I do not have identification. M.'

A minute later, she received confirmation of receipt of her message. Satisfied that she was indeed inconspicuous, she stayed in place.

Shamir broke the silence first and began to tell his story.

"Consider this, my friend: A beautiful, quiet, and peaceful mountainous winter vista is spread before you at moderate distance, completely filling your field of vision. The sky is filled with gray clouds heavily laden with moisture. It is snowing lightly somewhere among the mountain peaks. Then, without apparent cause or warning, a giant avalanche cascades toward you down the side of the tallest mountain with an ominous distant muffled roar. It pushes over 10 million tons of snow, ice, trees, and tumbling boulders before it at almost 300 kilometers per hour, perhaps even finally continuing along a flat valley floor for a while before it comes to rest in a formless white pile somewhere far below its subtle birth. After the chaos, a peculiar calm and peaceful, almost deadly silence remains. Perhaps some wild animals stumbled helplessly in its path and were buried alive without any true awareness of their location or the physical strength to dig themselves out. Maybe even a mountain climber or an adventurous skier or two–perhaps more–met their agonizing deaths as well after becoming disoriented in the cold white violence, or slightly later in the extended final frigid silence. Imagine how arduous it would be to find any survivors. Think of how difficult it would be to view the future the same way as before."

Umar looked at him without obvious facial betrayal of his thoughts and waited for him to continue.

After a few seconds of silent impatience, he responded, "Well? What's your point?"

"Please humor me for a few moments, and stretch your imagination, Mr. Kasana."

With suspicion that the driver was deadly serious about *something*, and no doubt did not have a habit of wasting his time or anyone else's, he waited patiently with some effort and the beginnings of some unfamiliar and unsettled curiosity. He endured a momentary and uncharacteristic dearth of intuition or creativity. Men like Shamir did not hire men like him, nor drive expensive luxury automobiles during a life of common ignorance and stupidity.

After brief contrived mental effort, Umar said, "Okay…. I give up!"

"Think for a moment about the old Arabic principle of the straw that broke the camel's back," the driver said with the slightest and almost evil twinkling in his dark eyes.

Umar just stared blankly back at him, waiting impatiently for a familiar, or even a new or reluctant mental synapse to occur. After a further brief pause, Shamir continued.

"A sudden shift in the wind, the far-off cry of a lone wolf, or perhaps a small bird landing at a critically fragile point, or maybe even a distant minor earth tremor of unknown origin disturbed the mountain just enough to break the delicate integrity of millions of tons of snow and ice tenuously clinging to the slopes of prior snowfalls. Or maybe even just *one little snowflake* fell at just the right delicate and strategic spot at precisely the right time to start a swift chain reaction of unalterable natural events, obeying the ever-present fundamental forces of gravity, and mother nature took over with obvious accelerating destructive consequences, yet with a certain kind of beauty… at least from a distance. Mother Nature can often exhibit such awe-inspiring beauty with her power…, even when she is violent and destructive beyond all imagination. Do you agree?"

"Perhaps so, but *what is your point?*" he said with calculated impatient emphasis.

"The right kind of persistent fear…, widespread fear of the unknown…, can be an engine of social disintegration! If we can create enough fear to disrupt the economic system, the orderly transportation of goods and services, adequate supplies of food and fresh water, and eventually the entire social order, then we shall have punished the infidels as the prophet Muhammad has instructed us, and they will be ripe for our domination. We shall have prevailed in a completely unexpected and significant manner never before accomplished nor even imagined, and even those remaining will then turn to Allah for guidance and truth, and we will become stronger yet, and much closer to our ultimate goal of righteous Islamic world domination!"

"And just how… are *we* going to do *that?*"

"I have a plan…."

After a few seconds, Umar responded, "And that will produce another pin prick, like the USS Cole, and 9/11!"

"Maybe…. And then… maybe not," Shamir said in an ominous manner that even Umar could not dismiss.

In sincere bewilderment, Umar said, "Exactly *what* are you talking about?"

"You will know soon enough. The entire world will know when that 'one extra snowflake' falls at just the right spot and unleashes the avalanche of power of Almighty Allah Himself!"

"You are crazy! An avalanche will not destroy much of anything because avalanches usually occur in the middle of nowhere and away from meaningful population or industrial centers!"

The other man quickly responded in an elevated and bitter tone of condescension, "When, exactly, did I become crazy? When I was born? A year ago? When I awoke this morning? Two minutes ago? Perhaps brilliance or even the sacred intervention by Allah can occasionally masquerade as madness!"

Kasana retorted, "Or perhaps the other way around!"

With evident irritation and a matching tone of native self-righteousness, he continued, "But it is the wish of Allah either way! I am convinced that He has given me the final plan to start the inevitable disintegration of the United States of America by destroying the infidels and at the same time free Allah's people from its tyranny!"

Kasana responded somewhat indignantly, "And... exactly *what* is this plan?"

"To facilitate the efficient execution of your responsibilities in this exercise, I prefer that you not know that right now. Your compensation justifies your essential ignorance of the plan until your own spark of realization finally occurs..., *as it most surely will*. And, incidentally, your initial period of ignorance may enhance the success of your part of the plan as well as your survival. You cannot confess a secret that you do not know, even under duress or accidentally in some unforeseen manner. I do not expect failure, Mr. Kasana! I expect only *success!* Now..., will you accept the diamond... or not?"

"Surely you understand that I will have this stone examined. You obviously know how to contact me, so you can rest assured that I shall return the stone with my decision. However, an agreement will not be binding until I am satisfied that my final compensation is worth the risks I most likely will be undertaking."

"Agreed. I will expect to find you at the Mikla Restaurant within the next five days. If you are not available at that location within that time, I must conclude that you have stolen the stone, and my people will find you and deliver very unpleasant and permanent consequences. Do we *understand* each other, Mr. Kasana?"

Umar answered with his characteristic confidence, "For the record, I do not *need* your token gem, and my reputation is far more important to me than your stone. If you do not trust me sufficiently, then we might as well part company right now without an agreement."

With a peculiar and ominous tone, Shamir responded, "I believe I have read you *correctly*, Mr. Kasana. We *will* meet *again!*"

Shamir's confidence was unnerving. After another half-minute of silence, the man in the dark gray suit in the Abarth near the other end of the parking lot turned off his ultra-sensitive high-tech Sennheiser directional microphone aimed at the Maserati. He then removed the small 64-gigabyte SanDisk SD card containing the electronic recording, placed it in its custom translucent plastic protective case, and put it in his pocket.

Satisfied that his plan was significantly closer to execution, Shamir drove Umar back to the Mikla restaurant without further meaningful conversation. Without the headlights on, the unremarkable dark blue Fiat slowly pulled out from its parking space in the shadows near the far end of the parking lot and followed the Maserati at a professionally adequate distance. Melek started her car and eventually followed the other two cars. Within 15 minutes, the Maserati stopped in front of the Mikla restaurant, and the man in black exited the car, walked briskly to the restaurant entrance, and continued to walk inside as the Maserati started to move forward down the street. The man in the dark gray suit rechecked the license number of the Maserati–66-EH-1477–committed it to memory and continued to follow the luxury sport sedan through a left turn to the south onto Ataturk Boulevard for another several minutes. Melek stayed behind the Abarth at a discreet distance. She watched it turn to the right onto Kennedy Road west, following the Maserati along the Sea of Marmara all the way to the Ataturk International Airport. At 10:10 that evening, she watched Shamir board a Boeing 737, Pakistan International Airlines Flight 1704 to Karachi, where it landed at 3:55 A.M. the following morning.

The man in black soon discovered that his 'lady of the evening' was no longer in the restaurant. Their table had already been cleared and prepared for the next patrons. He was so preoccupied with his current disappointment that he did not notice that the same man sitting in a corner alcove on the far side of the dining area before the American woman had arrived was still there. He could have been a tourist, or perhaps he was still waiting for a business associate who never arrived. Oddly enough, the man had never been the subject of the earlier 'identity game' he had played with the woman in the red dress. His camera was still well hidden under a white napkin on the table. Nikolay Mednikov was an expert in being inconspicuous. He was neither professionally nor personally interested in the woman in the red dress. The Russian GRU agent surreptitiously took several more photographs of the man in black, and immediately sent them through the internet to Colonel Vasily Koshelev.

Kasana paid his bill and left the restaurant with greater than usual curiosity and a recently squelched extremely lustful urgency.

CHAPTER 37
Monday, August 3, 2015

He had discovered in his original research that no hotels were within 30 miles of Krasnodon, so Colonel Kovalenko drove from Kamyshin to Luhansk, a city large enough to have ample public overnight accommodations. The 384-mile trip via the P-228 and E-40/M-21 highways under gray skies lasted eight hours and 45 minutes. He found a studio apartment for two nights in Luhansk on Zhukova Street, in the northern part of the city. He parked his rental car in the appropriate lot, exited the car and locked it, and then walked to the main entrance and entered the foyer. After completing simple arrangements and payment to the attendant at the front desk, he went upstairs. The second-floor room was comfortable enough for his simple needs and included a refrigerator and a television for about $22 a night. He used neither, but wearily removed his clothes and took a hot shower. Within 20 minutes, he eased his exhausted body onto the bed and immediately fell into a deep sleep with the scarcely adequate overhead incandescent light still on.

**** *LONDON, ENGLAND* ****

Because the theft of a rather substantial number of diamonds is not just a simple crime with ordinary insurance ramifications, Lawrence Thompson forwarded copies of the surveillance videos from the Zen store cameras to MI-6. Caroline Mayfair was a 37-year-old single woman, and competent lab technician at SIS–the British Secret Intelligence Service. She received the video im-

169

ages and refined them with various computer image-enhancement programs until she had several clear images of Umar Kasana. Given various assumptions and statistically acceptable relationships between the eyes, nose, mouth, chin, ears, and other points of reference on his face, she was able to create a three-dimensional facial image. Then, with a little more artistic creativity based upon the images of his entire torso, she created a curiously accurate and detailed image of the entire stature of the man.

CHAPTER 38
Tuesday, August 4, 2015

**** SINGAPORE, PHILIPPINES ****

After five days of traveling over 1,650 miles, Destiny stopped at Singapore harbor as an overcast dusk approached and lights started to appear throughout the vast array of skyscrapers near the water's edge. The crew once again topped off her fuel and water tanks and brought an adequate supply of fresh food aboard. Two hours later, she was again at sea heading east into the night.

**** LUHANSK, UKRAINE ****

Colonel Kovalenko was awake early, and dressed by 7:30 A.M. He got in his car and drove south toward the center of the city, across the Luhan River for about two miles to Lomonosova Street, turned left and drove a few blocks to the da Vinci Art Bar to have a light breakfast of buttered cinnamon toast and coffee. After he finished eating 22 minutes later, he started the final 30-mile leg of his trip from Luhansk to Krasnodon. After 46 minutes on the M-4 highway, he was certain that no one would recognize him at such a great distance from the military base in Chelyabinsk. He continued to roam about Krasnodon under cloudy skies, regularly checking his rear-view mirror while looking for the church. He knew that Roman Catholicism was not popular in Russia. Only slightly fewer than 150,000, or less than 0.1 percent of the total Russian population admitted to being Roman Catholic, and therefore represented one of the least likely probabilities of a critical leak to Russian authorities above his position about the information he needed to convey to someone *other* than the

Russian authorities. After another 20 minutes, he deliberately drove past the church to his right, and then parked his car more than two blocks away. He walked back to the church in a circuitous manner with habitual subtle peripheral visual scanning of his environment. He stepped toward the old outer gate of about two acres of church property outlined with a perimeter five-foot high stone wall in need of repair. With only slight dissipation of his anxiety, he reached for the heavy iron knob of the arched gate smoothed and polished by more than three centuries of human contact. With final commitment, he turned it and pushed with mild force against the old dark metal bars with his left hand. It started to creak with the expected symptoms of age as the rusted hinges broke free from their most recent rigor, and then squealed slightly as he continued to push the gate open only far enough for his body to pass through. Then he turned around and tried to defeat any further inevitable noise as he carefully started to close the gate behind him while slowly looking around inside the lush green grassy courtyard. The gate again groaned defiantly until he closed it fully while turning the knob to avoid most of the expected final heavy metallic impact of the closing latch. With a slightly elevated heart rate, he walked the remaining 50 feet or so to the main entrance, again glancing around him within the ancient courtyard stone walls, looking into the drab shadows of overgrowth near the perimeter walls for anything that did not appear to belong there. A few bright yellow wild dandelions obstinately interrupted the otherwise plain perimeter of the main building. He continued with the slight confidence of having come this far undetected across the walkway of stones smoothed by centuries of footsteps, ascended the four steps to the doorway, and opened the large, freshly painted red main door to the church. It did not creak or squeal as the outer iron gate did, but it groaned softly as if secretly trying to announce his presence to someone inside. After a few moments of mild disorientation, he recognized the confessional built into the wall about 30 feet to his right in the fading afternoon light admitted through the colored glass windows in the western wall to his left. He walked deliberately toward it across the flagstone floor with slightly increasing determination. The sanctuary was quiet except for the mild echoes of his footsteps. Two women wearing black veils and plain, unremarkable dark-colored dresses sat in pews two rows away from the ancient well-polished mahogany altar and farthest from the entrance behind him. He passed through a sudden burst of sunlight streaming through the colored shapes of ancient glass forming an image of the Virgin Mary in one of the western windows. He kept his head down, briefly enduring some cautious fear of recognition in those few seconds of bright illumination. The late afternoon sunlight from between constantly changing cumulus clouds outside periodically filtered brightly through the richly colored pieces of glass in the old image of Jesus Christ in another window in the west wall, adding a small dose of comfort to the otherwise stark interior of the sanctuary. Somehow, it had survived through World War II when the Nazis occupied the city between July 20, 1942, and February 14, 1943. However, a few bullet marks in both the internal and external stone walls were evidence to the most careful observers of old and permanent obscure battle scars–insults to the architect who designed it and the proud artisans who built it. He turned slightly to his left to glance into the far reaches of the sanctuary.

It is remarkable how lunatics deface, destroy, and try to change or eradicate particular elements of human history and culture. They have no respect for human accomplishment and tradition. Who are those two women in the pew? Agents of the old KGB perhaps? No. Enough paranoia!

He hesitated slightly, and then turned back to face the confessional. After reassuring himself that it was indeed unoccupied, the colonel entered a confessional for the first time in his life. He sat heavily upon the old worn, dark-brown wooden seat and sighed with the broad experience of many years on this planet, with the burden of the possible fate of a nation weighing upon his shoulders, and concern for his own future. It was a private enclosure, deliberately designed to avoid visual contact, effectively hiding the language of the eye and the face, permitting only the rare experience of interpersonal isolated aural communication. He surmised that the ritual in the confessional had been designed to minimize personalities and identities as much as possible to encourage expression of the bare truth, which was usually embarrassing or heavily laden with guilt, and even more so, face-to-face. The confessional gave a feeling of privacy and secrecy, hidden from prying eyes and ears and therefore encouraged expression of sensitive truths as anonymously and readily as possible. The only relevant or known elements of the ritual were the exchanges of speech, inflection, and the inferences of gender, and approximate age. Even though a face-to-face confession was possible, it was not required in religious practice, so he had chosen the personally more comfortable and private anonymous method. Several seconds passed before the priest slid the internal wooden partition aside as an indication of his readiness to listen, and then waited patiently. The colonel slowly gathered his intended thoughts from the many possibilities that had been rushing through his mind during the last several hours and exhaled as silently as he could.

The priest sensed his difficulty, and out of habit, unaware of the age, life experience, beliefs, or social position of his confessor, asked, "What troubles you, my son?"

Viktor sighed once again and waited briefly for his courage to return. The almost claustrophobic old wooden enclosure with the chestnut brown lattice panel between him and the priest did not impress him with the security he needed, even in the Catholic presence of God. He could not see into the sanctuary. He could not be sure whether someone else was not within hearing distance near the confessional. But surely, no self-respecting Catholic would dare stand within listening distance of a confessional! But then, not everyone in this part of the world was Catholic... and officials of the state could stand any damned place they chose to stand.

I must do this! I have no choice! I am a dead man if I live, and I am a dead man if I die, so I shall forestall the inevitable with all my being while I still can.

Again, the voice tried to comfort him, "I can assure you, my son, that I have heard many troubled hearts, perhaps as heavy as yours, but even those who question the faith have found salvation, peace, and forgiveness."

Another 15 seconds passed silently before he finally spoke in a controlled and quiet tone, just above a whisper.

"Father, this is not easy for me. I am before the spears of destruction from both those I trust and those I have no reason to trust, and no doubt also from others I do not even know, in effect destroying all trust, because the secret I bear is beyond all that I could ever have imagined. If I speak to the wrong person, I will surely bring attention, if not death to myself, and also to those I love, and... and I greatly fear... also to many, many other people I cannot know. I am not here to save myself, but to save others. The right people must know what I know before I am eliminated. Time is critical, because even those who would kill me do not know the importance of what I know. This is not a time for political correctness, but only truth and rapid action!"

With slightly increasing alarm, the old priest tried to control his professional demeanor, and said with a slightly elevated heart rate, "Tell me, my son. The Lord will forgive even the gravest of sins with sincere repentance...."

The old priest was speaking only from the perspective of wisdom and experience, quietly serving his fellow man in this small Ukrainian community. However, he was also serving only with the experience of known history and was limited in his appreciation of the future threatened by the evil application of man's technological creativity–man's driven but innocent discovery of many of the secrets of the universe. Despite his position and his sincere wisdom, he could not know the weight of the colonel's heavy heart.

"I am not interested in forgiveness, Father. I am beyond all forgiveness. I have a beautiful 24-year-old daughter. Her name is Karina. She is the light of my life. She is a dancer, and she has always dreamed of dancing in New York City. I have not been able to persuade her to stay in Russia. Her dreams possess her heart and her future. I am a cynical old man. I have seen and heard too much to have enough hope for the future. She, however, has the advantage of youth and does not see any limits to the future. She has not been around long enough to see her fellow human beings make the same mistakes and fail to learn the same important lessons–those experiences that lead to wisdom and offer perspective and true appreciation of life. She is blissfully blind with all the wonderful attributes of youth, and I love her all the more for that, because young people are the only evidence of hope that I can see for us all."

"So..., it seems there *is* hope, after all...."

"That is not the half of it, Father...."

The old priest started to battle the fear inside him. Something about this confession was bringing a lighted match to the fuse of his deepest and most explosive personal theological doubts, to his simple humanity, even to his very soul.

"Please..., continue...."

The colonel did not hear the phrase 'my son' and started to wonder whether even this 'priest' might not be an agent of the old KGB, or the NKVD, or even the GRU. This omission might have been only a minor mistake for a professional spy, or maybe it was just an innocent breach of habit by an old and perhaps forgetful priest.

Oh, shit! Am I paranoid? Why did I come here in the first place? Did they follow me and let me come here anyway... knowing that I might say something they want to hear? But I cannot be silent! I cannot bear this secret by myself! I must get it out of me! Damn conscience! Damn the KGB!

"I am a colonel in the Russian army and the commanding officer of a Russian military base, from which a nuclear explosive device mysteriously disappeared recently. Within a few days of assuming command, I ordered an inventory of all weapons on the base.... After I received the report from my executive officer, I personally toured the facility and verified his report. That is when I discovered, should I say... 'accounting anomalies' between his report and the report transmitted to me on the initial date of my command by my superiors. His report was accurate. The official inventory I originally received was *inaccurate*. The vault contained one extra device with no serial number and was not on the official inventory. That discrepancy puzzled and disturbed me, but when I mentioned it to my superiors, they brushed me aside! When I insisted that I was correct, they treated me like the little boy who cried wolf! After that, I simply kept quiet about it until I knew exactly *why* they were ignoring me and why the discrepancy existed in the first place, lest they accuse me of creating the discrepancy myself. That is when I was doomed by circumstances beyond my control and subject to beliefs that served the truth only when it was convenient for those in power above me. The prospects for my personal future appeared contingent upon events well beyond my ability to influence or control, as well as powerful people well above my position, authority and pay grade. It seems my position of responsibility was designed or used by the old KGB, or someone else in collusion with them deliberately as a 'weeding out' exercise in efforts to identify those officers with the proper sense of national and military allegiance necessary for promotion to positions of higher and more sensitive responsibility... or perhaps to other unknown organizations or political purposes. Those who 'failed' were reassigned shortly thereafter. Those who 'passed' remained at the facility for only several more months before being transferred elsewhere. Then a new commander was assigned to the facility. The secret had a lifespan longer than the service term of the commanders at this installation. Therefore, when new commanders arrived, they had to be tested to be worthy of knowing the secret–that an extra device had been kept apart from the known arsenal. It was probably intended to be used as a bargaining chip under the proper circumstances to maintain the integrity of the old KGB. But then maybe someone else might get it and use it for some other purpose. It took me a little too long to figure this out. The Russian government claimed they had all 'loose nukes' inventoried and accounted for, and that no danger of 'loose nukes' existed. However, statements of political or military policy are by their nature never from the heart, precisely because organizations have no heart–no conscience, or honor. In the case of large organizations, sometimes such statements are based upon only partial or incorrect information. I fear I have unintentionally branded myself as a political liability, which is not a healthy position, and is almost impossible to correct or escape. It has also occurred to me that if I am such a liability, then perhaps my daughter's life may also be at risk to control or influence me. I fear that whoever is behind this anomaly does not care who or what stands in his way. A long time ago, I took an oath to follow orders from those above me, but I had a conscience before I became an intelligence officer, and I have gained a wealth of experience in the military that challenges my faith in certain portions of government, if not human nature itself."

The priest listened carefully to the colonel, and to his own heart–the truth in what he did not want to hear. It was time to stop the charade–this abusive entrapment of the human soul. The colonel's tangential awareness of the platitudes of the Catholic faith provided little, if any practical solution that respected his perception of his own soul. The priest could not just tell him to turn himself in to the authorities above him, and he could not tell him just to 'tell the truth,' and 'everything will work out.' He knew the history of Russia and the former Soviet Union, and the probability that groups of 'old line' bureaucrats throughout that empire were intent upon restoring it. And then, of course, former KGB kingpins may have been involved. One could not rule out their potential interest in a political trump card–something they could use to increase or solidify their actual or merely perceived power and influence. They may not have been in *official* power, but nevertheless, they still had influence, effective patience, and some *degree* of power–and an historical reputation. Their priorities did not include mercy for those who would speak or otherwise reveal the inconvenient or politically incorrect truth. Besides, the priest now knew the secret, and his conscience could not contain it. That weapon might even find its way into terrorist hands. The unexpected poison of special critical knowledge within the confessional had contaminated him, and he had to contain it until he could guide it to the proper people before higher Russian authorities or someone else, with evil intent, could squeeze it out of the colonel–or him.

Age has its advantages–among them: perspective, patience, and a particular sense of priorities. The greatest portion of my earthly life is behind me, but I can still do what I know in my heart to be right.

After momentary dread, he took that intuitive leap of faith that he was doing the right thing by speaking honestly and sincerely before a stranger, and said, "Listen to me very carefully. I believe you are sincere. Maybe God has sent you here for a reason. You must go to the American Embassy in Moscow, and tell a woman named Andrea Sokolov very privately what you know–*carefully*, my son! Tell her Father Pavel Dryzhensky told you to ask for *her*–absolutely *no one else!* She will know who I am. Do you *understand* me, Colonel?"

The priest's message and unexpected, almost conspiratorial tone of voice increased his anxiety, but he managed to say, "Yes, Father. I understand."

"I wish you well. You have God's blessing…, and *my* blessing."

I need more than a blessing! I am proceeding blindly!

The confession was over without a 'Hail Mary,' forgiveness, further ritual, or a sense of peace for either of them. Colonel Kovalenko left the confessional, looked once more around the church for any evidence of someone interested in his presence–or absence. Satisfied that no one was deliberately watching him, he left the sanctuary. Just before he closed the entry door, he looked back into the church one more time. It answered him with silence, but not peace of mind. He walked slowly back down the empty street to his car, casually glancing around. He opened the car door, got behind the steering wheel, and started his trip back to his motel room in Luhansk. More than 400 yards behind him, a blue Opel Astra car maintained the same speed behind him as he left Krasnodon.

Still in the confessional, the priest exhaled heavily. The burden of listening to others' confessions and secrets over the years was bearable only with deliberate effort, discipline, concentration, and experience, along with the habit of taking long walks. He had taken a sacred vow never to reveal to others the information he would receive within the confessional. Most of what he heard in that small enclosure was typically personal, understandably human, and sometimes even relatively trivial from a day-to-day living point of view, or sometimes even from a larger social perspective. Sometimes the stories he heard were laden with intensely personal or serious moral or religious dilemmas. However, he had never heard a confession of such disturbing magnitude and potentially devastating consequences as this one. Even his 76 years of life and religious experience had not prepared him to harbor or dissipate knowledge of this kind. He had no choice. He reviewed the experience in his mind.

The man sounded sincere. He could not be joking. No man could invent such a complex and detailed story, let alone tell it to a priest, if it were not true! He appeared completely sane. He had traveled a great distance to unburden his heart.

Then the priest thought about the early history of the confession, and how it could never have had such threatening implications. No credible threat of real mass destruction existed during the early history of the church. He simply could not separate his religious life from his personal life. How a priest is supposed to behave professionally and how a simple private individual should behave were in severe conflict within him. His mind was racing almost out of control and his heart rate increased. A myriad of implications and possibilities were multiplying in his imagination without his consent. He knew that he had not relieved the confessor's burden. He had simply duplicated it. He waited anxiously for the next confessor, hoping it would not be someone who wanted to know about the confession he had just heard. He started to pray. *Was it habit, or desperation?* Minutes slipped by in his racing reflection. No one else came. The church was silent. He continued to wait, trying to find peace. Gradually, he was somewhat more secure in this most recent passage of quiet unoccupied time.

Later that evening, he retired to the privacy of his bedroom and logged on to System 13 on his laptop computer and relayed his information and thoughts to the only human being with the right kind of influence he knew he could trust with sensitive information in the shortest possible time. He sent a message to Duke Chancellor summarizing the very disturbing story he had heard from the colonel. The implications of the story were clearly too important to overlook or put aside. He did not trust official agencies, police, government bureaucrats or politicians in general… nor *Russian* ones in particular. He also did not believe that conveying this information to his Catholic superiors would result in effective action.

Would they even believe me? Would they punish me for revealing a private confession? If they did believe me, and gave me the benefit of a doubt, whom would they tell, if they told anyone at all? What would the consequences be in the real world, let alone in my life–personal or professional–if what the colonel told me is true?

He began to type on the keyboard:

'I received a man in confession today, a Russian Army colonel, who told me that he was the commanding officer of the Chelyabinsk military base, where he said certain Russian nuclear weapons are stored. He said that he discovered a discrepancy between the official weapons count and his personal count of the weapons inventory. He believes that one weapon no longer in storage is unaccounted for, and his superiors have not believed him. He fears for both his professional and his personal life, and by implication, his daughter's life. He said she is a beautiful 24-year-old dancer named Karina, who also may be at risk because of his discovery. He believes that he is vulnerable to serious accusations of having stolen the missing device himself, or of official incompetence. I told him to contact Andrea Sokolov at your embassy in Moscow. I believe the man is genuinely sincere. I was strongly obligated although greatly conflicted in passing this on to you. P.D.'

****** MARYLAND ******

Duke Chancellor read with mild alarm the message on System 13 from Pavel Dryzhensky. He trusted the old priest. He knew that the implications of a missing nuclear device were clearly beyond his ability to manage, despite his wealth and influence. He immediately contacted the only person he could really trust within the entire United States federal government or military establishment–General Richard Murray at the Central Intelligence Agency.

His daughter? Karina? A dancer? Oh my God! She's the one I brought over here! This is very disturbing! Was Valentin following the people who had the stolen nuclear device from Chelyabinsk? And Sammy's discovery of the internet chatter word frequency. Mead... Could whoever has that nuclear device be trying to transport it to Hoover Dam? Blow up the dam? What would that mean... exactly? It certainly has the flavor of terrorist behavior. Maybe I'm jumping to unwarranted conclusions. But, when the stakes are this high, what is an unwarranted conclusion worth? We must investigate this possibility. It's better than dismissing it out of hand without the effort to confirm or deny with a little more conviction. No one wants to see that dam destroyed with this kind of suspicion ahead of time. We must investigate this! And what about Karina? Is she in danger?

**** LANGLEY, VIRGINIA ****

General Murray's cellphone chirped briefly with the unique ring signal from Duke Chancellor. It was 2:07 P.M. and the general was in a hallway between meetings at CIA headquarters. He knew Duke was trying to find him in the most immediate, personal, and urgent manner possible–his secure cellphone.

He walked directly to a secluded part of the hallway, lifted the phone to his ear and said quietly, "Talk to me."

"The message is unclear."

He recognized Duke's voice, the unique message, and responded, "Unclear–acknowledged," terminated the connection, and casually replaced his phone in his pocket as he continued to walk back toward his office.

Although the short conversation was over, General Murray experienced real fear for the first time in decades. He entered his office without saying a word to anyone. He had just heard the code word for 'nuclear' coming from Duke Chancellor. They had never used that code word before. It was based upon the unique spelling of the two words 'unclear' and 'nuclear,' where the interchange of the first two letters determined the coded meaning of the word and the message. Not only was the message unclear, but it was also *dangerously* unclear, and General Murray knew he had to understand as soon as possible and in a more secure manner why Duke had conveyed that message personally. He sat at his desk and put his hands against his forehead in a habitual posture of intense concentration. He tried to calm his body with several controlled deep breaths and isometric arm and abdominal exercises. Within the next several minutes, he was ready to go down the next unplanned path of his life.

As the general walked out of his office and past his secretary's desk, he muttered, "Daisy, I've got a serious dose of indigestion. Cancel the rest of my day."

Her name was Jennifer. He did not say 'please.' What she just heard from her boss meant that she was to cover any inquiries about his location and activity with credible solid excuses until he contacted her or returned to his office. She knew that he was going somewhere unusual, off the record, and in his own automobile, because he did not request a driver. She also knew him well enough to know that he was deeply concerned about something–probably unexpected–and did not have indigestion. She was very good at her job and took good care of him. That is why he took very good care of *her* with respect and thoughtful personal benefits, like regular birthday presents once a year and tickets to shows and fine restaurants during many of those months when she did not have a birthday.

General Murray walked briskly out of the building to his 2011 gray Cadillac STS in the parking lot, entered it and drove out of the CIA compound north toward The Plymouth Building.

**** *MARYLAND* ****

Less than an hour later, he parked in the underground garage space cryptically reserved in stenciled red paint for a 'visitor,' left his car and walked quickly to the elevator. After about 15 seconds of impatiently scanning his environment, he entered the elevator as soon as the doors had parted sufficiently, waited for them to close, and then rode it to the top floor. Few people had the code to reach the top floor, so Duke knew that General Murray would appear in his office within seconds of the chime announcing the elevator arrival outside his office. Duke left his private office door open in anticipation of General Murray's visit.

The general walked in and said with well-disguised anxiety, "Hello, Duke. What's going on?"

"Have a seat, Richard. I have reason to believe that an extremely sinister development is under way. I received this message on a secure channel from one of my sources in Ukraine. Read it, please."

With rare anxiety fighting his trust in Duke, General Murray reached for the printed copy of the message and read it.

> 'I received a man in confession today–a Russian Army colonel–who told me that he was the commanding officer of the Chelyabinsk Military Base, where he said certain Russian nuclear weapons are stored. He said that he discovered a discrepancy between the official

weapons count and his personal count of the inventory. He believes that one weapon no longer in storage is unaccounted for, and his superiors have not believed him. He fears for both his professional and his personal life, and by implication, his only daughter's life. He said she is a beautiful 24-year-old dancer named Karina. He believes that he is vulnerable to serious accusations of having stolen the missing device, or of official incompetence. I told him to contact Andrea Sokolov at your embassy in Moscow. I believe the man is genuinely sincere. I was strongly obligated although greatly conflicted in passing this on to you. P.D.'

General Murray knew that the theme and variations about lost or stolen Russian nuclear devices had already made the rounds in official as well as unofficial secret Washington circles and various reports and publications periodically for decades without concrete proof or verification. A cloud of Russian denials not entirely credible or unexpected from both the official Kremlin and various knowledgeable defectors' actual and alleged statements usually accompanied such reports. Furthermore, he suspected that if this situation were forwarded through official channels at the upper levels of diplomacy and government officials, then it would put the source of this information in danger. He knew from experience that when Duke Chancellor's organization came to a conclusion about otherwise unverified or unusual information, then it was best to act quickly, if not decisively upon that conclusion, and ask questions later. This development also implied that the CIA, FBI, and other clandestine organizations in friendly countries had not yet noticed what Duke had just discovered, and that was both disturbing and critically important. The rare trust relationship between Duke Chancellor and General Murray was forged over years of working toward solutions based upon discovering the essential truth with a shared sincerity and respect for what is ultimately right in the increasingly complex world of terrorist belief systems responsible for 9/11, the USS Cole attack, and the Fresno incident, as well as numerous smaller, but still vicious acts against humanity. They both knew that the rules of western cultural civilization were often irrelevant, if not naïve and harmful in the battle against terrorism. General Murray knew that The Chancellor Organization could act decisively and innocently in ways and places not always available to the CIA, the United States military, or other official organizations, precisely because it was a *private* and *super-secret* organization, and it was in no way a representative or functional arm of the United States government. For those reasons, it had become a highly valued special and independent source of information outside 'the system.' General Murray understood that a priest who reveals a confession to other people is in big professional trouble, and absolutely would not do so without some *extraordinarily* thoughtful consideration beforehand.

After another several moments, he looked up at Duke and said, "This obviously has the makings of potentially very serious consequences. I know Andrea. She's one of our best. However, we obviously need to be careful, especially with this priest."

"I agree. I am rather limited in what I can do, and this is a little outside my normal business, so I wanted you to know as soon as possible so the right people get the right message as soon as possible and can get going on whatever needs to be done."

"I appreciate your heads up, Duke. Is that all?"

"No, unfortunately…, it isn't. Another one of my people, a bright young reporter from Kazakhstan was murdered 12 days ago at a pier in Karachi. Apparently just before he died, he sent me this message."

Duke reached for the message that was still on his desk and handed it to General Murray, whose heat rate was now increasing.

> 'Urgent. Personally witnessed transfer of heavy satchel from a truck to a dirty white Mercedes southbound in the Anzob Tunnel. Followed Mercedes toward Pakistan. Noted apparent bribe paid near Spin Buldak at Pakistan-Afghanistan border Route A-75 by driver of dirty white Mercedes–license tag 7786AB01. Followed Mercedes south to Nakka Kiri, where two men lifted same unknown canvas package out of Mercedes and put in blue Toyota, license plate RIZ-6645. Followed Toyota to current location–pier at Karachi. Mercedes location now unknown. V.M.'

General Murray made a mental note of both license plate numbers and then looked up at Duke with a serious expression creased into his brow as he said, "I'm *very* sorry, Duke. Your people should not have to make such sacrifices. It's sad enough that our people take such risks."

Duke responded in a cautiously low tone, "Thank you, Richard. He was a fine, intelligent, and admirable young man, and I shall miss him as I would a son, if I had one. I am going to pursue further efforts to clarify what he was working on. He deserves at least that much from me. But wait just a moment, please. I have something else."

General Murray was still on edge. Duke then turned around to the finely polished mahogany credenza behind him, opened the lower right drawer to retrieve paper copy of the message from General Arshad, and then swiveled back around to face General Murray holding it out across the desk for him to see.

"This is a precise transcription of a phone call I received on one of my secure lines from General Arshad of the Pakistan Special Services Group on Friday, July 31, just five days ago. You remember him, I'm sure."

"Of course! We made a deal with him and arranged to restore his son, Amir's sight in Miami, and in return he found, arrested and handed over the Fresno terrorist!"

General Murray grasped the message and read it.

Fatih Abdul-Kaliq: We are seated in the middle of an ancient city that still bears the evidence of man's struggle for truth and peace. I will soon be the new leader of the Islamic State, which will eventually prevail in its quest for a caliphate. We strongly object to the interference of the United States of America against our struggle for self-determination. We have plans to eliminate the United States from its current dominant world position with the help of Allah, peace be upon Him. It is inevitable! God willing, we will put our plans into motion this year.

Mr. Murat: Is there anything else you can tell me about your plans, Mr. Abdul-Kaliq?

Fatih Abdul-Kaliq: God willing, the United States will experience devastation unlike any other in its history. It will be crippled forever!

Mr. Murat: I see. And exactly what is this devastation, and how is it going to come about?

Fatih Abdul-Kaliq: You would be a very foolish young man indeed if you expect me to answer that question. That is my message to the world. Our time together is over.

General Murray held the document on his lap as he looked up at Duke.

"It is clear to me that something quite unusual and sinister is brewing, regardless of whether these events are related. You were right in contacting me about this as soon as possible. I have heard nothing even resembling this kind of information in the everyday traffic or from other contacts I have in the agency…, or elsewhere in my network. If Director Miles knows about any of this, he certainly hasn't told *me!* Thank you for sharing this with me. I will take full responsibility from this point. I do not want you exposed for any reason whatsoever, nor do I want you or your people to take any further unnecessary risks in this matter. I–*and this country*–cannot afford to have you exposed under any circumstances. Now, are you sure this is all you have?"

"Yes. That's all I have right now… except… for one other disturbing thing…"

"Lay it on me!"

"I have no legal or scientific 'evidence' in the manner implied by what I have shown you here, but one of my people has been experimenting with relative word references and frequencies in communications traffic across the internet, and his work has given me the impression that Hoover Dam could be the target of that missing nuke."

"Can you be a little more specific…?"

"Richard, I honestly cannot go further with my information and reasoning at this point, but I have enough suspicion to conclude that we had better *act* as though Hoover Dam is the target. I would be *devastated* if indeed that is the way the future might unfold and I did not say anything, regardless of the persuasiveness or quality of my intuition."

General Murray said thoughtfully, "I see.…"

"The stakes are rather high, so if we spend the money and put forth the effort as necessary, and I am completely wrong about this, then I am prepared to bear the appearance of a world-class fool. However, if that is indeed the target and we are fortunate enough to stop such an attack, then we will have won another battle–a critical psychological battle I would think–in the apparently never-ending war against terrorism."

General Murray already knew that Duke Chancellor was nowhere near a world-class fool by any stretch of the imagination—not even a common clown's fool. One does not run a successful information business, acquire great wealth, and influence many people in important positions, both public and private around the world, by being a fool of any order whatsoever. He silently considered his alternatives at this point for several moments. He had to be prepared to sell his suspicions and recommendations to those in authority above him. At the same time, he had to protect not only a valuable personal friendship, but also an extremely important source of information that had been critical to the security of the United States in the past and would continue to hold that degree of importance in the future. He had made up his mind and spoke with assurance.

"First, I will get in touch with Andrea Sokolov to get her take on this. Then I will advise people out in the field to be more focused upon the implications of this information and start looking a little more carefully to connect these, and some other 'dots' that may develop."

Duke responded, "I will pay particular attention to anything else related to these items and notify you as quickly as possible."

"Thank you, Duke. I must get going on this immediately!"

They shook hands with sincere trusting eye contact, and then General Murray let himself out, rode the waiting elevator back to the underground parking garage, walked briskly back to his car, and wasted no time returning to Langley.

**** LANGLEY, VIRGINIA ****

Jennifer cheerfully welcomed her boss back to his office but he had an unfamiliar degree of urgency in his step, an unusually rigid facial expression, and his color was ruddier. The general greeted her politely, but without humor.

"Jennifer, please find Lou Bischoff, and tell him to get down here as soon as possible."

"Yes, sir."

She was 'Jennifer' when his life was troubled. Otherwise, she was 'Jenny.' She knew something unusual had developed during his absence, and he would require much more than usual from her in the very near future. She immediately sent a secure message to Lou's cellphone.

'Boss needs you here ASAP!'

Lou Bischov, one of the general's most capable and trustworthy field agents casually walked into Jennifer's office 10 minutes later.

"How did you get here so fast?" she said with obvious surprise.

"Magic..., and your magnetic personality!"

She sent a distinctly deliberate facial expression of incredulity right back at him, and snapped, "This is not the time for fairy tales, Mr. Bischov! Something's up. He wants to see you immediately, so get in there and *don't* joke around! He's in a hyper-serious mood!"

"Actually, I was just upstairs when I got your message."

She just looked at him impassively and shook her head without acknowledging his typical flirtatious behavior around her. He got the message loud and clear, quickly turned and walked into General Murray's office with a straight face.

Once inside the general's office, he closed the door behind him, turned toward his boss, and said, "Okay, General. What's going on? I got some really negative vibes from Jenny...."

"Remember after 9/11, when just about everyone in this business was accused of not 'connecting the dots?'"

"Yeah, I remember. Why?"

"Ominous 'dots' are in that folder. Read it right now and commit what you read to permanent private memory. Top Secret Crypto. Then we'll talk."

The Bishop picked up the only folder on the general's desk, sat down on a cushioned chair adjacent to his desk, and opened the folder. He knew his boss was on edge.

Seven minutes later, after apparently having read it twice, he said, "Okay..., I got it. What do you want me to do about it?"

"I want you to connect the dots between those dots. I want you to find out whether a nuke was taken from Chelyabinsk, and if so, where it is now, and while you're at it, find out where it's going, along with a timeline and a reason. Get a name, address, shoe size, political or religious preference and location for everyone even remotely connected to anything you just read. My hunch is that we have absolutely no room for error in this assignment. You will have anything you need to accomplish this objective–people, material, equipment, transportation, information, money–whatever! Work as quickly and as quietly as possible because time is obviously not our ally, and we cannot afford to go much higher up with this right now without some *facts*. So far, other avenues of inquiry have not yielded anything useful in that regard. If I do not get some *facts* from you–or anyone else–in a *very timely* manner, I shall have to proceed to higher authority with too much unsubstantiated information and associated conjecture. That might imply a lack of conviction, leading to insufficient support from the people upstairs. Unfortunately, my intuition tells me that will eventually lead to a tragedy of *extremely* regrettable proportions. *Have I made myself perfectly clear, Mr. Bischov?"*

The Bishop registered unfamiliar dread internally, knowing that General Murray was being hyperbolic in his instructions, but was deadly serious to an extent he had not experienced before.

Lou remained officially impassive on the surface, as he replied, "I understand completely, sir! I'll get right on it!"

"Report anything of substance or even remotely credible intuition that you encounter directly to me as soon as possible, so I can coordinate with others, and whoever or whatever else develops. I don't care what *time* of day it is or what *day* it is. I don't care whether you are on the can or farting in a cornfield! YOU CALL ME IMMEDIATELY!"

The Bishop left General Murray's office without flirting with Jenny on the way out. Her intuition started vibrating with unfamiliar concern, but she knew that she was obligated to keep her thoughts to herself. Even the most casual or innocent related comments could get to the wrong ears and create bureaucratic interference or lead to unpleasant real-world consequences... even a disaster. The people she worked for kept certain information secret for very good reasons. Secrecy had become essential in an increasingly competitive and dangerous world during the last few centuries, particularly since the beginning of the twentieth century, and even more so since the end of World Wat II.

When the major pros exude concern, when the Bishop doesn't flirt, there's definitely big trouble around the corner!

Within the next 15 minutes in another part of the vast Langley headquarters complex, Leah Cummings walked into her office with the fork from the Mikla Restaurant in her handbag.

General Murray finally got through to the director, Marvin Miles, on his cellphone.

"Marvin, we need to talk…, right now."

"I've got meetings in three minutes, General. What's going on?"

"I'll be in your office in exactly 90 seconds."

"General! You can't just…"

The phone connection was dead. Precisely 88 seconds later, General Murray walked into the director's office, continued past his secretary's desk, opened the heavy dark mahogany door of the director's office, walked in, and tossed the manila folder he was carrying onto Marvin Miles' otherwise tidy desk.

"You need to read this, Marvin…, *right now!*"

"General! You're out of line! I don't have the time right now, and we have procedures…"

"We won't have any 'time' for anything else if you don't read this right now…, sir! I already put the Bishop on this with a promise of top priority and full support–anything he needs. I'll need your support and the agency's support to back me up on that! That's why I had to get this to you as soon as possible. I don't know exactly where this is going, but I don't think we have much of a choice, so we need to be on top of it with everything we have!"

Marvin Miles stared at the general with small evidence of confusion as he picked up the folder and then briefly glanced at his watch.

He scanned the material in silence with habitual efficiency, then dropped the folder on his desk and uttered, "Holy shit! *Where* or *how* did you get this information? I have not seen anything like this coming in from the field!"

General Murray hesitated for a few moments, weighing his personal honor, his professional position, and his responsibilities, and then said, "Trusted and sensitive source, sir. I am honor-bound to protect my sources. If I betray trust, I destroy access to information. That is how this business works sometimes, sir. You, of all people, should know that!"

"General, you are testing my patience! WHO… or WHAT… is your SOURCE?"

With habitual daring, the general replied, "Sir, I would sooner resign my commission and leave the agency than reveal that information!"

"You are asking me to put this country's entire primary intelligence community to work on a very serious threat without giving me something resembling solid ground to stand on, something that the president will be able to use to justify supporting us…. I am *duty-bound* to inform the president of this kind of information, and I need to do that with credible *evidence* and *conviction!*"

"Sir…, my source is the same one that helped us get Rasheed Shirani, the mastermind behind the Fresno incident. You did not question my sources then. And, if I recall correctly, you had me make the presentation to the president myself."

For several seconds, Miles carefully considered the trust he needed to have in his people, even though he could not always have the same confidence in certain 'sources' that they might have. He looked into the general's eyes for another 10 seconds, obviously weighing the personal and professional risks he would be taking in this unexpected development. He knew that the general had not arrived at his current position by chance or by making any stupid decisions.

After a quick reassessment, he said, "All right, General…. You will have what you need. But keep me in the loop on this at least once a day and notify me *immediately* with any specific further developments…, especially if this situation becomes even more critical!"

General Murray responded with his unique military intonation, "Yes sir!", turned on his heel, and left the director's office.

**** I STANBUL, TURKEY ****

Shamir left Istanbul Ataturk International Airport at 5:50 A.M. on Lufthansa Flight 1305, an Airbus A321 bound for Frankfurt. His portside seat, 20A was next to the window over the wing, but he spent little time looking out. The plane landed on time in Frankfurt three hours and five minutes later. He had a layover of two hours and 20 minutes to contemplate his master plan further and the details immediately ahead in the United States that he believed required his personal attention. During that layover time, he arose from his seat in the departure gate waiting area several times to take a stroll down the hallway before returning to his seat. As more people entered that same waiting area for Lufthansa Flight 442, he walked shorter distances, and never lost sight of his seat. The Lufthansa flight attendant watched his behavior. As time for boarding drew near, 28-year-old flight attendant Hanna Dietrich prepared for boarding the Airbus A340 bound for Detroit. Within a few minutes, she started calling passengers for boarding by seating sections, from the rear of the aircraft forward. Although this part of her day could often become tediously routine, and sometimes hectic, she maintained her discipline in checking every boarding ticket for names she had memorized according to her most recent instructions. When she saw the name Shamir Rahmani, she looked up briefly into the eyes of the man who had been nervously walking in the hallway. Without deviating from her check-in routine, she quelled a mild chill, and subtly grasped her cellphone from her pocket. She surreptitiously quick-dialed her immediate superior officer, held the phone up to her right ear as she continued to check boarding tickets in a professional, practiced, and efficient multi-tasking manner, while Shamir continued to walk forward into the Jetway. Within seconds, the familiar voice answered.

"Rosenberg."

She spoke briefly and softly into her phone, "SR23 is boarding Lufthansa 442 from Frankfurt to Detroit. Seat 24B. Confirm."

The voice in her phone replied, *"Confirm you said SR23 is boarding Lufthansa 442 from Frankfurt to Detroit, seat 24B."*

Her silence confirmed the response. She disconnected the call and continued to check boarding tickets as she smoothly returned her cellphone to her pocket. In the nine hours and 20 minutes it would take for Flight 442 to traverse the 3,990-mile distance to Detroit, David Rosenberg had added a few more notes to his three-year-old file about the man known as Shamir Rahmani.

For what it's worth, I find it rather peculiar that someone allegedly dedicated to an extreme jihadist philosophy is traveling to Detroit. Maybe he is on an educational lecture tour. Then again, maybe he is up to something else… entirely different.

Shamir was traveling to Detroit because a few remaining details of his grand plan required his personal attention.

****** *TEL AVIV, ISRAEL* ******

David Rosenberg made two secure telephone calls from his office. The first one was to Ariel Romanovsky.

"Ariel, this is David. I need some assistance with a very sensitive matter."

"I am unemployed. You will have to look elsewhere." (I am available–standard compensation.)

"Encrypted details will follow over the M66 secure internet line. Key is from unit four protocol, code is 'Sunday.'"

The call ended. Ariel was a survivor. Her talents were in sufficient demand to relieve her of fears of capture or internment by either of her two main competing employers–the Russian GRU, and the United States CIA. Occasionally she would do 'favors' for the Israelis. David terminated that conversation, and immediately called Joe Czarzhynénsky.

After three rings, Joe answered from his office in the back of his restaurant on Franklin Street in Reading, Pennsylvania, *"Hello, David. I really didn't expect to hear from you so soon. What's on your mind?"*

"We have been aware of a certain Middle Eastern subject named Shamir Rahmani, who we suspect has extremist interests. He is a highly educated and reputedly extremely wealthy Pakistani citizen, but he was born in Iraq. I have just learned that he is on a plane from Frankfurt heading to Detroit–Lufthansa Flight 442–just a heads up, nothing urgent that I am aware of, but I suspect you should learn about him if you do not already know about him."

"Thank you, David. I'll pass this along to our people immediately."

So ended another brief thread of information, one of billions, in an increasingly threatening world.

Joe activated the secure System 12 on his laptop computer and sent a message to Duke Chancellor.

> *'From D.R. who just noted a wealthy individual with possible extremist ideas named Shamir Rahmani on Lufthansa 442 bound for Detroit from Frankfurt. DK the name, but I suggest a tail would be appropriate. From anyone else, I would not be so concerned.'*

Within 10 seconds, Duke responded:

> *'Confirm from D.R. Shamir Rahmani on Lufthansa 442 bound for Detroit from Frankfurt. Source recommends tail.'*

He then sent a message through the super-encrypted System 14 to General Murray:

> *'I was just informed that a wealthy suspected terrorism backer, Shamir Rahmani is on Lufthansa Flight 442 out of Frankfurt bound for Detroit. Reliable source thought you might need to know that and recommends tail. D.C.'*

Within 30 seconds, he received a response from General Murray:

> *'Acknowledge Shamir Rahmani on Lufthansa 442 from Frankfurt to Detroit. Recommend tail. Thank you.'*

Within another 20 seconds, a secure message reached the Bishop. He glanced at his phone, knowing the unique sender code:

> *'Immediate–tail name Shamir Rahmani at Detroit International Airport, arriving on Lufthansa 442 from Frankfurt. Unknown history, but source indicates possible extremist person of interest.'*

Lou Bischov was driving northbound on I-95 toward Philadelphia from Washington when he got the message. He immediately headed for the Philadelphia International Airport with the first indication of definitive urgency in this otherwise nebulous task. He increased his speed slightly above the speed limit, and weaved deftly through and around traffic, but without obviously risking a police stop. He correctly assumed he did not have any time to spare. After arriving at the airport long-term parking lot, he drove another 12 minutes to find a parking spot. He quick-dialed Jenny.

"Get me the ETA for Lufthansa 442 at Detroit, pronto!"

He knew she could get the information faster on her computer than he could find it while looking for any number of television monitors listing arriving and departing flights for all airlines in the airport. He exited his car and walked about as fast as most men could jog through the parking garage, across the pedestrian bridge, and into the domestic flight departure terminal.

Within one minute of his call, she texted back, '3:21 P.M.'

He quickly responded 'ty,' and continued to hurry into the main terminal area. Along the way, he politely, but effectively nudged and elbowed his way through various small crowds and lines of waiting passengers to the ticket counter, keeping his CIA credentials in his hand for immediate persuasion if necessary. For $552, he got one of two remaining seats on Delta Flight 1339 scheduled to arrive non-stop in Detroit at 2:25 P.M., leaving him just enough time to find Rahmani before he could leave the airport terminal. After collecting his boarding pass and ticket, he ran to the departure gate and arrived there after the last of the passengers had boarded over a minute before. He quickly handed his boarding pass to the young male agent at the Jetway entrance as he continued to breathe heavily, but with increasing control. The agent quickly scanned his boarding pass and looked at the Bishop with implicit permission for him to board. Delta 1339 taxied for 15 minutes in heavy traffic to its departure runway. By the time the plane arrived at the runway takeoff point, heavy smoke started to billow out of the starboard engine. Within seconds, a small explosion occurred, and the smoke gave way to a small inferno. Emergency sirens and other warning devices sounded in a dissonant chorus. The airline crew quickly ushered passengers to the emergency exits. Inflated rubberized plastic slides deployed immediately from the aircraft and passengers slid down them to the tarmac in a rather steady manner as if they had practiced it before. The Bishop cursed a few ancient deities as he slid down the chute in an unflattering posture.

By this time, Ariel had decoded the message from David Rosenberg:

> *Subject Shamir Rahmani, Iraqi by birth, wealthy, likely extremist jihadist philosophy, traveling to Detroit. Find out what he is up to.*

CHAPTER 39
Wednesday, August 5, 2015

A light rain fell outside as Father Pavel Dryzhensky spent much of the morning in deep prayer.

The world is indeed a dangerous place. Almighty Father, I have broken my vow of silence. I beg for Your forgiveness—a sign that Thy grace will cleanse my soul. I stand anxiously between faith and human conscience, burdened by fear and unable to embrace peace. If my work is done, I pray not only for Your forgiveness and mercy within me, but also within the lives of those under the yoke of the confession I could not in sincere human conscience keep within me.

After five minutes of absolute silence, he stood up slowly, stepped to his left, and retrieved his copy of the Code of Canon Law from the built-in bookshelf occupying one entire wall in his small study. He turned the pages rapidly until he found Canon 983.1 and read it silently, as if to make sure of what he already knew.

'The sacramental seal is inviolable; therefore, it is absolutely forbidden for a confessor to betray in any way a penitent in words or in any manner and for any reason.'

> *Have I lost my faith? Is there no allowance for the heretofore unthinkable? The inconceivable? I did not betray a penitent! I have conveyed information of immense importance! Am I not to do everything I can to save lives, to attempt to make right what I know is wrong? Am I not bound by God-given conscience to do everything I can to prevent a catastrophe? He obviously wanted me to know*

his concerns and to convey those concerns to others who can act upon them in an effective manner! Canon law was created over 1,600 years ago without any human awareness of the secrets of the universe known today, and their potential for good or evil. And now, I fear humanity will experience unnecessary and unique preventable evil for which they are unprepared. Is conscience not the voice of God? Am I to suffer forever the choice between nefas and the vital inescapable conviction of informed conscience?

He knew that Canon 983.1 clearly explains that the sacramental seal is inviolable and that it is absolutely wrong ('nefas') for a confessor in any way to betray the penitent, for any reason whatsoever, whether verbally or otherwise. However, the official Latin text of this canon is much stronger. The word nefas, which translates as 'absolutely wrong,' has no clear and direct equivalent in English. The term nefas refers to what is so wickedly sinful, so abominably execrable, that it is obviously impossible to do it! Regardless of what word English translators may have used, it fails to convey the true meaning of the original Latin. All priests are aware that the penalty for violating the seal of the confessional is excommunication, and they certainly do not take that consequence lightly. One of the several criteria that must be in place for an excommunication to occur is that the perpetrator must be *aware* that the sanction of excommunication is attached to its commission. From the Catholic perspective, it is impossible, if not sinfully false for a priest to claim ignorance of the penalty if he were to repeat the contents of someone's confession.

**** LANGLEY, VIRGINIA ****

In the biochemistry lab at Langley, evidence analysis technician Julie Anderson carefully removed the fork from the plastic bag Leah Cummings had brought back from Istanbul, and then conducted standard DNA gathering procedures to isolate and identify the genetic material remaining on it. Within the hour, she had determined that sufficient DNA material was left on the fork for duplication of enough testing samples to conduct all the tests she needed. Within the next few hours, she had identified all the adenine, guanine, cytosine, and thymine markers that in a certain sequential order defined a unique human source and entered that code into her computer database. Then she executed the program that would search the entire database looking for a name, event, tag, or date placeholder to match with that DNA code. About an hour later, she found absolutely no evidence of a match, and immediately reported that result to her superiors, who had already gotten the urgent word from Director Miles to start looking more carefully for unusual events and relationships among those events and other discoveries.

General Murray answered his desk phone with inadequately veiled impatience, "Murray!"

"General, this is Julie Anderson at the lab. The fork that Leah Cummings brought back from Istanbul after a meeting with a suspected Turkish arms dealer named Kasana had a good sample for DNA analysis. However, we could not find a match anywhere in our database, so it looks like he has not crossed our path in the past…, or he has been extremely careful."

"Thank you, Ms. Anderson. Please find a way to get that sample DNA code to the FBI, Mossad, SIS, MI-6, and Interpol ASAP–but plain vanilla delivery, routine with no background–and then get back to me with whether any of them has any information or a computer match and what the details are. I don't want any 'delivery bias' or preconceptions to contaminate any of their responses. Furthermore, I don't want any unnecessary questions or threads of thought available to someone we don't know to start putting this together before we do, and perhaps leak something we don't need leaked that might get to the wrong people prematurely and possibly complicate our task. If someone asks why we want to know, then refer such requests directly to me. Understood?"

"Willco…. We can do it securely encrypted over the internet. I'll be back to you as soon as I have something to report."

"Thank you!"

Two seconds later, his phone rang again.

"Murray!"

"This is Lou. I find it rather curious that the plane I was on bound for Detroit from Philadelphia in time to find my man in the Detroit airport terminal developed an engine fire just prior to take-off, and I had to get another flight to Detroit. I missed that guy I was supposed to tail, but now that I'm here, I am going to snoop around in the city anyway to see what I can find out."

Dammit! There are no coincidences!

"I think you'd better find him…. Intuition suggests he's part of something really nasty coming up…. Keep me informed."

"Understood."

**** CHELYABINSK, RUSSIA ****

Halfway around the world under overcast skies, Colonel Kovalenko returned to his office feeling more committed to conquering his unusually threatening and increasingly nebulous future. Once again, he made a personal inspection of the contents of the storage vault and returned to his office with the same result–all 90 accounted for.

I know one is missing! Where is it now, and who is responsible for removing it?

CHAPTER 40
Thursday, August 6, 2015

Colonel Kovalenko exercised one small privilege of his rank by taking a brief personal leave. He flew non-stop in common civilian business attire from the Chelyabinsk airport to Vnukovo International Airport just southeast of Moscow on Ural Airlines Flight C268. After deplaning two hours and five minutes later under partly cloudy skies, he rented a late model small white Lada Kalina automobile at the airport. Then he drove out of the airport parking area and continued northeast on the M-1 highway toward downtown Moscow and the American Embassy, which is slightly more than 20 miles from the airport, and close to the geographical center of the city. He arrived near the embassy in just under an hour and 15 minutes. After he found a parking space on Devyatinskiy Bolshoi Street adjacent to the south perimeter of the embassy compound, he left his car, walked back to the main entrance, and entered the guardhouse immediately to the right of the main gated vehicle entrance, and spoke to the United States Marine guard on duty.

"My name is Viktor Kovalenko. I am here to see Andrea Sokolov."

The guard responded in official manner, "Please step over here, sir."

He endured the expected electronic 'frisking' and 'body patting' at the symbolic front door of the United States of America. He deliberately avoided mentioning his position, rank, or any other indication of his affiliation with the Russian military. After apparently passing the brief examination satisfactorily, he waited patiently with only mild apprehension for recognition of his presence to find its way through the personal and electronic embassy maze to a responsible person. The guard deliberately waited for several unproductive minutes to see whether the visitor displayed any subtle signs of suspicious nervousness or anxiety while he waited for any possible negative response to the name Kovalenko on his computer monitor.

"Identification papers, please."

I must not even look military! Damned training!

The guard examined his credentials without facial evidence of any concern or question.

Apparently satisfied that the visitor posed no credible threat, the guard said as he raised his right arm and pointed, "You must take this pass, and go to the tallest building over there, and then go in the front entrance. You can't miss it."

He handed Colonel Kovalenko a numbered plastic yellow badge with a metal bead chain through a hole at one end, obviously designed to be worn around the neck, and impassively waited for his response. He did not detect any sign of trouble.

As he accepted the pass, the colonel said absently, "Thank you."

He walked deliberately in the direction the guard indicated toward the center of the compound, entered the lobby of the large gray 11-story cement office building, proceeded to the reception desk, and showed his pass to the United States Marine guard on duty.

"My name is Viktor Kovalenko. I am here to see Andrea Sokolov."

The Marine examined his pass carefully for several seconds, and then returned it to him. He looked up at the colonel and studied him carefully with a straight face, but in a non-threatening manner for another several seconds.

"Sign here, please, and have a seat over there. I will let her know that you are here."

He then lifted a black phone receiver on the desk in front of him, waited only about 10 seconds, and then said, "A gentleman named Viktor Kovalenko is here to see Ms. Sokolov."

Within seven minutes, a tall, slim, and moderately attractive woman on the young side of middle age in a simple gray business suit with shoulder-length nicely styled wavy red hair and smart-looking designer glasses framing her mesmerizing clear green eyes walked from the elevator bank across the lobby to where Colonel Kovalenko was waiting near the reception desk.

She approached him and asked innocently, "Mr. Kovalenko?"

"Yes."

"I am Andrea Sokolov. Please follow me, sir."

She turned and walked silently back toward the elevator bank and pressed the 'up' arrow. Within 25 seconds, the elevator car arrived silently, and the doors parted as she turned toward him with a visual invitation to enter the empty elevator car ahead of her. The two ascended to the second highest floor without conversation as his heart rate increased slightly and the elevator doors parted. She indicated subtly with her hand that he should leave the elevator before her on the tenth floor, then led him to the right and entered one of two interior rectangular meeting rooms. The room had cream-colored walls and no other doors. Five colorful abstract oil paintings of several square feet each with black illegible signatures in the lower right-hand corner hung on three walls. With another obvious silent hand gesture and a reassuring moderate business smile, she offered him a comfortable cushioned seat at the modern round oak table with polished chrome legs centered in the fully carpeted room. She turned away from him briefly and closed the heavy solid oak wood door with the slightly muffled sound of closing against foam rubber insulation. Then she locked it by turning a spring-loaded dead-bolt knob until it answered with a dull metallic thud, and then approached the table and sat across from him in an identical maroon chair in a confident and deliberately relaxed manner.

"We are perfectly secure here, Mr. Kovalenko. No listening devices or hidden recording equipment of any kind whatsoever are anywhere in this room, or anywhere else in a position to detect sound from inside this room, from either inside or outside this building. The reason you are free to express yourself without monitoring and recording equipment is due entirely to Father Dryzhensky. I am not at liberty to clarify that explanation any further. As of this moment, you and I are at a level of parity..., meaning that you took the unusual initiative to come here at Father Dryzhensky's suggestion, and in response, I have offered you the special privilege of confidentiality. Now..., our slate is clean, and it is your turn to speak."

Something about this woman relaxed Viktor. She was self-assured, very professional, evidently quite capable, and 'official.' She sounded like she had at least some respectable degree of responsibility and authority that he needed to perceive. He briefly thought of Karina, strikingly more beautiful and much younger than this woman. But, she was still *someone's* daughter. His natural curiosity surfaced.

What path had she taken to arrive at this position? What was her education, training, and experience? What is her rank? Exactly who is she? What is her level of authority?

After another few moments of silence, fully realizing that the momentum of his recent decisions had propelled him to this uncertain point of no return, he started to speak.

"My name is Viktor A. Kovalenko. I hold the rank of colonel in the Russian Army. I have personally witnessed evidence of the removal of a small nuclear device with no serial number from the inventory of such weapons stored at the Chelyabinsk military installation, of which I am, or perhaps *was* the commanding officer."

After a few seconds, she responded carefully, "Why are you here telling this to *me*, and not to your own superiors?"

"Because I do not know whom to trust! I have taken a very significant risk merely by coming *here!* About three weeks ago, my superiors brushed aside my initial efforts to inform them, and they did so with an undertone of ominous personal implications. After that experience, basic human conscience drove me to tell someone who I would have some reason to expect would really *listen* to me without bias or agenda and would not carelessly tell someone else who could harm me or my daughter, or further expose my information to the wrong political people. At the time, the only way I could imagine respecting both the sensitivity of what I had to say, and my personal sense of security was to confess to a Catholic priest. With respect for the sometimes dangerously intertwining grapevines of certain kinds of information in Russia, I chose to travel secretly for two days far from my base to find an independent and innocent secret way to reveal my information. As you must know, few Catholic churches exist in Russia. I simply could *not* keep it inside me! It was becoming a major distraction in my personal and official life. That is how I came to see Father Pavel Dryzhensky."

She took a subtle deep breath and released it slowly, realizing that the meeting with Pavel had been mere coincidence, and nothing more.

Then she said, "I see…. Continue, please."

He struggled mightily before taking his next leap of faith, briefly thinking again of Karina in hopes of living to see her achieve her dream.

"I must request asylum in the United States of America. I have reason to believe that if I remain in Russia, I will eventually become a scapegoat, political roadkill, or a victim of intentionally clandestine extermination, or more likely, all three. As you Americans say it, I am a 'dead man walking,' particularly from this moment forward. However, I firmly believe that I can offer extremely valuable assistance in efforts to find this missing device if I am granted asylum. I am aware of the names of certain people who allegedly deal in such merchandise in Russia–our version of your mafia–and I have a rare true friend in the GRU, whom I would trust with my life. Actually…, I have already done that. I am already beyond the point of no return, Ms. Sokolov. *Please* try to understand my situation…."

She watched the man cut his personal and official ties to his homeland right there before her eyes, as if desperately eviscerating himself. The scene ripped at her heart, despite her intelligence training and exceptional professional experience from other 'special' assignments within the Central Intelligence Agency around the world. She deliberately waited in silence for about another 30 seconds while her brain shifted into overdrive, weighing the pros and cons of what she had just heard, and of her developing intuition.

How much time and effort should I spend trying to verify what this man just told me, when time is most likely a very critical factor? What kind of maniac could tell a story like that if it was not true? What if he is not really a military officer? My sources could check on that. It would be next to impossible for him to have known Pavel Dryzhensky's 'secret life' beforehand. The world is much too dangerous to ignore this kind of potentially beneficial chance coincidence, particularly with increasing terrorist activity, various rumors and other information about allegedly loose nukes in the last several decades.

After several more thoughtful seconds, she said decisively, "I believe you, Colonel. I have certain trusted contacts as well. I will do what I can to elevate the importance of what you have related to me to the people who can do something about it. For now, however, I need not emphasize too strongly that you should be very careful in your associations and activities until we can get you out of Russia. That may take several days to a week…, possibly longer. I am going to give you a special single-channel, sealed cellphone with a unique encryption system. Guard it *carefully*. We will want it returned in its *original* condition. If you attempt to open or disassemble it, it will self-destruct. I will call you on that phone when we can get you out. I will use only your first name, and tell you the time is 1700, or 1800 hours, regardless of what time it really is. That is how you will know that I am making the call, and when you must be back at this embassy. If I say 1800 hours, then you know you have no less than 17 hours and no more than 18 hours to get to the embassy from the time of the call. If I say 1900 hours, then you will know that you must be here within 19 hours, but after 18 hours after my call. No one else will be able to intercept or trace that call. If you deviate in any way whatsoever from these instructions, then the deal is off. This is the time to ask questions–not later. I will give you a special pass now for your entrance at that later time. Do you understand completely everything I have just told you?"

He hesitated less than two seconds, realizing that he had just placed his entire fate in her hands without a comfortable period of preparation, and said, "Yes, I understand completely."

She tried to offer the reassurance he needed to hear, "I have done this before. We *will* get you out."

Her assurance soothed him enough. He needed to trust her.

"Thank you, Ms. Sokolov. Thank you very much!"

How odd! I, Colonel Viktor A. Kovalenko, a once proud and valuable Russian Military Intelligence officer am now in a position of trusting an American woman I do not know, with information that could be the end of me, or even extremely dangerous to someone else, and perhaps many others I cannot possibly know. I must be either truly desperate, or not in full control of my fate. The die is cast.

She said, "Please wait here until I return in several minutes with the cellphone you will need."

Colonel Kovalenko waited as she instructed, while trying to control the rush of thoughts colliding in his mind.

I have stepped out through the window of familiarity upon the ledge of uncertainty and danger. I know that the next step will put me at the mercy of people and events that I cannot completely know, anticipate, or control. God help me!

Only a minute had gone by when Andrea returned to the room and again closed the door. She sat down, handed him the phone, and then wrote out a special pass on an official-looking yellow pad, stamped it, and handed it to him.

Then she accompanied him in silence out of the room, down the hall into the elevator, and rode down to the lobby, where she finally said in an official business-like manner, revealing absolutely nothing about their conversation or relationship, "Goodbye, sir."

He imitated her manner with an equally neutral, "Good day."

He turned away from her, strode across the lobby, and left the embassy, retracing his steps back to the main perimeter entrance guardhouse, where he returned his original yellow badge without incident, and then walked away to his rented car. Within seconds after he checked his side view mirror and pulled out into the street, a small blue car also pulled out into the same street, traveling in the same direction behind him. He continued southwest along the M-1 highway back to the Vnukovo International Airport so completely absorbed in his anxious contemplation of his unknown future and getting to the gate on time that he neglected to notice the small blue car following him at variable distances. The other car went to a different parking lot at the airport as he returned his rental car. He had little time to board the Ural Airlines return flight back to Chelyabinsk. If the 'wrong people' really knew what he had just done, they would most likely have had him in custody by now.

They do not know anything yet. So far, so good. If they do know, then what are they waiting for? Do they want to discover more about my activities?

After he returned his car to the rental lot, he walked briskly to the main terminal, trying not to betray concern. He found a bank ATM kiosk, looked around the immediate area cautiously for a few seconds, and then withdrew as much cash from his HBSC account as he could get. A fit-looking young man followed him at a respectable distance, but only to the lounge gate, and observed him boarding the aircraft.

Andrea Sokolov sent a message to Duke Chancellor because she did not trust CIA channels of communication with this degree of sensitivity at this stage of an unconfirmed potential crisis. If the Russians had managed to compromise the official embassy communications facilities, they more likely would not have been able to break the Chancellor Organization's communications. Probabilities were that they were completely ignorant of the Chancellor Organization in the first place. If the story were false, or at least questionable, then repercussions would be more uncomfortable within the CIA than they would be within the Chancellor Organization, which was much smaller and more flexible. Duke Chancellor could control, absorb, or diffuse the information with much greater efficiency and confidence, and without burdensome official government records, procedures, or injury to her personal or professional reputation or career.

**** ATLANTIC OCEAN ****

Captain James R. Kilroy received special orders early in the morning to proceed to the coordinates of exfiltration: 57.073619 degrees latitude, and 17.97706 degrees longitude, southeast of Iceland, and west of Ireland. He knew that he had to make a 158-degree left turn. Many sailors would sense the sub turning and wonder why. Little did he know as a small boy 44 years ago at the Lexington Middle School between Grant and Washington streets in Lexington, Nebraska that he would eventually ascend to high military rank and deadly responsibility in the United States Navy, commanding the latest in submarine technological marvels at an annual cost of $50 million, and that would not need more fuel for about 33 years. He also could not know how close fate would take him to the periphery of danger from the thoughts of a truly evil mind. The Virginia Class USS Mississippi, SSN 782, was cruising at moderate speed 200 feet below sea level south of Iceland and west of Ireland at 50.838691 degrees latitude and -24.082031 degrees longitude. Those on duty among her crew of 132 officers and enlisted men were working at normal duty stations without adverse incidents. No one other than Captain Kilroy and the sailor driving the sub was expecting a turn, but they all recognized the subtle change of speed and direction to the port side. An off-duty sonar operator heading back to his bunk after a shower sensed the turn, and momentarily leaned against the adjacent starboard side wall to maintain his balance before continuing down the hall.

Okay, Skipper…. What the hell are you doin'?

Captain Kilroy coincidentally answered him in the sharp metallic naval version of high-fidelity sound over the intercom within six seconds, *"This is the Captain…. We have a new assignment. We're heading for the Baltic Sea to pick up a passenger. That is all."*

The sonar operator–and everyone else, regardless of duty shift–sensed their speed increase as the four Curtis turbines forced the giant aft propeller to its maximum rotation with its characteristic subtle sound, pushing the mammoth sub to 40 miles per hour within minutes.

Another sailor just getting to his bunk after his duty shift mumbled to himself, "Must be somebody pretty important to race over there like this."

CHAPTER 41
Friday, August 7, 2015

**** *MOSCOW, RUSSIA* ****

Andrea Sokolov awoke early this cool morning, and prepared a simple breakfast of kasha, dry toast, and a boiled egg. She had been expecting an acknowledgement from Father Pavel Dryzhensky during the last two days but had not received any. With increasing concern, after she finished her breakfast, she sent a secure message to Duke Chancellor.

> *'P.D. has not acknowledged my messages during the last two days. This is distinctly out of character, so I am fearful about his current status. A.S.'*

The response from Duke appeared within 28 seconds, confirming that her channel was functioning properly.

> *'Acknowledge your most recent message re: P.D. Will investigate from this end. D.C.'*

He immediately sent a message through the System 19 channel assuming that Pavel would respond to Duke even with the unlikely possibility that he might be suspicious of his contacts to and from Andrea. Duke waited for more than 16 hours with no response and assumed that the elderly Pavel Dryzhensky was in trouble or was severely ill, or possibly even dead.

**** ISTANBUL, TURKEY ****

Umar Kasana exited the Ciya Sofrasi Restaurant at number 43 on Gunesli Bahce Street into the clear warm day. Two GRU agents were sitting in a parked black Hyundai rental car across the street. Igor immediately set the Canon D70 digital camera to dual exposure, fast repeated automatic shutter release, and set the 400 mm lens to automatic image stabilization. Then he aimed the camera at his subject directly through the open driver's side window and pressed the shutter release button. The camera responded with six rapid 'shutter sounds,' each in dual exposure mode, in less than two seconds until his subject disappeared around the corner. Within the next two minutes, he transmitted the 12 rapid-fire images he had just recorded directly from the camera through the internet to Colonel Koshelev at GRU headquarters. Colonel Koshelev recognized the images of the man he knew as an international arms dealer. He immediately sent a secure phone message to his most effective field agent.

> *Major Z. Subject K6 confirmed Istanbul. Interrogate regarding any possible nuclear transactions. Priority highest. V. Koshelev.*

CHAPTER 42
Saturday, August 8, 2015

**** CHELYABINSK, RUSSIA ****

The fastest way Boris could get to Istanbul from Chelyabinsk with the least inconvenience was by a commercial flight via Moscow. The distance to Moscow is about 1,107 miles, and from Moscow to Istanbul is about 1,091 miles. An unscheduled direct military flight could have aroused suspicion in either Russia or Turkey, not to mention the notice of NATO air defense satellite systems, and he did not want to draw even that kind of attention to himself or his mission. He boarded Aeroflot Flight 1423, an Airbus A320 at 7:40 P.M. and arrived at Sheremetyevo two hours and 25 minutes later, at 8:05 P.M. local time, one time zone farther west. He waited through a one-hour and 20-minute layover, and then continued to Istanbul at 9:25 P.M. on another Airbus A320, Aeroflot Flight 2134, seated next to a starboard window.

Colonel Kovalenko was in his office with the door closed, going through the motions of being the base commanding officer while internally trying to stabilize his biochemistry with stale leftover breakfast coffee and intense personal concentration—so far, with little success. He almost jumped out of his chair when the special cellphone from Andrea Sokolov buzzed in his pocket. He inhaled, and then mentally counted to three for no reason other than to regain and maintain his composure. He opened the phone to its operating configuration, put it next to his left ear, and waited without saying anything. A woman's calm voice came on the line.

"Viktor, It is now 20:00 hours."

The line went dead–no dial tone, just absolute silence. He listened for another 10 seconds, but he heard absolutely no sound. He held the device in front of him, examining it. The little green power light went off. Nothing was wrong with the phone. It was completely silent because it was programmed to shut itself down at the termination of that call so it would not continue to transmit a signal unnecessarily that someone could intercept or trace. He was sure he had just heard Andrea Sokolov's voice. He had just enough time to get to the embassy on time if he left immediately.

Very clever, these Americans! It is time to leave. This is really happening!

He could catch a flight leaving Chelyabinsk at 2:35 that afternoon on Aeroflot Russian Airlines Flight 5829 operated by Orenair and arrive non-stop at Vnukovo Airport two hours and 30 minutes later, which would be 3:05 P.M. local time in Moscow. He would then have plenty of time to get to the embassy by 7 o'clock that evening. He secured the door to his office, and then changed into his civilian clothing from the closet in his office. Then he hung up his duty uniform in the closet and closed the door. He looked briefly around his office for anything that might reveal his intentions to someone else. Then he put the special cellphone in his pants pocket and checked for his own cellphone and wallet. He left his office for the last time and closed the door. No one else was in the hallway. He went down the hall, out the back door to his car, and drove to the airport. It wouldn't matter if he left his car there. They would eventually know that he had left, and by then it would not make any difference. His flight was uneventful and arrived on time at Vnukovo and taxied to the arrival terminal. He could not see anyone unusual waiting for deplaning passengers. With elevated heart rate, he maintained a cautious respect for everything around him as he went through the arrival terminal. Suddenly he thought that someone whose official governmental business was to observe other people might find it peculiar that he did not have any luggage. He could not do anything about that now, but his vigilance continued. He again went to the HSBC kiosk to withdraw as much cash as he could get from his savings account, and then casually walked out of the arrival terminal to hire a cab. After waiting only about 90 seconds, he told the next arriving cabbie to take him to a location he knew was near the Moscow Zoo, from which he would assess whether he was being followed, and then walk less than a mile to the United States embassy. No one could interrogate the cabbie productively about the true destination of his passenger.

So far, so good....

After he entered the silver Renault taxi and closed the door, he surreptitiously looked around through the rear window. No one rushed to any cabs behind the one he just entered. He continued to look back periodically and as inconspicuously as he could. No one was following him in any obvious manner in any kind of vehicle.

Of course they are invisible! That's what they do! They are very careful, unless they want you to know they are watching!

He paid his fare and then exited the cab near the entrance to the Moscow Zoo. After waiting several minutes for the cab to disappear into traffic, he started to walk around the outside perimeter of the zoo. Pacing his time carefully to arrive at the embassy on time within the specified hour, he continued to stroll around the zoo, appearing to find something of interest every several minutes. Then, when the time was about right, and he was satisfied that no one had followed him, he started to move in the general direction of the embassy. He carefully checked the streets and intersections for people or vehicles that did not move along independently of his behavior. He made sure he did not walk in the most direct path toward the embassy. That didn't always mean anything either, since the pros often used disguises, tag teams and clever communications devices to observe and inform from innocuous stationary locations—inside buildings, on rooftops, as well as from moving or parked vehicles. He watched his time carefully. He was a subconscious victim of his own training. About 34 anxious minutes later, he arrived nervously at the entrance to the embassy at 7:14 P.M. and presented his special pass with as much self-control as he could muster.

The guard at the entrance said, "Take this pass to the main building over there, sir, and present it inside at the reception desk."

He held onto it with slightly more finger pressure than necessary. He did not want to put it in his pocket, and he did not want to drop it. That innocent mistake might convey nervousness to a trained eye. He needed to have it in his hand where he could feel it, where he knew exactly where it was. Without it, he would feel naked, insecure, and vulnerable. He walked innocently to the main building and entered through the front entrance. Somewhat more relieved inside the building, he continued to the reception desk and again presented what he was almost beginning to believe was his 'magic' pass.

"Take the elevator to the tenth floor, sir."

He looked at his pass one more time.

The last time she came down to the lobby to get me. Seems like this is going to work…. I hope.

By 6:20 P.M., he was in Andrea Sokolov's office on the tenth floor. She closed the door behind him. Another man was standing behind her next to the wall. He wore dirty dark blue coveralls with tool pockets that obscured his girth. He was about six feet, three inches tall, and had dark sandy unruly hair. His hands were rough and large with a few small, dried blotches of what could have been black paint, grease, or some other dark stain. He had several days of beard growth, and small, dark, penetrating brown eyes set in a disproportionately large bony face. He appeared to be both innocent and strong.

Andrea greeted Viktor in a friendly, but official voice, "Good evening, Colonel. The clock is ticking, so please forgive my direct manner. I could not get you a credible set of false identification papers. It was too risky, because we did not have the time necessary to do it the usual way, given the information you provided. Put these coveralls on. You are a plumber known as Nikolay A. Semenov. You will have to get in the trunk of a car just outside this building. After you leave the compound, M.R. over here will drive the car to a garage on the outskirts of Moscow, where the car will be loaded onto a transport truck for the trip to Saint Petersburg. M.R. will be in the truck cab and will do some of the driving. You will remain in the trunk of the car until you meet your next contact in Saint Petersburg, but the ventilation will be adequate. The journey will be long and a bit uncomfortable, but I am confident you will arrive at your destination safely without discovery. M.R. is quite experienced in deception and various methods of 'persuasion.' You will know him only as 'M.R.' for security reasons. He will not continue the trip beyond Saint Petersburg. The transport truck driver is also a trusted and reliable 'associate.' We have used him before. The entire trip should take only about 10 and a half hours, and the roads should be relatively clear of traffic since it will be dark outside for most of your journey. Expect one stop about halfway between Moscow and your destination–near Novgorod–for fuel. The next stop after that will be your destination in Saint Petersburg. Since you will not be able to see outside, I want you to be prepared and understand as much of what will be happening as possible, so you do not suffer any unnecessary anxiety and so you will understand if anything unexpectedly adverse develops. The journey should be successful, but prudence dictates that you be aware of what is supposed to happen, and roughly when, so you can identify and prepare for unexpected events. Obviously, silence is the best policy. We do not expect any inspections along the way, but again, prudence is best. If the authorities discover you, then I am afraid I will not be able to help. After you arrive at your destination in Saint Petersburg, you will get out of the trunk, and go to a fishing boat, where you will again need to be hidden until your rendezvous with the United States Navy. I do not know who will be on that fishing boat, but they are friendly and reliable helpers. Now, before you leave, do you have any questions?"

Colonel Kovalenko swallowed with difficulty but had understood from the start that this adventure would be unusual, to say the least, and he was not disappointed in that regard.

With quickly remanufactured resolve and the hope of seeing Karina again, he admitted, "I have no questions. Here is your phone."

With a friendly smile, Andrea extended her right hand to shake his, accepted the phone in her left hand and said, "Good luck, Colonel. I will discover in due time whether you have arrived safely."

M.R. offered a weak, but sincere smile and gestured with an open hand toward the door as he looked confidently into Colonel Kovalenko's eyes.

Viktor turned toward Andrea one more time, and said quietly with genuine sincerity, "Thank you! Thank you *very* much!"

Five minutes later, the two men left the embassy through a back emergency door and walked only a few steps past a trash dumpster toward a small two-door black sedan at the side of the building. M.R. went to the back of the car and unlocked the trunk lid, stood aside, looked around briefly, and then motioned to Colonel Kovalenko to step into the trunk compartment. With effort, Viktor entered the trunk and managed to approximate a fetal position on his right side, with minor extra room for repositioning himself, as necessary. He looked up out of the trunk with obvious concern in his face at his new companion. M.R. smiled confidently and nodded, as if to assure his passenger that he would not suffer any negative consequences or injuries before he reached his destination while under his care. Embassy maintenance people commonly used the car, so it would not arouse any suspicion. M.R. then closed the trunk lid without slamming it, locked it, and entered the driver's seat and closed the door. He started the engine and drove slowly through the compound toward the front gate. He was now fully committed. His movement at this point was routine. If he stopped or changed his mind, or drove in some other direction, he would attract suspicion and official attention, and would have to face questions to which he had no answers. He continued deliberately toward the main gate, as if he were leaving on a routine assignment and stopped for the obligatory cursory search and handed the guard a white pass. The guard took the pass, looked only briefly at it, and then nodded at the driver. M.R. took his foot off the brake and started the long journey to the sea and the fishing boat.

About 12 minutes later, Andrea left through the front entrance to the embassy to get her car in the compound parking lot. Within two minutes, she got in her car, masked her anxiety effectively, and drove to the main gate. The guard gave her a subtle 'thumbs up' with his right hand. She acknowledged him with an imperceptible nod, and then drove out of the compound, let out a long sigh of relief and returned to her apartment in moderate traffic without adverse incidents.

After an unknown period, Viktor sensed the car behavior consistent with Andrea's description of entering a garage. He mentally verified the sounds and motions consistent with the car being loaded upon a transport truck. Then the jostling ceased, and several minutes of silence followed. He heard at least two voices, but not clearly enough to understand the conversation. Then he heard the unmistakable sound of a closing vehicle door. Then he heard the transport truck engine start, and he started to move with a jerk. After that, the truck appeared to continue in a steady manner with constant speed and normal slowing and mild turning as if traveling on a well-paved road, as opposed to a dirt road or a major high-speed highway.

Within two hours, the truck slowed to a halt, as if approaching a stop sign or a checkpoint. Colonel Kovalenko became warily alert as the engine and road noise decreased to a lower idling sound. In the darkness of the trunk, his eyes were wide open, ready to take in any visual clues of what might be happening outside. He dared not make a sound. The car jostled slightly, and then he heard one of the truck doors open. M.R. obviously got out of the truck, as the car jostled only slightly on the truck as the driver stepped outside of the truck cab, removing his weight from the left side of the truck. Viktor's heart rate ramped up quickly, and he started to hyperventilate, even though the air was stale and cool. Moving his eyes despite of the absence of light was a natural reflex but provided no information. He was not yet afraid, but he knew fear might not be far away. He knew that the unexpected and the unexplained or misunderstood intrusions upon life often led to fear. His body's natural preparation for flight or fight started to emerge. He knew what it was, but he could not control it completely. He had to endure it for some unknown period. His mouth was dry, and he continued to breathe the stale cool air faster than he wanted to. He heard the obvious sound of a heavy truck engine approaching. The sound increased in volume but changed to a lower pitch as the truck obviously came to a halt somewhere nearby, and then apparently stopped as the engine noise continued at an unstrained steady idling pace and volume. He heard voices but could not understand what they were saying. Two men were talking to each other. No! Another voice interrupted! Someone was becoming irritated. He did not know the sound of M.R.'s voice because he had been silent since the two had met at the embassy. An argument was developing, and he did not know who was getting the upper hand, or who had authority. He wanted to live to see Karina again. He had been trained in ways to maintain discipline and tolerate or absorb torture, but those methods were not working. This experience was completely new to him. Then Andrea's voice echoed in his head… *'then I am afraid I will not be able to help.'* Without the familiar or clear input from his senses, he was at the mercy of his imagination, intelligence, and training. Nevertheless, he was mentally 'treading water.' The seconds ticked by too slowly. The present became an almost unbearable weight. He was increasingly uncomfortable physically and did not dare to move in a way that might make a sound or rock the car in a noticeable manner. He could not know whether someone capable of delivering negative consequences was out there, or what he might be looking at, or thinking. Then a door closed. Suddenly the truck engine revved faster and louder. Then another door closed. Then the truck gears engaged and the sound of low gears rotating at accelerating speed dominated his dark theater. The other truck was moving away. Within the next half minute, those truck sounds diminished into the fearful dark silence. Then at least two voices resumed. The apparent sound of a body being punched startled him. Unintelligible grunts and sounds of a physical struggle became clear for the next minute. Suddenly absolute silence resumed for the next 15 seconds. Then he heard the unmistakable sound of a pistol being fired, and then again. Almost 10 minutes of silence passed. His eyes widened in the empty darkness. Then footsteps approached the truck, the car door opened, and the weight of a heavy person rocked the car. The car door slammed shut. The truck door slammed shut. Viktor's heartrate rocketed higher.

Was that M.R..., or someone else? Someone just got into the car!

The truck engine started, and the car lurched slightly as the truck accelerated at a greater speed than he had experienced since he left the embassy, implying a different driver.

Then he heard an elevated voice from inside the car attempting to overcome the truck road noise, "We have a necessary change of plans!"

About 10 minutes later, he heard conversation, but he could not understand everything he heard. The man who got in the car was apparently aware of his location. He was having a telephone conversation, but Viktor could not hear clearly what he was saying. Suddenly, the conversation stopped. For the next two hours or more, the truck sped along the highway without interruption. As Andrea had told Viktor, they would stop for fuel at Novgorod. After a while, the truck decelerated, and then it stopped. Again, he heard voices, and whoever was in the car got out. The truck filler cap was being unscrewed. He heard the faint metallic sound of the fuel nozzle being inserted in the filler opening, and then the slight hollow rushing sound of liquid pouring into the almost empty gasoline tank. About two minutes later, the rushing sound diminished, but with higher frequency as the tank filled to its maximum capacity. The metallic bumping sound occurred again, and then the sound of the filler cap being screwed back into place followed. After further muffled sounds, someone slapped the outside of the car trunk lid three times. In about five seconds, the car door opened. Again, a heavy weight caused the car to rock slightly to the left side. The car door slammed shut and the truck engine came to life.

Then an elevated unfamiliar voice obviously coming from the front of the car said, "M.R. had to leave. I am Yevgeny. I know the plan. I am going with you to your destination in Saint Petersburg."

How do you believe a total stranger? How do you put your faith... your life... in the hands of someone you have never met nor even seen before, whose voice you have never heard before, and cannot see now? Especially when you carry secret information!

Why is he in the car and not in the truck cab? Is someone else in the cab with the driver? Does he know who I am? What will happen to M.R.?

For most of the next five hours, second by second, minute by minute, hour by hour of constant droning road noise without adverse incidents or conversation, the trust developed–or at least the fear diminished. The development of a norm, a predictable continuation evolved. Physically and emotionally exhausted, Viktor easily succumbed to a semiconscious sleep in the monotonous road noise.

The driver and the 'third person' must be 'them'..., the good guys. I hope they are... the good guys.

Time returned to its normal pace in the monotonous road noise.

Did they shoot and kill someone to save me from discovery? How could I ever repay these people?

CHAPTER 43
Sunday, August 9, 2015

**** *Saint Petersburg, Russia* ****

Suddenly he awoke to the subtle transition from no traffic in rural areas to increasing traffic noise and different road conditions, with more turns and lower speeds, different sounds, until he could finally detect the faint odor of the sea–salt air, subtle vague fishy odors.

This must be Saint Petersburg!

The car stopped. The engine stopped. A car door opened and closed. He heard footsteps approaching. The trunk lid swung open. He was in an old, abandoned metal garage. He struggled to get his stiff and aching body out of the trunk, onto the truck bed, and then finally down onto the firm cement floor. He stood unsteadily for several seconds before he stretched his arms, legs, and back.

Yevgeny smiled genuinely at his passenger and said, "Here is your new work uniform!"

For the first time, Viktor met the man who gave of his time and energy to perform a duty clearly illegal, dangerous, and unclear, to transport him to this location, and in the process may have saved his life. He accepted the fisherman's overalls and struggled to put them on over his clothing.

After he adjusted the obvious fit of his new costume, he looked into Yevgeny's friendly gray eyes and said, "Thank you for what you have done for me!"

He could not yet say, *and for the lives of many other innocent people.*

Yevgeny pointed to the old fishing vessel tied to the nearest pier outside the garage, and said, "That is your next transport."

Yevgeny could not know the full extent and implications of the mundane task he had performed in transporting Viktor from one innocuous location to another and may knowingly have risked his life in doing so. They shook hands firmly with understood sincere eye contact. Then Viktor turned and walked quietly to the fishing boat tied to the pier. His eyes took in the sights of the real world again, albeit a world unfamiliar to him. He continued to stifle his gratitude with necessary discipline.

**** KRASNODON, UKRAINE ****

The usual early worshippers from the surrounding community gathered under cloudy skies outside the old church, met with others, and exchanged friendly pleasantries as they did every Sunday. Several entered the old church and started walking down the aisle between well-worn wooden pews toward the narthex. Others went immediately to their favorite pews. An elderly woman wearing a gray sweater struggled with her new aluminum walker before her as she stepped slowly and unsteadily through the main door of the church toward the confessional. She could see that the little red light at the front above the door was on, indicating that the confessional was occupied. She knew that the priest had never heard confessions at this hour before the first service. She waited, sensing a faint unpleasant odor while staring at the confessional for several minutes. She was a 'regular,' and always walked that way to her favorite pew. She had waited long enough and followed her intuition. Some others stopped in their tracks, sensing something out of place or not right in the church. She approached the confessional and bravely opened the side door. The body of Father Pavel Dryzhensky fell out onto the floor. His throat obviously had been cut, and his bloody white robe was evidence of recent severe bleeding. She screamed with both shock and fear and then crossed herself and clasped her hands together at her chest in prayer out of ingrained habit. Other parishioners from inside and outside the old church suddenly gathered in an urgent rush near the confessional to see that their priest was obviously executed. Someone called the local police on a cellphone. Officers responded within 13 minutes to secure the crime scene and question the parishioners. No one reported anything unusual. Clearly, the crime had been committed only a short time ago, but before the parishioners had arrived, since some traces of blood were still slightly moist. The manner of execution was symbolic–perhaps a warning of what can happen to someone who talks, or hears, too much.

**** MOSCOW, RUSSIA ****

Andrea Sokolov made her fourth attempt on Sunday to contact Pavel Dryzhensky to confirm that Colonel Kovalenko had been taken out of Russia and was on his way to the United States. Again, his channel was inactive. She finally contacted Duke, indicating that Pavel Dryzhensky was no longer responding to her communication efforts. Later in the day, her private cellphone buzzed with an unfamiliar caller identification number: 011-7-499-884-2339. She did not recognize the number, ignored the call, and continued her work. About 20 minutes later, her phone buzzed again with the same caller identification number. This time, with a mix of increasing curiosity and apprehension, she pushed the answer button, held her phone up to her left ear, and then waited 10 seconds without saying anything, expecting the caller to identify himself.

After hearing nothing further, she said cautiously, "Hello?"

A male voice responded, *"Are you Andrea Sokolov?"*

"Yes, this is Andrea Sokolov... Who are you? How did you get this number?"

"I must remain anonymous, but I am highly placed in GRU. My message is for good reason for all concerned. A Chechnyan Islamic radical murdered your friend in Krasnodon. If necessary, make sure your superiors know the Russian government was not involved in any way... politically, militarily, or otherwise. I am obliged not to use official channels."

She whispered forcefully, "Who *are* you?"

"I am... a friend. You know what to do. You will not hear from me again."

He wants me to inform my superiors. How did he know about my 'friend?' How did he know my phone number? I won't hear from him again...? Something tells me that is not true.

The caller terminated the connection. Andrea was now breathing rapidly with the mild fear of approaching nausea. She hyperventilated and looked with a furrowed brow at her phone as if it were contaminated. Momentarily frozen in mental limbo, she sat heavily upon her reading chair, holding her phone on her lap, just staring at it for several seconds. Then the rush of thoughts began, coming from the improbable, the impossible, and then the most likely assumptions. Regardless of the veracity of the call, the message was consistent with her inability to contact Pavel Dryzhensky. That was simply too much of a coincidence to be unimportant. She needed to inform Duke as well as her superiors at the CIA because someone from a foreign clandestine service had contacted her. She would be obligated to inform her superiors of that fact eventually according to standard CIA operating procedure and rules. It was clearly always better to do so immediately, rather than later, during a scheduled mandatory annual review or under other unknown, unexpected, coincidental, and career-threatening or even criminal circumstances. The worst scenario would be that a whistle-blower or someone of higher rank, or even someone else entirely unknown to her might discover or somehow learn of the event before she reported it. There would be no tolerance for excuses and no forgiveness. Some people like Robert Hanssen could fool the FBI for years, but she knew she was definitely not one of them, nor did she even remotely desire to be. She had to report the incident.

But the man said she would not hear from him again. Exactly why was that? Can I believe him? He said he was a friend. Dammit! Who? What kind of 'friend?'

Duke would know how to handle this. He would certainly look out for her in a much more sincere and thorough manner than the CIA would. It would be easier for her to go through him first, rather than go directly to her superiors. He had reliable connections with the CIA anyway, and she was simply more comfortable with telling him first. She lurched into action and opened her laptop computer to activate her secure link to Duke Chancellor.

'A.S.–Received strange unsolicited telephone call on my cellphone this evening from 011-7-499-884-2339–someone who said he was 'highly placed' in the GRU, said he was a 'friend.' Told me a Chechnyan Islamic radical murdered 'my friend in Krasnodon' (I have to believe he was talking about Pavel), and that the Russian government had nothing to do with it 'politically, militarily, or otherwise.' He also said he was obliged not to use official channels, and that I would not hear from him again. I don't know what to make of this right now, so I am passing it along to you as soon as

possible, rather than informing my superiors first, in case you have some important suggestions, insights or advice I am not likely to get from them.'

Duke responded within six minutes:

'Acknowledged. You must notify your superiors immediately. I will handle all other matters from here. You should be in the clear, because he called you, and not the other way around. However, if necessary, I will make sure you do not suffer any official adverse consequences. D.C.'

**** ISTANBUL, TURKEY ****

Boris arrived at 1:05 A.M. under a clear star-filled sky at Ataturk International Airport and rented a white Fiat Linea compact car from Avis for the equivalent of about $45.37 per day. After completing the rental paperwork, he walked outside to find the car, which obviously had been washed recently because it still had a few drops of water on it during a clear night. He settled into the driver's seat, started the engine, and then drove to the Best Western Tashan Airport Hotel just a few miles east of the airport for some much-needed sleep. Several rooms were available, but he took the smallest one. All he wanted was a good night's sleep. His room had a view of the Sea of Marmara to the south that he would not enjoy until after daybreak. He lay on top of the bed to relax, but his body quickly succumbed to sleep and shut itself down for the night.

**** WASHINGTON, D.C. ****

Her immediate superiors at the Washington Post had assigned Susan Wong temporarily to their office in Tokyo with instructions to 'be creative' and to look for unusual human-interest stories in the hopes that the bright young woman could improve their publication circulation with interesting stories about Japan and general East Asian events. After several moments of curiosity about why she was selected for this assignment, she relaxed enough to look forward to the experience, and to enjoy herself during this unexpected opportunity to travel. She picked up her flight ticket in the company travel office just before leaving the building for the day. She was surprised to note that the flight was non-stop, which cost more than one with connections, and wondered why she was receiving the special treatment.

**** MARYLAND ****

Duke sent a secure message to Sammy in San Francisco:

> *'ASAP Find out where this telephone number is based, and who owns it: 011-7-499-884-2339. Keep your search quiet and under the radar. Thank you. D.C.'*

**** LANGLEY, VIRGINIA ****

He grabbed his desk phone abruptly and barked, "Murray!"

"General, this is Julie Anderson again. That Kasana DNA sample came up zero from Interpol, MI-6, Mossad, and the FBI. If this is a bad guy, he must be very careful, General."

"Thank you, Ms. Anderson. Keep looking around and let me know anything you discover about that DNA, immediately!"

"Yes sir!"

He replaced his phone receiver with thoughtless emphasis and unspoken epithets.

**** MARYLAND ****

Duke was still in his office just before 6 P.M. when he called General Murray on his dedicated cellphone.

"What's up, Duke?"

"I received a message from Andrea Sokolov earlier today. She said she received an anonymous telephone call from someone who said he was highly placed in the GRU and indicated that the Russian government and their military organization had absolutely nothing to do with 'her friend in Krasnodon'—meaning, I'm sure, Pavel Dryzhensky—and that he had been murdered by a Chechnyan Islamic radical. They gave her no further information or explanation, other than that he was a 'friend,' and that 'she would not hear from him again.' She is going to report the contact officially. I am simply trying to make you aware of something in advance that might become important. I told her I would see that she did not suffer any adverse consequences for contacting me first, rather than her superiors, so please do all of us a big favor and make sure she remains officially clean on this. She is too good a person to damage or lose over this."

"Absolutely! That contact is quite interesting! It suggests that something unusual is brewing in Moscow… or somewhere where they have some interest… and it may have… embarrassing consequences for them… or something else entirely is going on. Maybe someone with influence or power over there is acting on his own—and that in itself would be quite unusual! I was not aware that we had any 'friends' in the GRU!"

"That's what I was thinking…. Maybe if we have a friend we don't know about…, then something of significant importance is occurring that, in and of itself, turns former adversaries into friends, or at least encourages if not cements a new cooperation. It has the feel of a shift in priorities, like the fox truly and sincerely offering to help the farmer catch a stray chicken, but without ulterior motives. That would suggest *significant* motivation, don't you think?"

General Murray responded, *"Yes. I agree. Please keep me informed about anything else that comes up that might be related to this."*

"Of course."

The conversation was over, but both men were unsettled.

CHAPTER 44
Monday, August 10, 2015

**** *Istanbul, Turkey* ****

Sunrise occurred at 6:08 A.M. with clear skies. Since Boris had never gotten around to closing the blinds, the room filled with the light of a new day and awakened him with only mild and brief disorientation. By 8:10 A.M., he had showered and dressed in comfortable casual working attire, including black rubber-soled laced shoes, just in case the day's action escalated beyond vehicular pursuit of his prey. He left his room and went to his rented car and drove toward the Mikla Restaurant. Within 20 minutes, he parked his car, walked to the restaurant, and entered through the main door. By 8:45 A.M., he was seated at a table in one of the more secluded areas of the dining room. A middle-aged, dark-haired man came to his table and offered a menu.

"My name is Kemal. I will be your server this morning. May I get some coffee for you?"

"You are just the man I want to see…, and no, I do not want any coffee, thank you."

"You want to see *me?*" Kemal said in genuine confusion.

"Yes. Do you recognize this man?"

He showed a photograph of Shamir to Kemal.

Kemal looked carefully at the photograph, and after waiting cautiously for a few seconds of indecision to pass, he looked away from the photograph and into to Boris's eyes and said, "Yes, I recognize him. Why do you ask?"

"*I* will ask the questions, Kemal," he said in a firm, but discernably menacing tone, and then continued, "Now, do you recognize *this* man?"

He showed Kemal another photograph of a relatively young, tall, fit-looking man wearing a black suit.

After studying the image carefully for about 15 seconds, he said flatly, "Yes."

Kemal was beginning to feel uneasy, as if he had just stepped into a dark and unfamiliar room for no good reason. He did not need 15 seconds to identify the man in black. He was stalling, hoping for inspiration, or the comfort of understanding, but neither developed.

Boris looked up at Kemal with a forced wry smile and said, "Now, my friend…, please tell me *exactly* why you recognize both of these men."

Kemal sensed that it would be best to answer the man truthfully and quickly, and said in a subdued tone, "It was one week ago today that I saw both men."

"Where?"

"Here…, I mean… one inside and one outside the restaurant."

"I need you to tell me everything about that day, Kemal…, *everything!* Do you understand me?"

"Yes sir! This man, the first one, he gave me a note to give to the second man, and then he left the restaurant. It was near the front entrance where I was making a telephone call. He never actually came into the restaurant to eat, but he knew that the other man was in the restaurant. I do not know how he knew that, but I did as he asked. It was a just simple favor from a potential customer, so I did it. I went to the table where the second man was seated with an attractive American woman, and I slipped the note into his hand without her seeing it."

"How do you know she was American?"

"I heard her speak at the door… before she went to her table."

"Tell me more about the American woman."

"She wore a red dress, blue scarf, white shoes…, nice figure, honey-blonde hair with a red band in it."

"You're *sure* of this… Kemal?" he said with a withering stare.

"I said she was pretty. Men do not lie about that kind of woman…, right?"

Boris already knew that the man in black was a womanizer of almost pathological proportions. He accepted Kemal's story so far.

"Were they related–the man and the woman?"

"I do not think so."

"What was the message on the note?"

"I do not know. I did not read it."

"You're sure you did *not* read the note?"

"Yes, I'm sure!"

He continued in a subtly menacing tone, "You were not the *least bit*... curious?"

Kemal was clearly becoming uncomfortable, as he said with mild alarm, "No!"

After a few seconds of reconsideration, Boris concluded that he could not easily intimidate Kemal if he were truly not involved with either of the two men beyond the innocent exchange he described, so he changed tactics with a more civil conversational attitude.

"So..., what happened after you gave him the note?"

"I think he hid it in his hand, so the woman would not see it, I guess."

"What happened next?"

"I do not know. I had other duties to perform, so I left their table."

Boris paused for several seconds, looked intently into Kemal's eyes, and then said, "Very well, Kemal. Here is my card. If you think of anything else about these two people, you call me immediately, day or night. *Understand?*"

"Yes sir. I understand completely!"

"That's good, Kemal.... That's *very* good..., because I do not want to discover later that you have lied to me, or withheld information..., *and neither do you!*"

Kemal swallowed surreptitiously and managed to offer a meek smile as he sensed with mild relief the approaching end of this increasingly uncomfortable exchange. He hoped he would never encounter this man again. Boris stood and responded with another uniquely withering stare for a few seconds before turning to leave the restaurant.

After about a 20-kilometer drive west from that location, Umar boarded Turkish Airlines Flight TK11 at 6:35 P.M. due to arrive at JFK International Airport at 10:30 P.M.

Susan Wong waited in the departure lounge area next to Gate D at Dulles International Airport for United Airlines Flight 803, a Boeing 777 aircraft, leaving at 1:15 P.M. and due to arrive at Narita International Airport about 47 miles east of Tokyo at 4 P.M. local time the following day.

**** GOGLAND ISLAND, SEA OF FINLAND ****

Gogland Island is slightly wider than a mile at its greatest east-west width, and about five miles long, located about 120 miles west of Saint Petersburg, Russia. A mile west of that isolated island on the overcast and 58-degree moonless night of August 11, 2015, the calm, dark, cold surface of the Sea of Finland began to stir and roil slightly about 200 feet north of the old, dark-gray 45-foot fishing boat idling near 57.073619 degrees latitude and 17.977066 degrees longitude. To those on the fishing boat, the submarine announced its hidden presence with a foreboding subtle change in the surface of the sea. Within seconds the upper 18 feet of the massive black bridge of the USS Mississippi broke through the water's surface as the sound of rushing seawater around it increased, and the deck of the sub became visible as it rose to normal surface posture. Most of the 377-foot long 7,800-ton submarine remained hidden beneath the dark surface of the sea. Among the crew of 145 officers and enlisted men, two seamen wearing blue duty uniforms with holstered pistols, stepped out through a hatch in the forward deck. Then the boat's executive officer appeared at the top and toward the front of the bridge. He brought a pair of powerful binoculars to his eyes and quickly scanned the calm dark surface of the sea in all directions. Within seconds, four flashes of red light appeared to the south, then four flashes of bright LED white light came from the same location. One of the seamen on the forward deck responded with four half-second bright flashes of red light and four similar flashes of green light, indicating acceptance of the pre-arranged signal from the fishing vessel, and giving permission to approach. The engine in the fishing boat came to life as the boat turned toward the massive submarine and cut smoothly through the dark surface of the unusually calm sea for about six minutes until it was within 45 feet of the waiting sub as the captain reduced power to the engines, slowing its drift toward the submarine. Viktor was the only man who looked out of place on the deck of the fishing vessel, illuminated by only a few cabin lights and several flashlights from both vessels. Despite his increasing anxiety, he reflexively reached out for the apparently brand-new bright orange lifejacket at the end of a yellow rope one of the sailors tossed toward him from the forward deck. Viktor caught it in mid-air as his heart rate increased. He put his arms through the appropriate openings and secured the vest around himself with the black strap on the front side. He was alone, proceeding like a robot, almost blindly, one necessary and daring second after another into the unknown future. He briefly patted the waterproof bag secured around his waist containing 350,000 rubles (about $8,134 in United States dollars), as much as he could withdraw from his savings in the time he had available. He fastened the life jacket securely one more time, just to make sure that would not become an extra worry. The sailor indicated he should fasten the rope around his chest and under his arms. He did so, and then in a fortuitous moment of relative calm with the fishing vessel idling within two yards of the sub in remarkably calm water, he cast his fate with determination and trust in the sailors and jumped to the ample rope ladder hanging down the side of the sub from the location of the two sailors near the forward hatch. He knew that if he failed to grasp the rope securely, he would fall to the surface of the sea between the two vessels. A dozen old tires hung by ropes from the fishing boat at the water surface, intended to cushion incidental contact between the fishing boat and the sub. However, if the two vessels got that close, they could still crush him to death as the fishing boat periodically moved closer with the occasionally capricious surface of the sea toward the hull of the sub despite the captain's efforts to prevent exactly that. Viktor focused with determination and grasped the rope ladder firmly with the vital strength of both hands. He found momentary security with a strong hand and foothold on the rope ladder as one of the two obviously strong sailors assisted his ascent by pulling on the rope around his chest. He looked up slightly with mild anxiety to concentrate upon the distance he had yet to climb to final safety, briefly trying to imagine his uncertain future while reluctantly leaving the familiar comfort of his homeland, for the last time. Sufficient strength from his younger days of training remained in his fit but aging body to sustain his labored ascent up the steepest side of the sub, but he continued with determination as his climb followed the contour of the sub toward the essentially flat and horizontal deck level. Then he slowly pulled his straining body higher and more horizontally with his arms as his right foot found the next higher cross-rope. With the continued assistance of one of the two strong young sailors pulling on the other end of the lifejacket rope above him, he grasped the top cross-rope of the ladder, and the other sailor helped him over onto the deck as if he had done it thousands of times before. The two sailors assisted his standing security and ushered him toward the open hatch. One sailor then removed his lifejacket and conducted a polite, but thorough military body search. He opened the waterproof bag, noted that no weapons or other dangerous materials were inside, and then closed it. Colonel Kovalenko silently cooperated in tolerating what he had expected and knew was necessary. After about 30 seconds of further efficient searching, the sailor turned to Commander Morris on the bridge and nodded with an affirmative facial expression as well as a hand signal of 'Okay.' Out of habitual military courtesy, Colonel Kovalenko looked up and saluted the man he correctly assumed was the senior officer on the bridge. Commander Jeffrey Morris confirmed that his new passenger was unarmed and bravely appeared to be masking at least some anxiety as he returned the salute. Commander Morris then waved off the fishing vessel. The captain of the smaller boat offered a quick, unpolished, and contrived salute and then engaged the twin propellers in reverse with a noticeable deep mechanical 'thud' from somewhere inside the boat's mechanical heart, slowly pushing his boat away from the massive submarine. He turned the bow to the east while changing the transmission to forward power with another deep mechanical sound, increased his engine speed, and cruised back into the anonymous and uncertain protection of the quiet international night. He would have his nets out early that day, again trying to earn a living from the sea, as he wondered with unfamiliar dread whether someone might eventually find out what he had just done. At least his wife would be comfortable. The universally persuasive language of cash secured his cooperation. The equivalent of $750,000 from the vast fortune of Duke Chancellor moved completely anonymously and circuitously to a Swiss bank. Half of that total went to an account in his name, and half to another account in his wife's name.

Commander Morris turned back to the others and issued a subdued but firm command, "Okay, gentlemen, let's get out of here! We're going home!"

Within a minute, Commander Morris left the bridge and descended into the sub. The two sailors and their new passenger also were on their way down into the interior, and the last sailor inside firmly secured the forward hatch above them. Within the next minute, the massive deadly military machine slowly and silently slipped back completely under the dark surface of the sea, which obscured its presence, eventually leaving only a few small bubbles, which soon vanished. Just 14 weeks after its commission on June 2, 2012, in Pascagoula, Mississippi, the latest United States high-tech submarine and the fourth so-named naval vessel, had started its first significant exfiltration task that would end just six days later at its home port of Groton, Connecticut. The two sailors took Colonel Kovalenko directly to Captain James R. Kilroy. The Captain's orders were to 'take good care of' their guest and get as much information as possible from him as soon as possible and then relay that information to CIA headquarters immediately. The captain ensured that their guest was comfortable before any debriefing.

"Smitty, you and Cashman stick to our guest like glue! Accompany him to the showers, see that he gets a fresh set of clothing, and then get him a square meal. After he has finished eating, bring him back here to my quarters, and remain outside my door until I tell you otherwise. I do not want any interruptions."

In perfect unison, the two sailors replied, "Aye, sir!"

Colonel Kovalenko understood that he was being given more than fair and courteous treatment, and mentally started to relax, which is exactly what the captain wanted. The two sailors escorted Colonel Kovalenko, one ahead of him and one behind, through the cramped submarine toward the showers. The executive officer entered the captain's quarters and closed the door behind him.

"So..., what do we have here, Captain? Who is this guy?"

"We're going to find out soon enough, since I will be debriefing him shortly. Your function here will be as a witness. I will do the talking. I do not have much detail myself, but I understand that he has something important to tell us. It is obviously important enough for someone very high above me to order me to leave the prior mission on short order and change course. This mission is at the highest order of secrecy, so I will remind you that whatever you hear in this interview stays inside your head until someone of appropriate higher authority with a need to know *asks* for it. If you have any doubts, then err on the side of silence and refer any inquiries *directly to me!* Understood?"

"Yes sir!"

About 50 minutes later, Smitty and Cashman returned Colonel Kovalenko to Captain Kilroy's quarters comfortably refreshed and satisfied with a full stomach of surprisingly tasty United States Navy food. He nodded to the two sailors before they closed the door behind him, and then sat on the only empty chair across the sturdy grey metal table from the two naval officers. He prepared himself with a deep breath and subtle exhalation. Captain Kilroy started the conversation.

"I am Captain Kilroy, and this man is Commander Morris. He will serve as a witness. We understand you have something important to tell us, so please begin…."

"Thank you, Captain. My name is Viktor A. Kovalenko, colonel in the Russian Army. I thank you for your hospitality, gentlemen. Now, I must talk to you without further delay. I have reason to believe that my fate has already been determined, so I shall do what I firmly believe I must do while I am still able. I am… *was* the commanding officer of the Russian military installation in Chelyabinsk, from which an unregistered portable nuclear device was mysteriously removed. I had been aware from my own inspection that a discrepancy existed between my personal count of the weapons stored at this facility, and the written official accounting I received when I arrived to take command on Tuesday, July 14 of this year–less than one month ago. My personal count was 91. The official inventory I was given stated 90. When I informed my superior officers, they were not interested in my contention that this discrepancy existed and told me that I had the 'authority' and the 'responsibility' to resolve the 'alleged' discrepancy. Shortly thereafter, it occurred to me that I had failed a critical 'test' of my loyalty by insisting that I was correct. Because of this apparent lack of interest in my discovery of the discrepancy, I became suspicious of those in command above me, and did not know whom to trust. I began to suspect that it would not be long before I was made to 'disappear,' with the assistance of the old-line KGB, or maybe the Russian mafia–or perhaps someone else completely unknown to me. Time was of the essence from that point forward. Since I did not know who was trustworthy in the chain of command above me, I confided in a Ukrainian priest, who oddly enough, directed me to a certain person in the United States embassy in Moscow. Admittedly, I took a chance by going to the priest, but doing so appeared to present the least possible negative consequences for me and the least possible damage from unknown or unintended exposure of my information within the military system. Gentlemen, I have some reason to suspect, although I am not entirely sure, that an independent international arms dealer has acquired this device. I suspect that in turn means that the location or ultimate destination and possible use of this device is unknown to current responsible world leaders. I am leaving Russia because I believe the nature of my knowledge and the degree of awareness of my most recent activities by the various powers above me in my country suggest that I am a target of either military intelligence, or the former KGB, or both. That is a situation from which few are likely to escape in a healthy manner. And more importantly, I was the responsible officer in charge of the Chelyabinsk installation and was therefore the primary target of those in power above me who would eventually want either answers or blood… or both. Obviously, you can expect my government to deny that one of our nuclear devices is lost, or worse, has been stolen from Russia, even if it is only because that 'official' written inventory now *accurately* represents the actual number of such devices stored at that location. Furthermore, that fact now conveniently stands as evidence to those above me that my prior contention was incorrect and therefore severely injures my reputation, credibility, and usefulness. Regardless, I am morally responsible for following my conscience, beliefs, and intuition by informing those who I have reason to believe are in a credible position to determine whether I am in fact telling the truth, and who could therefore act upon my information to help avert a potential disaster."

Their guest appeared to have finished his story, then took a deep breath, and exhaled as inconspicuously as possible. Captain Kilroy and Commander Morris glanced briefly at each other with similar subtle elevations of respiration and heart rate as they briefly tapped their pens upon their identical pale yellow legal pads in front of them on the table. Then they both wrote some notes.

Within about 15 seconds while Commander Morris was still writing, Captain Kilroy took advantage of his guest's apparent pause, looked across the table at Colonel Kovalenko with just enough doubt to invite the beginnings of unaccustomed fear and asked, "What is the name of the priest you spoke to?"

"I know him only as Father Pavel Dryzhensky."

Still fighting a flicker of fear, Captain Kilroy continued, "Where is he located?"

"In Krasnodon, Ukraine."

"How did you get into Ukraine?"

"I am an intelligence officer, gentlemen. I have been trained to accomplish certain tasks without notice. I used effective false identification, makeup, and drove a leased automobile."

"What is the name of the church you visited?"

"I'm not sure…, but it was a Roman Catholic Church. Not very many of those exist in the former Soviet Union."

"What is the name of the person in our embassy he told you to contact?"

"Andrea Sokolov."

With sincere doubt Captain Kilroy asked, "How would a *Ukrainian priest* know the *name* of *anyone* in the United States Embassy in *Moscow*…, Colonel?"

"I do not know, but I believed him. I already indicated to you that I could not trust anyone with Russian military or civilian governmental authority. He spoke with deliberate and unusually convincing persuasiveness, and satisfied my immediate intuition that he was sincere, and could not be a member of any state authority. I did not see any other realistic alternatives. I firmly believed I had no other choice but to follow his instructions precisely. What else *could* I have done after revealing that kind of information to him?"

Ignoring that question, Captain Kilroy continued, "Describe this woman, Andrea Sokolov, you said you spoke with at the embassy."

"She was between 30 and 36 years of age, I would guess. She was between about 170 and 180 centimeters tall, attractive, and about 62 to 68 kilograms in weight. She had a light complexion, medium length wavy red hair, some facial freckles, wore black rimmed designer glasses–never removed them–wore a nice light-gray business-like suit. She projected a confident and professional attitude and appearance…, as if she knew certain things–*secret* things, and how to get things done. She was quite self-assured… never smiled."

Captain Kilroy continued to study his guest, looking into his eyes for several seconds, studying them with a blank facial expression before continuing.

Rather precise memory!

"Exactly *what* did you tell her?"

Colonel Kovalenko's demeanor remained solid and patient as he immediately answered, "I told her essentially what I just told you, and that I was requesting asylum in United States of America."

Kilroy jotted down a few notes and responded immediately, "Why do you expect asylum?"

"I have a beautiful 24-year-old daughter. Her name is Karina, and she is a ballet dancer. She is already in the United States, and I wish to reunite with her. My wife died unexpectedly from cancer several years ago. Karina is all I have now. Of more importance to you, however, is the fact that I have a good friend highly placed in the GRU, as well as knowledge of certain people I have good reason to suspect are involved in the disappearance of this nuclear device. I should expect to be of invaluable assistance in efforts to find certain people involved in, if not actually responsible for this theft. Furthermore, I can help to avert potentially disastrous consequences from this device getting into the wrong hands without wasting valuable time unnecessarily. I fear that certain people in Russia, or maybe somewhere else, perhaps connected with those who desire to have this device and use it, may resort to action against my daughter in retribution for my presumed official behavior, or my secretly leaving Russia, and possibly telling others what I know."

"Why didn't you tell your 'very good friend' in the GRU your story?"

"I *did* tell him! As if reading my mind, he indicated to me that it would be extremely difficult for him to ask 'certain questions.' His friendship would have limited his level and depth of inquiry without prompting unwanted curiosity from higher authority. I already told you my superiors did not believe me, so it did not surprise me that he was apparently in a position similar to mine. Not everyone in Russia is of questionable integrity or loyalty to humanity, gentlemen!"

After another brief period of quiet assessment and reflection, while still focusing upon his guest's eyes, Captain Kilroy asked, "Exactly *why* should I believe you, Colonel?"

With deliberate firmness in his voice, Colonel Kovalenko responded confidently, "Primarily because what I have just told you is the *truth*, Captain! I have already taken significant risk and gone to great personal trouble and in-convenience–*with the assistance of your government*, I might add–to arrive at this table. Surely someone above your rank with influence and authority decided to task you with picking me up. I cannot believe such a person was either a fool or completely ignorant! More importantly, I have left my home country, professional livelihood, and career, certainly at considerable risk of my life, and maybe my daughter's welfare. Do you not know what it means to *leave* your country of birth under duress..., *permanently*, gentlemen? Can you understand the kind of motivation that forced me to jeopardize the life or welfare of my only daughter–*my own flesh and blood?* I have also left behind many meaningful personal friendships and acquaintances and have sacrificed much of my own personal comfort and peace of mind.... I have cast my life and future into uncertainty! Do you have any idea how *frightening* that is for someone of my age? No man would willingly do such a thing unless he were absolutely *compelled* by beliefs of extraordinary strength and significance! No one without principles well beyond the value of his own life would act this way! No sane person could ignore such truth! Furthermore, I strongly suspect that someone unknown to me was killed in the process of getting me out of Russia. I *owe* that man my continued best honest efforts going forward!"

After a thoughtful pause, Captain Kilroy continued evenly, "That is an interesting story, Colonel..., but some very talented, dedicated, and crafty Russian agents with questionable or obscure motivations could say the very same things."

With further steady confidence, Colonel Kovalenko responded, "*Perhaps* that is true, Captain. But *they* are *not* at *this* table! *I am!* Believe it or not, I have a conscience–much like I imagine and sincerely hope yours to be. But I am the *only* one who can eventually and credibly prove what I say, and you, sir, would be in a *very uncomfortable* position indeed, as would your superiors, if what I say is true, and you do not believe me! Time is *not* our ally in this matter, Captain! That nuclear device is no doubt moving even as we speak. Whom would you rather have me tell what I morally cannot keep within me? The Greeks? The Chinese? The British? The French? The Australians? The Iranians? Like it or not, gentlemen, you serve a country representing 'the last best hope for mankind.' And yes, I *am* educated! I am aware of the history of the world! More directly, gentlemen, can you afford to have vast and devastating destruction of innocent human lives and property on your consciences because of your doubts? Will you be able to live with yourselves after eventually learning the undeniably horrific consequences of what I have just told you–*perhaps even in your own country?* Shortly after dissolution of the Soviet Union in 1992, your CIA agents in Riga, Latvia did not believe Vasily Mitrokhin, when he walked into your embassy and said he had complete copies of archives of KGB's First Chief Directorate, including historical details of KGB's systematic repression of the Soviet people during the prior six decades. Your CIA agents thought the documents he had were fake, and simply dismissed him. So, he took them to the British, and a young MI-6 agent wisely accepted his story. The British came away with a historically significant intelligence treasure, and it appears that your agents had, as you say, egg on their faces! Can you afford to make a much more serious… and more *dangerous* mistake…, Captain?"

Captain James Kilroy suddenly imagined himself as the lone white king at the side column of the chessboard in the immediately adjacent unobstructed attack paths of two black rooks. *Inevitable, certain checkmate!*

**** ISTANBUL, TURKEY ****

Boris left Ataturk International Airport at 4:35 P.M. on UTAir Aviation Flight 4415 operated by Turkish Airlines, and arrived at Vnukovo International Airport in Moscow at 8:25 P.M. After a three-and-a-half-hour layover filled with careful thought and planning, he boarded UTAir Aviation Flight 555 at 11:55 P.M. to continue his journey to Chelyabinsk.

CHAPTER 45
Tuesday, August 11, 2015

**** *CHELYABINSK, RUSSIA* ****

Boris arrived at Chelyabinsk Airport at 4:15 A.M. under partly cloudy skies without anything more to eat than a single sticky and almost stale cherry breakfast pastry. By 4:40 A.M., he went out into the cool air to find only one taxi available just outside the main terminal building. Within 30 seconds, he awakened the driver from a sound sleep by forcefully slapping his hand upon the roof. Then he opened the rear passenger door and entered the car.

"Take me to the military base," he ordered in a firm but polite manner.

Within seconds, the cabbie worked himself into a completely alert posture and mental state. He glanced at his passenger in the rear-view mirror and started his car. By 5:20 A.M., Boris was at the main vehicle entrance to the base. His taxi stopped at the main gate and a sentry approached the taxi while another armed guard stepped closer to the passenger side of the car. Boris rolled down the window as the first sentry approached the driver's side.

The second sentry directed his focus upon Boris as he spoke, "State your business here, sir."

Boris immediately showed him his official GRU identification and a letter from Colonel Koshelev designed to deflect any further questions during occasions like this.

Boris asked with an official tone, "Who is in charge here?"

"Colonel Alexander Grushanin, sir."

"Then I must see Colonel Alexander Grushanin immediately."

"Very well, Major. This way."

Boris exited the cab, paid the driver less than the full fare, and told him to wait until he returned. Then he followed the sentry to the drab gray building housing the administration offices. The sentry led Boris through the front door and down the cream-colored hall to the commander's office. The door was open, and Boris invited himself in, holding out the letter from Colonel Koshelev.

"I am Major Boris Zhukov, on special assignment representing Colonel Vasily Koshelev, GRU, Moscow, sir."

The balding Colonel Grushanin nodded in his direction, picked up his glasses from his desk, put them on, and read the letter.

After a minute of thoughtful silence, he responded, "Very well, Major. You may verify the weapons count. Come with me."

After the two men entered the vault and each counted the weapons stored inside and agreed upon the final tally of 90 weapons, they returned to Colonel Grushanin's office, where he signed the letter, indicating that he had read and complied with the written instructions. Major Zhukov counter-signed, and then left the building with the letter. He entered the waiting cab and again awakened the driver.

Colonel Grushanin was satisfied that this little wrinkle in his day had passed smoothly without further consequences. Although both officers had agreed that 90 devices were stored in the vault, Major Zhukov was not satisfied. He returned to the Chelyabinsk airport and boarded his return flight to Moscow. He took another cab directly to GRU headquarters and hand-delivered the signed letter to Colonel Koshelev.

**** LANGLEY, VIRGINIA ****

CIA Director Miles had assigned to Reya Robinson the task of identifying the Mercedes automobile license registration 7786AB01 through both the internet and the CIA's own computer resources and relevant field offices. She eventually came up with the name Askhat A. Karimov, which turned out to be an alias of the owner of one of the mansions along the Varzob River in Tajikistan near Dushanbe. That person could not be located.

**** DEARBORN, MICHIGAN ****

Shamir rented a white 2015 CTS Cadillac from Hertz at the Detroit Metropolitan Wayne County Airport and then drove to the heart of an Islamic community within the city of Dearborn, Michigan. He registered for a room at the Hilton Doubletree just west of Southfield Road and north of Ford Road for $120 per night. At least 23 Islamic buildings, centers, or institutions of Islamic worship or learning are within a 50 square mile area including Dearborn.

He drove from one location to another where he expected to find sympathetic jihadist youth. When he found a group of young Islamic men, he asked well-crafted and innocent questions, subtly searching for anyone who might know of potential soldiers–two young men willing to join his ultimate plan to reduce the United States to a second or third-rate country. However, he never explained anything about his plan beyond the specific task he required of committed jihadists. He ended his search on the first day without success and retired to his room for the night. However, he had accomplished at least a part of what he had intended. The local Islamic rumor mills started to buzz with enough credible sources to establish the 'fact' that an important foreign visitor was in town looking for two special soldiers for jihad. The subject matter was sufficient to ensure that the message traveled only through the darkest and most secure communication paths to those whose job was to protect the Islamic community. This was not a typical open 'want ad' in the local newspaper. It was an insidiously implied underground request for at least one willing suicide bomber, preferably two, but not more than three.

The next morning, he left his room and went to his car in the parking lot. Two unfamiliar men were leaning against the trunk, obviously waiting for him. Both were dressed in casual clothing–denim blue jeans, Nike sneakers, light blue open-collared shirts. They looked strong, suspicious, and quite serious.

He approached them with his natural self-confidence and social charm, and calmly asked, "May I help you, gentlemen?"

The older man responded, "Is this your car?"

"It is a rental, and yes, it is mine. What can I do for you, gentlemen?" *They obviously followed me here.*

The two men glanced at each other as they simultaneously stood away from the car one step toward Shamir, and the older one continued, "We know people who say you have been asking certain… *questions*. Is it true that you have been asking… certain *questions?*"

He had no assurance that these men were sympathetic to his plan, although he had already concluded that they were Islamic. He wondered how dedicated they were to his version of Islamic principles.

Shamir responded cautiously with a brief mild smile, while trying to maintain credible innocence, "I have made some… discreet inquiries. Yes. Surely that cannot be a problem, can it?"

The older one ignored his question and continued evenly, "Where did you come from?"

"I am from Pakistan…. Why do you ask?"

They could easily overpower me if they wanted to, and have yet to do so or threaten to, so they are not yet sure about me, one way or another.

The other two men did not answer, but they did look around the parking lot, and the older one put his hands in his jeans pockets. Shamir glanced at him.

That had to be a signal. Others like him must be watching nearby. They must be very careful out of habit.

Shamir continued with a disarming smile, "Gentlemen, perhaps we should continue our conversation somewhere else–a more comfortable place, perhaps?"

The older man said firmly, "Get in your car. I will tell you where to go."

The younger man opened the back driver's side door and entered the Cadillac. The other man waited for Shamir to get behind the wheel, and then opened the front passenger door, got in, and closed the door. He rested the Glock model 26 9-mm pistol he had been hiding during the last several minutes on his lap. At his direction, Shamir drove about six blocks west on Kirkwood Avenue toward The Islamic Center of America, on the north side of the street, opposite the Center. About a block east of the Islamic Center was Saint Sarkis Armenian Apostolic Church. About one block west was the Warrendale Community Church, and one block west of that was The Detroit Catholic Renewal Center.

The older man said, "Park here. This is where we will continue our conversation."

After Shamir stopped the car and both men got out, the younger man got out of the Cadillac and joined the other two as the older man indicated that

Shamir should enter the building across from the Islamic Center. It looked like someone's home, furnished simply for reasonable comfort, but currently not occupied.

"This way!" the older man commanded.

The three men continued through the front living room, past the staircase to the second floor on their right, through the next room, which was obviously a dining area, and then into the rear of the first floor, which was a kitchen. They sat around a simple small wooden table finished with a light stain, using three of the four chairs available. They were not visible from the outside there as they could have been in the front living room through the picture window facing the street. The older man kept a grip on his pistol but held it on his lap out of sight. He had made his point in the car–he was armed and quite willing to use his weapon.

Shamir took the implied initiative, "Well, gentlemen, what would you like to talk about?"

The older man responded, "Why are you here... asking these questions?"

Shamir waited several seconds before answering, as he made a quick reassessment of the two men, and said, "I am looking for two brave young men who will fight the infidels."

The younger man finally spoke up, "Fight how?"

Shamir weighed his progress so far, concluding that these two were not a threat to him, and sought him out because of the seeds of speculation and rumor that he had planted around the local Islamic community yesterday.

The older one is obviously the decision-maker, and the younger one is probably the potential soldier.

Shamir interpreted their appearance at his car within 24 hours of his arrival as evidence of their curiosity and apparent eagerness to learn more, if not make a commitment.

Shamir said confidently, "I have a plan for jihad, including a significant attack upon this country, and I have need of at least two strong, competent men–who can drive an automobile as well as operate a small speedboat, and give up their lives in this world in service to Allah. I know many young men in this country are willing to be martyrs, but I need two very *special* men. That is why I came here–to look for those two special young men *myself*."

The older man moved in his seat, obviously putting the gun in his pants pocket.

After a moment of hesitation, he said, "What is the plan?"

"I must hear you swear before Allah your devotion to His will before I tell you. Otherwise, I will leave, and continue my search. My time schedule is already under way. I cannot waste my time with indecisive people."

"How do we know that you are who you say you are?"

"I cannot prove who I am. I can only act in accordance with what I say with Allah as my witness, Peace be upon Him."

Shamir's intuition told him that he had found at least one of the two that he wanted, and to elicit a commitment, he reached with his right hand into his pocket and slowly brought it back to the surface of the table as a clenched fist. Shamir studied each man's interested gaze upon his fist, waiting for that final sign from Allah that he had indeed found the ones he was looking for. Then they both looked him in the eye expectantly. He took that as the expected sign of divine confirmation. Then he slowly opened his right fist and dropped a 3.57-karat, perfect clear round cut diamond onto the tabletop–the equivalent of over a quarter of a million dollars in United States currency. Their eyes widened despite their recent doubt as they gazed at the gem.

"That gemstone is how you know that I am who I say I am. I have sworn before Allah to give one of these to each of the parents or the proper nearest kin of the chosen ones. I will reveal the plan only to the chosen ones. If you take it, then Allah will know that you are committed. If you do not take it, then I will keep it and continue my search."

The older man reached for the stone and picked it up, fascinated by its clarity and brilliance, even without direct sunlight, just as countless men from all cultures had reacted to diamonds throughout human history. He was not immune to the implications of its imagined value. Nevertheless, he sat in silent mild impatience, finally looking away from it without visual focus into the future, weighing his decision.

Within the next minute, he said, "This is my nephew Navid (meaning 'glad tidings,' or 'good news') Khadem. He has not been here in this country for very long. He will be one of your soldiers. I am Anwar Khadem, his father's brother. Both his parents were killed by United States bombs in Syria. His brother is one year younger, but he is strong and loyal. He will be your other soldier."

After studying Shamir's face for another few seconds, he yelled, "Khuram! Come down here!"

In less than 15 seconds, footsteps of another young man coming down the stairs announced the arrival of Navid's brother.

Khuram (meaning 'tiger') stood wide-eyed in the entryway to the room, and asked firmly, "What do you want?"

"Your time has arrived. You and your brother will avenge your parents' deaths and punish the infidels at the same time!"

Navid was only 22 years old, and Khuram was 21. Neither of the brothers had ever fired a lethal weapon. They did not even speak English beyond several dozen memorized phrases but understood much more than one might assume at first glance. Neither had ever operated a speedboat, but how difficult could that be for two brave and strong young soldiers–those who needed to step forward and prove their self-worth, who could finally call themselves *men*, or even *martyrs*? Navid was convinced that he had finally found his purpose in life–to punish the United States because Anwar had always told him that the United States had interfered in the Middle East by putting Israel in the middle of rightfully Arab lands. That, Anwar maintained, had increased disruption in Islamic life in the Middle East after the First World War, and eventually caused unending grief and strife. Khuram got the same message just by living in the same household. Anwar had implied that a time would come when he could punish those responsible, and that time had just arrived. He never mentioned, however, that the historical bickering between Sunni and Shia Muslims had also contributed to civil unrest throughout that region and had absolutely nothing to do with the United States, since their 'misunderstanding' developed its historical roots centuries before the United States even came into existence.

Shamir quietly studied the two young men for several moments and convinced himself that they were indeed there because of fate–part of Allah's plan that he needed to execute. He stared intently into their eyes searching for some small sign of hesitation or doubt and found none.

Then he spoke quietly, "You must remember the code words, 'Akbar Vegas' to accomplish your mission–when you pick up your cargo. Do you understand?"

The young men looked at each other briefly, and then turned back to Shamir and nodded in affirmation. Shamir pulled a folded piece of paper from his pocket on which Arabic script detailed what the brothers were expected to do, step by step, and handed it to Khadem.

"These are your instructions. Follow them exactly, and you will find paradise! Never let this out of your sight, until you have memorized every detail, and do not show it to anyone else! After you have memorized your instructions, you will destroy this paper! Do you understand completely everything I have told you?"

The two looked at their uncle briefly, and then back to Shamir, and said with newfound confidence and purpose, "Yes! Praise Allah!"

CHAPTER 46
Wednesday, August 12, 2015

**** *CAMBRIDGE, MASSACHUSETTS* ****

Among the more than 35,500 people who work for the Federal Bureau of Investigation are 21,726 professional staff members and more than 13,600 special agents. Two of those agents, Jason Carlisle, and Anthony Stokowsky, left their office in Suite 600 at One Center Plaza in Boston, Massachusetts, rode the elevator to the first floor, strode across the spacious lobby, and walked out through the front entrance into the sunny warmth. They entered the waiting 2014 black Chevrolet Tahoe. The driver immediately pulled away from the curb and drove past the nearby Irish Pub and the FedEx office toward Cambridge Avenue, which from his approach was one way opposite to the direction he needed to go. After finding a place to make a U-turn, he headed back down Cambridge Avenue. For the next 26 minutes, he threaded his way through the paved, but convoluted 'colonial cow paths' of Boston into Cambridge to his destination at 39 Essex Street. By 4:23 P.M., Carlisle and Stokowsky left their vehicle on a 'fishing expedition' and entered the building to find Rahim Nazari's apartment on the fifth floor. Their driver began a slow 'parking violation avoidance' maneuver by driving endlessly around the area until he found a legal empty parking space. After the two ascended the stairs to the fifth floor, Stokowsky knocked on the apartment door four times while trying to control his more rapid breathing–evidence of exertion and his physical condition, not fear. The two men looked at each other as they listened carefully for any evidence of people beyond the other side of the door. After another five seconds, he knocked again. The sound of something hard dropping on the floor betrayed someone's presence in the apartment. The door opened. A tall, thin, barefoot young woman with long disheveled natural red hair, and sleepy, but startling emerald-green eyes stood before them, leaning her head against the door. She was wearing tight white denim shorts with no belt zippered up the front of her flat stomach, and an oversized, faded red and white Boston Red Sox T-shirt that did not obscure her obviously erect nipples. Carlisle involuntarily registered due internal appreciation of her small twin peaks, recovered quickly, and cleared his throat.

"Is this the residence of Rahim Nazari?"

She responded lazily, "Yup."

The two men held out their FBI credentials and badges so she could see them as Carlisle announced in a subdued, but professional tone, "Is he here, Miss…?"

She said softly, and almost seductively, "Name's Fantasia."

"Fantasia…?"

"Witherspoon."

Stokowsky asked with faint trepidation in official FBI tone, "Is your father a federal judge… Judge Clarence T. Witherspoon?"

She smiled broadly and cocked her head slightly to the left as she murmured coquettishly, "Yup!"

Carlisle continued in habitual official tone, "Well, Fantasia…, is Rahim here now?"

"Yup…. Sleeping."

Stokowsky continued the halting labored alternating conversation, "May we come in?"

"Yup."

She lazily pushed herself away from the door with delicate, artistic hands and opened it more for the two agents to enter the small apartment. After mentally choking upon the sight of too many things in abundant disorder and inadequate space, the two men carefully stepped farther into the room. Carlisle looked across the room at the still form of a person curled up under the sheets of the bed by the outside wall, and then glanced over at Fantasia with a suggestive nod, raised eyebrows, and a facial expression clearly implying that he wanted her to awaken him. He then cocked his head with moderate emphasis in the direction of the bed.

Fantasia understood that they would certainly wake him up carelessly if she did not awaken him gently, so she slowly sauntered over to the bed, leaned over him and stroked his hair as she said softly next to his ear, "Rahim, you have two visitors from the FBI…. Wake up, sweetie…. Rahim? Rahim…, you have some visitors, sweetie…."

He finally responded as if struggling to overcome a deep REM sleep, and turned his head toward the wall, recognized his misdirection, and then turned toward the middle of the room, squinting at the three fuzzy forms in his dimly lit apartment. Then, as if poked with a cattle-prod, he immediately almost levitated into a sitting position with his hands instinctively clasped together over his crotch. He was wearing only light gray boxers.

He leveled a suddenly alert alternating stare at the two men and said in an elevated voice as quickly as he could, "Who are you and what are you doing here?"

As they both flashed their credentials in front of him Carlisle said, "We are from the Federal Bureau of Investigation, Rahim. We need to ask you some very important questions."

Fantasia quietly disappeared into the bathroom and silently closed the door behind her as the two FBI agents stood awkwardly in the dissipating residual privacy of apparently very recent intimacy.

Rahim asked in cautious resentment, "Do you *mind* if I get dressed, first?"

Despite his 'all-business' attitude, Stokowsky said as politely as he could, "No, not at all. We'll wait."

Carlisle was already at the window, pulling the shade up so he could see better in the apartment and to accelerate Rahim's return to reality with some direct sunlight. The two agents remained standing because typically common seating arrangements in the room were not obvious. The only cushioned chair in the room was piled high with books, papers, and clothing. Rahim stood as the two agents conveniently turned away from him and looked out the window, giving him time to get to the bathroom without any further undue embarrassment. He hurried by them, grasping a rumpled pair of trousers and a similarly wrinkled casual light blue shirt from a table as he approached the bathroom. As soon as he closed the bathroom door behind him, Fantasia pressed herself against him and planted her long tongue deep into his mouth, while grinding her pubic bone against his now resurging erection.

He reluctantly disengaged from her and whispered desperately, "What are you *doing?*"

She whispered back, "I'm giving you energy to confront the dragons out there, tiger!"

He scowled at her and urgently whispered again, "That's *not* funny!"

She smiled mischievously, giggled innocently, helped him dress and then buttoned his shirt with a smile of admiration. Then she stepped around him and opened the bathroom door. They both went back out into the main room– she with more confidence than he.

She turned deliberately toward the two agents and subtly pulled her shoulders back as she said softly with a subtle suggestive smile, "I'll leave you men to your worldly inquisition.... *Ta-ta!*"

She walked to the apartment door, opened it, and then turned back to blow a kiss to Rahim before she smiled, turned again, walked out, and closed the door behind her. The men could hear the diminishing clatter of her clogs banging on the bare old hardwood stairs as she descended the five floors to the street level.

Carlisle said, "Do you mind if we find a place to sit down?"

Rahim quickly went to the bed and straightened out the rumpled blanket at the foot of the bed, spread it haphazardly across the mattress and sheets, and motioned the two agents to sit on the bed. They looked briefly at each other with raised eyebrows and complied without further reaction. Rahim brought a weak wooden chair from the all-purpose desk/dining table and placed it in the middle of the room opposite the two agents and sat down carefully upon it as it registered a clear squeak in response to his average weight.

He said meekly, "I would have offered you the chair, but it is old and unreliable. Now, what is your visit here all about?"

Carlisle started with, "What are you studying, Rahim?"

After a few seconds of deciding to cooperate, he said cautiously, "I am finishing my graduate work in geophysics. Why do you ask?"

Stokowsky ignored the question and continued, "The tuition here is over $40,000 per year, and the expenses of living in Cambridge are a bit on the high side. How do you manage to pay your bills here, Rahim?"

Still with cautious cooperation, he responded, "I have a scholarship from Iran, my home country."

Carlisle continued, "What, exactly, is the source of your scholarship?"

"I do not know the original source. All I know is money from the Ministry of Education comes into my account here on time every year, and I get deposits in my bank account for living expenses. I also work in the library. As you can see, they are not large amounts of money, but I can get along happily enough."

I already got that impression.

Then Stokowsky asked, "What are your career plans, Rahim? I find it hard to believe that you have a scholarship to study at a very prestigious university in a foreign country without any life goals."

Rahim responded genuinely, "I am trying to prepare myself for a career in the energy production industry in my country. That is why I am here to study. My country will benefit from my knowledge, expertise, and abilities when I return to Iran, or wherever my employment opportunities take me. I may even be able to work here, in the United States!"

Carlisle continued, "What about your family, Rahim? Where are they?"

Rahim hesitated, and Stokowsky read some subtle signs of anxiety in Rahim's face as he slowly appeared to prepare to answer, "My parents live in Iran. They are good and decent people. They taught me the difference between right and wrong and how to live a good and respectable life. They work hard to earn a living but could not afford to send me to the United States to study here at MIT. I was quite lucky to receive my scholarship. Otherwise, I would never be here."

Stokowsky continued with calculated gentle curiosity, "Where do your parents live in Iran?"

Again, Stokowsky detected some subtle indications of anxiety as Rahim responded only briefly, "They live in the city of Shiraz."

Carlisle continued, "Any brothers or sisters, Rahim?"

"No."

Stokowsky stepped in, emanating genuine curiosity, "What about Fantasia… who is she?"

"What's to tell? She is a woman, and I am a man. We love each other."

Carlisle followed up, "You are Muslin, are you not, Rahim? And I would guess that she is not. Correct?"

With mild beginnings of defiance, he retorted, "What difference does that make either way? No, she is not Muslim, and yes, I am Muslim. *So what?*"

Stokowsky cracked a few knuckles as if by habit, but it was a signal to change the subject to maintain cooperation, so Carlisle followed up with a tangential question, "Is she a student at MIT also?"

"Yes. She is younger than I am. She is an undergraduate senior, studying electrical engineering and mathematics."

Carlisle continued, "Sounds like a challenging course of study!"

With only a slight smile, he responded, "Yes, it is…. She is *very* intelligent–probably *much* smarter than I am!"

Then in a deliberately abrupt change of subject, Stokowsky asked sharply, "Exactly *what* is your graduate thesis about, Rahim?"

He responded genuinely, "I am studying the effects of earthquakes and other forms of shock disturbance upon various geological formations in and around drilling sites. I do computer simulations to calculate the degree of force that drilling operations can withstand near different kinds of geological formations and at various depths of a drilling site and then try to assess the production value and damage implications and repair costs under adverse conditions. I expect to use this knowledge to assist energy companies in determining new drilling techniques, and where and how they can safely and cost-effectively drill, and where they should not drill."

Carlisle and Stokowsky looked subtly at each other with brief visual messages of agreement that they should terminate the interview, reassess, and then think about where they should go next, either physically or figuratively.

Carlisle said, "Thank you for answering our questions, Rahim. We have nothing further at this time. However, we may need to speak with you again, so please do not leave the country without notifying us. Here is my card, including my phone number on the back."

Rahim sustained a momentary anxiety response, but had nothing further to say either, so he simply watched the other two men leave his small apartment and close the door behind them. He sat quietly thinking, as their footfalls on the wooden staircase steadily faded into distant silence. For a few moments, all he was aware of was his heavy heartbeat. The stairwell was quiet again. They had left the building. He was sure he had not revealed anything. He wanted Fantasia again. He needed her non-judgmental, gentle, soothing warmth and softness.

Their driver had just circled by the apartment building for the eighteenth time as the two agents came out through the front door. The driver stopped just as they quickly entered the black late model Chevrolet Tahoe. Stokowsky got in the back seat, and Carlisle got in the front passenger seat.

Carlisle spoke first as the driver pulled out into the street, "That guy is as innocent as a fawn in a sunny green grassy field with bright yellow daffodils! He's also not a really serious Muslim. Doesn't exactly fit the profile of a terrorist, either."

Stokowsky replied, "That may be, but I have a persistent suspicion that he is hiding something. What do you think about the girl?"

Carlisle responded, "Outer space! Gut says she's got nothing to do with whatever he's into."

Stokowsky said, "Yeah, that's what I think also…. Helluva tease, though!"

Carlisle mumbled philosophically, "Yeah… refreshes the soul somewhat," and then chuckled.

CHAPTER 47
Thursday, August 13, 2015

**** *CAMBRIDGE, MASSACHUSETTS* ****

Rahim Nazari was alone in his apartment, sitting in his ratty cushioned chair constantly recycling his fears from the FBI warning not to leave the country, when he finally called Shamir's special cellphone number–963-42-128-3577. Shamir answered after an unusually lengthy nine rings.

"Hello, Rahim! How are you?"

"Two FBI agents were here in my apartment yesterday asking me where my tuition payments are coming from. I told them I have a scholarship. I suspect they do not believe me, and I am getting scared. They told me not to leave the country without telling them. Why is the FBI asking me questions? What am I supposed to do?"

"Just relax, Rahim. They cannot do anything bad to you. You are in the United States of America! You have rights that cannot be violated! Just tell them the truth about whatever they ask. Nothing you can tell them truthfully will get you into trouble. This is not Iran! I would never, never, ever put you in a position of danger or harm! Your father would hate me forever if I did that! This is your opportunity to get the education and the degree that you have always wanted, so do not worry about the FBI getting in the way. Believe me, absolutely nothing you can tell them will get you into trouble–ever! You have never done anything wrong in your entire life!"

Shamir had deliberately anticipated situations just like this. His meticulous planning kept Rahim ignorant of certain facts and implications that would arouse suspicions about his mission. Rahim could not reveal anything at all, simply because he was deliberately kept ignorant of his unwitting part in the master plan. Shamir correctly reasoned that the most honest and conscientious person in the world cannot either deliberately or even accidentally reveal in a credible manner what he never knew in the first place. Even threats or torture could not elicit information that was never there. Only the most profound or impossible fateful coincidence could betray him.

"But I am afraid!"

Shamir responded smoothly with another fabrication, *"All right, Rahim. Would you feel better if I hired a lawyer for you? I could have a lawyer sue the FBI for harassing you. He could force the FBI to stay away from you so you can complete your project with peace of mind. I will find a lawyer for you today. Do not worry! Everything will turn out according to Allah's will!"*

Rahim responded cautiously, "Are you sure about that?"

"Rahim… You are a student! You are not a criminal! They cannot harm you! After you complete your studies, then you can go home, and they will never bother you again! I promise! When will you finish?"

"I am almost finished. If I get enough computer time, I can run the remaining computer simulations and finish up in about a week or two if I do nothing else."

"That's wonderful, Rahim! Then you can receive your degree shortly thereafter and go home… and the FBI will never visit you again!"

After sensing that Rahim had apparently relaxed with that assurance, Shamir terminated the phone connection simply, *"Goodbye, Rahim. You will be just fine! I promise!"*

Unknown to either of these two men or the FBI, the Bishop was visiting the MIT Computer Science and Artificial Intelligence Laboratory at the achitecturally unique Stata Center, building number 32 on Vassar Street in Cambridge. He had a court order signed by Judge Clarence T. Witherspoon at the John Joseph Moakley United States Courthouse in Boston, requesting records of all MIT graduate student campus computer usage for the last calendar year. He walked up to the clerk at the reception desk and announced his name.

"My name is Lou Bischov. I work for the Central Intelligence Agency, and I have a court order requesting all the MIT graduate student computer usage records for the current calendar year."

He placed the court order on the counter before him so the young shapely woman behind the counter could read the front page, and then presented his CIA credentials. She was wearing designer blue jeans with a white short-sleeved shirt with five white buttons down the front, the top three of which were straining to withhold the pressure from within.

She looked up at the Bishop with a naïve questioning expression and said, "Will you please wait for just a moment while I get my supervisor?"

He appeared not to reveal any appreciation of her figure as most men did, and stated flatly, "No problem, Miss...?"

"My name is Carla."

Within a minute, she returned behind a 30-something confident-looking geek with unruly brown hair, but without the geeky glasses. The medium-built young man wearing a dark blue sport shirt and neatly pressed tan slacks smiled at the Bishop as he approached the counter briskly, stepped between Carla and the counter, and then spread his arms out with his hands flat on the counter, as if protecting her.

"I'm John Seward, Computer Facilities Supervisor. What can I do for you, Mr. Bischov?"

The Bishop scrutinized the young man with significant natural cynicism, but continued smoothly, "Mr. Seward, I need to have all the graduate student computer usage records for the current calendar year, please. This is a court order authorizing me to have those records."

He held up the court order so the other man could see the official title, summary, and the judge's signature on the front page.

"Oh! May I ask why?"

"You may..., but I am not obligated to provide any answers that cannot be found in the court order."

The Bishop did not want to imply any potentially revealing or counter-productive information or needlessly escalate a confrontation by using such phrases as 'national security' or 'privileged information.' His patience was already beginning to dissipate.

"I'm really very sorry, Mr. Bischov. I'm sure you have a job to do, as do I. I am going to have to ask you to wait while I contact the Dean of Graduate Studies about this."

The Bishop leveled his signature icy stare from his occupationally useful dark eyes directly into John's inexperienced academic eyes, and through them as well.

"Listen to me *carefully*, Johnny. This is a court order! Refusal to comply will put you in contempt of court, and subject you to some *very* inconvenient penalties. I sincerely doubt that you or your Dean of Graduate Studies, or *this university* would want to defy a court order!"

John sighed subtly, and then bravely picked up a nearby black phone and dialed the number for the Office of the Dean of Graduate Studies, while the Bishop continued to carve up the other man's retinas with his signature non-verbal communication skills. Carla could not hide her dreamy-eyed admiration of John's standing firm before the intimidating CIA agent. The upper-most fixed button of her shirt suddenly popped through its buttonhole. She blushed slightly, as she buttoned it subtly and quickly without calling any further attention to herself.

"Dean Preston, please…. Yes…."

About a minute of unanswered questions, ignorance of evil, and small random personal thoughts passed before the task at hand resumed for all of them.

"Sir, a CIA agent is standing here in the lobby of the Computer Science and Artificial Intelligence Laboratory with a court order to release to him all graduate student computer usage records for the current calendar year…. Yes…. It sure looks official…. Yes, sir…. 10 minutes? Okay, I'll ask him to wait."

The Bishop said dryly, "Don't bother. I got the picture." *Even the gods of academia have a bureaucracy!*

About 12 minutes later, the Dean of Graduate Studies walked through the front entrance to the computer facility and introduced himself to the only unfamiliar person standing in the lobby.

"I'm Doctor James Preston, Dean of Graduate Studies. What's this court order business all about?"

The Bishop looked up into the other man's eyes and said firmly, "Let's take a walk, Doctor Preston."

The six-foot, four-inch-tall lanky bespectacled former UCLA college basketball star forward ran a hand through his remaining sparse and unruly gray hair and smiled weakly at the younger tough-looking agent with a permanent five-o'clock shadow, and said, "Well…, okay…."

The two men left the building and walked east on Vassar Street toward a large parking lot a little more than a block farther down the street just beyond Amherst Alley. The Bishop walked through the parking lot speaking in a faint voice, so Doctor Preston had to bend down slightly to hear him.

"I'm going to say this just *once*, and you will *never* speak of it to anyone else. If I do not get those records *today*, you and this institution will be in contempt of court. One of your graduate students is receiving significant financial aid from a source that we believe is involved in terrorist activities, and we believe that this student is working on a project that is related to a planned terrorist attack, most likely upon the United States. He may or may not be aware of his participation or the consequences of what he is doing. If this individual is alerted to my request for this information, I am going to hold you *personally* responsible for obstructing a federal investigation, and anything else I can find or invent to express my *sincere* disappointment if you do not cooperate. I am working on a tight time schedule, Doctor. I do not know when this possible attack will occur, so I do not have the luxury of wasting my time or being unnecessarily polite. You do *not* want to be downwind when the shit hits *this* fan! If I am wrong about this possible at-tack, then maybe some feathers get ruffled and some faces turn red, but no one gets hurt. On the other hand…, if I am right, then you and I, and many other people are going to land face-first in some highly toxic and possibly fatal fecal regret. Now…, do I need to *clarify* anything about this request…, Doctor Preston?"

He stopped walking, turned, and looked up at the Dean, and started to carve into the man's retinas with his unique stare. Doctor Preston was still in deep thought as he tried to digest this potentially explosive information. The Bishop waited with infinite patience, still staring at Doctor Preston.

"I'm getting some very bad vibes from you, Doctor Preston! Do *not* put your lawyers between me and my objective! You will be risking un-known consequences that could haunt you for the rest of your academic and earthly lives…, and beyond! Not only that, but you would piss me off *significantly*, and your lawyers will eventually endure *excruciating* profes-sional federal blowback–and believe it or not, I am being politely… *deadly… serious!*"

The dean briefly looked up at the mostly blue sky with a thoughtful squint as if looking for his decision among the few pure white stratocumulus clouds drifting ever so slowly to the east far above them.

After about 12 seconds, he looked back down at the stolid CIA agent and said, "Let's go back to the lab and get your information."

CHAPTER 48
Saturday, August 15, 2015

The message coming in to Duke's computer through System 18 was from San Francisco:

> *'That 011-7-499-884-2339 phone number belongs to an unregistered disposable cellphone within a Moscow, Russia telephone exchange. That's as deep as I could get.' Sammy.*

Duke responded:

> *'Nice job, Sammy. I can work with that. Thank you.'*

He then called General Murray and waited through four rings.
"Hello, Duke..., what's on your mind?"

"Can your people identify the owner of a specific telephone number in Moscow?"

"Well, Duke, since the Snowden affair, we have lost a significant number of our assets and some technical abilities have been degraded somewhat, so I would guess we might possibly have a problem with that at this point, but I'll see what I can do. What's the number?"

"011-7-499-884-2339."

"Got it. What's the background on this?"

"Andrea Sokolov said she got a call from this number. The caller said–and I quote Andrea here– 'I must remain anonymous, but I am highly placed in

GRU. My message is for good reason for all concerned. A Chechnyan Islamic radical murdered your friend in Krasnodon. Make sure your superiors know the Russian government was not involved in any way, politically or militarily, or otherwise. I am obliged not to use official channels.' My guess is that this person had to mention his position to establish immediate credibility, which implies that he apparently did not have much time to make his point and may even have been acting without official higher authorization. What concerns me in addition to that is how he got her number, how he knew about 'her friend,' and obviously what his identity is. Despite all that, I don't believe he was aware of Andrea's place in my organization. It may not have been an official published number, but I find it hard to believe that the Russians are completely ignorant of our embassy personnel communications."

"Oh? Very interesting…! I'll get back to you as soon as I can!"

Duke was unsettled.

Who would kill an elderly priest… and, more importantly, why?

**** PHILIPPINES ****

After 11 days at sea and 2,935 miles from Singapore, Destiny approached the Philippines under overcast skies and sailed into Manila Harbor toward the Philippine Coast Guard Station. The crew topped off her fuel tanks and paid in cash. No one was suspicious, and no one asked any questions. After her fuel intake caps were closed and secured, Destiny's side thrusters pushed her away from the fueling pier for about 15 seconds. Then the thrusters stopped, and the main propellers pushed her forward into a turn taking her out of the harbor. The twin Caterpillar engines roared to full power once again as she set course directly to the east.

**** JFK INTERNATIONAL AIRPORT ****

Delta Airlines Flight 473, a Boeing 777 airplane, was idling on the tarmac in a light rain, about take off at 12:09 P.M. After the 13-hour and 46-minute flight to Tokyo, Umar would arrive at Narita International Airport at 2:55 P.M. local time the next day. When he was not sleeping, he could at least look out the window from seat 4A on the port side of the Business Elite section just forward of the leading edge of the wing. He started to rehearse his plans for the next transaction with yet unknown representatives.

CHAPTER 49
Sunday, August 16, 2015

**** GROTON, CONNECTICUT ****

The Groton naval yard near New London is home port for six Virginia class submarines, including the USS Mississippi. The sub cruised north under overcast skies into the Thames River from Long Island Sound and finally eased alongside a long pier on the east side of the river slightly north of the city of Groton. Sailors in their white dress uniforms lined the deck in a ceremonial show of normal official return to the home port. No public media had indicated that the sub was returning unexpectedly, and no obvious unusual activity was evident throughout the naval base. However, a small contingent of FBI agents had arrived surreptitiously during the preceding week as a precaution and stationed themselves at strategic observation points throughout the greater pier area, disguised as sailors, civilian maintenance people, and typical shipyard workers. Director Kingman did not tell them the whole story but indicated that a special visitor would be arriving on that submarine, and that certain designated agents would secretly escort him to a temporary safe house in Brooklyn, New York as quickly as possible.

Diogenes Kikos, a 32-year-old fifth-generation Greek descendant born and raised in New York City would be responsible for Colonel Kovalenko in the United States. The colonel would not be able to urinate, steal a candy bar, jaywalk, or wink at a pretty young woman without his awareness. He majored in Philosophy and Russian studies at Dartmouth College, where he also played middle linebacker on the football team. He gambled on a chance with the pros after graduation, and the New York Jets finally drafted him with no fanfare from deep in the list of prospects. After two years of only periodic playing time, he decided that professional football was not a viable career for a realistically secure future. His native intelligence, physical presence at six feet, four inches in height, 230 pounds of solid physique, and natural street smarts easily drew the attention of his interviewers after he responded to public FBI employment ads seven years ago. Even though Viktor Kovalenko spoke English quite well, Diogenes could understand Russian, and speak it passably.

Diogenes wore a naval officer's white summer dress uniform as he stood next to a late model black government Chevrolet Tahoe SUV at an inconspicuous, but unobstructed area of a parking lot near the pier. It was ready to make an efficient and rapid exit from the naval base onto public roads, consistent with Director Kingman's instructions to effect a quick covert departure and a secure journey south on I-95, eventually to a temporary safe house in Brooklyn. One of those 'sailors' on the deck of the submarine also in a white uniform was Captain Kilroy. Another 'sailor' was Colonel Kovalenko. They were unnoticeable in the semi-orderly but choreographed uniformed throng of sailors leaving the deck and walking down the gangplank onto the pier. With a contingent of a dozen sailors instructed to 'stay with their captain' until ordered otherwise, the group of men in white uniforms approached the 'naval officer' standing next to the SUV and with contrived activity effectively obscured the identity of the 'sailor' who entered the back of the SUV. After some further fake ceremonial behavior mixed with careful observation, random milling about and saluting, the sailors and their captain dispersed in different directions toward several small groups of waiting civilians, friends, and relatives for an unexpected respite from their tour of duty before again retuning to the sea in three days. Diogenes, Colonel Kovalenko and another agent had already entered the SUV, and the driver immediately drove away from the pier. An unmarked Ford sedan with two FBI agents inside followed the SUV from just outside the entrance to the base. Inside the Tahoe, the 'sailor' removed his uniform, and dressed in his selection of casual jeans and unremarkable shirts from several sets of clothing provided by the FBI. His handler even had a pair of tan casual Nike shoes in his correct shoe size and a pair of dark tan socks to complete the appearance of having no unusual appearance at all. Shortly after 2:30 that afternoon, the two vehicles moved out into the City of Groton, and then onto I-95 South through Connecticut and into New York to exit 6A for the Hutchinson River Expressway–I-678–south to the Bronx-Whitestone Bridge and continued south to the Jackie Robinson Parkway, passing by a vast cemetery to the south. They continued west to Cypress Avenue, farther west to Cooper Street, then southwest onto Wilson Avenue to the northwest, then turned left onto Menahan Street. The safe house was immediately to the right of the Pope John Paul II Family Academy. A cyclone gated fence stood across the deteriorating macadam alley between the two buildings.

After the SUV stopped in front of the house, Diogenes and the colonel exited the vehicle, then ascended the six cement steps to the front door of number 137 and entered the house just before 7:10 P.M. Unknown to all of them, they were just 13.4 miles north of Karina's apartment–a 30-minute drive in light traffic. The driver and the other agent waited outside the front door. While the colonel waited in the living room downstairs, Diogenes briefly searched every room in the house and looked around for anything that might appear unusual or out of place but found nothing worthy of his concern. The house had simple furnishings for adequate comfort. Several non-perishable food items were in the kitchen pantry, and two frozen hot dogs and three Swanson chicken pot pies were in the freezer. The refrigerator was bare, except for a yellow plastic bottle of French's Classic Yellow Mustard and six unopened plastic Dasani water bottles, which were already showing initial signs of freezing. Obviously, the last occupant had left the refrigerator temperature control at the maximum cold position.

Diogenes said, "This place is a temporary residence, Colonel, where you will stay safely until we arrange for a more permanent location elsewhere, probably in Virginia. I will be here for as long as you are here and will help you become at least slightly more comfortable during that period. Our driver will be available, as necessary. We will, of course have further phone interviews with those in Washington who need to work with your information. We might be traveling between this location and Washington periodically until we have a new identity for you. You understand, of course, as your arrival has been un-planned. The more we learn about you, the more effective our new identity for you will be. As soon as a new location is available, we will move you to that location. We obviously want your identity and location to be impossible to discover. Now, if you will tell me what kind of food you would like to have available here, I will do my best to find what you would like. We are close to a Russian neighborhood just south of here near the coast, with more typically Russian food in some of the grocery stores. If you would like to indulge in some local American tastes, we can arrange for that as well."

Although he was still adjusting to the vast changes in his life during the last few days, Colonel Kovalenko announced clearly, "I hope you understand that it is highly likely that former KGB or GRU or some other less-civilized people have agents in the United States, and if they discover or are informed of my disappearance from Russia, I strongly suspect they will come looking for me. My guess is that my disappearance has already been noted with prejudice, and orders for my abduction or removal from life have already been given to those who specialize in such dark operations."

"We are aware of several of your 'friends' in our country, Colonel, and we keep pretty good track of their activities, so I do not anticipate any difficulties that we cannot handle effectively."

"You do not know how efficient and *devious* these people can be!"

"*Perhaps* not…, but we can be quite crafty and 'efficient' as well, Colonel."

Viktor hesitated with skepticism for several seconds before responding, "Let us all hope so!"

**** KRASNODON, UKRAINE ****

Just after 2 P.M., Boris parked his rented car on Ekskavatomaya Street in a residential area near the physical center of the city of Krasnodon and walked about two blocks southeast to the police station. Inside the building, he presented his official GRU identification credentials to the duty officer at the front desk.

Boris announced with subtle authority, "A priest was murdered at a church near here about eight or nine days ago. I need to see the relevant police reports."

With foolish audacity, the duty officer inquired, "Why is that a matter of concern for the GRU?"

Boris responded as if explaining a simple logical concept to a schoolchild who obviously had not done his homework.

As Boris looked at the other man's nameplate on his uniform, he said casually, "Hypothetically, Sergeant Kosovo…, according to my orders, if I were to answer that question, it would be your *last* question. So, I will do you a big favor, and not answer it. I repeat–*I need to see the police reports!*"

Sergeant Kosovo responded with moderately controlled fear, "I see…, Major. Please…, have a seat, and I will bring them to you."

Boris continued with obviously contrived politeness, "Thank you!"

Sergeant Kosovo returned about four minutes later with a letter-sized manila envelope that had a label on one side with a hand-written identification of the contents of the envelope and the date the file was created. He handed it to Boris and waited while Boris opened the envelope, removed the report, and began to read it.

Date: August 9, 2015
Name of deceased: Pavel Dryzhensky.
Occupation: Catholic priest.
Age: 76 years, four months (approx.)
Nearest relatives: None.
Location of death: Mary Mother of God Church, Krasnodon, Ukraine.
Time of death: Approximately 9:10 A.M.
Cause of death: Single anterior gunshot wound, 32-caliber–penetrating the heart. Death was instantaneous.
Witnesses: None.
Comments: None.

Boris looked up at him with a subtle questioning stare before saying, "Thank you, Sergeant Kosovo. Now, please tell me who wrote this report…. It has no signature…."

"I… do not… know…."

"Was the body examined by a pathologist?"

"Of course!"

"Who?"

"Doctor Oleg I. Usenko."

"Thank you, Sergeant. I will be back if I have further need of your help."

Sergeant Kosovo nodded with a mild tinge of disguised fear as Boris glanced one more time at him, and then left the police station. He walked thoughtfully to his car just a block down the street. After he got behind the steering wheel, he called the coroner's office on his cellphone and asked to speak with Doctor Usenko.

"Coroner's office...."

"I am Major Boris Zhukov, GRU. May I please speak with Doctor Usenko?"

"Just a moment, Major...."

About one minute later, Doctor Usenko picked up the call.

"This is Doctor Usenko, Major. What can I do for you?"

"I need to know exactly how a Catholic priest was murdered recently at his church in Krasnodon."

"Someone slit his throat with a very sharp instrument, Major–probably a knife. He bled to death."

"Are you absolutely *sure* about that, Doctor Usenko?"

"That was the only murder in this city in the last six months, Major, and the only murder of a priest in this city for perhaps the last six centuries! Of course, I'm sure!"

"Did you find any other injuries besides the knife wound?"

"No, there were no other injuries.... What is all this about, Major?"

"May I see the body?"

"No. It has already been cremated. Why are you asking these questions, Major?"

"I am not at liberty to discuss the matter any further with you at this time. Thank you Doctor."

He ended the call abruptly and made a mental note about the discrepancy between the police report and what the coroner had just told him.

Who was the more reliable informant? Why was the body cremated?

Boris pondered these questions as he returned to his rented car and drove back to the Krasnodon Airport. Several hours later he boarded Aeroflot Flight 6061 at 11:15 that evening for the two-hour and 25-minute flight to Vnukovo International airport near Moscow. He spent that time involuntarily sleeping in seat 12F next to the starboard window over the wing. The Boeing 737-800 airplane landed on time at 1:40 in the morning. After he deplaned, the chilly outside air purged his mind and body of the recent urge to sleep as he waited for a taxi to arrive at the pickup area to take him to his apartment.

**** ISTANBUL, TURKEY ****

Michael Winston was on Turkish Airlines Flight TK1979 leaving Istanbul at 7:55 P.M. and due to arrive at Heathrow at 10:05 P.M. local time, four hours and 10 minutes later. After the plane landed and he deplaned, he took a cab directly from Heathrow to MI-6, the British Secret Intelligence Service (SIS) Headquarters at Vauxhall Cross in London. He immediately researched the Turkish license number 66-EH-1477 through Interpol and found that it identified a 2014 model Maserati Quattroporte purchased with cash by a man named Shamir Rahmani on Wednesday, September 13, 2014, in the Italian cultural center of Turin, the city where that car is manufactured.

He wondered: *Who is this Shamir Rahmani... talking to someone in Istanbul... named Kasana... about an avalanche, and a plan... 'those remaining will then turn to Allah for guidance and truth, and we will become stronger yet, and much closer to our ultimate goal of world domination...' World domination? Those remaining? Remaining after... what? What kind of lunacy is this?*

He quelled an unwelcome brief shiver, and then sent a casual friendly inquiry through official secure channels to Marvin Miles, director of the Central Intelligence Agency in Langley, Virginia.

> *M. Miles: Request any identification and background if available re: name Shamir Rahmani. Highest priority. Very grateful in advance for your assistance, old chap. M. Winston MI-6.*

CHAPTER 50
Monday, August 17, 2015

The huge Shiodome City Center office building in the Shiodome area of Minato, Tokyo, Japan was completed in 2003. It contains the headquarters offices of All Nippon Airways, Mitsui Chemicals, Air Asia Japan, and several other Japanese companies, as well as a multitude of smaller retail businesses. The Oregon Bar and Grill occupies about one fifth of the forty-second floor. From their window table in the crowded restaurant, two men gazed out through remarkably clean windows into the unusually clear blue sky about 62 miles to the southwest at the highest of the 'Three Holy Mountains.' Mount Fuji is a 12,389-foot-high stratovolcano composed of both lava and ash, with an unusually symmetrical conical contour. It has roughly a 78-mile circumference at its base, and a diameter of approximately 30 miles. It was formed during four main volcanic periods during the last 600,000 years. The mountain is most likely named for the Buddhist goddess of fire, Fuchi, and is usually covered with snow most of the year. This special inspirational place of scenic beauty last erupted for 16 days from December 16, 1707, to January 1, 1708, spewing fatal hot smoky gas and ash high into the atmosphere. Despite the relatively long time since its last eruption, it is still considered 'active' today.

The man dressed in black reached into his right inside coat pocket with his left hand and retrieved a small black velvet pouch, which he could effectively hide within his large grasp. He carefully slid it under his rumpled large red linen napkin near the edge of the table, and then withdrew his empty hand to his lap. He faced the other man, and briefly recited with a false smile in contrived friendly conversation some of the cultural and geological minutia associated with Mount Fuji as he glanced furtively at the rumpled napkin and pushed it in several short subtle nudges with his fingers toward the middle of the table. The beefy middle-aged Korean man with a short military-style haircut sitting across from him nodded appreciatively, looked out at Mount Fuji for a few seconds, then returned his attention to the table and just as subtly reached toward the napkin. He gathered both the napkin and the pouch beneath it firmly in his left hand and carefully slid them together toward his stomach and then off the table and onto his lap. Within a few seconds, he peered casually toward his lap as he removed his fake eyeglasses and rubbed the lenses with the napkin, and surreptitiously opened the pouch enough to view its contents briefly. Then he casually replaced his glasses on his face with his right hand, while holding the pouch with his left. He looked up briefly and innocently toward the other man with a slight nod, and then turned slowly to his right to look at his male associate three tables away, and again nodded subtly as he carefully and slowly placed the pouch in his outside right coat pocket.

The Korean said quietly, "Please excuse me for a moment. I will return shortly."

He moved his chair back from the table with ease and stepped away to go to the nearest men's room outside the restaurant near the center of the forty-second floor. His associate was shorter by an inch or two, and had longer, but still relatively short straight black hair. He was dressed in an average modern western dark blue suit and white shirt tailored to hug his obviously solid and muscular body. He arose innocently from his seat and followed the other Korean. He positioned himself resolutely outside the restroom and crossed his arms in front of his chest, straining the seams in his jacket as the other beefy Korean disappeared inside. He looked around inside the restroom for several seconds and listened carefully for any evidence of another person in the room. After concluding that he was indeed alone, he then went to one of the six toilet stalls and removed 10 square pieces of tissue from the dispenser, placed them in his pocket and returned to the sink. Still listening carefully, but satisfied that he was indeed alone, he returned to the entrance door, knocked on it twice, and again removed his fake glasses. Then he went back to the nearest sink, wiped the metal shelf under the wall mirror thoroughly with a tan paper towel, and then wet his hand and dropped several beads of water from it onto the metal shelf. After washing and drying his hands thoroughly, he reached for the pouch in his pocket, and picked out four of the gems, and then replaced the pouch in his pocket. After carefully wiping each of the four stones with the tissues, he placed them on a dry portion of the shelf away from the sink. Then he removed a pen from his inside coat pocket and used it to nudge a stone into a drop of water. The water appeared drawn around the bottom of the gem. A perfectly clean diamond appears to 'magnetize' water and will keep the water from spreading. A fake diamond would not disturb the water in any way. In the same manner, he nudged each of the other three gems into a bead of water and observed the same result. Just to eliminate the most remote possibility that he had selected the only four genuine diamonds in the pouch, he removed one more, conducted the same cleansing procedure, and nudged it into another drop of water on the shelf in the same manner. Again, the stone attracted the water. Then he took a jeweler's loupe out of his inside left coat pocket and retrieved one more stone from the pouch and examined it carefully with the loupe. Convinced now that all the gems in the pouch were genuine diamonds, he carefully dried the five wet test stones and replaced them along with the sixth one inside the pouch, put the pouch back in his left coat pocket and wiped the shelf dry with a paper towel. Then he turned and walked to the entrance door and knocked three times on the door. His associate outside returned to his table in the dining area. After waiting inside for another 15 seconds, the beefy Korean left the men's room and returned to his table.

A few seconds after he sat down at the table, he said quietly to his counterpart, "My people will initiate delivery five days from now. This is a new and untested device, but it is modeled after recently successful devices, and is easily transported because it is smaller. We will not meet again, unless of course the quality of our compensation cannot be verified. That would be bad for business. In that case, of course, you will be eliminated. Upon final verification within the next five days, we will notify you about the location of the operating instructions. You will receive an e-mail from 'Uncle Harry.' A password is required to open the attached message. You will need this one-time code pad to decode the message in the attachment. It was not designed for speed of decryption, but for security. If the message falls into the wrong hands, it will require many hundreds or thousands of computer hours of analysis and expert interpretation to decode it without the pad, but nevertheless, theoretically it could be done. But, of course, you will not let that happen. Therefore, so you should have no fear of discovery before you implement the instructions. Use only the pad page dated three days after the 'sent' date on the e-mail. All the other pages are filled with random or misleading characters."

Out of habit without moving his head much at all, he carefully scanned the ceiling of the room, mostly moving only his eyes, looking for possible hidden cameras. He then wrote on a piece of paper: 'PW = OPEN1776' and then slowly pushed the paper and the code pad across the table. Anyone watching would see only what looked like a brand-new book of 'post-it' sheets of light blue paper. The ink was invisible.

Susan Wong was a junior member of the Chancellor Organization on her first assignment, but she approached it with enthusiasm and the philosophical foundation she learned from Professor Michalik at Harvard eight years ago. Her official livelihood was from the Washington Post as a freelance journalist, and unofficially as the eyes and ears of Duke Chancellor within the Washington Post organization. She also was admiring Mount Fuji from an interior table on the far side of the restaurant from the window table occupied by the Koreans and the man in black. She noticed the subtle exchange of something between two of the men.

At the second table away to Susan's left and closer to the window facing Mount Fuji, sat Lei Chang. He was reading a newspaper while periodically glancing around the room, habitually mapping the interior of the restaurant into his photographic memory, while occasionally sipping tea from one of the restaurant's unique fine China cups. Unknown to the Koreans, the man in black and Susan Wong, they all had just acquired permanent status in the remarkable brain of Lei Chang. Following his equally fine intuition, he casually arose from his table with his cup of tea and invited himself into Susan's world.

Deliberately standing within her clearest peripheral vision, he said politely with practiced smooth international charm, "It is said that an attractive young lady should never sit alone for more than 20 minutes, lest certain men notice and assume that she is unattached, and therefore possibly open to some of life's more rewarding social adventures!"

He smiled in his uniquely disarming and friendly manner that so far had never suffered a rebuke. She looked up at him and responded internally with a reflexive warm smile while thinking, *this guy is good–really good!*

"My name is Chang…. Lei Chang. You may call me Lei. And you are…?"

With minimal and rapidly dissipating defenses, she responded readily with a smile, "Susan Wong."

Feigning mild surprise, he said smoothly, "Ahhh! You are American!"

She looked surprised and blurted out, "How did you know?"

"I am a natural student of human behavior! Your lack of a Chinese accent in perfect 'American English' with obvious Chinese heritage pretty much pegs you as American. I have traveled quite a bit, so I have learned much about people and the way they speak. Let me guess…. You are… from… California!"

Visibly stunned, she said, "That's right! What gave me away?"

"The answer to that question is a *state secret*," he said with feigned seriousness and then chuckled.

She laughed easily, and he readily joined in her laughter.

I don't like getting comfy with guys this easily!

He asked softly with convincing sincere interest, "So, what does an attractive young lady like you do for a living,"

She responded with a slight challenge in her voice and a hint that she actually was not an easy mark, "I work for the Washington Post. I'm a freelance reporter…. And what does a clever bachelor like you do for a living?"

He responded without missing a beat, but with rare, though subtle surprise, "What makes you think I am not married?"

She smiled with a slightly enigmatic expression, "I am obviously a woman, and therefore possess certain talents unavailable to men…, like… women's intuition."

He smiled more broadly as he said, "I see!"

He paused just a moment, thinking to himself, *Touché!*

Then she responded quickly without letting him off the hook, "*Well…?*"

"Oh! I work for the Chinese Ministry of Trade. I try to encourage mutually beneficial trade agreements between China and foreign countries."

That outright lie satisfied her for the time being, because he was handsome, friendly, sophisticated, and sounded genuinely sincere. And then he smiled again and added a very curious statement that planted a seed of concern in her mind. She had a fake pen on her table–the kind that contains a miniature electronic camera. *Is she also something else, perhaps in addition to, or instead of a Washington Post reporter?*

He continued, "I have learned over the years that one should never underestimate the value of an apparently chance encounter."

She wondered, *Meaning what... exactly?*

Her subtle facial response betrayed retention of that remark deep in her durable memory–precisely what he wanted. He surreptitiously photographed her with his tie clasp camera.

She watched his face carefully and silently for a few seconds as her brain remained in high gear.

Meaning... that he obviously wants me to remember him... for some reason....

In his left peripheral vision, one of the Koreans stood up and bowed ever so slightly toward the man in black, and then turned to leave the table. As the Korean man turned away from the table, Lei could see his face. The unexpected flush of instantaneous recognition and concern briefly quickened his heartrate.

What the hell is he doing here?

With a practiced internationally acceptable apologetic tone and only remnants of his recent smile, he said, "Please excuse me, Susan.... May I call you Susan?"

She responded with a facial hint indicating that she valued her independence, "You already have..., so my permission appears moot."

As he stood to leave her table, he looked down at her face and again smiled easily.

She's pretty sharp. I must remember that....

Then he casually announced, "I must be on my way. Business beckons unexpectedly!"

She smiled slightly with a quizzical expression on her face as he turned to leave, and her gaze followed him after he abruptly left, *just as the Korean men left their table together.*

Interesting coincidence!

She took as many photographs of the four men as she could under the rushed circumstances–the two Koreans, the man in black, and Lei Chang. Within several seconds, those images found their way from her pen through the internet to Duke Chancellor's desk halfway around the world.

You never know when photographs can come in handy later.

When they were completely out of sight, she sent an encrypted text message with her cellphone to Duke:

'Am in a restaurant at Shiodome in Tokyo. Regarding the images I just sent: The frontal photograph of a smiling Chinese guy–calls himself Lei Chang–claims to be a representative of the Chinese Ministry of Trade. Women's intuition suggests something else, but I'm just not sure what. I think he was hitting on me. That may or may not be important. However, he left the restaurant just as two really tough-looking Korean guys left–too much of a coincidence. The guy in black was at the same table as the two Koreans. I pass this along for what it's worth–maybe something, and maybe nothing, but as I said, my intuition said send it. S.W.'

'Images acknowledged and thank-you. D.C.' appeared in her text app about seven minutes later.

Lei followed the Koreans out of the dining room and disappeared from her sight. Then he innocently joined the Koreans as they stepped into the only available elevator on that floor at that time, along with several Japanese women and a Caucasian man. None of them spoke and no one made eye contact as the elevator smoothly made its way down to the street level. A soft metallic chime sounded one second before the doors opened within the silence of efficient Japanese engineering. The people left the elevator and headed across the large, elegant marble floor of the lobby toward the main building entrance. Lei followed the Koreans out of the building.

Immediately outside that entrance, a minor confrontation between a bicyclist and a pedestrian in the already crowded street drew increased attention from curious onlookers as two nearby police officers exited their marked patrol car and quickly turned their full attention to the developing commotion. The size of the crowd increased quickly. Vehicular street traffic nearby stopped in both directions as the pedestrian became unusually agitated and stepped farther into the street, screaming, and yelling, waving his arms in the air. Lei was uncharacteristically distracted, as the crowd momentarily obscured his subjects. The cyclist started yelling in Japanese with a Korean accent that someone had attempted to push him off his bicycle. The cacophony of dissonant human voices and angry yelling increased for several seconds. Lei made his way through the crowd as well as he could, but his progress was not enough for him to regain sight of his subjects. The commotion started to dissipate.

The Koreans had already disappeared into the vast urban complexity of Tokyo, the largest metropolitan area in the world. Lei was simultaneously intrigued and frustrated after realizing he had lost them, because he believed they were professional members of a clandestine network. Only a well-trained agent could have eluded Lei Chang that quickly because he had learned his craft from some of the best in the spy business.

**** BROOKLYN, NEW YORK ****

Viktor was restless at 2:36 in the morning while pondering the consequences of telling Vasily his new address. After another 10 minutes, he dialed Vasily's personal cellphone number from his own cellphone and waited.

It is about 9:46 in the morning in Moscow, so he should be in his office.

Vasily recognized Viktor's phone number, but responded officially, just in case someone else might be using Viktor's phone.

"Koshelev."

"Vasily, this is Viktor. I am in Brooklyn, New York at an FBI safe house– 157 Menahan Street. I have told them everything about the missing MK-4 from Chelyabinsk, and I think they believe me, so I am hoping that they will start to look for it as soon as possible."

"That's wonderful news, Viktor! My superiors are still hopeful of a quiet and timely solution to this problem. I will keep this to myself until and unless it becomes necessary that I let them know. Please keep me informed."

"I will, Vasily. I have not yet seen Karina, but I am eagerly looking forward to reuniting with her."

"Perhaps all will work out for the best, Viktor, but I believe we should be brief. You understand, of course."

"Yes. I will be in touch. Goodbye."

The connection ended abruptly. Viktor placed his phone on the nightstand and lay back on his bed. Within only minutes, he was snoring and Vasily was calling Boris to relay this latest information from Viktor.

The time between his conversation with Vasily and smelling the coffee downstairs appeared immediately sequential, as if he had never fallen asleep. He got out of his bed, showered, and shaved, as was becoming his new morning routine. Within 45 minutes, he was sitting in the kitchen, having a cup of coffee with Diogenes.

Diogenes asked, "So, what do you think of Brooklyn so far, Colonel?"

"It resembles parts of Moscow somewhat, but it obviously has its own distinctive 'American' character, I suppose. Why do you ask?"

"I'm just trying to break a little 'ice,' Colonel."

"Excuse me, please?"

"I am simply trying to establish some rapport, so I can learn about you to the extent I believe is necessary, given what you have said and done to get here."

With a slight smile, he said, "Oh! I understand! I am sorry, but that phrase was new to me!"

They both chuckled for a few seconds, and then Colonel Kovalenko continued, "The sun rises here in the east just as it does at a different time in Moscow or Chelyabinsk."

"Colonel, the sun rises only because you *think* it rises. From your earthly perspective, it seems to rise, but it really doesn't."

"What do you mean, Diogenes?"

"I mean that the sun is in a different location in the Milky Way galaxy and the larger universe at any given instant, and your position on the rotating Earth orbiting around it facilitates the *appearance* of the sun rising from your earthly perspective."

"Oooh…. Okay…, now I understand what you are saying!"

"I am trying to emphasize that what we see or believe is not always the ultimate or real truth, or what we know as 'reality.' We reveal only our interpretations, assumptions, and opinions most of the time, and many times unknowingly incorrectly, or according to custom or habit, instead of what is actual reality or ultimate truth. Sometimes either deliberately or subconsciously we delude ourselves into thinking that what our senses reveal is always the real or ultimate truth. Most of the time, we can all get along in life according to these admittedly imprecise and common sets of misinterpretations. Sometimes we even deliberately lie to distance ourselves from potential discomfort or to accomplish our selfish objectives by taking advantage of the vulnerable aspects of human nature in others, like the need to trust, and the desire to please or be liked."

"So…, why am I getting astronomy, philosophy and psychology lessons, Diogenes?"

"Because what we are dealing with, Colonel, is so frightening that we cannot afford to be lost in mere unexamined opinions, biases, and possibly false impressions or inaccurate understanding. We must be brutally frank and completely honest with each other about what is true and not a function of our selfish needs, politics, misperceptions, misunderstanding, fears, or desires. We do not have the luxury of unlimited time, politics, or convenient delusions. And, most importantly, I suspect we do not have the time for *distrust*."

"Does that mean you believe my story?"

"I have already read the report from Captain Kilroy about your exfiltration and debriefing, along with his personal notes. Yes. I believe you. I will proceed by trusting you as much as is humanly possible, if not more. That means that if you *ever* deliberately lie to me, or in any way mislead me, or allow me to be led astray, either I or someone else in this or some other investigative organization *will* eventually discover that. You *must* believe that! Right now, we, and possibly many other people cannot afford an adversarial or distrustful relationship between the two of us."

After a brief but thoughtful moment, Viktor responded, "I have not met many men like you, Diogenes…. I believe I am going to like working with you! I am very hopeful of success!"

Diogenes arose from his seat and indicated to Viktor that he was to follow him toward the living room, and said genuinely, "And I with you, Viktor! Take this cellphone. It is not an ordinary cellphone. It is specially encrypted and will allow communication with me under any circumstances. This device has no 'blind spots' or 'dead zones.' Guard it carefully. I am now going to call the director of the Federal Bureau of Investigation on the house phone, so your information gets directly to the top man without misinterpretation."

After they were comfortably seated on opposite sides of a round maple coffee table, Diogenes called the director of the FBI, Robert Kingman, on the secure house phone. Within 10 seconds, the first debriefing proceeded over a speakerphone on the table.

"*Kingman.*"

"For the record, Mr. Kingman, I have you on speaker phone. Only two people are at this end of the communication: Colonel Viktor A. Kovalenko, and me, special Agent Diogenes Kikos. Colonel Kovalenko is a 47-year-old Russian Army Intelligence officer, formerly the commanding officer at the Chelyabinsk Army base, one of several Russian nuclear armaments storage facilities."

"Also for the record, you are on speakerphone here, with me, Robert Kingman, and the assistant FBI director, Calvin M. Baker. Colonel Kovalenko, welcome to the United States! This is a completely secure encrypted communications line, so please feel free to speak frankly. Now…, we would like to hear what you have to say in your own words."

"Thank you for your interest in this matter, Mr. Kingman, because it is indeed of the utmost international importance. Immediately after having taken command at Chelyabinsk on Tuesday, July 14 of this year, I personally conducted an unannounced inventory verification of the status of nuclear weapons held in the Chelyabinsk storage vault. My initial command assignment orders included an inventory report stating that 90 MK-4 type devices were held in storage at that time. I personally counted 91 such devices, one of which had no serial number. I reported my discovery to the Verification Command in Moscow, to a General Rusanov. He made it quite clear that I had both the authority and the duty to 'correct' the inventory discrepancy. He was obviously telling me that I had to make a mental adjustment to a reality different from my personal experience. I could *not* do that. I became suspicious of him and started to wonder where I fit in an apparent conspiracy of some kind. I began to suspect remnants of the old KGB, which according to some, still has aspirations of returning to the old Soviet Russian glory days. Later, I returned to the storage vault again unannounced and rechecked my count. I was surprised to see that only 90 weapons were in the vault! Maybe the old-line KGB may have wanted such a device to use as a bargaining chip, possibly in efforts to reunite the old Soviet republics, or, I fear, for the new radical Islamic terrorist efforts, or perhaps just to sell for cash. Maybe some connections exist between Chechnyan radical groups and others in the old broken Russian military-industrial complex. I am not well-versed in such possibilities. Although my experience as an intelligence officer has revealed no specific facts indicating such a conspiracy, my intuition is unsatisfied. It has appeared obvious to me that the only person who could have been instrumental in removing one of those devices was my executive officer, Major Leonid Logonovsky. He was the interim commander immediately before I arrived to take command. I do not know the man personally very well at all, but I cannot think of any other individual with both the opportunity and the authority to accomplish or contribute to such a theft. I am shocked and ashamed that a Russian military officer would do such a thing! After I verified that one of the 91 devices I had counted before was indeed missing from the vault, I wanted to confront Major Logonovsky, but, again to my complete surprise, he had already been reassigned to another military facility in Moscow without any input from me. Someone higher up had to have pulled a slight-of-hand. That simply confirmed my suspicions and elevated my concerns about my personal future as well as the potential for this device getting into the wrong hands. From my perspective, it was *already* in the wrong hands. Furthermore, I discovered that it was precisely that one device with no serial number that disappeared. Now, you should also know that I have a contact in the upper ranks of the GRU organization, whom, I must confess, I will not identify, because he is a loyal friend from my early military training days whom I absolutely will not betray under *any* circumstances whatsoever. I believe you know the rest of the story."

Kingman responded after several seconds of apparent efforts to digest what he had just heard, trying to reconcile a distant historical fear with the very real present, *"That's quite a story, Colonel! What can you tell me about this General... Rusanov?"*

"My 'story' is, unfortunately quite real, sir! I do not know General Rusanov personally, so I cannot say much about him. I have learned, however, that he is from a military family background, and apparently has the ability, connections, and talent to achieve positions of power and authority more easily than one might normally expect."

"What about this Major Logonovsky? What else can you tell us about him?"

"Again, I do not know the man personally. My first impression, however, was that he is a competent military officer with good leadership qualities. He appeared self-assured, intelligent, and had expected knowledge and command presence. From what little interaction I had with him, he was quite organized and efficient in executing his duties and responsibilities, and obviously knew the structure and organization of the base inside and out."

"Could anyone in the official Russian political leadership have arranged or facilitated this theft?"

"Absolutely not! That would be the epitome of insanity and grotesquely *stupid!* Completely unthinkable!"

"Well, apparently <u>someone</u> with some kind of higher authority had a hand in this!"

"I understand your suspicion, but since the old Soviet Union dissolved in the early 1990s, it has not always been entirely clear who has what influence. Money tends to operate in Russia in much the same way as it does in the United States, or anywhere else, for that matter. You have your version of crime, as do we. Some people are willing to bend certain rules to achieve financial comfort and security, or to achieve imagined power and influence during times of uncertainty. However, I also fear that the essential rules of humanity and civilization are readily broken in service to beliefs of extreme religious nature as well as greed."

"What makes you so sure your government is not involved?"

"As I told you, I have a very good and absolutely trustworthy friend in a position of knowledge inside the system. He assures me that the official governmental structure has had *absolutely nothing* to do with this! Furthermore, they themselves are working quietly behind the scenes to find this device before it becomes a much more severe problem—not only for them, but for others in the international community."

"I am having some trouble accepting all of this, Colonel, as perhaps you might imagine. What is your motivation? Why are you here? Why can't you just let the official Russian military and intelligence organizations solve this problem?"

"My *parents* taught me right from wrong, Mr. Kingman! They taught me the value of truth, honor, and responsibility. They taught me the value of education and service! Mr. Kingman, I have a conscience! If I believe that a sinister disaster using a Russian or any other similar nuclear device is being planned anywhere in the world for no sanctioned military reason, then I have the absolute personal as well as military obligation to try to prevent that. I also have a beautiful and talented daughter who now lives in New York City. I have no other immediate family members. If that device ever gets close enough to my daughter and explodes, injuring or killing her, along with many other innocent people, then how do you think I would feel if I had not done *everything* in my power to try to prevent that? Do you have a daughter, Mr. Kingman? A son?

A wife? What would *you* do if you were in my shoes, knowing what I know? To get to this most recent point in my life, I had to persuade a Ukrainian Catholic priest, an agent in your Moscow embassy, and a United States Navy Submarine Commander of my sincerity. I am acting upon my personal belief and conviction because *I... have... no... other... choice!*"

Kingman was silent for several seconds, weighing what he had heard up to this point, and then said, *"Very well, Colonel. I appreciate your candor. We may need to speak with you again. For the record, unless you have something else to add, this interview is concluded."*

After a brief pause, Viktor responded with mild resignation, "I have nothing else to add, Mr. Kingman..., except that I would not want to be in your shoes... if you do not believe me."

The connection fell silent. Diogenes looked into Viktor's uncertain moist eyes. Viktor looked anxiously into the younger man's eyes.

Did they believe me?

**** *WASHINGTON, D.C.* ****

Kingman looked intently at Calvin Baker and said cautiously, "Well? What do you think?"

The assistant director said, "If there were ever a time to trust a complete stranger, this is it! We had better put everything we have into this! I am not going to live with what this man just said and do nothing about it! Rightly or wrongly, I simply *cannot* do that!"

Kingman sat silently for three seconds, and then said in complete resignation, "I agree. Let's get busy!"

Immediately after Calvin Baker left the director's office, Kingman's phone rang.

Agent Delmont Hathaway said, *"Mr. Kingman, I traced the tuition money in Rahim Nazari's account back from MIT to what I believe is its source."*

"Okay.... Lay it out for me."

"It looks like the original money came from the National Bank of Kazakhstan with the SWIFT code NBRKKZKX. Every bank in the world has a unique SWIFT alphanumeric code–either eight or 11 characters, where the first eight characters are used as identification only for the primary office, and the additional three refer to a

specific branch. Over 40,000 active codes identify all banks, the country they are in, and their specific locations within each country. 'SWIFT' stands for 'Society for World-wide Interbank Financial Telecommunication.' This particular bank in Kazakhstan sent a wire transfer in the amount of 8,391,928.59 Kazakh tenge (KZT) to the Dolati Branch of Bank Keshavarzi, with the SWIFT code KESHIRTH340 in Tehran, Iran. Someone in that branch converted that amount into 1,328,586,480 rial for deposit in a private business account at the same bank. That amount was then withdrawn and converted into USD $44,720 and wired to the HSBC bank at Canary Wharf in London. From there, it went to Bank of America NA, at 100 Federal Street in Boston, Massachusetts, with the routing number of 026009593 to the MIT account. I used the amount of $44,720 and traced backwards for that amount only. Whoever arranged this transfer did not think to disguise it within larger amounts or use a collection of smaller amounts adding up to $44,720. That suggests to me that the financial institutions themselves are not knowingly involved in any kind of conspiracy. They just appeared to be doing business as usual. Otherwise, I don't believe we would have discovered this trail of events at this time. It seems odd that such a circuitous transfer route was used without going all the way with a more effective or sophisticated disguise for the amount. Whoever sent this money could be an individual amateur trying to act like a professional, or is just… well, naïve…, or doesn't care who knows about his financial activities."

"Okay…, so, who owns the original account in Kazakhstan?"

"Someone named Shamir Rahmani."

"And…, who the hell is Shamir Rahmani?"

"I haven't a clue."

"Well, *find* a clue!"

"Yes sir!"

****** MOSCOW, RUSSIA ******

Two men sat in the back seat of a shiny black four-door 2011 ZIL military sedan outside the main entrance to the Domodedovo Airport. Behind the driver was Colonel Vasily Koshelev in dress uniform, and to his right sat Major Boris Zhukov dressed in a simple dark blue civilian suit, white shirt, and dark blue tie. The Russian president had learned about the missing nuclear device through internal secret military intelligence and created his own internal solution. He had reached down into the ranks through the layers of bureaucratically sensitive or suspicious generals and marshals to a hand-picked and trusted colonel–Vasily Koshelev of the GRU.

Colonel Koshelev turned toward Major Zhukov and said, "Major, my orders are from the very top–to find Colonel Kovalenko and the missing nuclear device as soon and as quietly as possible. Report to me immediately upon finding either Colonel Kovalenko or the missing device. Do not harm him! His information is invaluable, so he must remain alive. I am putting you in charge of the field operations of those two efforts. That means you will take orders from me and *only* from me. It also means I will do anything and everything in my power to assist and support you. All you need to do is ask. Our agents around the world now have explicit orders to respond with utmost haste to my requests and with the highest secret priority. This is a particularly sensitive assignment, Major, and obviously has political and other more critical and unique implications within Russia, as well as in the greater world community. That is why we will be using the latest in encrypted telecommunications technology. Officially and politically, Russia does not have much elbow room in this matter, so I need not emphasize too strongly how vitally important your role will be. I have chosen you because of your reputation, intelligence, accomplishments, demonstrated loyalty, dedication, creativity, and *common sense*. Our country cannot afford failure in this assignment, Major Zhukov! It is *our* nuclear device that was stolen! I have utmost faith in you. Use all your natural talents…, and for the sake of us all…, you must *succeed* in your mission!"

"I fully understand the gravity of the situation, Colonel. I shall give it my all."

Colonel Koshelev looked the younger man in the eye and offered his hand as a sincere basic human statement of trust, hope and admiration for the young officer, instead of the robotic official salute out of impersonal military habit. Then Boris opened the car door, stepped out, and then firmly closed the door without slamming it shut. He inhaled, then slowly exhaled, and started the most important job of his life. He walked directly to the main front entrance, entered the terminal, and proceeded confidently to his departure gate with only 25 minutes to spare. He boarded Etihad Airways Flight 68, an Airbus

A321 aircraft, and took his assigned seat–14F–next to the window on the starboard side over the right wing. He closed his eyes and concentrated upon the nature of his assignment and how he would proceed. The plane departed on time at 12:55 P.M. and flew for five hours and 25 minutes and over 2,320 miles before landing in Abu Dhabi at 7:20 P.M. After decelerating on the ground, it taxied to Terminal 3 and parked. Within 15 minutes, he and the other passengers had deplaned and entered the terminal building.

CHAPTER 51
Tuesday, August 18, 2015

Boris spent much of his time during the eight-hour and 20-minute layover in the United Arab Emirates thinking about the difficulty of his assignment and what he needed to do. He needed to get to the principal people as soon as possible to get participants' names and as much information as he could from each of them before identifying who would possibly be subject to 'persuasion' or execution if necessary. He needed facts, and he needed them yesterday.

Who could have stolen that device? Someone on the inside... An intermediary... Someone had to transport... Someone must deliver it to the target... Who? Where? Someone in command at the storage facility? Was the plan political? Purely mercenary? Religious? Or simply to threaten... to kill people, or to destroy property... or all of those? Was the motive terrorist-inspired? If so, to what end? Could the Chechnyans be involved? What about the former soviet republics? What about ISIS? Or is some heretofore unknown person or group at work here?

After a little more than a four-hour nap, he was still unsettled. He stood up from his seat and paced casually up and down the walkway to the departure lounge, observing everyone and everything in his field of view. His thoughts kept circling around the suspicion of a terrorist link, but without conviction. Shortly thereafter, he boarded Etihad Airways Flight 151, a Boeing 777, and took economy class seat 30K in the starboard section just behind the emergency exit door above the starboard wing. Within 17 minutes, the plane lifted off the runway two minutes late at 3:42 A.M. for the 7,261-mile journey to O'Hare International Airport in Chicago, Illinois. The plane easily made up the two-minute late departure in the 14 hours and 50 minutes of total flight time and arrived as scheduled at Terminal 5 at 9:30 A.M.

**** BROOKLYN, NEW YORK ****

Diogenes returned from a nearby grocery store with some food items and a copy of the New York Post and placed them on the kitchen table in front of Colonel Kovalenko. Viktor glanced at Diogenes, and then picked up the paper and looked at several headlines about world events. Then he sat down and paged through the paper scanning each page, noting pictures of arrested assault and murder suspects and two stories about house fires, complete with large sensational photographs. In another section, he glanced at several graphic pictures of three mangled automobiles at the scene of a collision on the Long Island Expressway. He skimmed several other minor articles, and then came across the entertainment section as Diogenes went back outside to his car. The sub-headline announced, 'Russian Ballerina Debuts Friday.' Underneath that title, he continued to read, 'The beautiful and talented Karina Kovalenko will perform at the David H. Koch Theater at the Lincoln Center for the Performing Arts at 8 P.M. on Friday, August 21.' He was bursting with pride as he dialed the special number ending in '1408' on his personal cellphone for Vasily Koshelev and waited for about 15 seconds, listening to the distant uneven gurgling ring tone.

After the ring tone stopped, a quiet, bland voice said, *"Koshelev."*

"Vasily, this is Viktor. I am still at the same place in Brooklyn, New York."

"It's good to hear your voice, Viktor! How are you doing, and how is Karina?"

"I am safe and well, but I have not seen Karina yet. She will be performing at the Lincoln Center for the Performing Arts in Manhattan this Friday evening! I hope to be there to see her perform!"

"Viktor? Are you still there...? Viktor...?"

"Vasily...? Vasily...? I do not hear you...!"

"Viktor...?"

**** MARYLAND ****

Duke's cellphone rang with the distinctive sound identifying an incoming call from General Murray's cellphone.

He brought the phone up to his left ear and said simply, "Hello, Richard. What's up?"

General Murray said, *"Feedback on that telephone number–I just discovered Kovalenko's contact in Moscow! It's a guy named Vasily Koshelev! He must be the one Kovalenko said was a friend in the GRU! The other phone number is the one you had asked me about: 011-7-499-884-2339. With a little effort and some cooperation from the FBI, I also got William Hickey's group at the NSA to research all signals including the phone the FBI gave Kovalenko. Apparently, this is the first time he used it."*

"That's very interesting! Now…, I have something else for you, coming through System 16 shortly."

Duke Chancellor maintained a steady respect for the people in his organization throughout the world who served as his eyes and ears and learned often enough that their observations and reports eventually became the pieces or the glue in otherwise unknown puzzles not always within the radar of official governmental clandestine organizations, either domestic or foreign. It was precisely because of the nature of his private corporation that his people were able to operate as private citizens, innocent but careful observers completely outside the realm of governmental bureaucracies and their politically correct and cumbersome disclosure and accountability procedures. He sent the images from Susan Wong to General Murray along with his comments:

> *'I received the attached photos from one of my people in Tokyo, who noted suspicion about the identities and coincidental behavior of these people. The two Koreans were meeting at a table with the man in black. The frontal photo is a Chinese man she said called himself Lei Chang, who claimed to be a representative of the Chinese Ministry of Trade. She expressed suspicion about that employment status. Of particular interest, however, is the Caucasian man in black. We have encountered other references of a curious or suspicious nature to a man dressed in black, so I am not sure what this means, but it appears as one independent coincidental reference too many to be acceptable without at least some suspicion. D.C.'*

Within a minute of his receipt of Duke's message, he responded:

'Acknowledged. Will look into this ASAP. R.M.'

**** C*HICAGO*, I*LLINOIS* ****

Boris had just settled into room 225 at the Hilton Chicago O'Hare Hotel for $85 for the night when his cellphone rang.

He recognized the caller identification. In a quiet, bland tone, he answered, "Boris."

"Koshelev. On Wednesday of this week, tomorrow, you can expect to meet your 'business associates' at Capri's Pizza Restaurant, located at 8820 South Commercial Avenue in Chicago. They will know only your first name—nothing else about you, your organization, or the mission, except that it is of the most urgent nature. They understand that they are to take orders from you alone and will suffer severe consequences if they do not cooperate."

"Understood."

The connection fell silent. Boris knew that the international connections of the Russian GRU had just firmly ensured the cooperation of these people with an offer they could not refuse.

CHAPTER 52
Wednesday, August 19, 2015

The interior walls of Capri's Pizza were painted several times over many years and at least once in red, and very recently. Various paintings of different artistic quality representing a variety of Italian cities and landscapes throughout time adorned every wall. Photographs of Italian Olympic soccer teams hung in frames of various sizes and degrees of wear and tear on a dark green wall behind the varnished wooden counter. Someone's slightly faded brownish ancestral photographs occupied yet another section of the red wall to the left. Also, in the corner to the left of the counter was a charcoal sketch of a nude woman admiring her reflection in a mirror. Maybe it was trash–but then, perhaps it was priceless art, depending upon one's point of view, experience, or motivation. The obviously old cream-colored square linoleum tiles on the floor had been cleaned recently but were not pristine by any means. Two men sat on two of the eight chairs around a long rectangular dining table adjacent and parallel to the large plate glass street window in selfish recognition of the current dearth of patrons. A checkered red and white vinyl tablecloth unevenly spread over the table hung equally unevenly over the sides. A four-foot-wide red neon 'PIZZA' sign hung with uneven picture-hanging wires from round eye-screws in the upper window frame. It was positioned roughly in the center of the window and just slightly askew from horizontal. On the table in front of each man was a slice of plain pizza from a 14-inch pie on a simple off-white paper plate with scalloped edges. Two open cans of Classic Coca Cola, moist with external condensation stood on the table, one near each plate. The men appeared to have spent much of their lives exclusively in places other than boardrooms, ballrooms, 70-foot sailboats, fine white beaches, and expensive restaurants. A young woman with dark hair and a plain physical appearance dressed in unremarkable casual blue denim clothing sat alone on the other side of the dining area, finishing a plate of angel hair spaghetti and large meatballs.

Shortly after 2:10 P.M., Boris entered the restaurant, and slowly looked around the dining area. He glanced only briefly at the woman. He concluded she was not a factor in his mission. The two dark-haired clean-shaven young men wearing red T-shirts and dirty off-white denim aprons behind the counter at the rear of the restaurant were preparing take-out orders for pizza, Stromboli, calzone, and subs, while simultaneously gesticulating and incessantly chattering in animated Italian. One was of average height, unremarkably pudgy, and probably could not do even one pushup if his life depended upon doing so. The other was taller with obvious high regard for his physique. He also apparently took considerable pride in the ornate tattoo on his muscular upper right arm from his shoulder to his elbow portraying a well-endowed, long-haired nude woman with the name 'Veronica' emblazoned in fine red ornate script across the figure. They looked his way briefly, suspended their activity for a few seconds, and then continued about their business. The two beefy, unshaven Caucasian men with dark complexions seated at the window table, apparently just finishing their pizza slices, were the ones he was to meet. He walked slowly toward them.

Within their hearing distance, he said clearly in a quiet commander's voice, "My name is Boris. I am looking for two men to do an important job."

He waited expectantly with a questioning facial expression and somewhat threatening raised dark eyebrows, but with increasing confidence as they turned their heads slightly toward each other and then briefly nodded to each other. He concluded correctly that these two were indeed the men that had been ordered to do the job he wanted done. While studying their faces carefully, he reached into his shirt pocket and withdrew a folded white paper on which he had printed legibly in capital block letters in black ink:

157 MENAHAN STREET, BROOKLYN, NEW YORK, BACK DOOR DOWN THE ALLEY, ON THE RIGHT.

He unfolded it and placed it face up on the table between the two men.

After about five seconds, Boris asked firmly with obvious intolerance for anything other than the expected answer, "Questions?"

They had nowhere else to go, and Boris knew that. The culture from which they were selected had strong motivational codes of obligation to certain higher international authority.

The older man, Alexander, grasped the paper with his meaty fingers, studied it for a few moments, and then folded it and put it in his shirt pocket as he responded in a firm deep raspy whisper while looking up at Boris, "No questions. It will be done."

Both men glanced at each other in apparent agreement and commitment, and then picked up their soda cans and gulped down the remaining semi-flat sweet dark liquid. The meeting was over. Another small portion of the future had just been determined. The 'pizza boys' behind the counter innocently watched the three men walk toward the front door. After the other two men walked out of the restaurant, Boris intuitively turned around at the exit door and leveled a virtually castrating stare across the entire 40-foot-long dining area into the young pizza men's suddenly widened eyes. They immediately returned their nervous self-conscious attention to their pizza dough with slightly elevated heart rates for the next 30 seconds or more before regaining a sense of normalcy.

**** TOKYO, JAPAN ****

For the last two days, Lei Chang had been searching unsuccessfully for the two Koreans he had seen at Shiodome. With unaccustomed injury to both his personal and professional pride, he concluded that the urgency of his assignment required that he continue to the United States without further delay, despite the probability that Jo-Mung Suong had disappeared. He hailed a taxi and told the driver in perfect Japanese to take him to Narita International Airport.

**** GROTON, CONNECTICUT ****

After two weeks in Detroit innocently trying to discover information about Shamir Rahmani, Ariel returned to her apartment in Groton. She composed an encoded message to David Rosenberg:

'It is my opinion that Shamir Rahmani was in Detroit to recruit soldiers for jihad. I could not get specific information regarding names or places. All I could find was a registration at the Hilton Doubletree just west of Southfield Road under the name Rahmani, which was also the registration name for a late model Cadillac automobile rented from Hertz at the airport. Although I learned that a white Cadillac was seen within the main Islamic community, no one in that vicinity was able (or willing) to provide any useful information. I left it at that because I was beginning to sense that I would soon lose my anonymity with any further presence or inquiry. A.R.'

CHAPTER 53
Thursday, August 20, 2015

**** *TOKYO, JAPAN* ****

While waiting in the departure lounge, Umar Kasana surfed the internet on his smartphone. Several advertisements scrolled by about the upcoming debut of the young Russian ballerina at the David H. Koch Theater in New York this very night. Within the hour, he left from Terminal 1, Gate 42 at Tokyo Narita Airport on a Boeing 77W airplane, United Airlines Flight UA7999 at 11 A.M. All 212 passenger seats were occupied. Although he was certainly not a dedicated patron of ballet, he was thoroughly smitten by the young Russian beauty. He was determined to see her perform. The nonstop flight arrived at JFK International Airport at 10:45 A.M. local time at Terminal 7. His total flight time was 12 hours 45 minutes, so he was tired and more than eager to stretch his legs. After the plane landed and all the passengers had deplaned, he walked inconspicuously with the last of the crowd into the main terminal. He proceeded to the luggage claim area and waited for about 15 minutes just a few yards past the beginning of the luggage carousel. Within a few minutes after the carousel started moving, he gathered his travel luggage and proceeded through customs without any adverse events. Several minutes later, he took a taxi from the airport to the New York Marriot Marquis at 1535 Broadway and 45th Street. He paid the $224 in cash in advance at the front desk for the first night of an uncertain stay. After checking in, he rode the elevator to his room on the 40th floor of the 49-story building and settled in for a nap on the queen-sized bed before going to the theater.

**** MANHATTAN, NEW YORK ****

Early evening temperatures fell to the low 70s, with minimal breezes and clear skies directly overhead after a late morning thundershower had passed through the city from the west. Broad dark gray storm clouds still hung slightly above the horizon to the east. Even near the end of the day, the atmosphere was clean and fresh after having sustained unusually frequent lightning during the storm. Only a few widely scattered puddles of rainwater remained on several streets and sidewalks. People began entering the David H. Koch Theater by 7 P.M. for the opening performance of Shakespeare's 'A Midsummer Night's Dream,' scheduled to start a half hour later. The New York Times, The New York Post, The Daily News, and The Wall Street Journal had published brief articles during the prior week about the upcoming opening performance, along with professional rumors and thoughtful discussion among critics throughout the greater New York world of theater and the arts about the young and unknown new Russian ballerina, Karina Kovalenko. Some of the more noteworthy critics pointed out that she had been refused a position in the Bolshoi Ballet and that the advance rumors and hype were a little overdone, if not merely premature. Those generally acknowledged as the savvy 'insiders' were gathering more than their usual degree of self-promoted attention by deliberately dropping hints in the media and on social internet sites about the thrilling surprise awaiting patrons of the theater. Since it would be her first performance in the United States, the audience was augmented by various writers and reviewers from other major metropolitan news centers around the country, including: Boston, Philadelphia, Chicago, Denver, Dallas, Miami, Saint Louis, Atlanta, San Francisco, Kansas City, Seattle, Detroit, and Los Angeles. As usual, the sharks of the critical media were circling around another source of potential controversy to inflate and amplify opinions for their own egos and the financial bottom lines of their employers. They knew that they did not have to be right. They just had to be flexibly controversial, if not deniably so. Several local captains of industry, political kingpins and their spouses were also in attendance. They no doubt often competed with one another to be among the first to see, hear, like, dislike, or do anything in the lofty circles of New York City society. The critics from other cities had to be there to bolster their personal and professional reputations, if indeed the young Russian dancer was as good as the rumors implied. They could always melt into the background if she was not as good as the hype. However, they could not afford to skip her performance if indeed she was exceptional. By the time Karina made her appearance on the stage, however, mistaking any of the prior discussion and rumors was impossible. She was in dancer's heaven, living her dream, building her future with happiness. This time, even the 'inflated' prior hype was unusually accurate.

Umar radiated utter joy while scarcely suppressing hints of internal lust as she performed flawlessly in Shakespeare's 'A Midsummer Night's Dream.' He was in the front row of the third balcony, seat A115, focusing upon her lithe and incredibly flexible body. He was jealous as she would periodically join a male dancer and imagined that man surely felt the soft warmth of her agile and angelic body next to his.

I must know how her young, warm and soft smooth skin feels against mine... how she feels deep inside... the scent of her beautiful long blond hair!

He was accustomed to having whatever he wanted through the well-practiced application of his personal charm, physical strength, or the proper application of enough money in the proper hands to align someone else's behavior, personal perspective, ethics, or sense of priorities with his.

By the time the performance ended, even the traditionally or most habitually dour, wrinkled, and unforgiving critics in attendance had to admit with at least mild sincerity that Karina Kovalenko was indeed 'a remarkable sight,' 'a stunning sweetheart,' 'beautiful, both physically and artistically,' and 'supremely gifted beyond comparison.' They said so with further superlative embellishments in their internet blogs immediately after the performance and in their published newspaper reviews the next day. Even the traditional 'talking heads' made time in their daily television broadcasts to depart from their regular barrage of reports about the dark side of humanity and its unfortunate encounters with natural disasters, law enforcement, or military forces to include video clips from the theater area, including brief interviews with departing patrons on the sidewalk outside the theater. They all expressed some variation of the theme of having just experienced a rare appreciation of both exceptional natural female beauty and rare physical talent. She had indeed become the new 'star' of her profession.

"... I'm 83 years old, and I fell in love with her!"

"… I want to be like *her* when I grow up!"

"…Absolutely *marvelous!*"

"… I didn't know such movements were even *possible!*"

"… I'm speechless!"

"… I really think I just saw an angel!"

"… I've seen plenty of ballet in the last 40 years, both here and abroad, and I can *guarantee* you… Karina is *by far* the best!"

****** NEW LONDON, CONNECTICUT ******

The Brass Rail Café is just west of the Thames River, about 2.5 miles south of the big naval yard on the other side of the river. It provides food, drink, and periodic opportunities for meeting the opposite sex, usually male military and female civilian. On this evening, a woman with long wavy dark hair, friendly blue eyes, and medium-to-dark complexion enhanced with little makeup was having a small plate of lasagna and a house salad for her supper. She sat near an interior corner of the dining room at a chestnut brown wooden table with a limited window view of Bank Street just outside the building. Smitty walked into the café with a few friends and took a table closer to the front window next to her table. The young men were simultaneously juggling and cross threading several shallow conversations among themselves with rapidly changing subject matter of little apparent significance to others. All four young men simultaneously glanced appreciatively at her. She smiled briefly in return, but immediately turned away from them without further invitation or encouragement. Smitty continued his prior conversation.

"Yeah, we had to quit the mission we were on and go pick up 'a passenger' in the Baltic Sea, the captain said, and then hightail it back here. What a screwed-up Navy!"

One of the other young sailors was still on an emotional high from his second major experience outside the State of Arkansas, and offered, "Yeah, sometimes it seems like the big brass just likes to play a different game every once in a while… y'know? Like… the Navy gets *boring* for the big guys!"

Another asked, "So, who was your 'important passenger'? Had to be important, right? Else the Navy wouldn't have provided *limousine* service!"

They all laughed for several seconds, completely unaware of the nearby woman who was innocently toying with her meal. She had not taken a mouthful of food since the young men sat down and continued talking. Instead, she took small sips of her unsweetened iced tea through a straw as she concentrated to remember what she was hearing. Her listening skills, memory, and intelligence were far superior to theirs.

"Dunno, really. I was posted right outside the briefing room, but I think he was like a Russian colonel or somethin'–name was Cola Venko, or somethin' like that."

She carefully glanced toward their table to see who was talking and created a mental picture of him for possible later reference. One of the other sailors glanced back in her direction and smiled. She turned away innocently and sipped her iced tea, picked up her fork, and took a bite of lasagna. She briefly appeared to study the initials and phrases etched into the wooden table next to her placemat– *'Angel & Bobby forever,'* *'Mine in Yours,'* phone numbers, –evidence of someone's version of simple and innocent romantic love that she had never experienced, except for a brief encounter at the Philadelphia Museum of Art. She had grown up too fast. Nevertheless, Ariel Romanovsky was a confident woman, completely aware of her femininity. Seven years of experience as a double agent for the Russian GRU and the Central Intelligence Agency with brief intermittent experiences with Mossad kept her senses and self-awareness in peak form. She was attractive, though not a classic beauty, and usually chose not to present herself in a manner that typically drew seldom-wanted male attention, primarily because her employment usually required less visibility than most women might ordinarily desire. She was nevertheless effectively physically attractive to almost any man who took the *time* to look at her carefully for more than 15 seconds. When she chose to go out 'full-female,' most civilized men might describe her with a simple three-word phrase– she had *'it'*–that ill-defined, and often misunderstood female quality that elicits subtle and sometimes surprising sexual desire from almost any man on the planet. That quality is not simply physically 'sexy' in its entirety, but something much more subtle than that. She could be intellectually and verbally engaging, if not intimidating at times, and could discuss fluently in several languages a wide variety of subjects spanning the spectrum from ancient history to current events. She could adjust her humor, charm, and wit to any generation or culture, and could communicate quite effectively non-verbally. One might easily imagine that even the Pope would buckle at the knees in unfamiliar desire before her after she had 'turned it on' within perfume distance... after she knowingly and deliberately had activated her special female charms and talents. One of her favorites was Jo Malone Vanilla & Anise. She was physically exceptional not in an abundance of female features, but in a rare degree of both proportion and shape well carried on her five-foot, eight-inch frame. Part of her unique quality, however, was in her profound knowledge of *exactly* how and when to use her feminine talents. To say she had multinational 'charm' would be only a pathetic approximation of her capabilities.

Once tasked with acquiring certain manufacturing secrets from the Siemens company over six years ago, shortly before she was unexpectedly obligated to have two opposing employers, she innocently allowed a 55-year-old executive just an inch or so shorter than she was to buy her a drink at the fashionable Neidklub at number 25 Reeperbahn in Hamburg, Germany. In the laser-light-filled discotheque she offered only a mild degree of resistance to his suggestive invitation to go to his room at Cityhotel just down the street. Once there, she further exercised just the right amount of coy reluctance to accept his increasingly obvious amorous advances. She allowed her prey to develop his maximum degree of desire, and when the time was right, she easily sensed it and casually suffocated him with her breasts during his helpless rapture until he suffered an unexpected fatal heart attack. She was almost like the female praying mantis calmly devouring her mate during the sex act. Then she casually showered and reassembled her innocent demure appearance, stole his briefcase full of the required 'information,' innocently walked out of the room with it and an hour later delivered it to her Russian handler as if she had just returned from a brief refreshing vacation. After several weeks of her subsequent intentionally devious disappearance, her handlers 'offered' her another assignment in the United States, where, unknown to them, she acquired an innocuous one-bedroom, 772 square-foot apartment–number 207 at 2775 East 12th Street in Brooklyn, New York. That was in effect, her 'hideaway,' to which she retreated on occasion when she chose to be invisible, if not non-existent. Her 'visible' and official civilian life, however, was based in New London on the west side of the Thames River across from Groton and the naval yard on the east side. She lived at number 66, a two-bedroom unit at the Winthrop Square Apartments and adopted the life of an artist, since she had enough genuine natural talent to supplement her 'government' work. Her neighbors knew her as a normal, sweet young woman with unusually good artistic talent.

CHAPTER 54
Friday, August 21, 2015

**** SOMEWHERE OVER PENNSYLVANIA ****

Boris was in an airplane about 27,000 feet above the earth, heading east over farm fields near the central Pennsylvania-New York State border.

Interesting… how these Americans produce and even export so much food without large state-run farms.

His mind was churning as he looked out from his port-side window in economy class seat 28A of the Airbus A320 airplane. He had left Terminal 3 at O'Hare International Airport in Chicago at 5:52 A.M. on Spirit Airlines Flight 224, due to land at LaGuardia Terminal B two hours and eight minutes later at 9 A.M. local time.

**** GROTON, CONNECTICUT ****

Ariel read some of the many internet reviews of Karina's 'beautiful,' 'brilliant' and 'flawless' debut performance in New York. She prepared to go see the rising young star that the Bolshoi had mistakenly, foolishly, or now at least regrettably turned away. It was an opportunity for her to reconnect in a small and subtle way with her nominal homeland, now that she was not entirely in control of her own life. She rode the afternoon metro train from New London to Grand Central Station in Manhattan just like many other innocent weekend travelers to the Big Apple, and killed some time shopping before taking a cab that arrived at the theater at 6:10 P.M. She negotiated with a street scalper about a block south of the theater for an admission ticket for a mere $125 in cash. Then she registered his appearance and personal characteristics in her remarkable memory for possible later reference or retribution if necessary and offered only a manufactured smile and a silent visual epithet in return.

**** BROOKLYN, NEW YORK ****

Colonel Kovalenko read many of the same reviews in the newspapers that Diogenes had collected for his benefit. He had to see his daughter perform, regardless of international crises, and no one was going to deny him that privilege, with or without a ticket.

"Diogenes, we are going to see my daughter perform this evening! I must see her while I have this opportunity, because I fear I may not have another chance in my uncertain life… and you could use a dose of Russian culture!"

Diogenes knew no way around this development. FBI training had not yet found a consistent way to overcome genuine orchestration of heartstrings. Standard operating procedure, responsibility, rules and regulations, political posturing and traditional consequences gave way before the universal right of a father to see his child. The difference in this case was that Colonel Kovalenko was not just any father, and his daughter was not just any pretty young woman. Diogenes had absolutely no choice in the matter, and he knew it. The avenues of potentially immediate or eventual retribution and regret upon denial were both enormous and ominous.

**** MANHATTAN, NEW YORK ****

Leah Cummings boarded the 4 P.M. Acela train at Union Station in Washington, D.C. and after a series of mild variable catnaps arrived at Pennsylvania Station in New York at 6:52 P.M. She took a cab to the David H. Koch Theater at Columbus Avenue and 62nd Street to see the recently widely advertised young Russian ballerina perform. At 7:26 P.M. she deliberately walked past the nearby scalpers with her own internet ticket, ignored their hawking with private disdain, and continued to the main entrance and entered the theater. She walked up the stairs in a conscious effort to maintain her habitual respect for exercise and sat in the second ring center section–seat number C110–near the middle of the third row back from the forward edge of the balcony directly facing the stage. She did not indicate any special awareness of the handsome man wearing a coal black suit seated nearby in row A, seat 115.

Colonel Kovalenko and Diogenes arrived early near the theater in a black 2014 Ford sedan with dark tinted windows. Viktor was beaming and overcome with anticipation and paternal pride. After they got out of the car, their driver left the immediate vicinity to find a nearby waiting area for the return trip to Brooklyn. By this time, Diogenes was infected with the same desire to see the young woman in person as her father was. The scalpers could no longer demand a premier opening price, so Viktor negotiated with one of those obvious 'small businessmen' for a reduced price. The scalper was wearing a white leather jacket, designer blue jeans, sunglasses, a black T-shirt, and large circular plastic earrings.

He announced brazenly to Viktor, "I can sell you a ticket for just $250, in cash, sir."

It is a good thing they do not know I am Karina's father. The price could have been much higher! Damned capitalist bastards!

Viktor was reaching for his wallet when Diogenes approached the young 'entrepreneur' and pulled out his FBI identification badge, stepped ominously between the scalper and Viktor, and said, "I think that's a little *high… sonny!* How 'bout we get *two* tickets for $150 *total!*"

For a brief second, the scalper caught sight of Diogenes' nine-mm Glock service handgun in his black shoulder holster, and correctly interpreted the much larger man's visual message. He had never been this close to the FBI in his entire young borderline criminal life and was not the least bit interested in risking any potential inquiry into his identity or past 'accomplishments.' He would compensate later for his lack of sufficient profit with other, more-naïve customers in typical capitalistic fashion.

"Like I said, gentlemen…, two tickets for $150! Thank you very much! Thank you *very* much! Enjoy the show, gentlemen! Thank you! *Thank you!*"

Viktor headed for the main entrance while Diogenes turned back with a lingering visual warning toward the scalper, and then quickly caught up with Viktor. With some direction from an usher, the two men found their way to their seats, A117 and A116, in the second ring balcony next to an attractive young woman with wavy black hair sitting in the aisle seat, A118. She was wearing a dark green evening dress with a very noticeable plunging neckline, a gold necklace, matching earrings, gold bracelet, and a gold watch but no rings. Her fingernails were only slightly on the pink side of natural. The men had to excuse themselves to get by her to their seats immediately to her left. She stood with a typically understanding smile, as she looked each of them in the eye before they were past her and all three of them sat down in their seats. Since Viktor was seated between the woman and Diogenes, he caught a strong whiff of her perfume–vanilla and anise, *in spades*. Within seconds, she sensed a slight mental interruption–a brief flash of something, like an instantly disconnected mental synapse, or like a lightbulb that burned out immediately upon being switched on, as if the normal smooth continuity of time suddenly stumbled upon itself for just an instant. The performance would not start for another 21 minutes. Umair was in seat A115 next to Diogenes. All three men were aware of the feminine perfume scent.

He then turned to Viktor and said quietly, "Colonel, you know this is way out of line. I could get my neck in the ringer *big time* for this!"

Viktor responded lightly, "Yes, but you had no choice, and your superiors will understand that! I will stand up for you! They need me right now, and they cannot afford not to keep me happy!"

In mock anger, Diogenes retorted in an audible whisper, "You're really incorrigible, you know that?"

Both men chuckled as the woman next to Viktor suddenly sustained an unexpected and unwelcome vicious attack of professional intuitive heat.

Colonel?

All three were quiet for several seconds before Ariel turned toward Viktor and said in perfectly crafted innocence, "Please excuse me, sir, but... are you Russian? I'm sorry, but I could not help overhearing some of your words, and I thought I detected a Russian accent. I am from Moscow, so I have an awareness of such accents."

Taken completely off guard, Viktor responded, "Yes! In fact, I *am* from Russia!"

Diogenes folded his arms in front of his chest, and then jabbed Viktor in the left arm as subtly as possible with the three middle fingers of his left hand under his right arm. Mired in inescapable admiration of the young woman as well as intense paternal pride, Viktor ignored him and continued.

"My daughter, Karina, is going to perform here tonight. She was turned down by the Bolshoi about a year or so ago, but she was quite determined to show the world that she is worthy of such status!"

Ariel responded genuinely, "Oh, how *wonderful!* I know of her! I have read about her in the papers and on the internet! Many people appear to believe that she is indeed quite marvelous! She is certainly *remarkably attractive* in the photographs! What an amazing coincidence–that I am sitting right here next to her father! Well, you must be *extremely* proud of her!"

His face melted into an irrepressible paternal smile as he responded sincerely, "I *am* immensely proud of her, indeed! Here is a picture I took of her when she left Moscow for the United States!"

He retrieved his cellphone from his pocket and immediately touched the photo gallery icon to reveal as the first image the one taken at Sheremetyevo.

"Oh, my goodness! She's so *beautiful....!* May I please have a copy of that picture?"

Viktor was so lost in paternal pride that he was completely unaware of any implications of sharing that photograph. Diogenes was still absorbed in reading his program notes about Karina.

Viktor said, "What is your e-mail address, so I can send it to you?"

Ariel's smile never left her as she said eagerly, "If I may, I can do it quickly from your phone...."

She held out her hand, and that was all the encouragement Viktor needed to comply. She completed the minor task remarkably quickly and efficiently, implying thorough familiarity with his cellphone model, and then handed his phone back to him. She was in fact familiar with many internet modes of communication. She had also just memorized his cellphone number.

She said with quiet genuine appreciation, "Thank you very much!"

As Viktor pocketed his cellphone, Diogenes was mentally counting all the demerits he was accumulating. He was thinking how absurd it would be for him to lean toward the woman and lecture her about the fact that he was an FBI agent, that she was talking to a potentially valuable informant with knowledge about possible great danger, and that she should *shut the hell up* and mind her own business! However, he did not know that Ariel Romanovsky was also a pro–a very experienced and intelligent triple agent. She worked for the Russians, and she worked for the United States as well, and sometimes for the Israelis. She may or may not have been above his pay grade, but she was most certainly more experienced, and crafty, and a far better actress than he could ever become as an actor.

She continued innocently to confirm her memory, "May I please have your cellphone number? Maybe we could meet for coffee sometime…, yes?"

Viktor responded easily, "Sure! I would like that! Here…."

He wrote his FBI-issued cellphone number down on a piece of the program and ripped it off to hand to her–202-324-7793. *That's not the same number!* Now she had *two* cellphone numbers. She took the piece of paper just as the small insert from his program fell out onto the floor near her feet.

He said apologetically as he pointed down to the floor, "Oh… please excuse me."

He awkwardly leaned over to try to reach the insert that had fallen between her legs. She recognized what had happened and offered a polite innocent giggle as she moved both her legs out of the way to her right so he could grasp the insert directly below her seat. He enjoyed another brief whiff of her perfume before he returned to an upright posture in his seat. She smiled innocently at him with a facial expression as if to say dismissively, 'no problem at all.'

Viktor started to read the program, basking in rare authentic paternal pride, then turned his attention to the insert, and read it.

'Karina Kovalenko will be replaced in this evening's performance by Allison Connors.'

As if suddenly mortally wounded, he cried out, "Oh no! This cannot be!"

The people in the row of seats immediately behind and to the left of them turned briefly to look directly at Viktor. Ariel immediately turned toward him with sincere concern in her face, as did Diogenes.

Diogenes leaned toward him and whispered with intense alarm, "What's wrong, Viktor?"

Ariel now knew the man's first *and* last names–*Viktor Kovalenko! Karina Kovalenko's father! –Colonel Viktor Kovalenko, the 'passenger' the sailor called 'Cola Venko' who was recently picked up by a United States Navy submarine in the Baltic Sea!*

He showed Ariel and Diogenes the insert that neither of them had found up to that time, and then they both removed their own inserts and read them.

Within several seconds, he gathered his self-control, leaned toward Ariel, and whispered, "Please excuse me. I must leave."

She agreeably stood with a mix of both personal and professional concern in her face, simultaneously raising her seat cushion and pressing her firm toned legs back against the underside of the raised seat enough for Viktor and Diogenes to squeeze by her shapely torso. The man in black briefly looked over at Ariel as the two men entered the aisle. Viktor walked up the aisle ahead of Diogenes with a heavy heart, not clearly seeing anything around him, but concentrating on the red 'EXIT' sign now about 80 feet ahead of him. The two men passed through the balcony entry and Viktor raced ahead of Diogenes down the staircase to the lobby.

Viktor went directly to the nearest attended box office window without late patrons nearby and asked the young woman behind the glass ticket window, "Excuse me, please. Why is Karina Kovalenko not performing this evening?"

With evident surprise, she said, "I don't know, sir!"

"But I *must* know why she is not performing! I expected to see her perform this evening! I am her father! I *must* know! Surely you can *understand* that!"

Have I just revealed my identity? Have I ruined my opportunity for a new identity?

"Please wait just a moment, sir… I will call the production manager."

Diogenes stood by helplessly counting more demerits, as Viktor stood patiently at the window, effectively masking internal anxiety, and mentally racing through all kinds of fearful or unfortunate scenarios that could explain Karina's absence. He was also concerned about the possibility that someone had just overheard him, and that his identity–and his past–would eventually become known, like the resurgence of a dormant virus now awakened to blossom into further irreversible infection. He glanced furtively from one side to the other, and then slowly turned around only enough to see whether anyone behind him could have heard him. It was simply impossible to know. Then the woman behind the window replaced the modern angular black plastic phone receiver in its cradle on the wall next to her and faced out toward him with a bland 'public relations' facial expression.

She responded in a businesslike air of apology, "I'm sorry, sir, but she called in sick several hours ago. She did not show up for this performance. It happens occasionally. I'm sure you understand."

He wanted to say, *'Not to my daughter, it doesn't! And no, I do not understand!'*

He was fearful even behind his ingrained military facade. *The old-line KGB is still active, and they no doubt have agents in New York City! They may be trying to get to me through Karina.*

Yobani stos! (Shit!)

Diogenes said with a sincere effort at empathy, "Viktor…, I know you are upset. I certainly would be if I were in your shoes…, but I think we should go back to our seats. Russian culture…, remember?"

Viktor took a deep breath, held it briefly, and then exhaled as he stared into Diogenes' eyes with obvious frustration and deep disappointment.

With biting sarcasm, he finally responded, "Yes…. Some *Russian* culture…,while my daughter is the only Russian in the ballet… and is also *'sick'*…!"

Diogenes gracefully absorbed that subtle fury as they silently returned to their seats–both without effective concealment of their obviously serious personal, but different discomforts. Although she also was disappointed, Ariel stayed for the entire performance, uneasily enduring an uncharacteristic inability to convey her empathy to Viktor with convincing sincerity. The recent discomfort among the three dissipated only slightly during the performance.

After the show, Ariel finally expressed her disappointment in not seeing Karina perform, and said, "I realize that my disappointment does not even approach what you must be feeling, but I am sure we will have another chance to see her dance!"

Viktor managed to say evenly, "Yes, I am extremely disappointed, but thank you for your thoughts…. Good night."

Then she added with a hopeful facial expression and an attempted comforting smile, "We will meet again… for that coffee…, yes?"

He turned toward her and smiled briefly without further indication of his thoughts. Diogenes watched the exchange carefully with a fleeting unfamiliar and vague premonition. He and Viktor walked slowly within the orderly exiting crowd of patrons in silence. The man in black was also disappointed as he arose from seat A115 and walked innocently behind them. He could not avoid overhearing enough segments of the conversations during the last several minutes to realize that he also would not see the latest object of his brother's desires. They all descended the stairs down into the lobby and continued in silence out the front entrance. The FBI SUV was in the line of vehicles creeping along the curb heading west on West 62nd Street near the theater. He and Viktor walked more quickly to the vehicle, got in, and rode back to the safe house in Brooklyn without another word. In less than 30 seconds, the man in black disappeared into the city that never sleeps.

Ariel returned to her home on the 11:43 P.M. train from Grand Central Station, which arrived on time in New London at 12:43 A.M. She entered her car at the train station parking lot and returned to her apartment without incident. She opened her apartment front door, habitually turned around and closed it with a turn of the master lock knob. She then walked through her dimly lit living room to her bedroom, undressed and hung her clothing neatly in her closet. After she finished her personal daily routine with a quick shower, she dried herself with a large white bath towel, put on her favorite light blue negligee, and slid between the light blue sheets of her comfortable twin bed. Just before falling asleep for the night, she opened her eyes and sustained a mild but peculiar feeling–an odd combination of fear and hope she did not recall ever experiencing before.

That colonel... Viktor Kovalenko is strangely familiar, somehow....

Within seconds, she succumbed to a deep sleep while the image of the beautiful Karina Kovalenko that had been transformed into an electronic stream of ones and zeros on its way to Ariel's cellphone in the theater... also entered the vast computer network inside the National Security Agency headquarters at Fort Meade, only because her internet protocol address was regularly monitored as that of a known double agent.

**** LANGLEY, VIRGINIA ****

Jay 'Mohawk' Reppert just finished his report about Judge Witherspoon's court-ordered computer usage files from MIT. Jay was a unique individual, 30 years old, six feet tall, and lanky. His head was neatly shaved everywhere but within a precisely centered two-inch wide swath of short dyed bright green hair from the top of his forehead to the base of his skull. His black horn-rimmed glasses contained thick lenses, commonly described as 'Coke-bottle' lenses. He was blessed with unusually healthy teeth without any cavities and in perfect shape and symmetrical alignment. He habitually flashed a perfect brilliant white smile at whomever had the challenging experience of being within conversational distance. He was a former Rhodes Scholar with a Ph.D. degree in mathematics and physics from The University of California at Berkeley. He was also blessed with an IQ higher than 190, which the CIA valued despite his unique physical characteristics, and a curiously contrasting ability to date very attractive women of any age whenever the spirit moved him–or *them*. When he was not working or dating, he entertained himself by reading or playing original jazz music on his second-hand sitar. Late that afternoon, he called the Bishop to report that he had finished his official analysis of the computer usage records from MIT.

"Mr. Bischov?"

"Yeah, Mohawk…, whaddya have for me?"

Jay continued typing commands on his computer keyboard as he responded, "It's coming right up on internal e-mail, so you can look for it… in… five… seconds…. There she goes!"

"Thanks, Mohawk."

In the tone of an afterthought, he said, "Mr. Bischov?"

With effectively squelched impatience, the Bishop responded, *"What…?"*

"Did you ever notice that in English, the word 'live' spelled backwards is 'evil'?"

Obviously grappling with what he perceived as a complete non-sequitur, Lou replied with some impatience, *"No…, Mohawk…. I really… hadn't… noticed… that…."*

"Well, those same four letters also form the words 'veil' and 'vile,' as well as the masculine name Levi!"

"That's very interesting, Mohawk…, but I have some important work to get back to, so I'm going to hang up now."

The Bishop hung up and drummed his fingers on his desk, watching his email inbox. Just 10 seconds later, he had Mohawk's email at his desk computer with an attachment that was password-protected. He immediately called Mohawk back. Mohawk promptly answered his phone.

"Yo!"

The Bishop said with obvious impatience, "Okay, wise guy, what the hell's the password?"

"Oh! Sorry, Mr. Bischov! It's three six capital 'D' capital 'D' dash two three dash three six. No spaces. Got it?"

36DD-23-36. Jesus! Where do we get these people?

"Yeah…, I got it."

He hung up the phone with a little more force than necessary, then entered the password in the current dialog box on his computer monitor and read the message.

'Computer usage was shared among many students at the undergraduate and graduate levels, as well as by a significant percentage of the faculty, and overall usage time increased throughout the most recent 12 months. Most of the usage was spread consistently across all departments, with what appear as general standard research applications, statistical, and typical mathematical applications common in scientific inquiry. One user, however, was using incrementally more time than 80 percent of all other users. What appears unusual is that this user was running one program for more than 85 percent of his usage. This program seems to be a simulator designed to show effects of different kinds of forces upon boreholes, drilling equipment and various densities of rock formations at different drilling depths. Although similar simulation programs were run throughout the examined period by three other users, few others used this particular program, which was run under the charge code for Rahim Nazari. Standard computer procedures were employed for optimal computer facility efficiency. Each user would submit a 'job' (program and input data if required) with a user identification number, department, priority number and username. However, no other program used this identification information as input, and there can be no explanation for this other than an attempt to obscure or hide something. Further investigation revealed that a small routine hidden near the beginning of the program would take that identification input and examine it for the last letter in the field of the user's first name. If the last letter was an 'A,' then a variable was assigned the value of one. The letter 'B' caused the variable to have the value of 10. The letter 'C' would assign the variable a value of 100, and so on down the alphabet. This variable was used in the section of logic designed to show lateral pressure or force underground at various distances as a function of explosive force at various depths. None of the jobs in the period examined was run with any letter of the alphabet prior to 'D' immediately after the 'first name' field, and several runs contained 'G' and 'H.' That

313

variable was rahime, rahimg, rahimh, or rahimi, indicating forces based upon a factor of 10,000, one million, 10 million, and 100 million respectively. Although no specific units of force were specified in the program, in my opinion, it is hard to imagine that they were units smaller than one pound, given the nature of the simulation. Call me if you need anything further. M.'

**** VIRGINIA ****

General Murray was at home quietly eating dinner with his wife, Ginny, when his cellphone buzzed in his pants pocket with the caller identification of Lou Bischov.

He glanced at Ginny and said, "Sorry, Hon.... I've got to take this."

He stood up from his chair and walked purposefully to his study on the first floor on the opposite side of the house from the dining room. Then he closed the stained oak French doors behind him, and said in a low tone, "Yeah, Lou.... What's on your mind?"

"The MIT computer usage report from Mohawk–looks like Rahim Nazari was working on the effects of nuclear explosions at various depths underground. Maybe someone is thinking about blowing up some oil fields, maybe disrupting the world oil market."

"Did he say that?"

"No–my conjecture. You said you wanted my take on this, sir, so there it is."

"What makes you so sure?"

"You need to see the summary he sent me. I will forward it on your secure line. Password is 36DD-23-36."

"What?"

"He's very smart, and a rather unique geek, sir. Just enter that password and read the message. It will be coming through in about 10 seconds."

General Murray received the expected message on his smartphone, typed in the password while shaking his head with a passing thought of incredulity, read the summary message carefully, then sat back in his chair, concentrating in absolute silence, hoping for a new perspective, or an alternative theory. After he finished reading the message again, he looked off into the distance without focus.

Something tells me we are all going to be in very deep shit in the not-too-distant future.

****** SHIRAZ, IRAN ******

Shiraz International Airport serves the city of over 1.57 million people. It is the second largest in Iran after Imam Khomeini International Airport in Tehran and is situated just south of the city of Shiraz, between Route 65 and the Shiraz Ring Expressway. The leased Bombardier Global 8000 executive jet had just received take-off clearance during a short lull in commercial traffic shortly after 11 A.M. and started to roar down the more distant of the two runways from the terminal building in a southeasterly direction. The twin tail engines screamed at full power as the sleek white jet lifted easily into the clear sunny skies. Somewhere in the city below, a 52-year-old man and his wife huddled in a dark and unfamiliar room, in an unfamiliar building, worrying about their only son… and their own future. They heard the jet take off. It was only one of many flying into and out of the nearby airport. It made a slow and slight turn southeast of Shiraz and north of nearby Maharlu Lake to the east. Of course, they could not know that it was on a secret and sinister flight of more than 4,200 miles. The pilot, 32-year-old Saeed (meaning 'happy, prosperous, lucky') Hadad, and 30-year-old co-pilot Ahmad (meaning 'more commendable') Farahani flew the leased airplane because no convenient commercial flights were available from Iran to their destination. Their route was well south of the People's Republic of China. About eight hours later, they approached the Sea of Japan and then turned slightly north to follow the coastline of North Korea toward a former military airport on a peninsula near the coastal city of Kimchaek, in North Hamgyong Province.

Nocturnal satellite photographs show the country of North Korea as essentially a dark land mass, bordered by the overwhelmingly obvious lighted evidence of cities and towns with vibrant economies in all other countries. Similar time-lapse satellite surveillance of the location signals emitted from all sea-going vessels greater than 599 tons show significantly fewer instances of entering or leaving the greatest part of the North Korean coast. The only exception appears on the western coast of the country near Pyongyang, and even there the amount of implied traffic pales in comparison with most of the other international traffic to and from seaports of most other coastal countries.

The North Korean air force was curiously absent from the skies during that flight. The pilot headed for the asphalt runway–16/34–the longer of the two at 7,900 feet. The other runway–02/20–was concrete and measured 7,549 feet. The landing was uneventful as the sun approached the mountainous horizon among distant late-day rain clouds from the west. The remaining almost horizontal rays of orange sunlight between the clouds and the mountains pierced the cockpit as the plane taxied to the end of the runway. Saeed then turned the aircraft to his right off the main tarmac and taxied toward a small dark gray vacant metal hangar near the most remote wooded edge of the complex, and then shut down the two jet engines. Within 10 minutes, a gray fuel truck with no external markings arrived nearby. Two maintenance men wearing off-white denim coveralls began refueling the jet in silent obedience to their special orders. While jet fuel was still flowing into the tanks, another man in a casual blue open-shirt uniform walked around under the wings, and circled around the entire aircraft, silently checking visually and carefully with his hands for any adverse maintenance issues. Someone with influence and authority had obviously circumvented the procedures for unscheduled aircraft landings at this particular airport.

CHAPTER 55
Saturday, August 22, 2015

About 6,632 miles east of Kimchaek, early evening customers kept the restaurant full, as a few patrons waited for seats at the entrance to the Russian Tea Room at 150 West 57th Street. Boris checked in with his reservation. A tall, voluptuous young Caucasian woman wearing a dark blue dress and presenting a genuinely inviting smile led him to his table near the back of the dining room at the last booth on the right. The young woman with long dark wavy hair seated alone in the second-to-last booth on the right side innocently looked up at him as he followed the hostess to the last booth with a remote hint of internal recognition. She was wearing a flesh-colored sheer blouse without a bra, and a red silk scarf strategically almost covering her breasts in a manner that allowed her to reveal either more or less with only an innocent slight shrug. Her pale cream-colored jacket was folded next to her on the seat. She was apparently on the prowl, but ready to switch gears, if necessary, by putting her jacket on. Her matching pale cream-colored skirt was partially hidden beneath the table. Boris did not look directly at her, but registered vague familiarity with his peripheral vision. He could not make any connections with immediate concentration, so he reluctantly abandoned the effort, and sat down at his table facing away from her. She had already ordered Beef Stroganoff for $39 and omitted the one ounce of Siberian Osetra Caviar for $175. She was nursing a medium-sized glass of the least-expensive French red wine on the wine menu while she waited for her main course. He immediately opened the menu his server just placed upon the table in front of him and scanned the offerings, but his mind kept struggling to identify the vague feeling of familiarity emanating from the adjacent booth behind him. He quickly chose the Veal Chop á La Soblianka, at $42, but skipped the fancy caviar and wine. He was uncharacteristically not in a careful mood. He was unable to concentrate, and that bothered him. Such feelings could lead to trouble in his line of work, and he was not prepared for that. He just wanted a break from the continuous state of awareness and vigilance–the emotional weight of his assignment and his commitment to the success of his mission. He was unusually wary in a nebulous and unfamiliar manner before he entered the restaurant, but at least he was safe in the Russian Tea Room. It provided a temporary illusion of home turf and some degree of comfort or peace of mind.

But home turf is not always a safe place, either…, now, is it? Who is she?

She opened her purse on her lap, removed a small dispenser of Jo Malone Vanilla & Anise, surreptitiously sprayed some of the liquid contents upon her wrist, and then smoothly replaced the vial back in her purse. Then she innocently brought her wrist up to her neck and appeared to attend to some errant strands of hair as she applied the remaining wrist moisture to her neck, adjusted her scarf to a more revealing location, and then innocently grasped her wine glass and took another sip, allowing for some further voyeuristic reward before she put her wine glass back on the table. The vanilla and anise scent wafted over the back of the cushioned seat into Boris' booth in mere seconds.

As if suddenly struck by lightning, he remembered. *The Cherepovetsky School of Strategic Intelligence, class of 2006! We were through for the day after graduation when she 'accidentally' bumped into me next to a water fountain in the student center. I turned around with mild irritation, but she was smiling at me in a way that no other woman had before–or since. The 'chemistry' was immediate, obvious, and profound. I had a priapism that she deliberately glanced at with an even more suggestive smile. I was 22 years old, and she was only 20.*

She turned her head enough to direct her voice more effectively and obviously in his direction, and asked softly in a warm curious tone of wishful familiarity, interrupting his mild reverie, "Why are you here?"

He responded vaguely, but with a tone of invitation to further conversation, "I'm doing my patriotic duty for Mother Russia."

He was first in his class, and unbeatable in the mental games of espionage… and a formidable fighter. Why is a man of his superior ability in the United States? No doubt because he is following the scent of something… something important. Otherwise, they surely would have sent someone else.… Who sent him? And why?

She admitted her curiosity, "And, exactly what duty is that…, Boris?"

She remembers as well.…

"You know that I am not at liberty to discuss that…, *Ariel*. You have not changed much.… The charm is still very… *familiar*."

She said just above a whisper, "I expected you would remember as much…, but you might be surprised to know who is asking certain *questions*.…"

He responded evenly, "What do you mean by that?"

She gracefully arose from her seat without adjusting her scarf, again deliberately allowing some visual pleasure at eye level, and took two steps to stand next to him, looking down at him still seated in his booth and said, "Can I trust you?"

He answered carefully, very aware of her use of feminine charms, "That depends upon what we know, and whether we tell the truth…, does it not?"

She continued, trying to maintain communication, hoping for something meaningful to emerge, "Yes, I suppose it does. Trust is rare in our world, isn't it? Particularly in our business. Once it is broken, it would take a miracle or more to repair or replace it."

After a calculated pause, she asked softly, "May I sit with you?"

Masking his desire, he said evenly and equally quietly, "Yes…, of course.…"

She sat across from him and watched his eyes carefully, assessing his focus and presumed mental state. He was looking directly into her eyes, and never wavered, but also noted what appeared below in his peripheral vision.

He continued without missing a beat, "And sometimes, we do not have the option of trusting, or believing in miracles, because the momentum of time and events not completely under our control can often pre-empt, render impossible, or even waste our intentions."

She responded softly with a hint of premeditation, "Yes…, I suppose that is true.… May I make a suggestion?"

If I follow her lead, where will that take me? Does she know anything useful? Surely, she can be of some help. She has been here longer than I have, and she has CIA contacts. She could not have known I would be here, and I was certainly not following or looking for her. This is a pure coincidence–nothing more, and nothing less. I should play it for all it's worth.

He said with a friendly smile, "Sure! I am open to *suggestions*..., at the moment...."

Also with some recognition that their meeting was pure chance and should not be wasted, she said confidently, as if she were stating a fact like when the sun would rise the next day, "After you finish your meal, we will retire to my apartment in Brooklyn and share a drink and some pillow talk in comfortable privacy."

She knows something.... I'm sure of it!

He said with an irrepressible smile, "How could I resist?"

With the twinkle of further invitation in her eyes, she murmured, "You're not trying *hard* enough...."

Later that evening, they both succumbed to their rapidly developing and then urgent, but carefully orchestrated giving and taking of mutual pleasure. They both knew it had to happen, so they made the most of their natural urges, and then quietly shared the peaceful afterglow between the white silk sheets of her queen-sized bed for several minutes. His mission had so far survived her expert intuitive satisfaction of his senses–indeed his entire being.

Although regretting the inevitable return to daily reality, he finally said, "Now..., about that 'pillow talk'?"

Clearly back into her everyday world, she asked innocently, "Do you know a young woman named Karina Kovalenko?"

He deliberately controlled his genuine surprise and said calmly with veiled caution, "Yes.... Well, I know *of* her. Why do you ask?"

"She is a Russian ballerina, as you probably know as well, and was supposed to perform in 'A Midsummer Night's Dream' on Saturday, August 22, at the David H. Koch Theater for the Performing Arts in Manhattan, but she never showed up. An insert in that evening's program stated that her position would be taken by another performer by the name of Allison Connors. By sheer coincidence, I was sitting in the balcony of the theater that evening right next to a man I soon discovered was her father, Colonel Viktor Kovalenko. During a brief conversation with him before the performance was to start, I got his phone number. Actually, I got two phone numbers–one from his personal phone, and the other I presume was his FBI phone. He was obviously surprised and quite upset by what he read in the insert, and left his seat for a while, and then returned about 15 minutes later. Another man left with him and returned with him. I don't know who he was, but he was young, large, and probably very strong, and left after the performance with the colonel. My guess is that he was an FBI agent. Colonel Kovalenko was extracted from Russia on a United States submarine sometime before Friday, August 21. That's the day I overheard a United States Navy sailor at a bar in New London, Connecticut talking about recently having picked up 'a passenger' in the Baltic Sea. He did not know the correct name of the person they picked up but said something approximating his real name. I figured it out at the theater. I do not think Colonel Kovalenko was allowed to run free in this country after being picked up by a submarine, so that big guy was probably responsible for him after he left the sub. Now..., back to my first question: Why are *you* here?"

He was still recovering from the virtual onslaught of this remarkably coincidental and useful information as he said, "You might have some difficulty believing what I have to say, but before I say it, you must understand that I must trust you completely–first, because of the sensitivity of the information, and second, equally important, because I could use your help, and that personal phone number. You will understand what I mean by that after I tell you certain things that I had not intended to tell anyone at all. You must promise me that you will keep what I have to say to yourself. Are you willing to do that?"

She looked at him with a quizzical expression and started to wonder about the coincidence of their meeting, the ultimate in overdue refreshing sexual intimacy, and now this unexpected intuitive fear creeping into her life. She already knew Boris was an exceptional individual, but she had not anticipated this degree of 'unusual' and the current beginnings of completely unexpected fear. She knew herself well enough to believe that she could not just walk away from this series of coincidences and enjoy whatever scarcely sufficient peace of mind was still possible in her complicated life. She had been contaminated or infected with unplanned circumstances and their unknown origins and implications. However, the sex was great. She had to have trusted him enough for that, so she would trust him once again.

She responded as convincingly as she could, "Yes. For certain personal reasons, I do not believe I have much of a choice."

After a few final seconds of obvious reconsideration, he continued, "I am acting under the highest authority. My mission is twofold, but one does not necessarily have priority over the other, because I believe the two are connected in important ways. I need to find Colonel Kovalenko. I need to know what he knows."

She responded immediately with a business-like attitude, "I think I can help there, because I have already met him, I know what he looks like, and I know what his handler looks like. I also believe that he is currently located in the greater New York metropolitan area, and I have both of his telephone numbers after having suggested to him that we meet for coffee sometime. Now, what's the second part?"

He hesitated for several seconds, trying to appreciate what his life would become after sharing the second part of his mission with a known double-agent... an *attractive female* double-agent. Again, he did not have much of a choice. She was intelligent, experienced, quite capable, and his task required success, regardless of the methods employed. Time was not on his side, and he needed all the help he could get, and whenever he could get it.

He said directly and without emotion, "The second part is to find... and secure... a missing Russian MK-4 nuclear explosive device removed from the military installation at Chelyabinsk, of which Colonel Kovalenko was the commanding officer."

The 'coincidence' of their meeting that evening suddenly added another significantly different and more complicated dimension to her already complex life.

"*Ooohhh mmmyyy God!* At Cherepovetsky this scenario was just a theoretical classroom exercise! And now..., you believe this is real? It is actually... *happening?*"

"Yes! *Absolutely!*"

She waited several moments, uncharacteristically stalled without an urgent bright idea, but then asked an obvious question just to keep the conversation going and try to generate some useful new thoughts.

"Do you have any idea yet where it is or who is responsible for taking it?"

"I do not have many solid facts. I am proceeding according to my best evaluation of the few facts I do have, information fed to me by the people upstairs, intuition, and the implications of certain unsubstantiated rumors. My biggest problem is that I do not know anything about the time schedule. This could be immediate, or it could be merely in the early planning stages. I simply do not know at this point. If it is immediate, then we are facing a very unpleasant future indeed, particularly if retaliation or escalation develops as a consequence. If it is still sufficiently deep in the planning stages, then we have some realistic hope for a quiet, covert, and safe resolution. What disturbs me the most is that we already know that the device is moving. We just do not know how fast, where, or in what direction. I cannot responsibly assume that this problem is not of the most urgent kind. It is almost literally an enormous time bomb."

"If what you say is true, as I believe it is, because of the tangential, but consistent events I related to you about Colonel Kovalenko, then you are going to need all the help you can get! Your presence here suggests to me that you have some reason to believe that the target is in the United States. Is that what you are thinking?"

"Yes. But it is just a guess. My assumption is that money, greed, and fanaticism were the kindling for this fire. No competent government in the traditional nuclear club would willingly allow the release of a nuclear device under *any* circumstances! I still have that much faith in humanity, regardless of politics. However, to the best of my imagination, it appears that the United States is the most obviously hated nation by those who hate enough to want to use such a weapon without sanction. That kind of hate does not respect any political or religious foundation other than its own and obviously intends to maximize indiscriminate damage and death. So, who do we know about who preaches death so clearly for those who are not of the only 'correct' political or religious orientation? Who strives for death as opposed to life? If we were talking about some other conventional weapon, then I would have no clue. That leads me to believe that radical religious extremists are at work somewhere in the pipeline, and the source of the necessary money is criminal or private as opposed to state-sponsored, and it is very sympathetic to their cause. The most visible extremists lately are Muslim or ISIS radicals, or remnants of the former Bin Laden organization. No other people or group I am aware of would have the fanatical drive, political muscle, or money to orchestrate what I think is going on. No responsible or financially visible official agency would knowingly fork over the money necessary to finance a terrorist plot. Furthermore, a responsible government would not even attempt to do it even surreptitiously because of the inevitability of discovery and undoubtedly subsequent severe condemnation, or sanctions, if not worse, by the world community. The modern world is simply too complex to expect absolute secrecy to survive un-discovered forever. You and I are living examples of why secrets are variable in their durability. That is also the reason I require your trust and dedication to keeping what I know–what *we* know–strictly guarded until the time is right to enlist greater, and by implication, more visible support with more-convinc-ing information, organization, and facts. We cannot afford to look like fringe witch-hunters or careless paranoid psychotics crying 'wolf' in the dark. The world's political chess board is not a place where the players carelessly leave soiled shoes or footprints behind. Russian authorities are too proud and too embarrassed to go public with this yet, and they are quite fearful of internal collusion. Unfortunately, they are also under the cloud of suggestive rumors and certain small facts that point to this much larger potential danger. Ho-wever, they are not yet able to speak definitively enough to persuade the greater world community that the danger is actually *real* this time, *and* that they are *not* responsible for it! That is why I believe I was tasked with finding Colonel Kovalenko and the device as quickly and as quietly as possible. If the Russian government moves too many chess pieces on the world's chessboard within a narrow timeframe, then the other players will notice and wonder why, drawing incorrect conclusions or interfering with a timely and quiet solution by forcing Russia's hand. Such notice might also find its way to the perpe-trators, giving them advance awareness of forces or strategies arrayed against them. That might allow them to take evasive measures, change, or execute their plans earlier or in some other way different from what we might expect. My superiors still believe–at least for now–that they can subdue this threat quietly and not expose unnecessarily any apparent or potential weaknesses in the Russian political-military complex. If I fail in my mission, the consequences could be bad not only for Russia, but for the entire world community."

Ariel said, "You obviously know that I am caught in between. I have pres-sures of obligation from both the GRU and the CIA. I would appreciate your giving me the benefit of a doubt. I sincerely *do* want to help you. We will be a much better team working together than we would be as two completely in-dependent agents. I may need you to keep the GRU off my back."

Boris looked directly into her eyes and responded honestly and firmly, but with an ominous hint, "I will do what I can, but my mission comes first *at all costs*. You *must* understand that."

Her body sustained a rare flash of intense internal heat, fearing that he would indeed kill her–if necessary–as he said, 'at all costs.'

She responded bravely despite her hidden anxiety, "So…, do we have an understanding to cooperate?"

With finality, he responded, "Yes. Let's get the job done!"

**** CRAWLEY, ENGLAND ****

Lawrence Thompson took a taxi from his modest old home on Eglise Road in Warlingham to Gatwick Airport, about 29.5 miles south of central London on the M-23 highway. He did not know how long his business trip would last, and he did not want to pay the equivalent of $16.75 per day in parking fees at the airport. An hour after he arrived at the airport, he boarded the Boeing 737, Turkish Airlines Flight 1964, scheduled to leave Gatwick at 11:55 A.M. The three-hour and 50-minute non-stop flight arrived at Istanbul Sabina Gokoen airport at 5:45 P.M. local time. He gathered his minimal carry-on brown leather luggage, walked through the arrival terminal, and tolerated an unexpectedly brief customs examination. Then he proceeded out to the street, where he found one of the ubiquitous white Hyundai taxis. He told the driver to take him to the Adamar Hotel on Catalcesme Street, which is about a block away from the Zen Store on Cagaloglu Street. The driver nodded and immediately pulled out into the street, implying he had at least a mild conversational understanding of 'cabbie's English.'

CHAPTER 56
Sunday, August 23, 2015

CIA Director Miles sent a routine reply to Michael Winston at MI-6:

'All we have on the name Shamir Rahmani is that he was born in Iraq in 1976, lived in Pakistan for a time, graduated from Harvard College with the class of 1997, and inherited an Iraqi oil fortune shortly thereafter. His current location is unknown but is most likely not in the United States.'

A secure encrypted reply came back four minutes later.

Strongly advise you elevate your knowledge of Rahmani. We have curious evidence of potential terrorist plans which we believe contain his name. The following is a direct transcription of an audio intercept near the Bosporus during the evening of Monday, August 3 of this year in Istanbul:

First speaker (believed to be Rahmani): 'Consider this, my friend: A beautiful, quiet, and peaceful mountainous winter vista is spread before you at moderate distance, completely filling your field of vision. The sky is filled with gray clouds heavily laden with moisture. It is snowing lightly somewhere among the mountain peaks. Then, without apparent cause or warning, a giant avalanche cascades toward you down the side of the tallest mountain with an ominous distant muffled roar. It pushes over 10 million tons of snow, ice, trees, and tumbling boulders before it at almost 300 kilometers per hour, perhaps even finally continuing along a flat valley floor for a while before it comes to rest in a formless white pile somewhere far below its subtle birth. After the chaos, a peculiar calm and peaceful, almost deadly silence remains. Perhaps some wild animals stumbled helplessly in its path and were buried alive without any true awareness of their location or the physical strength to dig themselves out. Maybe even a mountain climber or an adventurous skier or two— perhaps more–met their agonizing deaths as well after becoming disoriented in the cold white violence, or slightly later in the extended final frigid silence. Imagine how arduous it would be to find any survivors. Think of how difficult it would be to view the future the same way as before.'

Second Speaker (A male named Kasana): 'Well? What's your point?'

First Speaker: 'Please humor me for a few moments, and stretch your imagination, Mr. Kasana.'

Second Speaker: 'Okay… I give up.'

First Speaker: 'Think for a moment about the old Arabic principle of the straw that broke the camel's back. A sudden shift in the wind, the far-off cry of a lone wolf, or perhaps a small bird landing at a critically fragile point, or maybe even a distant minor earth tremor of unknown origin disturbed the mountain just enough to break the delicate integrity of millions of tons of snow and ice tenuously clinging to the slopes of prior snowfalls. Or maybe even just one little snowflake fell at just the right delicate and strategic spot at precisely the right time to start a swift chain reaction of unalterable natural events, obeying the ever-present fundamental forces of gravity, and mother nature took over with obvious accelerating destructive consequences, yet with a certain kind of beauty… at least from a distance. Mother Nature can often exhibit such awe-inspiring beauty with her power…, even when she is violent and destructive beyond all imagination. Do you agree?'

Second Speaker: 'Perhaps so, but what is your point?'

First Speaker: 'The right kind of persistent fear, widespread fear of the unknown, can be an engine of social disintegration! If we can create enough fear to disrupt the economic system, the orderly trans-

portation of goods and services, adequate supplies of food and fresh water, and eventually the entire social order, then we shall have punished the infidels as the prophet Muhammad has instructed us, and they will be ripe for our domination. We shall have prevailed in a completely unexpected and significant manner never before accomplished nor even imagined, and even those remaining will then turn to Allah for guidance and truth, and we will become stronger yet, and much closer to our ultimate goal of righteous Islamic world domination!'

Second Speaker: 'And just how are we going to do that?'

First Speaker: 'I have a plan.'

Second Speaker: 'And that will produce another pin prick, like the USS Cole, and 9/11!'

First Speaker: 'Maybe.... And then... maybe not.'

Second Speaker: 'Exactly what are you talking about?'

First Speaker: 'You will know soon enough. The entire world will know when that 'one extra snowflake' falls at just the right spot and unleashes the avalanche of power of Almighty Allah Himself!'

Second Speaker: 'You are crazy! An avalanche will not destroy much of anything because avalanches usually occur in the middle of nowhere and away from meaningful population or industrial centers!'

First Speaker: 'When, exactly, did I become crazy? When I was born? A year ago? When I awoke this morning? Two minutes ago? Perhaps brilliance or even the sacred intervention by Allah can occasionally masquerade as madness.'

Second Speaker: 'Or perhaps the other way around.'

First Speaker: 'But it is the wish of Allah either way! I am convinced that He has given me the final plan to start the inevitable disintegration of the United States of America by destroying the infidels and at the same time free Allah's people from its tyranny.'

Second Speaker: 'And exactly what is this plan?'

First Speaker: 'To facilitate the efficient execution of your responsibilities in this exercise, I prefer that you not know that right now. Your compensation justifies your essential ignorance of the plan until your spark of realization finally occurs..., as it most surely will. And, incidentally, your initial period of ignorance may enhance the success of your part of the plan as well as your survival. You cannot confess a secret that you do not know, even under duress or accidentally in some unforeseen manner. I do not expect failure, Mr. Kasana. I expect only success! Now... will you accept the diamond or not?'

Second Speaker: 'Surely you understand that I will have this stone examined. You obviously know how to contact me, so you can rest assured that I shall return the stone with my decision. However, an agreement will not be binding until I am satisfied that my final compensation is worth the risks I most likely will be undertaking.'

First Speaker: 'Agreed. I will expect to find you at the Mikla Restaurant within the next five days. If you are not available at that location within that time, I must conclude that you have stolen the stone, and my people will find you and deliver very unpleasant and possibly permanent consequences. Do we understand each other, Mr. Kasana?'

Second Speaker: 'For the record, I do not need your token gem, and my reputation is far more important to me than your stone. If you do not trust me sufficiently, then we might as well part company right now without an agreement.'

First Speaker: 'I believe I have read you correctly, Mr. Kasana. We will meet again!'

Director Miles read the entire message with intense interest and curiosity, and said aloud to himself, "We definitely need to know more about Shamir Rahmani, and this Kasana guy!"

**** MOSCOW, RUSSIA ****

Andrea Sokolov was in her apartment, contemplating whether to alert her boss about her suspicions. She sent two identical messages–one to her boss, Marvin

Miles at the CIA using normal CIA channels. The other message was to Duke Chancellor, encrypted through System 16 to make sure her thoughts were not lost, misinterpreted, or disregarded by her superiors because she had no substantiating evidence.

> *'This is just a 'heads up'–The somewhat credible rumor around here is that a Russian nuke is missing from Chelyabinsk, and could possibly be headed for the USA, but as everyone would expect, Russian government officials deny that a nuke has been lost. However, I have reason to believe that they really do know that a nuke has been stolen, apparently by outside extremists with inside help, but are keeping it covered up while they are working very hard to find it as quickly and as quietly as possible. They are concerned about a very serious credibility problem if they reveal the story and also claim they are not responsible. A.S.'*

Duke responded within several minutes:

> *'Acknowledge your message re: missing item. D.C.'*

**** NEW YORK ****

Boris dialed the personal phone number for Colonel Kovalenko that Ariel had given to him and waited patiently through 10 rings.

Colonel Kovalenko looked at his phone display, and then finally answered cautiously, but with strong intuitive curiosity, since he did not recognize the incoming domestic phone number on his phone display, so the call was not from Vasily, "Who is this?"

"*Товарищ,*" (pronounced tah-VAH-risch, meaning 'friend,' 'companion,' 'colleague,' or 'comrade.')

Colonel Kovalenko froze upon hearing an unfamiliar voice speaking only the Russian word without a name. He waited with increasing anxiety for further communication but discovered that the other man was waiting for him to say something first.

This man did not call by mistake or dial a wrong number.... He is either Russian or an extremely good actor, and already knew who would answer at this phone number.... If he wanted to kill me, he would not call me first, giving me advance warning.... He would simply find me and eliminate me.... He does not know exactly where this phone is, so this is merely a communication..., probably useful.... But why is he calling now? Why didn't he call yesterday or the day before? Because he just recently made a connection..., or discovered something meaningful?

Unable to quell his curiosity, Viktor responded in a deliberately controlled, steady, quiet commander's voice, "Who are you and how did you get this number?"

The voice responded immediately, *"I am Major Boris Zhukov of the GRU. The highest authority has ordered me to find you and a missing MK-4 weapon removed from the storage vault at Chelyabinsk. We need to meet."*

"Under whose authority have you been so tasked?"

"Colonel Vasily Koshelev."

Viktor sustained a sudden unwelcome shiver.

Vasily would not send anyone to kill me..., would he...? That would be... unthinkable!

Several seconds slipped by before he continued cautiously, "Why do we need to meet?"

"Colonel Koshelev knows that you are trying to find the missing weapon. We have a better chance of finding it by working together than by working independently, and the longer we wait..., the longer we do not coordinate our efforts..., the greater the probability of a disaster, probably in the United States, with subsequent most dangerous international implications and serious embarrassment to Russia. We need to share our information and thoughts in private."

"How do I know I can trust you?"

"You will have to accept my honesty and sincerity for at least these two reasons: First, you know we do not have unlimited time, and second, I accompanied your daughter, Karina, from Moscow to the United States under orders from Colonel Koshelev..., to ensure her safety as a personal favor to you. I came to admire her in many ways. I would be worse than a fool—a complete idiot—to be insincere with you after having met her and, I must confess..., having fallen in love with her."

Viktor responded in obvious surprise, "You know Karina?"

"I was not at liberty to speak with her, nor engage with her in any manner whatsoever, because of my mission and the clandestine nature of my assignment. I was in

female disguise, and therefore could not speak to her or otherwise reveal anything—my true appearance, identity, or my feelings. When I was assigned to accompany her, I simply had no idea... that she was so... beautiful!"

This guy is either a world-class con artist, or he is genuinely truthful. I do not have the time for the former, so meeting could be acceptable. He obviously knows Vasily and I are friends. He would be an utter fool to jeopardize his professional position by dishonoring a close friend of his commander. However, I still must judge for myself. The GRU does not accept congenital con artists, psychopaths, or stupid and careless people. Nevertheless, to be absolutely sure, I will find out about him from Vasily.

"Major Zhukov, I have conditions before we can meet, as I assume you must understand. I cannot afford mistakes or deviation from my conscience and intuition at this stage of my life, nor during this critically most important mission. I need to verify your story with Colonel Koshelev. I will call you back to arrange a meeting if I am assured of both my safety and the wisdom of working together with you. Do you understand?"

"Yes, Colonel..., I understand. I will await your call."

"Then we must end this call now and proceed."

CHAPTER 57
Monday, August 24, 2015

**** *BROOKLYN, NEW YORK* ****

He walked slowly and as quietly as he could up the stairs to his room, but the old wooden stairway succumbed to his weight enough to groan softly under the partially threadbare patterned crimson carpet. The oak wooden boards hammered together over a century ago had eventually begun to squeak after having borne the footsteps of many immigrants, laborers, and more than a few lost souls with compromised pride during and since that time. No doubt, these stairs had sustained the weight of many others ascending to the second floor, where one room represented some small measure of refuge, familiarity, peace, and comfort away from the daily grind of earning a living from meager wages in an unfamiliar country–a new homeland. He sat heavily upon the bed for several seconds before reclining and closing his eyes, as the occasional mild traffic noise of the evening outside drifted into the background of his consciousness. Suddenly, his personal cellphone buzzed in his pocket. He reached for it and casually looked at the display. The caller identification was unfamiliar. He was not expecting any calls. With some natural curiosity and professional wariness, he opened the connection, and then slowly brought the phone up to his left ear.

"Yes?"

"Colonel, we have your daughter, Karina with us. At the moment, she is safe and healthy. We are honorable men, and we wish to make an exchange. You know the operational code for the MK-4 device, and we wish to have it. If you do not give it to us, then your daughter will die a very unpleasant death. Do I have your attention, Col-

onel... Kovalenko? By the way, Colonel, we are aware that you were in charge of the Chelyabinsk military base where 90 MK-4s were stored, where your inventory revealed 91 devices, one of which had no serial number. It may also become known to certain Russian officials that you were responsible for removing that 'extra' device, Colonel, unless of course, you give us the information we require."

"Who are you? How did you get this telephone number? I do not know who you are! You could be an imposter claiming to have my daughter!" *Is Logonovsky involved in this?*

"Karina was... kind enough... to tell us your phone number, Colonel.... Perhaps you will recognize her voice...."

He heard the background rustling sounds of the other phone being jostled and handled.

"Papa! They killed Mushka! Please help me! I am... NO! Stop! Mmmmfff..."

The muffled sounds of voices, movement, scratchy rattling sounds, and someone obviously covering the microphone of the other telephone, along with other sounds of a struggle and a female scream added to Viktor's hopeless fear for his daughter. Then the other voice came back on the line.

"Now, Colonel... I believe you know that was Karina, so you should also know that we are quite serious!"

Colonel Kovalenko knew the name of Karina's cat, Mushka, as his heart sank abruptly in realization that they were holding all the cards. He did not recognize any voices he heard other than Karina's. He was not accustomed to being helpless or not in control of any situation. His blood was virtually boiling with unfamiliar primordial rage.

"Exactly *what* do you want?"

"The operational codes, of course!"

"I cannot tell you what I do not know!"

"Surely you cannot expect me to believe that you do not have knowledge of the operational codes, Colonel! I know you were the commanding officer of the nuclear storage installation!"

"For precisely that reason I never walked around with sensitive codes in my head, and I certainly do not carry a note card with that information! You obviously know nothing about Russian, or any other kind of security! Those codes are in a secure location at the base! You are out of your mind if you think

I am going back there just to get those codes for you! The police or the GRU would arrest me or kill me at any moment between now and the minute I set foot inside Russia, or even one foot outside this country! Your evil plan, whatever it is, is obviously faulty and completely and insanely stupid! You have no leverage with me, and you know it! So set my daughter free, NOW!"

"I do not believe you, Colonel! Besides, she is such a... beautiful... insurance policy!"

With the greatest discipline and concentration humanly possible, if not more than that, Viktor responded in convincing, sincere, and resigned desperation as he faced the inevitable evil rushing at him.

"I must conclude that you will kill her, regardless of what I say or do, since I cannot bargain with you. I do not have, nor can I obtain the information you want in exchange for her life. I am saddened beyond measure..., and beyond words. Therefore..., I shall alert the GRU..., and the FBI, CIA, SIS, ISI, MI-6, Mossad, Chinese State Security and whoever else I can think of about your treachery with the world and with my daughter! I will make it my life's work during every second I have remaining on this planet to hunt you down! If I fail to find you on this planet, then in the hereafter I will identify your soul and exterminate it! I will punish you beyond your wildest imagination for what you are doing to her and to humanity! Your wretched belief system is full of holes and your morality is inhuman! You are evil at best! You have unleashed infinitely more determination to oppose you than you have the intelligence to comprehend! You are immune to truth and reality! But then, you are also too stupid to understand what I have just said! That is why I shall fight you–because you deliberately see the world with a blind eye, hear with a deaf ear, and think selfishly with a vacuous brain! Brute force is the only language you understand..., and *you shall have it!*"

"All life is expendable, Colonel! Maybe you can kill me. And... maybe not. However, many others believe just as strongly in the same cause. Our shared vision will survive any one of us. It is Allah's will and inevitable plan! If you find another one of us, and kill him also, then you will be just that much weaker for having expended the effort and energy to do so. Many others will follow us. We make many more babies than you do, and we teach our children the only truth! You are not the only tool of our effort. We love death and you love life, and that addiction to life is your fundamental and ultimate fatal weakness! We know others who have access to the secrets of your

world–the secrets that unleash the power of the universe to give us our kingdom in death! So, you see, Colonel, that you really have no choice! You must give us the code, or Karina will remain hidden forever, never to dance again until after you give us the code and we verify that it is indeed correct.... A pity, really.... She is such a beautiful girl, a sight to behold on the stage..., as well as off the stage..., providing so much earthly human pleasure to you infidels!"

Has this evil scoundrel seen her perform? Has he polluted her life with his vision? Was he in the theater during her debut? Was he there the day after? Has he touched her? Has he violated her? Allah's plan? He must be a truly extreme jihadist!

The phone connection terminated unexpectedly before Viktor could continue to vent his still steadily accelerating and expanding wrath. He was profoundly alone in his grief and misery beyond description for the first time in his life. He had never experienced, nor imagined such devastating grief and anger. The image of his little girl filled the theater of his imagination. He had the indelible pride of a young father, marveling at the miracle he had helped produce. Of course, she was the most beautiful baby. He watched her grow into the most precious little girl and the most beguiling teenager. Then she blossomed into the strikingly beautiful young woman who just wanted to dance. It was her life force and her unique passion. She told him several times that all she wanted in life was to dance. He knew, however, that one day her special beauty, vibrant personality, and warm natural charm would irrevocably captivate some young man somewhere. Perhaps that had already happened to Boris. She would meet someone who would give her the happiness she deserved, and who would protect her, taking some of the paternal burden away from him, and they would marry. It was inevitable. It was the design of life as he knew it. It was his most profound hope. But now, because of someone else's narrow-minded and selfish arrogance, some *evil* people had taken her, and in so doing, had taken most of his future and his fondest hopes. Life is nothing without hope, without that special bond between two people. He removed from his wallet the 6-year-old dog-eared photograph of Karina on her eighteenth birthday and just stared at it. She was certainly the most beautiful young woman. She had her mother's ice-blue eyes, and that inescapably captivating bright smile, her blonde hair was neatly trimmed in a shorter style. Then he activated his cellphone to view the most recent photograph of her–the one he had taken at the Sheremetyevo airport before she left for the United States. The same beautiful eyes returned his gaze. Her smile told him she loved him. Her hair was tied back in a naturally wavy ponytail, accentuating her delicate classic facial features. She was his little girl, striking out on her own for the first time and with such invigorating hope and promise. His reminiscence melted into unfamiliar anger and stifling rage as he looked away from the image on his phone. He could not defeat the constantly surging animalistic urge for revenge–the demand for the repair of his soul, and the need to save his precious Karina. He needed to eliminate her captors his own way. It would insult his self-image, his personal history, his military status, and his right as an individual in the human community, *but he would do it!* He would make it the purpose of the rest of his life and beyond that. Mentally exhausted, he instantly relaxed upon the bed, and quickly succumbed to overdue sleep, so completely overcome by torment that his body naturally shut down to save itself.

**** CHICAGO, ILLINOIS ****

Shortly after 4:05 P.M. near the corner of West 65th Street and South Ashland Avenue, two stocky men in their early thirties wearing cheap, dark rumpled suits and open-collared casual shirts with no ties walked innocently toward the rear of a vacant shiny black 2001 Cadillac hearse with a matching black vinyl top and a dozen common useless custom chrome ornaments. They casually looked around the vehicle parked on the north side of West 65th Street while approaching both front doors simultaneously, one from each side. As if he owned the vehicle, Yuri Kopov opened the driver's door, while Sergei Nikulin opened the passenger door. Within a minute, the driver efficiently hot-wired the ignition, and the Cadillac engine responded as expected. Yuri retrieved his portable Garmin Nuvi 2599LMTHD GPS receiver from his right pocket and mounted it on the inside of the windshield with its rubber suction-cup base, and then started following the directions from the shallow unemotional female voice emanating from its tiny speaker that sounded remarkably like the one at a McDonald's drive-through order station. He drove a little more than a block to South Ashland Avenue and turned left onto West Marquette Road. A hearse in that area of Chicago was not unusual, since several funeral homes were within a quarter of a mile radius of that location, and temporary street parking was customary and often ignored by the police. The driver continued to a right turn onto South Lafayette toward the I-94 East ramp, which then joined I-94 southbound traffic. Within 15 minutes, the hearse moved onto I-57 South toward Memphis. An hour later, the driver took exit 212 onto US Route 36 toward Tuscola, and then to Illinois Route 130 South to Illinois Route 33 East, which then became Main Street in Oblong, Illinois. Yuri turned right onto South Grant Street just before the Pulliam Funeral Home and continued south to East Kentucky Street. The hearse with Illinois license plates then turned east onto East Kentucky Street, past North Johnson Street on the left, still moving cautiously just under the 25-mile-per-hour posted speed limit. Yuri was trying not to provoke the nearest unseen suspicious or conscientious local police officer patiently waiting in a hidden patrol car. They continued through the unfamiliar, quiet, and peaceful old residential area filled with hard-working, God-fearing, grass roots American citizens. The hearse headlights illuminated the mostly empty streets in the early evening dusk under overcast skies almost four hours after leaving South Chicago. Yuri drove slowly toward to the edge of town and approached the southern perimeter of about 34 perfectly flat acres of grassy land filled with final resting places, some of which were sacred, and others probably not. The mostly uniform lush green grass had been mowed recently, but a few hardy dandelions close to several stone markers had escaped the mower blades, and made their defiant presence known with bright yellow flowers. For more than the past two centuries, the important and the insignificant lives of some of the generations within that period of history melded into the earth at that location, leaving skeletons in various degrees of preservation, some in formerly elegant wooden boxes under a wide variety of markers, and others not so carefully deposited. Near the eastern border of the burial ground, the hearse followed the slightly cracked and inadequately repaired macadam road that curved to the north, and then veered to the left at the beginning of an interior oval circuit marked 'One Way' leading clockwise. The hearse continued closer to the center of the cemetery, then followed the pavement north before it turned to the right toward the eastern perimeter, and again curved back to the south and the entrance to the loop. The hearse stopped about halfway along the eastern length of the oval next to a small headstone about 22 feet west of the road, toward the middle of the cemetery. The rectangular two-foot-high dirty granite marker tilted slightly north from vertical and lay not quite parallel either to the road or to most of the other stone markers along a mostly straight line to the north. Small cheap plastic facsimiles of the American flag stapled to thin pine dowels stood proudly next to a few surrounding stone monuments farther toward the west. Yuri stopped the hearse, put the transmission lever in the 'park' position, and disconnected the ignition circuit, leaving the wires dangling under the dashboard for easy reconnection later. He glanced about 40 feet to his left, where a small decaying bouquet of chrysanthemums rested against a four-foot tall finely polished granite stone marker. It made absolutely no impression upon him. His focused only upon his safety and his assignment. Silence filled the hearse as the two muscular men in the front seat sat and waited. A few pairs of bright high-beam headlights moved east on Route 33 about half of a flat mile in front of them. The distant slightly muffled roar of an approaching Kenworth T880 tractor-trailer engine and the singing tread chorus of the rig's 18 tires on the road called from a distance and then steadily faded with a slightly lower frequency as the truck disappeared to the east with diminishing Doppler effect. Within a few minutes, absolute silence returned to the mass resting place. After another 15 minutes of peaceful mid-western evening and increasing darkness passed without incident, the two men exited the hearse and went to work, satisfied that no one had seen them. They spread a black body bag neatly on the grass next to where they would dig. They were efficient and steady in their efforts, as if they had done it many times before. The moon was high in the sky, and slightly more than three quarters full. The focused beams of white light from their small LED headlamps provided enough extra illumination for the task without unnecessarily attracting attention from anyone beyond the perimeter of the cemetery. They carefully removed about three inches of topsoil containing the grass cover throughout the area where they would dig. The two men alternately checked their surroundings periodically as they continued to shovel dirt away from the marker until they hit the solid target below within 20 minutes. After they cleared most of the dirt from immediately above the old wooden box, Yuri swung the pick over his right shoulder and then brought it down with force upon the top of the cheap pine box, which immediately split open with the impact of the pick. They wasted no time opening the box, retrieved the remains from the simple coffin, and hoisted them into the body bag on the ground near the pile of dirt. The two men climbed out of the hole, wrapped the human remains in the body bag, and carried it to the hearse. Sergei opened the rear door with one hand while clutching the body bag with the other. Then they pushed the wrapped human remains into the hearse, closed the door quietly, and returned quickly to the dirt pile. They rapidly shoveled as much of the dirt pile back into the hole as they could but had to leave small amounts of dirt within the grassy area where the pile had been, and their efforts still left an obvious depression next to the marker. They obviously could not replace all the grass as if it had never been disturbed, but they did a good enough job to extend the time before anyone could discover their activities, allowing as much time as possible to leave the area, the town, the county, and the state without detection. After futile final efforts to eliminate residual evidence of their presence, they returned to the hearse and got in. Yuri drove slowly away from the cemetery to Illinois Route 33 East, and followed that road to Illinois Route 1 North, just east of the town of Robinson. He continued farther north to the small town of Marshall, Illinois. A few miles north of Marshall, they stopped to eat at the Burger King on East Trefz Drive. They relieved themselves in the men's room and wash their hands. Later, after each of them finished eating a medium-rare double hamburger and a large order of slightly soggy salty French fries, they drove across the street to the Marathon gas station to fill the hearse gas tank with regular 87-octane gas instead of the recommended 93-octane fuel. After replacing the gas tank cap, Yuri entered the hearse, started the engine, and returned to Route 1 North. Less than a mile farther down that road, he exited to the right onto the entrance ramp to I-70 East.

**** BROOKLYN, NEW YORK ****

Diogenes was still asleep. Viktor looked at the clock in the kitchen and calculated that it was around 11:30 A.M. in Moscow. He dialed Vasily's private number and waited.

In a cautious business-like tone, Vasily answered, *"Koshelev."*

"Vasily, this is Viktor...."

Vasily got up from his desk, limped slightly toward the door to his office and locked it, turned and limped back to his desk, sat down, and then continued, *"How are you doing? Have you seen Karina yet?"*

"Vasily, I am well, but heartbroken, because I have not seen Karina…, and may never see her again!"

"*WHAT? What do you mean…?*"

"Someone called me recently, claiming to have abducted Karina, and said they will kill her unless I provide them with the activation code for the MK-4 that was stolen. They said Karina gave them my phone number. That is how they knew how to call me. I believe they forced her to tell them my phone number. As proof of their intentions, they gave Karina the phone, so I recognized her voice. She said they killed her cat, Mushka. I knew her cat's name, so they had to have been in her apartment. Then they took her away or took the phone away. As you know, I do not have those codes, and they did not believe me when I told them so. I must conclude that they will kill her, regardless of what I do. That is why I am completely heartbroken…, and angry beyond all imagination! However, right now I urgently need to verify a few things. Did you order a Major Boris Zhukov to accompany Karina on her trip to New York?"

Still astonished internally, but with immediate recognition of Viktor's discovery and the necessity to honor his friendship, Vasily responded sincerely, "*Yes, I did. I am so very sorry he was not close enough to Karina to prevent this madness! I am so tremendously saddened beyond imagination!*"

In a non-accusatory, curious, but sincere manner, Viktor responded, "Why did you send this man with Karina?"

Vasily hesitated slightly before conveying his most sincere response, "*You know that the modern world is not always safe, Viktor…, particularly for an attractive young woman traveling a great distance to a big and unfamiliar foreign city. In addition to the heretofore normal problems and threats in international air travel, we have the world of terrorism to consider. My position affords certain privileges and autonomy. You are a sincere friend. Karina is your daughter. She is also a national symbol of Russia's best ballet dancers. I simply decided to assure myself that she would not encounter or suffer through threatening or dangerous circumstances alone during her journey. I had hoped you would not object, but I did what I believed was right by sending someone to watch over her and protect her during her travels if need be. In retrospect, I should have told you earlier. I apologize for not doing so.*"

"Vasily, I understand your motivation. I do not fault you for that. I truly appreciate your consideration. I asked you about Major Zhukov because he called me last night, and I had to verify who he is, and what his assignment is. I do not know how he got my phone number, but that is not critically important right now. According to what you have told me, he was forthright and honest in what he told me. He offered his assistance in finding the missing MK-4. I needed to trust him as much as I trust you, and you have given me the assurances I need to have. That is why I called."

"He is my best man in the field, Viktor. He is loyal, quite remarkably capable, and above reproach. You can trust him with your life! I told him to find both you and the missing nuke. So far, he has succeeded in half of his mission. He has the full co-operation of the rest of my field operatives at his command. Your knowledge and abilities can only enhance his probability of success."

"Thank you, Vasily. I intend to work with him and anyone else who can help. One final thing, Vasily…"

"What is it, Viktor?"

"I promised the man who has Karina that I would hunt him down through death and all eternity if necessary and punish him beyond imagination. I intend to serve appropriate justice upon these people for what they have done to Karina. I believe her captors will kill her, regardless of anything else that may happen. I am not asking for favors. I am simply telling you what I intend to do.… That is all I have to say."

Vasily thought for the first time that his friend may indeed not survive this tragedy, but he also knew Viktor was a very determined man. He absolutely had to help Viktor.

"I will give you as much protection there as I can through Major Zhukov and protect you as much as I can officially here in Moscow."

"Oh NO!"

"What's wrong, Viktor?"

"I just remembered how Major Zhukov must have gotten my cellphone number! In a moment of indiscretion, I wrote my phone number down on a piece of paper and gave it to a young Russian woman who spoke to me at the theater where I expected to see Karina perform last Saturday! Either she must have given it to Major Zhukov, or he somehow got it from her! My guess is that she gave it to him, which implies some relationship between the two of them!"

"Do you know her name?"

"No…, I do not know her name."

"Do you remember exactly what she looked like?"

"Yes… of course! I was sitting right next to her in the theater–on her left, to be specific! She was very attractive, with long dark wavy hair, nice figure, nice perfume, very friendly, tall. I had to squeeze by her to get to my seat. She was only 10 to 14 centimeters shorter than I am. She was wearing moderate heels, green dress, gold jewelry. I noticed her shoes when I stooped to retrieve an insert that had fallen out of my program–the one that announced that Karina would not be performing that evening. I remember because I was so upset that I would not be seeing Karina. She initiated conversation by asking me whether I am Russian because she said she detected a Russian accent when I was speaking to my FBI handler sitting to my left. She said she was from Moscow but spoke perfect English. I told her I was Karina's father, so she must have figured out my name somehow…. Now I know! The FBI agent said my first name, but not my last name when we were talking in the theater before the performance was scheduled to start! I inadvertently gave her my last name by telling her I was Karina's father. Karina's name was obviously in the program and the insert, so she already knew that! Do you have any idea who this woman might be, Vasily?"

Vasily sustained a rapidly increasing heart rate, but said only, *"Your description does not ring a bell at the moment…."*

Viktor could not detect his friend's flushed face over the phone, and continued, "Well, if you get any ideas about her identity, I would like to know…, just to understand more about what has been going on around me. It certainly cannot hurt to know at least her name. Maybe I can arrange with my handler to meet with her at some point and learn a little more."

After a brief pause, Vasily responded, *"I will keep my eyes and ears open, Viktor."*

"Thank you for everything, Vasily. I wish you well… and hope to speak with you again before too much longer."

Vasily did not want to say 'farewell,' or 'goodbye,' or anything else implying finality. He preserved his memory of Viktor simply by breaking the connection. The safe house was completely silent for a brief period. Then Viktor retrieved the phone number stored in his most recent incoming call list and called Major Zhukov.

Within several seconds, the now familiar voice responded cautiously, *"Yes?"*

Viktor asked quietly, "Major Zhukov?"

The voice said, *"Yes. Please forgive the caution, Colonel."*

"I have verified your story to my satisfaction. However, I doubt that we will be able to meet, because I cannot go anywhere without my FBI 'friend,' and I do not believe it would be wise for you to be identified by the FBI, because that could no doubt interfere with your mission. I am not sure how agreeable they might be to inviting you into their mission, even though you have the same objective. If your mission is compromised by identifying yourself to the FBI, then Russia might have to start over with other agents, and I do not believe either country has the time for that. We will have to work together the best we can with private telephone communication."

"Very well, Colonel. In that case, you should know that our people will visit you early Wednesday morning…, 5 A.M. exactly. You should be fully dressed and prepared to leave the safe house permanently, because it will be torched after you are taken away."

Viktor listened carefully to the instructions for a plan obviously already under way and of which he had been completely unaware. He was extremely anxious about the fate of his host. He had come to admire and respect Diogenes, but his own self-imposed mission eclipsed all others. Diogenes was a professional. He was still relatively young, quick, intelligent, and strong. He would have to fend for himself.

"Very well, Major. I will be ready."

"Two local contractors will take you west."

"Where?"

"You will learn that from them…. Goodbye, Colonel…, and good luck!"

CHAPTER 58
Tuesday, August 25, 2015

**** BROOKLYN, NEW YORK ****

By morning, he was despondent after a restless night in the safe house. In the early dim light of the new day, he lay in his bed, tense and unsettled, staring at the cream-colored ornate molding surrounding the nineteenth century ceiling in need of a fresh coat of paint. His thoughts tumbled about randomly in his unsettled psyche.

Yes, I have killed men, but not women–during the second Chechen war–not during peace. My taking of another's life occurred during a 'kill or be killed' condition. They say I killed Shamil Basayev, but no one knows for sure. I did not wantonly kill other innocent people. I did not walk up to someone who was not actively engaged in actions against the state and put a bullet in his head. I killed because I was ordered to kill, because I had a mission, orders, a purpose in upholding the state, and authorized by those in power. Whether they were right or wrong, they were not evil! That is the nature of war. I was not born a soldier. I was not taught to kill by my parents, grandparents, my neighbors, or my teachers. I was taught to kill by the army because that is what armies have done for thousands of years all over the world when reason, values, and perspective fail. They took Karina from me! She was Kristina's gift to me! She was God's gift to me, to Russia, and to the world! And now God has allowed them to take her away? They STOLE her from all of us–from the future! They acted with selfish vicious and unspeakable evil intent! They could not have perceived her as a threat! They should have felt transformed by her! They should have admired her beauty and her talent! They should have protected her! But they <u>stole</u> her! It would not have mattered what I *told them. The truth would have been irrelevant to those simply so easily driven and consumed by hate or madness, blinded by their own one-sided and unexamined beliefs. They took my child because of some selfish, psychopathic drive for recognition, or to make a statement, to cause some irrational brainless obedience to ideas long since buried in the 'progress' of civilization, to punish her for no possible rational reason—or to punish me or make me do their bidding, or because... because... why? What would I gain by having an answer? What truth or peace would be in that answer? What kind of message were they sending? If I risk my life to do what they want me to do, what assurance do I have that I will succeed? What assurance do I have that Karina will live? If they kill her, am I to go on my way and forget about her? Am I not to avenge her death at the hands of evil people? Who will speak for her, if not I? Who could speak for her any better, more truthfully, any more sincerely than I could? The entire history of humanity gives me the right, the obligation, and the duty to protect my child, my flesh and blood, and to speak for her! Am I to go back to my 'home?' I have no home! Without Karina's freedom, I have no peace! I cannot forget her! She is a part of me! I am filled with hate, and I hate them beyond imagination for filling me with hate! Someone is going to pay! Someone will experience the ultimate wrath of the soul that they must know they have ignited! On the other hand, are they so stupid as to overlook that consequence! They are evil, but are they that stupid as well? Is this the kind of evil shit that Christianity says I should forgive? I must do this! I have no choice! If God exists, He had better get off His butt and stop this insanity! Some say He works in mysterious ways.... That's a cop-out! Will He stop me? What about the state? Will the state speak for her? Avenge her death? Of course not! Am I now just as evil as those who took Karina? No matter what I do, I will never have her back! So, does that mean I should do nothing? Or does it mean I should fight them with all my being wherever and whenever I find them? How can any punishment be proportional or appropriate for what they have done? Am I so full of hate that I have lost my reason? What punishment could discourage maniacs like these, or satisfy civilized people as justice? Satisfaction is small compensation! Justice does not free the soul of pain! What life philosophy can draw them away from their idiotic concepts? Certainly, history and the truth as I know it have failed to do so. I simply cannot believe that they are acquainted with any truth more real or more precious than what I believe is true. Truth cannot be arbitrary! It must be real, universal, indelible, and constant!*

In a moment of frustration, he abandoned all hope and self-control for the first time in his adult life, and screamed at the top of his lungs, "I WILL FIND YOU…, YOU BASTARDS!"

He spoke to no one. 'They' could not hear him, nor would 'they' care to know his thoughts. One other man did hear him, however. Within 10 seconds, Diogenes raced up the stairs and knocked urgently and heavily five times upon the old solid cherry wood door to Colonel Kovalenko's room with the bare knuckles of his right hand.

"Hey…! Viktor! Are you okay? Viktor! Open the door, please!"

Diogenes waited about 20 seconds without a response, listening carefully. Unknown to him, Viktor was still simmering in unfamiliar rage.

Now with increasing anxiety, Diogenes called out more urgently, "Viktor? Are you there?"

He knocked again four times. Then, after another 10 seconds, the latch clicked, and the door opened slowly as one squeaky hinge challenged the current silence. The younger, clean-shaven man wearing a white dress shirt, dark blue trousers, maroon tie, and polished black Oxford shoes stood still outside of the threshold staring slightly down, but directly, eye to eye at the unshaven older man with unruly hair, wearing no shoes, and dressed in ill-fitting pajama bottoms and yesterday's T-shirt. The innocent look of unmarried youth, dedication to ideals, belief in the future, obedience to duty, moral and physical strength engaged with self-surprising effort the deep penetrating empty stare of the ultimate paternal loss, greater life experience, wisdom, anger, hate, emotional depletion, and unimaginable vital determination.

After several more uncomfortable seconds, the younger man said calmly and respectfully, "Let's go downstairs and have some breakfast, Viktor. I think we should have a talk…, man to man…. I'll make some scrambled eggs, bacon, coffee, and toast."

Viktor waited as if he were concentrating upon reassembling his self-concept from widely scattered emotional debris, but then said in a clear calm voice with a hint of indelible pride, "I will shower, shave, and dress in clean clothes first…, and *then* I will go downstairs."

Diogenes relaxed with a small mental breeze of admiration for the other man, and then said calmly, "Very well, Viktor. I will meet you in the kitchen when you are ready."

Just 26 minutes later, Viktor walked into the kitchen at the rear of the first floor and sat upon one of the two formerly sturdy chairs at a matching old round wooden kitchen table covered by a plaid red and white plastic tablecloth. The chair squeaked for an instant while accepting his weight as he sat down upon it. Diogenes turned away from the stove and looked briefly into his eyes expectantly. After about a minute of gathering his thoughts, Viktor finally spoke.

"Someone called me last night on my personal cellphone claiming to have Karina. He wanted me to give 'them' the operational codes to an MK-4 nuclear device taken from the vault at the Chelyabinsk military base, or, he said..., she will die a very unpleasant death. He also said that 'they' would inform senior Russian military officials that I was originally responsible for removing that device from the base storage vault, and by implication still have it, know where it is, or have deliberately disposed of it in a manner unacceptable to the Russian government. I do not now have, nor have I *ever* had those codes in my head, and I am not going back to Russia to get them under any circumstances, because I would not survive that effort! I most certainly do not know where such a stolen device is located! I will not sacrifice my daughter for any reason, and I will not cower before thugs, maniacs, and liars! *I WILL NOT!* Arming the mini nukes takes about 20 minutes, Diogenes, and can be done only by trained specialists. The weapons are maintained in a ready status with a battery-powered circuit. If the battery power gets too low, the device transmits a signal to Russian outposts where trained specialists can get to it and stabilize it with fresh batteries. These devices are designed to self-destruct if they are opened improperly. Major Leonid Logonovsky was trained to arm those devices correctly. He is the only person I can think of who could be involved with whatever this evil plan is. As interim commander before I arrived, he had access to the vault. His reassignment shortly after my arrival and without my input was suspicious at the very least and implies collusion from other people at either higher or darker levels."

Diogenes briefly looked away and finished placing the scrambled eggs and bacon on the two plates on the counter next to the stove, picked them up, carried them to the table, set them down on the table, and then sat on the chair across from Viktor.

After digesting that remarkable summary, Diogenes said with veiled anxiety, "Your character is quite admirable, Viktor. However, we have a very serious problem here! This is the real world–the one in which he who is 'holding all the aces' gets to do as he pleases. However, if you give them a code that happens to be credible and almost correct, perhaps that will buy us some time and…"

The fire returned to Viktor's eyes as he responded in his commander's voice, "That will not fly, Diogenes! *'Perhaps'* is unacceptable! I know very well what 'real world' is like! I absolutely refuse to participate in their plan to use that weapon! They will still have my daughter regardless of what I do or tell them, and after whatever they are planning, regardless of how much time you think you can 'buy,' *we all* will lose her for no good reason! I have absolutely no doubt that they will follow through with their threat to throw me to the remaining wolves of the KGB! Do you really think for even one second that these people are trustworthy? You are obviously not Russian! You do not appreciate the devious and self-serving character of the old KGB hard-liners! She means the world to me! I cannot, and *I will not sacrifice her life* for any reason whatsoever! Do you honestly believe that the thugs who have her will honorably return her to me unharmed, regardless of what I do, *even if I could* give them the real codes?"

Diogenes suddenly sustained an unexpected and unique chill of fear as that thought circled like a vulture in his mind. *We all will lose her?* Within a few seconds he recovered and continued with desperately manufactured confidence.

"Viktor, listen to me! We *will* rescue your daughter, and we *will* see that the Russian military and security forces *'understand'* that you are not an available target, bargaining chip, or pawn! Trust me! Not everything in this world is accomplished through official channels, by traditional means, diplomacy, or even noble deeds. There are 'dark' channels and methods, Viktor. You know that as well as I do."

Colonel Kovalenko was clearly unmoved by this brief appeal for trust, even though it was coming from a representative of a United States government agency whom he had come to admire.

In a tone of self-surprising calm, he answered thoughtfully, "Perhaps you could give me some comfort with knowledge of what is happening in 'the dark channels,' Diogenes?"

After a brief pause, Diogenes said, "Viktor, this is one of those *'situations'* in which *any* communication would kill both the process of finding a solution and the solution itself. The end game requires the strictest essence of secrecy and trust!"

Viktor hesitated for several seconds, and then said, "In that case, and with all due respect…, if you do not trust me, then I shall have to proceed on my own. You leave me no choice."

As if borrowing a little extra authority from above his rank, Diogenes replied, "With all sincere appreciation of your perception of your situation, Viktor, that would be *extremely* unwise!"

Viktor reached for his cellphone in his trouser pocket, without diverting his focus from Diogenes' eyes until he looked down at his phone briefly, as he pressed the correct keys quickly out of recent habit to access the picture he had taken of Karina inside the Sheremetyevo Airport departure terminal. He then slid it right side up from the other man's perspective across the table between them and then looked up at his face again, watching his eyes intently.

After several silent seconds, he said in that unique combination of a senior military commander's authority and a sincere paternal tone of love while Diogenes stared at the image, "It appears that you and I are at a standstill, Diogenes. Believe it or not, this photograph does not do her justice. What would *you* do…, if *you*… were in *my* shoes…, Diogenes?"

OOOHHH… MMMYYY… GOD!

Diogenes was neither her father nor her stepfather. He was neither her brother nor a family relative of any kind. He was not even a casual friend. He was not her lover. He was not even Russian. He really did not know her at all. He was not particularly religious. However, some heretofore unfamiliar universal masculine trait welled up inside him from his toes through every bone and fiber of his body, heart, and mind as he desperately stalled for time while he continued to stare at the electronic image of an astonishingly beautiful young woman. His next breath caught in his throat. He would most certainly choose to save his loved one. Such beauty was almost sacred to him. It would be a supreme violation of everything he knew as good if she were assaulted, or killed, and those responsible would be worth no more than absolute *extermination!*

It really does make a difference, doesn't it…? Whether beauty exists in the world…, whether art, human talent, creativity, accomplishment, love, culture, passion, have value…. What kind of person…, what kind of animal would even dare to hurt

*her? What does it matter that she is Russian? Why am I in the middle of all this…
this goddamned SHIT?*

After a few brief moments of further silent reflection, and then another
moment of intense and honest soul-searching, he looked up into Viktor's eyes
as he said clearly, honestly, and with unexpected sincere conviction, "I would…
try… to… save her… *at all costs.*"

Diogenes looked back down at the electronic image of the beautiful Karina
Kovalenko for several more seconds, hoping that someday he would see her
in the flesh, experience her living presence, hear her voice, speak to her, even
hold her hand…, or just watch her dance. Reluctantly, he looked back up. The
two men stared into each other's eyes during a brief period of silent and unique
male understanding. They had just bonded. They finished eating their breakfast in the silence of private thoughts.

**** TOKYO, JAPAN ****

Lei Chang boarded United Flight 838, which was scheduled to leave Narita
International Airport at 6:20 P.M. He would arrive at his destination in San
Francisco at 11:40 A.M. local time the following day.

CHAPTER 59
Wednesday, August 26, 2015

They stopped the hearse five times for fuel, bladder relief, liquid refreshments and snack food during the last 12 hours and 47 minutes before they arrived in Brooklyn and located 137 Menahan Street. Colonel Kovalenko was sitting alone at the kitchen table at 4:52 A.M., completely dressed in his 'average American' street clothes. He was contemplating his uncertain future as he sipped from a cup of lukewarm, but tasty Green Mountain coffee. He did not know exactly where Diogenes was, but he was not in the kitchen with him, and he did not hear him stirring. He assumed that he was still sleeping. Then his cellphone vibrated in his pocket, startling him out of a misty flow of images of Karina mixed with unwelcome memories of the dark gray concrete and cold metallic fixtures inside of the Chelyabinsk nuclear weapons vault, and his anxiety in the confessional at the church in Krasnodon. He read the text message:

'Must prepare to leave in three minutes.'

That message was intercepted and deposited in the vast NSA computer system along with several million other messages. He took one more sip of coffee, stood with uncertain bravado, took a deep breath, put his cup down on the table, and then walked to the rear door. As if he were a mindless robot, he turned the lock knob slowly to the unlocked position, firmly grasped the doorknob, turned it quietly counterclockwise, and then carefully pulled the door open. Step by uncertain step, he walked outside into his dark and uncertain future, closed the door quietly behind him, and then moved just to the edge of the side alley, but not so far into it where someone could see him easily from the street. He waited uneasily. Within a minute, the hearse headlights illuminated part of the front end of the house and the alley to the left and then immediately went off. The engine was running. Two car doors closed quietly, and then about 20 seconds later another car door closed with a slightly different sound. Shadows of two men carrying a large heavy bag from the back of the hearse hurried awkwardly but silently down the alley to the rear of 137 Menahan Street. In the early morning light, they acknowledged Viktor briefly in Russian as he quietly followed them in through the rear door. The two men warily checked the kitchen and the hallway as they carefully carried the large bag into the kitchen and laid it gently on the floor. Then they quickly unzipped the bag and quietly rolled an obviously dead and decayed body completely out of it and onto the floor. One of the men grasped Viktor's arm on the way out, and urgently indicated nonverbally that Viktor should follow him in a quiet rush down the alley to the front of the building and into the street, where they both entered the hearse. The other man still at the rear door of the building had already sprayed gasoline from an old plastic sport-drink container onto the floor, the body, and over the stove. He struck a match, which immediately flared to spawn its flame, and then threw it into the kitchen. He immediately picked up the body bag, turned around, and rushed out the back door with it. He ran as quickly as he could around the corner of the house, up the alley, and back to the waiting hearse. From the rear of the house, the flames started to project an erratic dull yellow glow visible from the hearse. He threw the bag into the rear of the vehicle, closed the door quickly but quietly, and rushed to the driver's door, opened it, got in, and again closed the door quietly. The vehicle immediately moved slowly down the street with the headlights off and the parking lights on, turned right at the next intersection, and continued down that street still with the headlights off.

Inside the house, Diogenes awoke with a start from a dream about a fire, and immediately smelled the smoke now wafting throughout the house. He sprang into a hyper-alert search for Viktor, starting with his bedroom. Adrenalin rushed through his body as he fought the urge to flee competing against his urgent need to find Viktor. His heart was already functioning at peak capacity. His guest was not there. He completed a cursory, but efficient search of the upper floor, including the bathroom, and then immediately worked his way with barely controlled urgency through the stifling smoke filling the first floor. He concluded that the fire was in the kitchen but had no appreciation of its intensity. He held his breath, ran toward the kitchen, and grabbed the fire extinguisher from the wall just inside the kitchen door from the dining area, and unleashed its pressurized contents into the kitchen. However, the fire was already too advanced, and the heat was intensifying beyond his ability to withstand it. He did not see the burning body through the smoke. It was time to save himself, no matter what happens. He turned around and raced through the first floor to the front door, struggling desperately to get a breath of air. He fumbled briefly with the lock knob, opened the door, and rushed outside, gasping desperately for fresh air. Within several seconds while still moving away from the building, he pulled his cellphone from his pocket and quickly dialed 911.

"What is your emergency?"

"This is FBI... Agent... Diogenes Kikos...! A suspicious... fire is raging... at 137 Menahan Street... in Brooklyn...! Possible human injury... or fatality... inside...!"

More than 10 minutes later, Yuri was still anxiously driving the hearse through Brooklyn when Viktor persuaded him in obvious desperation to drive the 13.5 miles to his daughter's apartment at 2911 Brighton Fifth Street. Sergei quickly entered the address into the Garmin GPS unit. Within several seconds, the artificial Garmin voice issued directions. Yuri turned south onto Bushwick Avenue and continued to Pennsylvania Avenue south to the Belt Parkway. The directions took them west to Brighton Sixth Street, then south to Neptune, and then a block farther to Brighton Fifth Street near the Erynn Apartment building. A black van was parked at the curb in front of the main entrance to the building. Two muscular, bearded, dark-haired young men were carrying a rolled-up carpet on their shoulders to the rear of the van from the entrance to the building. They looked briefly toward the hearse without any deliberate acknowledgment and continued their task as if it were a regular daily routine. They had no choice. Any evidence of surprise or fear..., or any immediate dash to escape would be an admission of guilt and draw the Russians' attention with unknown, and deadly consequences. After they pushed the carpet completely inside the truck, they closed the rear doors, and each walked deliberately to the cab from opposite sides of the truck as if it were business as usual. Then the driver started the engine, and the truck slowly pulled away from the curb and moved down the street. Viktor told Yuri to wait while he went into the building. He left the hearse and hurried to the front door, stepped inside the vestibule, and pressed the buzzer button for Karina's apartment. No one answered. He tried again and waited for a minute, still without an answer. Then he turned the knob on the vestibule door. To his immediate surprise, it opened. The 'moving men' did not check or bother to secure the door. He walked briskly up the four flights of stairs to her apartment. The door was open. He called out to her. No human voice or other sound emanated from within the apartment. A small bowl of milk was on the floor near the kitchen. The furniture stood haphazardly around the room near the walls, leaving an unusually large open space in the middle of the bare hardwood floor. The room did not look like Karina would have arranged it. She always kept her living environment clean and had a particular place for everything. A pink and light-blue woman's jogging outfit lay carelessly draped over a tan cushioned chair next to the window, which was open about four inches. He checked the other room—obviously, her bedroom. It was neat and orderly with just a minor lingering aromatic hint of feminine soaps, powders, and lotions. The double bed was neatly made and covered with a white quilted comforter. Three large pink and blue pillows were arranged carefully at the middle of the headboard. The closet door was closed, and her pink fluffy slippers lay next to each other on the floor at the side of her bed—left slipper to the left and right slipper to the right with the toe ends just under the bed. All the drawers in her second-hand cherry wood dresser were completely closed without any stray fabric jammed carelessly against the outside edges of the drawers. The top had been dusted thoroughly recently, and the two-foot square mirror in a narrow brass frame hanging on the wall above it was spotless. He checked the bathroom. A small gray cat was lying lifeless on the floor with a coaster-sized pool of blood next to its head. Now extremely unnerved, increasingly anxious, and completely disappointed, he rushed out of the apartment and down the stairs to the front door, almost stumbled through it, but regained his balance and continued to run back to the hearse and got in.

Then with sudden realization of what must have happened, he shouted, "She's not in her apartment. It is still early! She should have been in her apartment! That van! The two men with the carpet! That was Karina's carpet! They did not just take her carpet at this hour of the morning! They have Karina! FOLLOW THAT VAN!"

The driver turned toward him and said, "What van?"

"Drive down the street and look for that black van we saw before I went into the building, you dimwit!"

Yuri swore to himself in Russian and raced down the street. At the next intersection they all looked down each of the three streets–to the left, the right, and straight ahead–and did not see any black van... or any other moving vehicle. All three men were unfamiliar with the major metropolitan area and had absolutely no idea where to go to find the van. With obvious desperation, the three men interrupted each other with directions, opinions, and arguments about where to drive, as the hearse moved up and down many of the streets in Brooklyn for most of the initial stages of the rush hour. Finally, Viktor exploded with an unintelligible string of rare and quite severe Russian epithets, and then sank back into his seat, breathing heavily as the other two men just stared at him wide-eyed with a mixture of fear and awe, not knowing what to do or say.

I cannot even call the police, and I sure as hell cannot call the FBI!

He imagined the scene:

Hello, I am Colonel Viktor A. Kovalenko, a Russian informant with knowledge of a missing Russian nuclear bomb. Just after my escape from an FBI safe house early this morning in a hearse, I saw two men take my daughter away from her apartment wrapped in a rug, which they put in a black van that they drove away! Right! Such a credible story!

Viktor inhaled deeply, and then quietly slid away from the current reality into a dark and remote corner of his mind. He said nothing further and closed his eyes. Yuri slowly gathered his senses, and then impatiently followed the GPS directions back to the I-278 beltway west toward the Verrazano Narrows Bridge. He paid the $15 toll in cash and proceeded toward Staten Island. The toll clerk just looked blankly at the hearse bearing Illinois plates with three men in it. She took the money like a bored polite robot and went about her business. The hearse was just another of at least 200,000 vehicles that would cross the bridge by the end of the day. She could not know that her life had been brushed ever so slightly by the brief presence of men connected to a minor thread of the much larger fabric of worldwide events that would eventually dominate her life with raw fear in the not-too-distant future. Even if she could know, she was powerless to do anything about it. About halfway across the bridge, Viktor threw his FBI cellphone out through the hearse window between the bridge support cables and over the side of the bridge into the Lower Bay about 288 feet below the generously patched roadway. His life purpose was now profoundly clear: find the MK-4 and find Karina. He could not concentrate upon one or the other. He had to do both. About eight seconds later, NSA and FBI computer systems registered the death of Colonel Viktor Kovalenko's FBI cellphone. The FBI discovered it first and concluded that they had just lost Colonel Viktor Kovalenko. Silent alarms reached FBI Director Robert Kingman prompting that conclusion.

New York City fire department Engine #332 and Hook and Ladder #175 from 165 Bradford Street in Brooklyn arrived in typical Big Apple fashion with bright red LED lights flashing and penetrating deep bass horns and sirens blaring at carefully designed frequencies and ear-splitting levels. Within a minute of the first truck coming to a complete stop, the firefighters had all the hoses out and engines pumping water through them at, over, into, and around the burning building. They extinguished the fire in a routine and professionally efficient manner, but eventually left the FBI's former safe house in ruin. Nevertheless, they managed to save the adjacent house to the right from excessive damage. After most of the smoke had cleared out of the building, firefighters and fire marshal deputies entered the building carefully, looking for the source of the fire and other related evidence. They discovered the burned body on the floor in the kitchen, along with some unique and curious signatures of arson. All the gas appliance fixtures were intact with no evidence of breakage, malicious tampering, or damaged fittings. Since self-immolation is not a preferred method of suicide, the investigators concluded that foul play had occurred prior to the fire, implying at least one perpetrator. Someone could have transported the body from somewhere else and placed it in the house before the fire started. If that were true, then at least two people would have had to carry the body into the house. That would be more likely than one very strong person doing all the work, and implied conspiracy of some sort. Two firefighters carefully placed the dead body in a black body bag and zipped it closed for transport to the morgue.

Diogenes was still watching the entire scene from the other side of Menahan Street when his cellphone buzzed as if it were impatient. He recognized the caller identification of the FBI Director. He knew he was about to be sent to the far corner of his life wearing a dirty low-class dunce cap–but more likely, something even worse than that would transpire.

He answered out of habit and duty, but with increasing anxiety, "Agent Kikos."

"This is Kingman. I just got word that the cellphone you gave our guest has disappeared–no signal. What's going on Kikos?"

With almost blind further obedience to duty and fate, while imagining the rapidly approaching end of his career, Diogenes responded mechanically, "A fire broke out in the kitchen of the safe house, sir. Colonel Kovalenko was there before the fire, and he is not there now. I assume either he escaped during the fire, or he is the one burned to a crisp in the kitchen. Whether that was planned or not, either by him or someone else, I don't know. I also don't know whether his phone was burned. The house is totaled, sir. It will no doubt require reconstruction."

"You know there will be an official inquiry…."

"Yes, sir…. I realize that…, but…"

"There are no 'buts' in the FBI, Kikos!"

Yes, there are, you bureaucratic dipshit! "Sir, with all due respect, I followed procedure–as much as I could without sleeping with him!"

"Nevertheless, the powers that be know you were responsible for Colonel Kovalenko at that location, and now he is either dead or alive somewhere else!"

"Someone else may have helped him escape…, or, may have abducted him, or killed him. Absolutely no solid evidence exists about any of this either way yet, so I would like the field of possibilities to reflect that reality…, sir. I am not a klutz! With all due respect, sir, apparently whoever devised this safe-house plan should have included another agent if Kovalenko was that important!"

"Save it, Kikos! File your report and get on with the task at hand! You'll have your say in due time!"

I'm good, but dammit, I'm not superman! "So, what are you saying, sir?"

"Identify that body and find what you lost, Kikos! I don't have the manpower to spare. The chairman of the oversight committee, Senator Phinneus T. Huffer is going to have a field day with this!"

I didn't lose him, you political bat-head! He escaped! "Yes sir. Is that all?"
"Yes! Get busy!"

Diogenes immediately arranged for an official FBI bulletin to be sent to every FBI field office in the country, including as much subjective information about Viktor's appearance as he could remember, and a brief statement that 'this person has urgent national security information.'

Another three red pump trucks had already crowded the entire street for a block in either direction, for most of the last four hours. The fire was completely extinguished, and some of the inevitable sensation-seeking and the merely curious onlookers had started to disperse. A few local male youths remained, dressed in faded saggy blue jeans and T-shirts bearing a variety of obscure slogans you would not share with your grandmother. They wanted to get their several seconds of inane juvenile antics into the peripheral field of view of the two television cameras–one from News4 New York and the other from Channel 7 Eyewitness News. One of the cameras focused upon Becky Lindquist, the eager and professionally aggressive young correspondent assigned to cover the story, with the destroyed building visible behind her. As visual transmission started, but five seconds before live voice transmission, she stared seductively into the camera lens and habitually primped her reluctantly coiffed brunette hair and smoothed her gray Emilio Pucci suit jacket with her unadorned right hand, while holding a News4 microphone in her left, clearly, and deliberately displaying a large sparkling gem on her ring finger.

I know I'm a knock-out, boys, but I'm already taken! Soooo sorry!

In finely tuned, trained official television tone, but breathless and urgent 'breaking news' manner, she said with a practiced serious facial expression, "Fire officials have informed me that this blaze was of suspicious origin, and started sometime in the early morning hours, between approximately 2:30 A.M. and 5 A.M. The surrounding structures sustained some minor damage, but, as you can readily see, this house at 137 Menahan Street right behind me was completely destroyed! My sources in the fire department informed me that there was one human casualty in the house, but the body was burned well beyond recognition, so we really do not know who he or she was at this time. However, my sources in the police department told me that the dead person had been shot once in the back of the head, so it appears that this fire was an attempt to cover up a *murder!* I'm Becky Lindquist, Channel 7 Eyewitness News. Now back to you at the studio."

She offered her own naive conclusion without any consideration of deeper threads of significance in this most recent human tragedy. She could not know its eventual international implications. She had no need to think. Her job was only to report. The television cameras lingered on her face for an unplanned period of 15 more seconds of awkward silence, while the hearse with the three Russians moved farther away, but carefully along with traffic at the maximum 65-mile-per-hour speed limit, going north on the New Jersey Turnpike toward I-80 West. Yuri cautiously stayed out of the left lanes, where he knew typical speeds above the posted limit would attract the attention of the State Police. His livelihood at this point in his shady career ironically required judicious adherence to the law.

**** BROOKLYN, NEW YORK ****

Two FBI agents–George Roberts and James Scully–were at the morgue within a half hour after the scorched dead body from the safe house had arrived at the office of the chief medical examiner at 599 Winthrop Street. They held their identification badges up in front of the receptionist in an official blunt manner at eye level for her inspection, and asked to see the Chief Medical Examiner, Doctor Benjamin Nakazami. Roberts glanced at her nameplate facing out from the front of her desk as Diogenes was on his way to the same location.

The receptionist responded, "Doctor Nakazami is in a meeting, gentlemen. I'm sorry, but he will not be available for another 20 minutes or so."

Agent Roberts leaned over Nicole's desk to present his best official expression of urgency within a foot of her innocent hazel eyes, and said, "I guarantee you that our need for his services far exceeds the importance of whatever he is meeting about right now, Nicole! Please... *do* inform him that we need to speak with him *right now!*"

"I'm sorry, sir, but..."

Scully interrupted, "Miss... we don't ordinarily just barge into this office unannounced. This is important...!"

After having heard the elevated voices in the reception area, the bespectacled Doctor Nakazami opened his office door, and stepped into the hallway.

With genuine confusion Doctor Nakazami looked from one agent to the other, giving each of them equal exposure to his facial expression of annoyance and said, "What seems to be the problem, gentlemen?"

Roberts announced, "We are from the FBI, Doctor. We need your professional expertise right now in a matter of national security..., and I am *not* joking around! We need to have that burned corpse that just arrived thoroughly examined as soon as possible!"

"I'll get to it in about fifteen minutes, gentlemen, but it will take several hours before I can prepare a report for you."

By this time, Diogenes had arrived at the coroner's office to learn whatever he could before starting his latest additional assignment. The three agents sat patiently in the waiting room and exchanged information. Diogenes gave the other two a detailed physical description of Viktor Kovalenko from what he could remember.

Scully said flatly, "You know, Kikos..., you're going to be in some really deep shit for this...."

Diogenes responded sharply, "Tell me something I don't already know!"

About five hours later, Doctor Nakazami completed his thorough examination of the body, removed his light blue latex surgical gloves, and discarded them. Then he left his examination room to report to the FBI agents in the adjacent waiting room.

"Gentlemen, my preliminary report will indicate that the body you had delivered to me was a male Caucasian, approximately 44 years old at the time of death. The cause of death was a single gunshot wound to the back of the head prior to immolation–*about 10 to 12 years prior to immolation*. The bullet was still in his head, implying something less than thorough police or forensic procedures at the time, and deliberate avoidance of proper reporting standards. It was a .44 caliber round, and my guess is that it most likely was fired by a Ruger Blackhawk 44 Magnum Revolver–just a guess, mind you."

Roberts glanced at Scully with a questioning facial expression and then quickly turned back to Doctor Nakazami and said, "How do you know all that?"

"I am one of only about 500 forensic pathologists now working in the United States. It is a very demanding occupation, because oddly and sadly enough, significantly more deaths occur that require forensic analysis than can be handled by those 500 professionals. We need several hundred more than that to perform all the work properly. That's why many autopsies are done in hospitals. In New York City, with an annualized rate of 324 murders projected for this year, I am pretty busy, many times doing two autopsies a day, in addition to testifying in court at least as many times as I examine dead bodies. All that experience gives me a pretty good idea about how people are murdered with guns, gentlemen."

Scully said, "Oh…! Well…, thank you, Doctor Nakazami. We will be in touch if we need any further input from you."

Scully and Roberts left Diogenes in the Coroner's office, walked outside to their car without conversation, opened the doors, got in, and sat uncomfortably and silently in their seats for about 20 seconds. Scully grasped the steering wheel and stared at his hands as if he were trying to grasp the sense in what he had just heard from the coroner.

As he looked up through the windshield he said, "Well…, obviously, our friend Colonel Kovalenko has disappeared, and we have a lot of work to do!"

Diogenes was still trying to process the information from Doctor Nakazami and how he was going to accomplish his most recent assignment. He walked out of the coroner's office and back to his car.

****** WASHINGTON, D.C. ******

Kingman called Diogenes in a necessary effort to reestablish a better working rapport, and said, "Colonel Kovalenko most likely doesn't know much–if anything–about New York City. He could be lost. He could be anywhere. He might even have contacts here in this country that we know nothing about!"

Diogenes said with conviction, *"I would bet heavily that he is a man on a mission–a very determined mission. And, if he is even only half the man I think he is, he is definitely not lost! My intuition tells me he is a man of substantial character and broad intelligence. He is a hardened, well-trained, and resourceful military officer who still believes in right and wrong. They abducted his daughter, for God's sake–his only child! And I strongly suspect he will stop at nothing until he extracts his full measure of justice from anyone or anything his determination requires, even at the risk of his own life. He sees those who are responsible for taking her as completely evil destroyers of beauty—the beauty of her person, her talent, her heart and soul, her innocence and all that she represents in the best of humanity. She was pure, and she gave joy to countless others with her marvelous talent. Not only that, but he feels responsible for the theft of a suitcase nuclear device because it occurred on his watch, and not because he had anything to do with stealing it. That in itself was a vital blow to his ego and his self-image as an honorable military officer, but more than that, to his self-concept as a responsible world citizen—an honorable member of the human species. He is an unusually complex man with deep convictions, and more determination than any of us has ever experienced before. He is accustomed to being in command and getting the job done—and I strongly suspect he truly believes that he has absolutely nothing to lose from this point forward."*

"Well! That's quite an assessment, *doctor!* Do you actually *believe* what you just told me?"

Diogenes was convinced that he had nothing to lose, either, and fired off a passionate broadside response.

"Yes, I do, dammit! That was 'Dartmouth' on my resume, Mr. Kingman! <u>*You*</u> *hired me! I went through the FBI National Academy at Quantico with flying colors! The least you can do is respect my intelligence and experience!"*

The obviously frustrated FBI Director absorbed that mild rebuke with some reluctant respect for its truth, the young man's unusually mature guts, and continued in a more respectful and conversational tone, "So, tell me…, how do you come to these conclusions, Kikos?"

After several seconds of recalibrating his composure, Diogenes continued, *"We had several very sincere conversations—brief, but deep and meaningful enough for me to recognize that he is not just another military officer, nor just another Russian, nor just another father. He impressed me as a very wise and complex man who has been through unimaginable sorrow and has seen or experienced real evil at one time or another. He also has a deep respect for life and duty—duty not just to a particular country, government, political party, or other short-sighted principles and philosophies—but a much broader duty, well beyond politics extending to all humanity and its future."*

After several seconds, and with reconsidered respect for the young agent, the Director said, "Very well, Agent Kikos…. I'll keep that in mind."

****** NEAR BLOOMSBURG PENNSYLVANIA ******

Yuri had the hearse radio on to help occupy the silence between minimal bits of conversation as they sped west just under the 65-mile-per-hour speed limit across rural northern Pennsylvania on I-80. That bumpy section of the interstate highway was obviously still in urgent need of repair. He had passed several idling white State Trooper marked patrol cars in the wooded median within the last 50 miles and was not about to press his luck by exceeding the speed limit. He turned the volume up.

'... *And in other national news, the beautiful Russian ballet dancer, Karina Kovalenko has been missing for the last five days. Anyone who may have information about this young woman is encouraged to call Detective Vincent DeVito of the New York City Special Task Force at 800-788-8888. Again, that number is 800-788-8888. A reward for substantive information regarding her whereabouts has been set at two million dollars by an anonymous concerned citizen.*'

Yuri blurted out, "*Holy shit!* Did you hear that? Two million bucks! Must be someone important!"

Viktor was uneasy, battling his worst fears. His daughter had not been in her apartment. Her door had been unlocked and the cat was dead. Tears started to form in his eyes.

They said they would kill her. Someone took her in that truck! Is she already dead?

His body answered with unusual chest pain. He knew his body was healthy. He was not having a heart attack. This was intense paternal heartache–far worse than a coronary because he had to live with it. It was permanent. He was trying to deny what he intuitively knew but had not yet verified–the earliest visit of unexpected and unalterable truth–of acceptance of what he could not change... *ever.*

****** CHICAGO, ILLINOIS ******

The sun had set after another cloudless day. The hearse returned to the vicinity of West 65th Street and pulled over at the entrance to a partially filled, fenced-in parking lot.

Yuri kept the engine running as Sergei turned around to face Viktor, reached over the front seat with a no-frills black cellphone and said, "Take this. The phone is untraceable. You may need it when you least expect to need it."

He turned around and reached to the floor between his legs, grasped something, and again turned around to face Viktor, handing him $3,000 in hundreds, fifties, and twenties, a PMM Makarov 9x18mm pistol with all the serial numbers filed off and a box of 30 rounds of ammunition.

Viktor readily accepted the phone, the money, the gun, and the ammunition. He looked into Sergei's eyes for two seconds, then shifted his gaze of curiosity to Yuri for another second, and then turned back to face Sergei as he pushed the items into his pockets.

Yuri said in a tone that might have meant his words would be the last ones Viktor would ever hear, "Good luck, Colonel!"

Viktor hesitated during one more glance at them before he opened the rear door and left the hearse. Yuri and Sergei bid final, silent farewells to Viktor and then disappeared into the complex underground of the windy city. Viktor started walking. He walked several blocks north before he found an unoccupied taxi and waved his arms frantically as he stepped out into the street to get the cabbie's attention. The cabbie pulled over toward the curb and stopped. Then Viktor opened the rear passenger door, sat in the rear passenger seat, closed the door, and told the driver to take him to the nearest decent hotel. The cabbie dropped him off at the Courtyard Midway at 6610 South Cicero Ave, Bedford Park, about two blocks southeast of Midway International Airport. He paid the cabbie without comment and got out of the car and walked directly into the hotel lobby. He registered for a room and paid $189 in cash for the night for a king-sized bed and far more amenities than he had found during his trip to the church in Krasnodon. With his limited funds, however, he knew that he could not stay there long, nor did he even want to. He had a serious earthly mission, and an urgently unknown period within which he had to discover the location of the missing MK-4. It had to be moving toward the United States if it was not already here. Although Europe could be a target, and even Russia had suffered attacks, the most obvious enemy of the kind of mind capable of using a stolen nuclear device had to be the United States. He also had a cosmic personal mission–to find those who had taken Karina. Viktor still had $11,147–$3,013 in United States currency, and the equivalent of about $8,134 in 350,000 Russian rubles. He had to exchange his Russian currency. He had to eat, and he had to buy clothing.

The only possible source of the activation codes would have to be Logonovsky. No one else could have orchestrated this madness. Someone got to him and offered him more money than he had ever seen or imagined. It had to be for the money. He had no obvious political life or religious preference. He was not married and showed no evidence of a relationship. If he had thought that he could get money for a weapon with a clear conscience by not giving the activation codes along with it, he would have been gambling his life against the determination of an extremist mindset, and that certainly was a losing proposition. They would certainly kill him as soon as they squeezed the codes out of him. Greed often distorts the mind.

After settling into his hotel room, Viktor waited until about 11 P.M. before calling Vasily. He would most surely be awake at that time, which was 7 A.M. local time the next day in Moscow. He dialed Vasily's number on his new cellphone and waited for the connection.

Without waiting for identification from the other end of the call, he said, "Vasily. This is Viktor. I believe I know who is responsible for the theft of the 'doll.'"

Vasily responded with caution, *"I do not recognize your voice, whoever you are."*

"Please, believe me! I am in the United States and have escaped from under the protection of the FBI."

The FBI?

Vasily continued cautiously, *"How did you get this number?"*

"I told you, I am Viktor Kovalenko…, your friend!"

Viktor suddenly sensed that he might not be speaking with his friend Vasily Koshelev. Viktor spoke first without waiting for the other person to speak first–a minor, but sometimes critical mistake for an intelligence officer. Had he waited first, he could have verified the voice before continuing. He had not considered the possibility that his voice was unfamiliar because he was using another phone with different electronic quality and sound characteristics. This was the first time he had called anyone in Russia with the new phone. Nevertheless, the lack of the expected immediate familiarity created significant anxiety.

Had the power structure recently changed at GRU? Did someone discover something about Vasily he did not want discovered? Were they monitoring Vasily's phone?

Suddenly, Viktor inhaled with the internal heat of genuine and unexpected fear. He had just made a mistake out of habit and could not change its implications.

Was Vasily compromised? Was this someone who just sounded like Vasily? Surely, I had dialed the correct number!

Vasily said, *"If you are indeed my friend, then you must think of a way to prove your identity to me within the next 60 seconds, or I will terminate this call. Others will no doubt be listening shortly, so I suggest you get to it."*

Nine of the newly precious seconds passed in complete desperate silence before Viktor knew how to proceed.

"We dined across from each other at the corner table in the library at Pushkin in Moscow on July 26. You ordered roast beef. You gazed over my shoulder at a young beautiful blonde woman sitting across from a fat old slob in an ugly brown suit at a table on the far side of the room near the window—I saw you look at her, Vasily! I saw the look in your eye, and the small turn in the corners of your mouth. I know you, Vasily…. You *wanted* her!"

Vasily noted the precise details only an experienced intelligence officer could provide or would know to present as convincing identification. For the next 20 of the critical 60 seconds of what could have been their final conversation, Vasily pondered the subtle details of what only one other human being on the face of the earth could have known.

Of course, I wanted the woman—how could I forget? But then other GRU agents whom he could not have identified at the time, or former KGB operatives could have been inside that restaurant too, watching them, or could have gotten to him later and tortured the information out of him. That fat slob in the restaurant could have been KGB! But I had checked! I had indicated by my behavior that evening to Viktor that I was sure no one knew where I was going or had followed me or knew whom I would meet. Surely, Viktor also had been careful! Maybe he was sure. But obviously no one else could have seen and known…, could have read my mind at that table at Pushkin!

He had just pronounced a fatal and irrevocable death sentence upon someone who occupied a rare and sacred place of friendship in his life. Now he faced a decision that balanced that special friendship against his own future—a dim future indeed, if he were discovered and found guilty or even just suspected of harboring a fugitive, or of withholding information about a *military* fugitive–someone with secrets precious to the State or important to the old KGB! They certainly would eventually find out if they did not already know. Surely, the old KGB, and maybe others, knew by now that Colonel Viktor A. Kovalenko had disappeared, or more importantly, might have fled to the United States. Certainly, military officers do not simply disappear in Russia without official sanction, without someone at a higher level of authority knowing about it, if not orchestrating it. They had to know as well that Karina had gone to the United States. Surely, they knew by now that the Bolshoi had rejected her. They had to know that she was no longer in Russia. Where else would she go with such talent? It was a small matter to check the airline records. They had bored into his psyche during his intelligence training and produced a thorough psychological profile. They knew that family was essential to Viktor. They knew most of his life history. Where else would he go? True friends are rare and should not be sacrificed–especially with doubt or reservation.

"All right, Viktor. I believe you. I'm very sorry I doubted you, but I had to be careful. I hope you will understand. Please call me back in exactly one hour. Use the same exchange number but change the last four digits to 8041. I need to get to a secure location and take special defensive communication measures with another device."

If the new phone rang in exactly one hour, he would have the ultimate proof that it was indeed Viktor calling him. Only Viktor knew the secret code–to reverse the last four numbers to 1408. It was their most private secret from their youthful military academy days–one special simple secret securing the bond of friendship in a threatening military-political world where trust was routinely hunted down and executed–eliminated regularly like a pestilence. They had promised that each would watch over the other in times of potential crisis. This was one of those times.

At exactly midnight, Viktor dialed the new phone number and waited. It was 8 in the morning in Moscow. This time Vasily recognized the calling number, and the fact that it was exactly one hour since his previous conversation.

He said quietly, *"Koshelev."*

"Vasily, this is Viktor. You told me to call you back in exactly one hour. Now you know I am the same person who called you before, and surely you now know it is I, Viktor, your friend. Can you talk?"

"Yes.... Go ahead...."

"I have come to the conclusion that Major Leonid Logonovsky is heavily involved in the disappearance of that MK-4 from the Chelyabinsk storage vault. I do not have factual details–only a very strong suspicion. To the best of my knowledge, no one else was in a position to remove a weapon other than me, and *I did not do it!*"

"I believe you, Viktor..., particularly since the current location of Major Logonovsky is now unknown. I just discovered today that he never showed up for duty at the 821st Main Space Intelligence Center. I hate to be abrupt, but we have limited time before someone we both do not like will become aware of our discussion. Although I have taken defensive measures, one can never be entirely sure in this day of advanced technological invasion of what remains of privacy."

"I understand. Someone dangerous knows I am in the United States. They wanted the operational MK-4 codes. Someone has abducted Karina. They obviously forced Karina to give them my cellphone number and threatened Karina's life if I did not provide the codes. However, I believe they have already murdered her. In so doing, they have destroyed my life! I will stop at nothing before I have spent my all to avenge her death! I have become a nonentity. Officially, I no longer exist. Someone faked a murder in my FBI safe house in Brooklyn and burned the building. Two Russians took me away in a hearse. There should be no evidence of me now anywhere in the official world. You and those two Russians who drove me away from the safe house are now the only people in the world who know that I am still alive. I must assume that you were behind that escape from the safe house because you are the only person I told about my location, and the ones who got me out spoke Russian. Tell me, Vasily..., did you indeed arrange my escape?"

Vasily hesitated only slightly before he said simply, *"Yes. I did."*

"I had to know for sure, because if it was someone else, then that would be rather unnerving! I have made it my mission to stop this insanity, but I cannot do it alone. I must have your help!"

"What can I do for you?"

"Vasily, I fear that an historically significant terrorist attack is coming, perhaps before we or anyone else can stop it, and I believe that many, many people will die from this treachery, but we must try, Vasily! We *must* try to stop it!"

Vasily stalled, waiting for this potential nightmare to dissolve, and then out of sheer desperation, he said, *"Give me something to work with, Viktor. I need information..., facts, names, places, activity, contacts!"*

"The only *fact* I know is that the damned weapons count on the official report I was given when I assumed command was not accurate! I believe that Major Leonid Logonovsky, my former executive officer at Chelyabinsk and interim base commander before I got there, has questionable loyalties. I can think of no other avenue of inquiry. He had to know or be involved in conspiracy or falsehood. He knew about the discrepancy between the official recorded inventory and the actual weapons count. He had to know! He was the responsible officer! He might really be undercover KGB, or a GRU traitor, or some other nefarious waste of human flesh, for all I know! I trusted him as a military officer. Money had to be involved at some point in the trail. Find him, or find the money, and I believe you will find a loose thread at the border of a very dangerous fabric of conspiracy. But then, we also need to know who originated that weapons count. For centuries, or even just a few generations ago, treason used to have only relatively certain and historically small national consequences. Today it is different. The consequences are becoming international, very dangerous, and very uncertain. I am convinced that if it were not for Logonovsky's treachery, Karina would still be alive! You might also consider looking into General Rusinov's activities. He's the one who insisted to me that the storage inventory records in his orders were *correct!*"

"For you, Viktor, I shall find him! And for Karina, that her life shall not have been in vain, I shall find him and get to the bottom of this!"

****** WASHINGTON, DC ******

"Mr. Kingman, this is Debbie Heller in the research department. That body they found at the Brooklyn safe house is the former Ernest 'Rocky' Infelise—an underboss in the outfit, Chicago mob or Mafia—whatever you call it. He was arrested in Chicago in 1992 and convicted for a weapons violation, tax evasion, and running a prostitution ring. He was released on parole in 2003, apparently because of overcrowded prisons, and was then murdered somewhere in Illinois, allegedly by the older brother of a former

prostitute named Elizabeth Jones–maybe an alias–in February of 2005. We have no name for the murderer, who was never found."

"Thank you, Ms. Heller. That's very interesting...."

"Mr. Kingman?"

"Yes?"

"I have something else for you.... Off the record, please?"

"That depends upon the information...."

"Mr. Kingman..., I am <u>trying</u> to do my job! If I accidentally or coincidentally come across credible information that I believe will help the FBI do its job, then I believe I should pass it along, regardless of how I learned of it. You know as well as I do that not all our accomplishments have come from the letter of the law, deliberate intelligent planning, and official procedures.... Have I ever led you astray before?"

After several seconds of considering her point, he admitted, "No, Ms. Heller..., you haven't." *This had better be good!* "All right, go ahead..., off the record..., against my better judgement." *Now what?*

"According to the grapevine, a Russian agent by the name of 'Boris' is roaming around in this country–no prior record on file. We have no information about this guy at all–completely unknown!"

"Thank you, Ms. Heller. Now, if you will please tell me exactly which grape on which vine gave you that information?"

"I'm sorry sir, but this is one of those 'fuzzy' situations where the rules may have been a bit cloudy... a little complicated... unclear. I would suggest, however, that when you get a spare moment, you might want to check with the NSA to see whether a telephone conversation was intercepted on Tuesday, the 18th between 'Boris' and someone using a telephone number of interest: 011-7-499-884-2339."

Jesus H. Christ! We've just lost an important Russian informant with a story about a loose nuke because someone smarter than we were sprung him from a safe house no one else knew about, and now another unknown Russian named 'Boris' is paying us a visit for some reason. All this after the CIA finds an Iranian brainiac at MIT doing research with effects of large explosions, sponsored by a rich somebody from Iran or Iraq, or Pakistan. This cannot be coincidental! What the hell else is coming down the pike?

After a few moments, he called his secretary.

"Sharon, please get Marvin Miles over at CIA on the phone, ASAP!"

She responded quickly, *"Yes sir."*

Within two minutes, his phone rang, and he said impatiently, "Kingman."

Miles asked absently, *"What's on your mind, Bob?"*

Immediately, he said with a tone of casual curiosity, "What do you know about a Russian agent known as 'Boris'?"

After a few silent seconds, Miles said, *"Nothing. Why?"*

"Well, I just found out that he is a new arrival in the USA, and nobody I know knows anything about him. With all the other stuff that's going on, I can't believe his visit is unrelated. Consider this a 'heads up.'"

"Thanks Bob. I'll keep that in mind!"

Kingman hung up his phone and then called his secretary again. "Sharon, please arrange a personal meeting with General Joe Wilson, the director of the NSA *today!* It's important–any time, any place, any compromise!"

"Yes sir."

**** SOMEWHERE IN THE MIDDLE EAST ****

Among the more than six billion text messages sent every single day through-out the world, Shamir received the expected decrypted activation codes on his cellphone from Kasana, and then relayed them to Saeed's Iranian cell-phone number–09-909-221-4117–at precisely 9:11 P.M. local time in Damascus, which was 2:11 P.M. in Manhattan on the same day. The plan was proceeding smoothly and as expected, without evident discovery. The peripheral network of the NSA intercept systems snagged that digital information along with several billion other bits and bytes of data and sent it at the speed of light into the vast storage capacity of the National Security Agency computers at Fort Meade.

Then Shamir made a phone call on his cellphone to 313-713-4891.

After about 15 seconds, a deep baritone male voice answered, *"Wa-Alai-kum-Salaam."* (Meaning: 'And unto you, peace.')

Shamir spoke with self-appointed authority, "Tell Asim Haq that the plan will proceed. He must be at these coordinates–north 36 degrees, 8.468 minutes by west 114 degrees, 43.145 minutes–by 5 P.M. local time on the day of the attack and wait for a phone call. After he completes his mission, he will leave the country."

"I am the servant of the truth. I will give him money for a plane ticket and tell him to be there on time!"

That brief conversation also found its way via a secret satellite into the National Security Agency computer storage facilities to await discovery.

**** MANHATTAN, NEW YORK ****

Kasana was still in his hotel room when he received the e-mail on his smartphone from 'Uncle Harry' containing the activation codes. Within 15 minutes, he decoded the instructions according to the one-time code pad Jo-Mung Soung had given to him at the Shiodome building, and then texted the resulting two six-digit decoded numeric results to Shamir. Again, the NSA intercept systems grabbed the electromagnetic information out of the Ethernet, along with another several billion bytes during that day, and stored it in the oceans of bits and bytes inside the massive computer system at Fort Meade. His job was finished. He chose not to learn the ultimate purpose of his counterparty's activities. The device was small, and he could not imagine that more than a few hundred or perhaps a few thousand people somewhere might be injured or die because of his participation. He knew that in the universal struggle for life and peace, people on both major sides of a controversy die in noble and reckless or misguided efforts to assert their versions of the uncertain truth. Although he favored life over death, it was of no consequence to him that he was serving those who might prefer death over life. Perhaps a few buildings might fall somewhere as a message. It was not his fault that the world is a dangerous place. Thousands of people die every year in automobile accidents, gun violence, natural disasters, or simply being in the wrong place at the wrong time. Such massive death is the natural order of the universe at work in the modern social context–insignificantly paring down the growth of the world's population. They were very motivated buyers, and if they did not buy through him, they would have found someone else to get what they wanted. It was just a business deal, plain and simple, and they paid him well for his efforts. He did not judge his clients. What remained of his excuse for a conscience was free of guilt or concern.

**** FORT MEADE, MARYLAND ****

Chester Garfield was one of many proud young bachelors employed at the NSA. He was still at his desk at the National Security Agency headquarters building after 6 P.M., after a respectable majority of the 35,000 or so employees, many of them attractive single young women, had left for the day. He was idly listening to a classical FM radio station transmitting from Moscow, Russia. Then he changed the frequency for no reason other than his subconscious urge for momentary variety. While he was surfing the FM radio spectrum, he simultaneously scanned the most recent 48 hours of intercepted cellphone traffic on his computer terminal. He was not interested in voice chatter. That was usually unimportant because those who would not disguise their communications had nothing of interest to say that an experienced communications analyst would want to know. The exciting details of Ashley Doolittle's recent loss of her virginity was of absolutely no significance to him or his boss, the agency, or the country. It just interfered with the current mission. Those who communicated non-verbally and in code, however, obviously had something theoretically much more important, or at least interesting to communicate, and both the sender and the recipient were of greater importance than Ashley Doolittle. Otherwise, they most usually would not try to obscure their communication with non-verbal symbols or signals. He easily tired of listening, removed his headphones, placed them carefully upon an empty area of his workstation, and just watched his computer display of the current scan of stored traffic. He set and adjusted electronic filters to ignore signals associated exclusively with voice and to highlight digital signals more typical of encrypted or coded information. Within the next 10 minutes, something unusual appeared in his peripheral vision of his computer monitor. He stopped the scan immediately, and then carefully stepped it back in time second by second until he saw again what had just triggered his interest.

I wonder what the hell that is… two consecutive groups of digital information in a sea of vocal bullshit… identical in length, six characters each, but dissimilar in content… from one cellphone to another cellphone. That's not your everyday communication… not 'let's do lunch,' or 'I want you now,' or 'half pepperoni and half veggie.' Not in code, anyway…. What kind of code? If each character is either an English alphabet letter or a single digit, then the message in its entirety is buried in something like one in… let's see here….

He activated an Excel spreadsheet on his computer and quickly typed in numbers and commands.

That's… 4,738,381,338,321,620,000 possibilities! Super ouch! Few characters here that might reveal a pattern or a key…. Must require some kind of one-time pad, or a super-duper computer gizmo code. If it is in some other language, like Chinese, forget it! Let's at least just see… where this came from… and where it went….

It was after 9 P.M., and the challenge was becoming increasingly personal. Chester was still searching for the coordinates of the sending and receiving cellphones. He had zero tolerance for being defeated intellectually, because that might mean that someone else was smarter than he thought he was. Throughout his life, he could never leave a puzzle unsolved, regardless of how long it took him to solve it. Some took years. Giving up on a puzzle–or a code– would be a supreme insult to his academic career of straight A's from kindergarten in rural Franklinton, North Carolina through his Ph.D. in mathematics from the University of Chicago at the tender age of 22. By midnight, he had his answer. Somebody in Syria sent that message to somebody in New York City. The sending cellphone was near 33.522325 degrees north latitude and 36.273571 degrees east longitude, which he shortly discovered is Al Morabet Mosque, on Nazem Basha Street in Damascus, Syria. The receiving cellphone was near 40.7587 degrees north latitude and 73.9863 degrees west longitude, which is the New York Marriot Marquis Hotel near 45th Street and Broadway. He quickly composed a memo to the director of the NSA:

> 'I made the following discovery last evening, but without more specific detail. I thought it was worth your attention 'as is' and as soon as possible because of the very unusual circumstantial nature, and an unknown amount of time necessary to follow all the implicit leads. It is my belief based upon electronic signatures that someone in the Al Morabet Mosque on Nazem Basha Street in Damascus, Syria sent a coded message to someone in the New York Marriot Marquis Hotel near 45th Street and Broadway in New York City. That is not your everyday average unimportant communication in today's world of terrorist activities. I do not know what the message is, because I have not cracked the code yet, but I am working on it. Chester Garfield, Section 6.'

CHAPTER 60
Thursday, August 27, 2015

**** *CHICAGO, ILLINOIS* ****

Viktor awoke early, showered, and dressed. He found a branch office of Fifth Third Bank at 5241 West 63rd Street, just across the street from the southern perimeter of Midway Airport several blocks northwest of his hotel. He walked to the bank, went inside, and exchanged about $4,000 worth of his Russian money for United States currency with no noticeable extra attention from bank officials or other customers. He walked out of the bank and hailed a cab. Within three minutes, he entered a late model yellow Ford Fusion taxi. After he closed the door, he asked the driver to take him to the nearest place where he would find clothing stores.

**** *NEW LONDON, CONNECTICUT* ****

She heard the three sequential deep chimes of the C major harmonic chord of her doorbell, finished her last fork-full of salad, dabbed at her mouth with a patterned white paper napkin as she swallowed, arose from her chair at her kitchen table, and went to her front door.

They had their credentials out and clearly visible in front of them as the taller man said in a courteous but business-like manner, "Hello, Ariel. My name is George Roberts, and this man is James Scully. We're from the FBI. We would like to ask you some very important questions. May we come in?"

"Yes," she said cautiously, although she could not imagine immediately what they wanted to ask of her.

Roberts asked calmly, "Do you know the name 'Viktor Kovalenko?'"

Her heart rate immediately increased slightly as she recognized the symptoms of approaching complications in her life. She was smart enough to know that those complications would become quite disruptive if she lied. She had not prepared for this visit and certainly not this question, so she played it straight until a change became necessary.

She responded cautiously, "Yes, I recognize that name. Why do you ask?"

Roberts continued, "Do you know where he is?"

"No, I don't. Again…, why do you ask?"

"Has he ever attempted to contact you?"

"No. Not that I am aware of."

Scully said with obvious but subtle suspicion, "How is it that you recognize that name, Ariel?"

"I was coincidentally sitting next to him at the Koch Theater for the Performing Arts, in New York City, recently. During normal incidental chitchat, I discovered that he is the father of Karina Kovalenko, who was supposed to perform in the ballet that evening."

Scully continued, "So…, you don't really *know* him. You just met him coincidentally. Is that right?"

"Yes. That's correct."

Roberts was watching her very carefully and began to suspect something under the surface. His intuition was unsettled.

You just coincidentally met him, huh…?

Scully glanced briefly at his partner and intuitively read his hesitation. The two agents stood silently before her, watching her with unlimited patience, waiting for her to say something. They already knew what she did for a living. She shifted her gaze from Roberts to Scully and waited about 12 seconds for the courage to reveal her most recent and deepest secret. Her brain was racing to assess the implications of the most sincere and truthful answer– or a fabrication. She quickly concluded that she really had no idea what the implications might be.

She exhaled heavily, and then said with conviction, "I believe… that Viktor Kovalenko… is… my father."

Roberts was caught completely off guard with noticeable facial evidence of surprise.

Oh really?

After similar internal surprise, Scully continued, "Your name is Ariel *Romanovsky*..., correct?"

"Yes."

Roberts interjected immediately, "Explain, please...."

"Romanovsky is my mother's name. I never knew my father. When I had the time and inspiration, I asked her and others about him. I didn't know whether I should hate him or love him. I just didn't know him. I have gone through all my life not knowing him. Obviously, I was curious about who my father really was... or is. I cannot believe any woman on this planet can live a full or peaceful life without knowing both people responsible for her existence. After I was recruited by the GRU, probably at least partially because they knew I had minimal family ties, I periodically took advantage of their facilities and networks to try to find my father, but without much success. When circumstances changed, and I was obligated to work for the CIA, my search for him took a back seat to all the other matters I had to attend to, as I am sure you can appreciate. The bottom line is that I wanted to find the *truth*, to know all about who I am, really. I suppose the GRU believed that my relative lack of family ties would predispose me to taking obscure and dangerous missions more readily than others might agree to or be able to accomplish. I am not sure why they might have thought that. If they did, then they seriously underestimated me. I must admit that at times I wondered how I got into that secret life in the first place. I was like so many others, I guess, except that I was well above average in intelligence. I was only 20 years old, unfulfilled, alone and needed to feed myself, so I accepted the best offer that came along. Call it fate if you will. I have no other explanation. They educated me, trained me, and paid me, so I 'owed' them a lengthy period of my precious youthful life in service to the state. I became very 'proficient' at female spy craft. I suppose those very same reasons were also most of what caused the CIA to 'request' my services as a second employer after they learned about the Hamburg Siemens affair from the Bundesnachrichtendienst–the German foreign intelligence service."

Roberts continued, "I see.... So, what leads you to believe that Viktor Kovalenko is your father?"

"I received an anonymous telephone call from Moscow just four days ago, informing me that my mother had passed away due to a very aggressive form of leukemia, and that I was to consider myself to be on indefinite leave until further notice. I guess they suspected I might be under unusual emotional stress and would be ineffective in my official capacity for a while. I never knew she was ill. My work during the last several years prevented me from visiting her. That same day, I received a copy of a report compiled during the official investigation of my background prior to offering me employment. That report revealed evidence of an affair my mother had with a military man two years her senior about 28 years ago in Moscow, who she knew as 'Viktor.' The last name was not available. I imagine there weren't very many military men in that part of Russia at about the right age around that time named 'Viktor.' I have started researching that set of circumstances through contacts I still have in Russia, including some military officers, my GRU contacts and former friends of my mother. However, I have not yet received any information back from any of these people. I know my mother was not a promiscuous woman. She had very strong personal feelings and principles. I believe that she loved Viktor. Although I still have no proof, I have a strong intuitive belief that Viktor Kovalenko is indeed my father."

Scully continued with interest, "Who sent you that report?"

Ariel responded genuinely with a convincing blank facial response as she uttered, "I don't know."

Roberts interjected, "Isn't it a little unusual for your superiors to send you such a report?"

"Yes. I have been wondering about why someone did that."

Watching her face carefully, Scully said impatiently, "And…?"

She turned slightly away from him, as if trying to look into the future or find an answer somewhere other than in his face, and said thoughtfully, "I suspect that somebody upstairs knows something important, and for some unknown reason is trying to help me or protect me from something. I don't really know. I may be misinterpreting what little information I have. Maybe I have a real friend in a position of influence who I don't know anything about. Maybe someone is trying to position me for further work, or perhaps is manipulating me in some other kind of scenario beyond my current awareness or ability to comprehend."

Then Roberts shifted interrogative gears and said abruptly, "What do you know about a fire in Brooklyn on Tuesday, August 25 of this year?"

She immediately jerked her head around, faced him directly, looked into his eyes with a blank expression, and said, "Absolutely nothing! Why do you ask?"

Roberts ignored her and pressed on, "Are you *sure* you know nothing about a fire on Menahan Street in Brooklyn on that date?"

With obvious impatience and irritation, she snapped back at him, "*I just told you!* I don't know anything about it! Why are you still asking the same question?"

Scully interjected, "Because in our line of work, Ariel, sometimes people 'forget' things, and sometimes people tend to say things that are not completely true–quite *often* actually…. So, we try to help people *remember.*"

She said with evident confidence and sincerity with a touch of disdain, "You can believe what you will! I am telling you the truth! We work for the same people, do we not?"

Scully said, "We do–*full time.* You might, but maybe only *half* the time."

Immediately she responded sharply, "That does *not* mean that I do not tell the *truth!*"

Touché!

After noticing immediately that Scully had briefly lost his concentration, Roberts took over again, "Of course not. Where doubt arises, however, many times we choose what to believe, and sometimes we invent something to believe. Then again, sometimes we are simply… entirely *mistaken.*"

"Well…, you obviously don't believe in women's intuition, and you know absolutely nothing *important* about me!"

Roberts hesitated.

This isn't going anywhere. Time to look elsewhere….

Scully looked at Roberts with a suggestive facial expression, turned back to Ariel, offered his card, and said, "Well, Ariel, if anything comes to mind that you believe we should know, we would appreciate a call. We will be keeping an eye on you, of course…, and we prefer that you remain in the United States."

As she accepted his card, she responded with subtle sarcasm, "*Of course….*"

The two FBI agents let themselves out of her apartment and returned to their car. Ariel closed the door behind them and returned to her kitchen table unsettled.

THE KOVALENKO SECRET

The sun had set at 8:15 P.M., and another long twilight in Saint Petersburg had just begun under distant, orange-tinted stratocumulus clouds just above the horizon. Temperatures were falling into the high fifties, and the wind was gentle from the west. It had been another beautiful quiet day along the waterfront. In the calm Baltic Sea just north of Mikhaylovskiy Park in the western outskirts of the city, the body of a 45-year-old fisherman floated aimlessly about 56 yards offshore. Someone was sending a message. Either someone wanted the body found easily, or just did not care. Otherwise, they surely would have weighted it down to remain permanently on the floor of the sea to disappear, decompose or be eaten. The meaning of his life had faded in the diminishing memories of all but his wife and a reclusive American multi-billionaire. Duke had persuaded a proud and courageous but struggling middle-aged fisherman to transport a certain Russian defector with potentially invaluable information to a rendezvous point with a United States submarine just west of Gogland Island. Now the man was dead. Duke had used a small pittance of his personal fortune to gain the cooperation of another human being in executing what he believed was a very important task. He was determined to see that this man's death would not be in vain.

It seems inevitable throughout history that innocent human lives are lost in the efforts to save a greater number of other innocent lives. Must that always be the price? Why do I feel obligated to use my good fortune to save humanity from what I believe is wrong, or just plain evil? I am not God. I am simply human. Where is my guilt? Why must I fight those who believe just as strongly in another 'reality?'

Then he answered his own question:

> *Because they are hell-bent upon killing me and destroying my way of life…, because they obviously believe I do not believe what they believe. Or maybe another reason is plausible. What complete madness this is! Why can't everyone live peacefully with one other? Why is death the so excessively disproportionate price of not believing what is beyond proof or verification? Has the growth of the world's population itself devalued each individual life? Is that the principle of economics for humans–the greater their number the less value accorded each member? The only thing that truly sep-*

arates us is our beliefs. We all have a heart, a brain, and equivalent sensory capabilities. Skin color varies, but appearances are nothing compared to belief–the occasionally false but potent fuel that energizes the soul, passion, activity, accomplishment, and most of history!

**** THE ISLAND OF GUAM ****

After traveling 4,152 miles in the mostly calm Pacific Ocean interrupted by only two storms during the last 12 days, Destiny was visible on the southwestern horizon from the island of Guam. The moon would be completely full within two days. The yacht eventually approached the outer Apra Harbor on its way to the Cabras Marine Station within the harbor, where she would again take on enough diesel fuel to top off her tanks before resuming her fateful voyage to the east.

**** NEW LONDON, CONNECTICUT ****

The Bishop was just finishing a hamburger at The Brass Rail Café when Ariel Romanovsky walked through the front doorway to his right. He watched her walk by between his table and the cash register at the counter and continue to his left toward an empty table for two next to the back wall opposite and parallel to the front window behind him. He swallowed the rest of his glass of iced tea, stood up and took his meal check up to the cash register. He paid his bill in cash as he glanced over at Ariel, who still appeared to be studying a menu.

He walked over to her table, sat down across from her, and said, "These are treacherous times for an attractive young lady to be sitting alone in a café."

She put her menu down and asked in a calm, confident voice, "Who invited you?"

"I did. I'm the curious kind…, and I'm on a mission…."

She ignored him and picked up her menu again.

He persisted with an ominous tone as he studied her eyes for any subtle reaction, "I said these are treacherous times…, *Ariel*. We need to talk."

Now aware that this man obviously had an advantage, she put her menu down again, and calmly asked with an increasing heart rate, "How do you know my name?"

He reached into his coat pocket and retrieved his CIA credentials and placed them on the table where she had no choice but to see them, as he said, "It is my business to know people's names…, especially if they are attractive *Russian* women… who live near United States *military* installations… and do odd jobs for *opposing* employers."

He locked his signature penetrating gaze upon her eyes, and she knew that he still had the advantage for the moment, and at least polite cooperation would be best under the circumstances. He obviously knew who she was and what she did for a living, so guarded honesty would be the best policy.

She summoned a bit of residual daring and said, "If we are going to have a conversation, I prefer to know your name…, since you already know mine."

He looked carefully around the room for a few seconds, and then returned his gaze to her eyes and said in a barely audible tone, "Lou Bischov. I repeat– these are treacherous times. My information is that a Russian nuclear device has disappeared and is no longer under Russian control."

With ingrained discipline, she remained impassive only on the surface as his words registered in her head. *Oh my God! It really must be true–just as Boris said!*

He looked briefly around the dining area again, then looked back into her eyes, and continued in a soft voice, "I need you to find out whether that is indeed true, what people are involved, where it is now and where it is supposed to go, and anything else you can discover–as soon as possible."

"And… exactly *why* should I cooperate with you, Mr. Bischov?"

"First, because I want to prevent either a really tragic disaster or World War Three. Second, because you want to prevent the same things. And third, because I have friends in Hamburg, Germany, who know how a Siemens executive died six years ago at the Cityhotel."

She stared silently at his face, not flinching from his penetrating stare, weighing her position, contemplating the consequences of the possible truth in what he was saying about a missing nuclear device. She clearly understood that he still had the advantage. The Hamburg incident could become ugly, personally extremely disruptive, and unnecessarily time-consuming if he wanted to make it so. She correctly concluded that he knew a great deal more about her than she knew about him, and that he was *deadly* serious. *He* found *her*–not the other way around. Every instinct within her told her to cooperate. But she had promised Boris she would keep his secret.

She said with apparent sincerity, "I'll see what I can do. How do I contact you?"

He reached into his jacket pocket again, withdrew a business card, and placed it before her on the table. He knew that was about as much as he was going to get from her at that point, but he had planted a seed of inquiry. He had activated another relevant pair of experienced and disciplined eyes and ears in the desired direction.

"My secure cellphone number is on the back of my card. Call me–anytime, day or night. You must understand that we may not have much time to prevent what could adversely change both of our lives–forever."

That's what Boris said, also!

She just lost her appetite and slowly started to stand up away from her chair as if she was ready to leave.

He remained seated, still looking up into her eyes, and then added, "If I do not hear from you within a reasonable period, then I might get unusually suspicious. You don't want that to happen…, Ariel."

She turned to walk away but hesitated with a thoughtful facial expression, and then turned back to look at him one more time, and asked in a barely audible tone, "Are you the one known as 'the Bishop?'"

He already knew she was both clever and intelligent, and it would not be wise to be evasive. He needed her trust because it was the most efficient and fastest way to get to the fundamental and necessary truth. He had no time for games. Finding the missing nuke eclipsed *all* other professional and personal priorities.

"Yes."

Then she said flatly, "I understand you have quite a positive reputation for getting results. Is that true?"

He stood up and stepped toward her, and as he walked past her, he whispered, "Yes. Usually, I do," and then continued to walk out of the restaurant to his car.

**** *BRIGHTON BEACH, NEW YORK* ****

The storm had passed, and the sea was calm once again. The beach was peaceful and quiet just several minutes before sunrise. A couple slowly walked hand in hand parallel to the water's edge and away from the diminishing darkness behind them. Waves continued to roll farther up onto the beach with the advancing tide and then receded, as they had for tens of thousands of years. However, this morning they were more peaceful than during the prior week as if to apologize for the fury of the recent rainy, windy northeaster. Seagulls glided in the mild morning chill above the water and called out repeatedly, as they searched endlessly for any morsel of food. The regular gentle rushing sound of small waves breaking upon the beach continued with unlimited persistence. Sandpipers scurried toward the water's edge, poked their beaks into the sand here and there looking for breakfast, or merely playing. Then they turned and quickly ran back up the beach just fast enough to avoid the advancing shallow water's bubbly edge after another small and peaceful wave broke upon the beach. A mild breeze arrived from nowhere and then subsided into absolute stillness. More seagulls gathered above as the couple continued to saunter down the beach, completely absorbed in each other's presence during an infrequent period of natural tranquility. Still oblivious to their surroundings, they unintentionally walked toward the form at the water's edge.

"Martin… *Martin!* Do you see what I see? That looks like… "

"Oh my God! It's… it's… it looks like a woman!"

They broke out of their private lives with a simultaneous and urgent chill of unwelcome awareness and hurried another 130 paces ahead toward the water's edge as sandpipers quickly scattered in all directions. Cautiously, the couple continued to approach the still beautiful female form as the waves periodically lapped at her bare feet and farther up her torso and stopped just above her slim and firm waist before receding. She was lying on her back. Her striking ice-blue eyes appeared to be looking into the remote future far above her. Small waves in the steadily rising tide moved her perfectly toned young legs slightly. Her delicate hands remained at her sides in the wet sand. Her hair was soaked into a glowing long blonde silky tapestry, widening slightly over her left shoulder, firm left breast, and onto the beach. Several seagulls called out from about 90 feet above them. Martin quickly dropped to his knees, leaned over the body, and placed his right ear upon her chest. The seagulls flew higher and farther away. The most recent small waves were retreating again. For just a few moments, the human reality was completely silent during nature's peaceful sounds. He looked up at his wife and shook his head slowly from side to side.

"Sh-she's... *dead...!*"

Maria pulled out her cellphone from her pants pocket, quickly dialed 911, and brought the phone up close to her left ear as she stared at the flawless female form before her.

A metallic, heavy, bureaucratic female voice responded, *"What is your emergency?"*

"My name is Maria Stravinsky. My husband and I were walking on the beach, and just found a dead young woman at the edge of the water!"

Now sounding more interested and human, the voice responded, *"Are you sure she's dead?"*

Maria practically screamed, *"YES! I'm sure!"*

Finally, in an alert business-like tone, the voice said, *"Exactly where are you?"*

"Right near Deno's Wonder Wheel Amusement Park!"

"Please stay where you are. Someone will be there shortly."

Within the next 15 minutes, another dozen of the early morning curious, joggers and beachcombers started to gather at respectful distances from the four people standing around what was now obviously a dead female body on the beach. Two of those standing near the body were wearing dark suits, similar black laced shoes, white shirts, and dark ties.

After taking several photographs with a Nikon D7100 digital police camera, Detective Vinnie DeVito said, "My gut tells me that someone wanted this body to be found.... Either that, or it was an amateurish job. Wonder why she's not wearin' any jewelry.... Maybe someone stole whatever she was wearin'."

His partner, Dave Cassidy, responded, "You think she was murdered? Maybe she fell off a boat and floated here."

DeVito said dryly, "Definitely murdered."

"What makes you so sure?"

"I just *don't believe* that young, healthy, beautiful women just die of natural causes on a beach after a storm. Gut feel...."

Genuinely mystified, Cassidy asked, "How the hell do you know she was healthy?"

"Because her legs are toned and muscular, and her body is perfectly proportioned—no fat to speak of, belly's flat and firm. No obvious evidence of trauma. She was physically in shape. Not exactly a likely candidate for a fatal illness or a heart attack!"

Cassidy tried to assert his analytical self-image.

"You know you're not a doctor, and you're not being entirely rational here.... There's no obvious evidence that she was murdered!"

Unimpressed, DeVito said, "Evidence is not necessarily all in, and you know it. I'm a detective, damn it! I've been on the force for over 25 years! I've developed my 'detective's intuition' honestly and the hard way. You could use a little of that!"

"Okay... What gives..., *really*...?"

DeVito turned to face his younger partner squarely, toe to toe, looked him in the eye and distinctly spit out his chosen words with measured cadence, "I... absolutely... detest... the... killing... of... beautiful... young... women...! *Capisce?*"

He stepped back as Cassidy said quietly, "Got it!"

Then DeVito relaxed slightly and continued his analysis, "My bet says amateurs do not usually kill beautiful young women, and they usually leave physical evidence of a struggle. A pro did this, not long ago, and not here. The body is not cut, overtly mutilated, or even bruised, so someone wanted her identity known, or at least didn't care whether it was discovered. A message is here somewhere..., and I don't quite know what it is yet."

Another large gray and white seagull landed 15 feet from DeVito and looked around. Then the bird brazenly started to strut toward the dead young woman lying on the beach. DeVito looked at the gutsy bird, turned toward it, looked down, and stared it in the eye.

Don't even think about it! If you even breathe on that girl, I'm gonna kick your sorry feathered prissy ass all the way to Staten Island!

The bird looked up at him and just stared at his face for several seconds, then cocked its head slightly to the left. Then it turned and strutted away toward the water, while briefly shaking its tail feathers in what might have been a final parting expletive response.

Bright direct sunlight had just broken above the remaining distant storm clouds near the ocean horizon, casting long human shadows across the beach to the west from the small crowd around the fallen woman. The wailing sounds of emergency vehicle sirens somewhere to the northwest increased in intensity. Within a few minutes, an ambulance approached the crumbled end of the macadam street at the beach and then stopped abruptly. Another police car pulled up next to the ambulance. The glaring red flashing emergency lights from both vehicles continued in disparate cycles, periodically highlighting the nearby houses and parked cars on both sides of the street with red light despite the rising sun peeking through the distant remaining dark gray storm clouds. The two-man ambulance crew rushed with a stretcher down the beach away from the street to the obvious site of the tragedy. A uniformed police officer got out of her cruiser and surveyed the drama unfolding on the beach slightly lower than her position. She could see that she was not needed immediately on the beach, so she stayed with the vehicles to manage traffic control and keep the inevitably curious public at a distance. A loud metallic dispatcher's voice from inside her patrol car cracked through the early morning silence with alternating unintelligible words and electronic hisses. Within seconds, the emergency medical technicians were bending over the body, looking carefully for the young woman's vital signs, but she was already well beyond all hope of life. With rare real facial expressions of sorrow, they went about their business, lifting her carefully, as if she were a unique and delicate crystal figurine they were trying to move without breaking it. They had seen fallen bodies before, but never a young goddess like this one. They finally placed her upon the stretcher with just a little more care than usual, as if ensuring that she would be comfortable, and then covered her carefully and respectfully with a clean white sheet as they quietly talked to each other.

"Ain't never been this close to such a beautiful girl before, Archie.... Have you?"

"No, I haven't," said Archie. "A shame, really.... Whoever did this oughta be fried in pig fat!"

Dickie continued, "She's got really, *really* beautiful eyes..., y'know?"

Archie involuntarily clenched his fists and said solemnly, "Damn! *Why* did this have to happen?"

"Dunno, Archie…. Beautiful hair, too…. Never seen such striking blonde hair before, except in the movies, maybe…. A shame…. A real shame…."

"What did you just say?" asked DeVito suddenly from just behind Archie. "Huh?"

DeVito stepped around Archie, closer to Dickie and repeated himself with a clear tone of genuine interest, urgently, but without threatening, "What did you just say about her?"

Dickie said cautiously, "Uh…, I said…, uh…, I never saw such beautiful blonde hair before…."

"But you said somethin' else…, *after* that…."

"Uh…, except in the movies, I think I said…. Why?"

Detective DeVito, evidently distracted, ignored him, walked back to his partner, and said quietly in a somewhat conspiratorial low tone, "This young woman wasn't just any *regular* human being, y'know. I'm thinking she was an entertainer, a showgirl, someone in the movies, a fashion model maybe…. Women that pretty don't go unnoticed…. Too attractive, and my guess is that they usually draw a lot of attention. So, more than the average number of people should know who she is…, er, was."

"Maybe she was a really high-class call girl. You know… the ones that cater to the upper crust and the politicians, and charge thousands of dollars…."

DeVito turned and just glared at him face to face with obvious incendiary disgust.

Duly chastised, Cassidy responded, "Okay…. *Okay already!* I got your point!"

After calming down a little, DeVito said with evident doubt, "Maybe…. But I don't think so…. Let's look over on Broadway, Fifth Avenue, Madison Avenue, theater district…. Get your contacts in the media and entertainment people to help us out…. Call in some favors–if you got any left."

Sheepishly, he offered, "Got a few…, here 'n there…."

"As soon as he's done his job, we're goin' over to the coroner's office and get his take."

Detective Vincent 'Vinnie' DeVito was a seasoned professional police detective with over 25 years of service in the New York City Police Department. His dedication to finding 'the bad guys' as he called them was so intense that he pursued a case just one day longer than his wife was able to tolerate with his history of promises and protestations. That final evening together about a year ago, they both wrestled with the demons of their vital self-interests and the bare simple truths about their individual and marital lives. His arbitrary professional absence had worn her down to the bone. Everyone has limits–some deep and unknown, others shallow, delicate, and too easily bridged. Lenore had surpassed the one that required his personal and loving presence and could no longer abide his absence 'on a case.' They had lost 'it'–that precious mutual attraction that oozes excitement, fulfillment, warmth, comfort, and peace between a man and a woman, the closeness that requires regular, if not constant attendance, steady replenishment, nourishment, and tender loving care. They had unintentionally starved themselves of this vital marital nutrition–she out of traditional and eventually habitual respect for his need to work, and he out of this ingrained and mysterious fundamental need to do his absolute best to rid society of 'the bad guys.' It was hard and time-consuming work, and often mentally precluded intimacy. The decay of their marriage was an insidious and inevitable result of this clash of unexamined and unshared individual vital needs. Reluctantly, painfully, they agreed to part ways, admitting within their own hearts that they had not succeeded in fulfilling the idealistic dreams of their younger years, when sincere romantic promises and beliefs, profound sexual desire, and true love conquered all and surely would carry them to the natural sunset of their lives together. The only remaining evidence of their marriage was a son, Alphonso, now also a police officer in Chicago. After the divorce, Vinnie simply put even more of his energy into his work, and Lenore moved away. He never saw her again. Only a few two-term mayors ever learned of the reputation of Vinnie DeVito because that reputation was hidden so deep in the police department that it had acquired the character of seldom-expressed legend, known only to, if not protected by the most experienced members of the New York City Police Department. More than one term in office was usually required for even the mayor to deserve sufficient respect and rapport to be privy to that legend.

**** HWASONG GULAG, NORTH KOREA ****

A muddy olive-green 40-year-old Sungri-58 two-axle military truck with old and worn tires on the rear axle double wheels and only slightly less-worn tires on the front wheels was parked inside an unpainted and slightly rusted old corrugated gray metal garage in a remote and secret military outpost in north-central Hwasong Gulag. Wisps of light smoke rising from a single slightly rusted pipe chimney indicated a source of heat inside. The four windows, two on each side, had not been cleaned for several years. Hasa (Staff Sergeant) Paeng, the driver, checked his cargo in the back to see that it was secure, and then entered the driver's side of the uncomfortable single-bench cab. He started the antiquated 70-horsepower, noisy six-cylinder gasoline engine, originally of Soviet Russian design, and drove slowly out of the garage. Chunggup (Corporal) Seok hurried from the garage to the passenger side of the cab, jumped into the slowly moving vehicle, and slammed the door closed as the two started the 51.6-mile, one-hour and four-minute trip southeast on the Gulag 16 Road out of Hwasong Gulag toward the town of Kilju. Since North Korea had not developed an automotive industry of its own, spare military trucks were rare, and usually old. Dye-Jung (meaning 'great and righteous') Myong, minister of the People's Armed Forces secretly requisitioned the functional innocuous truck to transport a 12-kiloton device from the most recent nuclear test site near Mantapsan in northwestern Kilju County. He had taken it upon himself to sell to a Turkish international arms dealer an old reverse-engineered Iranian device with certain creative enhancements designed to increase its yield. His purpose might have been to improve his financial well-being as well as his military and political status. International assessments of the man were both scarce and minimal, but suggestive of an aggressive sycophant capable of contributing to the destabilization of the world community in efforts to elevate North Korea's international status as a country worthy of better world recognition or respect, as well as improving his position within it. The two unwitting soldiers followed their orders to the letter as they continued farther south onto Asian Highway 6 to the eastern coastal town of Kimchaek on the western side of the Sea of Japan. They knew it would be extremely unwise, if not fatal, to question, let alone disobey their orders. Compared with the undeveloped condition of North Korea, an oddly contrasting modern white Bombardier 8000 executive jet was already waiting at the western end of the only runway at the only airport within many miles of Kimchaek. It had a 104-foot wingspan, passenger capacity of 19, a maximum cruising range of 9,092 miles, and a price tag of $65 million in United States currency. The pilot's destination was 5,167 miles to the east–too far away for a return flight in the same aircraft without stopping to refuel. Such a stop would require too much time within which their location could be discovered and investigated. The aircraft normally needed 2,210 feet of runway landing distance, but its destination landing area had only about 1,800 feet of unobstructed pavement. The complex and daring nature of the mission required the perfect execution of every facet of the secret plan. Saeed was already an experienced pilot of jet fighters, but he would have to become very creative to accommodate the 410-foot shortfall in recommended landing distance. He had flown the Iranian-built Azarakhsh, modeled after and upgraded using technology from the Grumman F-14 Tomcat and the Northrop F-5 Tiger II under the Ayatollah after the fall of the repressive regime of Mohammad Reza Shah Pahlavi of Iran in 1979. The subsequent American hostage crisis in Tehran marked, if not sparked the beginning of the modern era of Islamic terrorism.

After overseeing the loading of their cargo onto the airplane, Ahmad Farahani, the navigator, and Saeed Hadad, the pilot, departed from the Kimchaek airport just before dawn into overcast skies. Within minutes after liftoff, Saeed turned off the plane's transponder. Without an operating transponder aboard the plane, it would be invisible to NORAD (North American Aerospace Defense) by any means other than radar. About 30,000 flights occur per day over the United States on average and about 80,000 flights worldwide every day. 40,516 landings occurred during the last 24 hours alone. At any given moment, about 5,000 planes are in the skies above the United States. In one year, controllers handle an average of 64 million takeoffs and landings. This particular business jet was essentially anonymous in the crowded skies.

He was unaware that the second in command under the North Korean defense minister, Jo-Mung Suong, had arranged the delivery of a reverse-engineered Iranian nuclear device, and not one of original North Korean design, so no one could accuse North Korea of sole responsibility for the outcome of his current mission. It was simply an undercover business deal between two selfish egocentric and influential men. Saeed pushed the throttles forward, urging the airplane to its maximum speed of 595 miles per hour, and set their course to the north over the Sea of Japan, around the northern Japanese island of Hokkaido, over the Sea of Okhotsk, and passing well south and then east of Kamchatka, Russia. Electronic intercept operators at the Japanese military electronic monitoring station at Chitose in the middle of the northern-most

Japanese island of Hokkaido appeared not to have detected the plane at all, or if they did, ignored it. Then the plane headed east over the vast Pacific Ocean, representing about 32 percent of Earth's surface. Theirs was just one unnoticeable airplane out of about 87,675 others that would be in the air at some point during that day throughout the world. Most of those other airplanes would be carrying people, but a significant number of them would be laden with cargo, feeding the voracious appetites around the world for the most immediate delivery of whatever promised to enhance economic activity, corporate and selected individual wealth, and the most current and fashionable life experiences of the all-important consumer, ultimately in satisfaction of simple basic individual human drives and desires. The two men were transporting something else–something entirely different and particularly unique. They were just past the most dangerous part of their mission. Neither the Russians nor the Japanese had noticed the private jet, or if they had, deemed it harmless enough not to send fighter aircraft up to intercept it and force it to land, or blow it out of the sky with a missile, as they might with a military jet. But then, maybe someone *ordered* them not to notice it. For about an hour, the only sound was that of the jet engines, the vital machinery that kept them from falling out of the lonely sky into the equally lonely, cold, and vast Pacific Ocean far below them.

Saeed's cellphone buzzed and simultaneously vibrated in his pocket. He pulled it out of his pocket to look at the screen. The text message was two numeric values: '45.277079, -122.599045.' In recognition of the message and with reaffirmed commitment, he looked out through the windshield as if he could see the location, the next important fixed place in his earthly existence. Finally, he was going to make his mark in life. He would establish himself in the history books and folklore as worthy of the greatest praise for his commitment to his religious duty and his supreme obligation to Allah. He knew the numbers were the geographic coordinates of his destination. Although he did not have the details of the master plan, he knew that his part was critical, and that Allah would reward him. That was all he needed to know.

Somewhere in the vast, defiantly warm, and dark air-conditioned electronic depths of the National Security Agency super-computers at Fort Meade, those numbers were recorded along with other electronic streams of trillions of bits and bytes.

**** *OREGON CITY, OREGON* ****

Slightly more than 10 hours later, flying significantly beneath the 2,100-foot cloudy ceiling and decelerating rapidly, their landing area appeared as they approached the given coordinates. Each man's heart rate accelerated to well over 100 beats per minute, as they briefly glanced at each other with raised eyebrows and faster breathing. They were definitely–and miraculously–far into the United States air space without any evidence of detection. The pilot had to decrease his speed without stalling until he could touch down just beyond the trees near the western cul de sac. The plane rapidly approached the only obvious place to land– the western-most end of an old, abandoned airstrip, now known as South Macdonald's Place, a residential street about halfway between, and parallel to Parrott Creek to the north and South Carus Road to the south in the semi-rural outskirts of Oregon City. They were in a foreign country without host permission, invitation, or official advance notice. If the local civil authorities caught them, they knew they could expect hostile treatment as unwelcome invaders, especially if no one believed their story about engine trouble over the Pacific Ocean. If their cargo were discovered, however, then the repercussions would be fatal. The greatest majority of the 35,000 residents located just south of Portland Oregon would not notice their landing, but the nearby residents obviously would. Saeed and Ahmad were counting on the elements of surprise, novelty, and confusion to give them enough time to complete their mission, and escape before anyone in the area could organize an effective response.

The six large and well-maintained houses built three on each side of the old runway were set back from the macadam street about 90 yards, and had similar long, dark-gray macadam driveways leading to the former landing strip. The absence of vehicles parked on the street made the landing much less difficult than it could have been otherwise. Saeed knew he could land the plane safely with only 2,210 feet of runway if he concentrated carefully on every nuance of the entire process, including wind changes. He had no control tower with radar or air traffic controllers to guide him or inform him of landing conditions. The sky was overcast, and the trees nearby showed no evidence of crosswinds. He had only his vision, experience, determination, and increasing adrenalin levels to complete his delivery mission and escape. No other planes were anywhere near this airstrip, because it had been abandoned decades ago, and had since become just an unusually wide residential 'street.' Saeed tightened his grip on the controls. South Macdonald's Place was about 410 feet shorter than the runway length that he knew he needed. He just missed the tops of the trees on his approach and then decelerated rapidly. After just one screeching impact of the tires simultaneously hitting the street about 100 yards beyond the western cul-de-sac, Saeed quickly understood that he would exceed the runway if he did not take extraordinary measures. He immediately reversed the engine thrust with full power and applied the brakes, but he would not be able to stop on the paved road. He dared not risk damaging the jet excessively, and by implication, his cargo. The airplane was expendable. His cargo was not. The momentum of the plane continued to challenge his efforts to bring it to a final stop until it finally skidded off the eastern end of the macadam pavement and into the edge of the open farm field ahead.

Already waiting near the eastern end of the road, a red 2006 Ford F-350 truck was idling in the shade just off the pavement on the south side near a small grove of oak trees. The driver held his breath as the plane skidded from left to right in front of his truck before stopping just off the pavement slightly to his right in the soft recently plowed dirt field. In anticipation of a cartwheel of the plane as the tail lifted into the air, the driver ducked under the dashboard onto the floor. After several seconds without hearing an explosion, he crawled back up on the seat and looked out at the scene before him.

The nose wheel assembly of the plane quickly sank into the fertile farm field, bringing the plane to an abrupt stop. The tail of the jet lifted higher than the nose and the main landing wheels under the wings lifted away from the roadway several feet, as the forward landing gear sank deeper into the soft farm field. Suddenly the nose of the plane dropped abruptly as the forward landing gear broke in the dirt and one final pull of gravity brought the jet to a complete upright standstill with an uncomfortable downward jolt of the recently dangerously elevated tail of the plane.

Saeed still had a virtual death grip upon the controls as he exhaled.

Allah has looked favorably upon us. The plane is upright, and we are not hurt. It is obviously a sign that our mission will succeed!

Within 30 seconds after the jet came to a complete stop, the side door on the left just behind the cockpit and forward of the port wing opened, and a folding stairway smoothly extended to the ground within 10 seconds.

By this time, several residents from four of the six houses on either side of the old runway came out of their homes to gawk at the sleek white jet located just beyond the far eastern end of their street, still sending a steady whining blast of violently wavy, super-hot idling jet exhaust into the otherwise peaceful residential area, distorting the view of the houses from one side of the street to the other. At least one woman immediately dialed 911 for the local police on her cellphone. Karim left his truck, walked quickly to the jet, ascended the stairs, and disappeared inside the cabin. Within a minute, he returned to the stairway and descended to the ground. Two other men followed him down the stairs, carrying an unusually large golf bag, with what looked like three blue golf club head covers visible at the top end. They carried the large and obviously heavy canvas bag between them to the truck. The truck cargo bed was empty except for an old gray slightly rusted warehouse dolly anchored to the forward wall of the truck bed. Then they carefully placed the bag in the bed immediately behind the cab and secured it with four bungee cords tied around the bag and hooked securely through thick metal eyelets on both sidewalls and on the floor of the truck bed. The jet engines continued idling, still pushing hot jet exhaust down the street with an impatient whine. The Iranians knew from the beginning of their mission that they did not have enough fuel to return to North Korea in that airplane. They also knew that their chances of flying to any safe haven after that landing without being discovered with suspicion would be zero, even if they could turn the jet around. But there was no time to repair the landing gear. By this time, surely someone else knew their flight had ended. Their window for escape was closing with each breath. They would have to exercise their vital commando training to escape and survive in a foreign country until they could complete their mission and eventually reach San Francisco International Airport for their flights out of the country. Despite the air turbulence on South Macdonald's Place behind the jet, the unfamiliar red truck moved past the airplane and raced down the road in low gear with the loud engine voice of a fully open carburetor. The sound from the jet engines finally started diminishing in pitch toward shutdown. The woman noted part of the registration number on the dented and dirty rear license plate, but she could not see the state name clearly as the truck faded into the distance ahead of a grayish wavy cloud of exhaust. The truck left the small housing development with the impatient roar of the V-8 6.2-liter 365 horsepower engine fading into the distance. The truck continued east onto South Carus Road past the Carus Elementary School to the right. Then Ahmad pressed the detonator switch on the radio transmitter he was holding. Within two seconds, the jet exploded into an unusually devastating white-hot conflagration. The small crowd of curious residents responded immediately with fearful and rapid retreats into their houses. After another few seconds, another explosion occurred, and the bright white glare of burning magnesium obviously stored somewhere in the jet illuminated South Macdonald's Place in brilliant sparkling white light. The air temperature closest to the fires soared to 4,000 degrees Fahrenheit.

During the next 42 minutes, the truck turned left to travel north on Oregon Route 213, also known as the Cascade Highway, until it ended close to I-205 North–the War Veterans Memorial Freeway–which eventually intersected with I-84 East near Portland. The driver proceeded up the entrance ramp to I-84 East and continued toward the approaching dusk along the beautiful and powerful Columbia River to his left. The road eventually diverged from the river just west of Hermiston as he continued toward Idaho Falls.

Deputy Sheriff Mack Mason arrived at South Macdonald's Place about eight minutes after the sheriff's dispatcher relayed the essence of the 911 call, turned east, and stopped his cruiser on the south side of the road a respectful distance from the burning ruins of the airplane. He immediately called the Clackamas Fire District Station #10 about 5.2 miles to the east.

"This is Mason from the county Sheriff's department. We have a burning business jet over here on South Macdonald's Place! Better get over here pronto!"

"Just had another call on that a few minutes ago. Was that the explosion we just heard a little while ago?"

"Probably was–but it's still burning pretty hot!"

"We're already on our way–we'll be there in less than 10 minutes!"

While shielding his eyes from the burning magnesium, Mason noted the unique rounded and wide double-impact skid marks from the plane landing on the roadway, obviously separated in width greater than a typical motor vehicle's tire tracks. The skid marks were a darker black color at the point of initial impact, which faded only slightly farther down the street consistent with the direction of the landing as the wheels had obviously quickly spun to synch with the plane's ground speed. This was not a case of 'burning rubber' in the manner of a typical dragster or a 'hot rod' stunt by some borderline youth with more testosterone than intelligence. The implications of the skid marks were as vaguely puzzling as they were sparse.

This is obviously going to be a very bad day!

He walked up one of the driveways to a woman who had retreated farther up her driveway and away from the fire, and asked, "What's your name, Ma'am?"

The 'soccer mom' with binoculars in her right hand responded with self-justified importance, "I'm Julia Kamber. I live right up here–number 4."

She turned slightly to her left and swung her pudgy left arm out to point to the comfortable-looking small brick mansion behind her, and then turned back to face Mason with obvious concern as he was writing down her name and address.

"What's your telephone number, in case I need to get back to you about this?"

"503-657-3307"

"Okay…. Now, tell me what you saw here, Ms. Kamber."

"Well, it was just a normal Friday around here–quiet and peaceful, you know–until I heard this loud noise, like a jet airplane flying too low nearby, so I got my binoculars and rushed outside to see what was going on. As soon as I got outside the front door, that jet airplane, or what's left of it, was landing on the street! I couldn't believe my eyes!"

"*Landing?* You mean… it didn't crash?"

By this time, four other residents who had been outside watching the drama continue had arrived next to Mason.

"Yeah! I know this street was once a real landing strip, but that was years and *years* ago–*way* before we moved here! Anyway, the jet went down that way and stopped just inside the farm field beyond the end of the street, where I saw a red truck parked. Then after the plane stopped, a man got out of the truck and went to the stairs of the plane, climbed up, and went inside for a few moments. Then he came out, and two other men followed him out with a big golf bag. It was odd that it took two men to carry a golf bag. Anyway, it had three blue golf club head covers sticking out of it. Sure must've wanted to play golf, I guess! They must have been a couple of rich guys ordering golf clubs special delivery, huh? Problem is, there's no golf course around here–not anywhere nearby, anyway. Then they all got in the truck and hightailed it out of here! Then after they must have gotten to the highway over there, I guess, the plane just blew up! Scared the living *hell* out of me! I thought I was going to *die!*"

"Do you think you could identify any of the men either from the truck or the plane if you ever saw them again?"

"I… I just… I really don't think so. They were down at the end of the street, and from where I was, I couldn't see around the tail of the airplane to where they were most of the time. What I could see of 'em was distorted by the wavy air from the jet engines. They fastened the golf bag into the back of the truck. It didn't take them much more than a few minutes or so before they were all in the truck and racing down the street here."

"Can you describe any of them?"

"I got only a glimpse of them through my binoculars. The two from the plane had black hair, and one had a dark beard–I would say they were from the Middle East, but I could be wrong. The guy from the truck was the tallest of the three, also had dark hair, but a darker complexion and a beard…, a little above average height, I would guess. Otherwise, there's not much I can say."

"What were they wearing?"

"Looked like average blue jeans for all three of 'em. The guy from the truck had a tan shirt on…, long-sleeved. The other two had lighter colored shirts–not white, though, and looked like they were wearing some kind of body armor."

"Body armor?"

Two of the other neighbors nodded in agreement, content to let Julia Kamber do the talking.

She continued, "Yeah. Black vests, like.…"

"About how long ago did they leave?"

"About 20… maybe 25 minutes ago, I think…, as a guess, anyway"

"How many jet engines did the plane have?"

"Two–one on each side in the back. Damn things were *loud!*"

"So…, as far as you could tell, there was no emergency or other kind of mechanical problem or difficulty with the plane or the landing…, right?"

"No."

"Ma'am?"

"I mean yes, there didn't seem to be a problem with the plane…, or the landing."

The officer was writing down what she said in his notebook, along with his interpretive notes.

"Did you see any markings–letters, numbers, words, names, colors, symbols–or anything that could help us to identify the plane?"

"No. It was just plain white."

He looked down the street at the wreckage and did not see any markings remaining on any of the pieces of the burning plane.

"Are you sure there was nothing on the tailfin or the wings–numbers, symbols, or letters?"

"No. It was just plain white like I said… at least on the side I could see from here."

"You said the truck was red?"

"Yes."

"Do you know what the make and model were?"

"I think it was a Ford, but I'm not really sure."

"Late model? Old? Any markings on it–dents, something broken, or… anything like that?"

"It was kinda dented a little here and there on the side I saw and had some minor scrape marks. It looked dirty and like it had been painted rather poorly, but I didn't see anything unusual other than that. It didn't look really old, but it definitely wasn't really a late model either."

"Could you tell which way the truck went after it left your neighborhood?"

"Couldn't see that far…, so I really don't know."

"Did you notice the license plate number?"

"I don't remember all of it, but it began with 'AH' I think."

"Oregon plates?"

"I don't know for sure, really…, but I don't think so. It was kinda dirty, like I said…."

"Anything else you can think of to tell me about this?"

She looked at him with a wrinkled drawn-out thoughtful expression on her face as she slowly turned her head from side to side, and said, "Nnnooo…, Can't think of anything else… right now. You have any ideas about what's going on here?"

He had no intention of sharing any intuition or other thoughts, so he said simply, "No Ma'am–at least not right now."

"Sure doesn't seem right, now does it?"

"No, ma'am—it sure doesn't. Thank you for your cooperation. I will get back to you if I need anything further from you."

"Okay," she said with resignation and a facial expression implying a head full of many unanswered questions.

He turned toward the other residents standing nearby and asked, "Any of you folks see anything unusual—any identifying markings on the plane?"

They all shook their heads indicating that they had not. Mason excused himself from the neighbors, left Julia in her driveway, and walked back down to the edge of the street. The sound of sirens became louder, as the first of four local fire trucks raced up the road to South Macdonald's Place, and then turned to the right toward the burning wreckage at the eastern end of the road. The other three fire trucks followed into strategic nearby positions shortly thereafter. Within a minute, 13 firefighters deployed from the trucks and quickly put all the fire-suppression equipment to work. Within an hour, the stubborn, bright magnesium fires were extinguished with foam, leaving only a few widely separated pockets of smoke and small fires. The firefighters quickly extinguished those with water or smothered them with more foam until the fire chief determined that the entire area was completely secure. For just a brief period, everything was quiet except for the muffled sounds of the fire truck engines as the firefighters started to collect the five hoses draped across the former runway and retract them onto their storage drums in the trucks. Fluffy mounds of dirty creamy-white foam remained over the skeletal wreckage of the plane for several minutes and then started to slide down on remnants of the fuselage and onto the street. The immediate fire danger was over, but the imaginations of those firefighters continued to smolder with unanswered questions. The fire chief removed his fire hat, wiped his brow with his left sleeve, and walked over to Mason.

The fire chief looked intently into Mason's eyes and bellowed with genuine urgency, "*What... in the hell... happened* here?"

Mason summarized in a mild official tone what the woman had told him, "That plane landed in the street. Two men wearing black body armor exited with a large golf bag, got into a red truck—probably a Ford—with the driver, and left the scene. Then the plane exploded and burned."

"You gotta be *shittin'* me!"

"Nope! That's what the lady up there told me!"

"This doesn't smell right, now does it?"

"Wuddya mean?"

"Well, that plane burned hotter and longer than I would have expected–almost like someone didn't want *anyone* else to know *anything* about it… and maybe even wanted to make it disappear *completely*. In addition to the burning jet fuel, there was burning magnesium and thermite. That black metallic ash is from burning thermite. They don't make those planes out of magnesium! Not enough to make that kind of fire, anyway. Must've been stored onboard. Everything–and I mean *everything*–burned to a crisp!"

Mason spoke with somewhat delayed urgency into his shoulder microphone, "This is Mason. Put out a BOLO on a late model red Ford pickup truck with some minor body damage and a poor paint job–male driver and two male passengers wearing black body armor wanted for questioning–left the vicinity of South Macdonald's Place in Oregon City about 40 to 50 minutes ago. Believe license registration begins with AH–alpha hotel. State of registration unknown. Witness says the truck has a large golf bag in the bed with blue club head covers. And call the National Transportation Safety Board and the FBI. Sooner or later, they're both going to want to get involved and learn what happened here at South Macdonald's Place."

He retrieved a Rolatape 412-D digital measuring wheel from the trunk of his patrol car, walked to the end of the cul-de-sac, turned around, set the wheel firmly on the pavement, and pushed it ahead of him down the entire length of South MacDonald's Place. By the time he stopped at the other end, it measured 1,890 feet, give or take the size of some large pieces of broken macadam road surface next to the farm field. Then he took some pictures of the entire scene and the remains of the aircraft with his smartphone.

The desk clerk in the Sheriff's Office called 503-224-4181, the number for the nearest FBI field office at 9109 N.E. Cascades Parkway in Portland, Oregon, and relayed the essential information. Within the next five minutes, that same information reached FBI headquarters at 935 Pennsylvania Avenue, NW in Washington, D.C.

**** SAN FRANCISCO, CALIFORNIA ****

He spent most of the nine-and-a-half-hour flight time from Narita International Airport to San Francisco somewhere between dozing and sleeping. After gathering his carry-on luggage and going through customs, Lei Chang switched his cellphone out of airplane mode. As he walked toward the bus stop for transportation to the car rental location, a message appeared on his Comm-S67:

> '*On Friday, August 28, 2015, Fourth Bureau and confirming satellite surveillance systems identified and tracked an unknown aircraft flight from eastern North Korea across the Pacific Ocean, terminating near the northwest coast of the United States. Last known coordinates: 45.277079 latitude and -122.599045 degrees longitude. Investigate and report. Code Shanghai. Priority immediate.*'

> *Too many coincidences in very little time–first the Shiodome meeting including Jo-Mung Suong, and now an urgent request from the people upstairs regarding a flight from North Korea to the United States. The North Koreans are up to something. The Fourth Bureau does not make mistakes.*

Although the complete structure and substance of the Chinese internet warfare and signals intelligence organizations are not known with certainty, it appears that a particular unit headquartered in Qingdao, known as the Fourth Bureau–also known as Unit 61419–is focused on Japan and Korea. Many of the Fourth Bureau offices, including the First, are in the Qingdao area. The Second Office employs Korean linguists. The Fourth Bureau's Seventh Office is in Hangzhou, and another office is in Jimo City, Wenlongzhen. Other subordinate offices appear to be in the Qingdao area, Dalian, Beijing, and Shanghai. The bureau was formerly based in the Shanxi provincial city of Xinzhou, specifically Huanglong Wanggou village just west of county road number 111 in east-central China. Although its headquarters moved to Qingdao, the Fourth Bureau may still maintain a training base in Xinzhou.

By 12:35 P.M., Lei was at the Hertz rental desk at the San Francisco International Airport Rental Car Center at 780 North Macdonnell Road, where he secured a late model Chevrolet Malibu. He carried his small tan Coach travel bag to the rental lot and found the gray four-door Malibu sedan. After storing his bag in the trunk, he settled into the driver's seat, activated his smartphone, and selected the GPS application. He entered the coordinates from the most recent text message he had received as a destination from his current location at the airport. Within several seconds the route to that location appeared as a turquoise line on a digital map on his smartphone. He studied it for about half a minute, and then placed his phone on the center console between the transmission shifter and the base of the center dashboard control panel. Then he carefully followed the polite but disinterested female voice issuing English driving directions out of the city. It would take him about 11 hours to travel north along the highlighted route for 632 miles. He drove as far as he could and stopped at a motel for the night.

**** OREGON AND IDAHO ****

Karim was driving the truck. Saeed was in the front passenger seat, and Ahmad was sitting in the back seat. They continued on I-84 to the southeast away from the Columbia River and toward Pendleton, La Grande, Baker City, and then through Boise, and on to the small town of Mountain Home, where Karim turned onto Idaho Route 20 north and followed it all the way to Idaho Falls. From there he drove north through Rigby, Rexburg, and then through Saint Anthony and farther into the mountains of eastern Idaho. They had been on the road for well over 11 hours, carefully staying within the speed limits, and stopped for fuel at isolated locations along the road after they left South Macdonald's Place. Local and State Police had not yet seen the truck, and the men inside it were unaware that a search had already commenced. However, they all knew that their time was limited and that a search was inevitable, given the evidence they left behind and their uninvited status.

They continued north under overcast skies on US Route 20 to Meadow Creek Road and turned right onto State Route 60, east-southeast of Henry's Lake. Karim continued for several miles, then turned to the northeast on State Road 63 into the sparsely populated mountains for several miles, leaving all evidence of civilization behind, and then turned onto a nameless unpaved road that appeared to lead to a dead-end in the middle of nowhere. Nevertheless, he followed the old scarcely visible brush-covered dirt road to even higher elevations. He had been here before, so he already knew the lay of the land. A brief opening in the clouds admitted rays of sunlight for less than 10 seconds as if showing him the way. Local temperatures were in the high 70s. A mild breeze periodically swayed some of the taller grasses nearby. The uneven road through the wilderness of wild grass, sagebrush, and shrubs became barely visible as a parallel pair of dirt and stony ruts marred every several yards with minor potholes and fist-sized and larger stones. Beautiful wildflowers punctuated the otherwise mostly empty landscape with bright yellow, blue, red, and purple colors in innocent contrast to the dark deed they were determined to accomplish. He checked his Garmin GPS coordinates carefully as he approached his destination. He pulled up to within 100 yards of the old wooden abandoned mine shaft entrance on the western side of a hill. At that point, the terrain was too uneven and steep for the truck, so he shifted the transmission lever into the 'park' position and turned the ignition key counterclockwise to the 'off' marker. Then all three men removed their bulletproof vests. Still muttering prayers under his breath, he opened the door and stepped out onto the dry and dusty ground. Only the periodic mild wind gusts disturbed the silence of this ghostly remainder of the frontier gold rush days of the mid-1800s. He stepped to the back of his truck and lowered the tailgate, still muttering barely audible words in Pashto, his native language. He reached for the bungee cords securing the dolly to the front of the bed of the truck and unhooked them. Saeed and Ahmad had already exited from the rear seat and silently helped pull the dolly from the truck bed. They set the upper handles against the open tailgate with the wheels on the ground and then secured the dolly in that position with their feet against the wheels. The driver reached for the old tan canvas 'golf bag' satchel, wrestled it along the bed of the truck toward the tailgate, and carefully eased it between the handles. Ahmad and Saeed helped guide and restrain its slide down the back of the dolly to the bottom slightly rusty support plate. Karim still had the youthful strength to carry the satchel for brief periods or short distances, but he did not know how long he could carry it, so he used the dolly to conserve his energy. An old military-style metal canteen full of water was hooked to his belt. Fastened to an army-green elastic band around his forehead was a powerful LED headlamp he bought at Cabela's in Springfield, Oregon during his first visit on June 18, a little over 10 weeks ago. With effort, he pulled the dolly over the uneven ground to the old mine entrance and set it down horizontally on the ground. He retrieved the three vests and secured them to the dolly with their straps so he could dispose of them in the mine. Then he went to the entrance, moved an old, rotted support beam from the hole in the mountain, and peered into its darkness with purpose and anticipation. He turned on his headlamp, still moving his lips in silent prayer. Then he returned to the dolly, lifted the handles, and started to pull the dolly over the rough ground toward the entrance to the mineshaft. The other two men followed. His steps were careful, but confident in the otherwise unfamiliar tunnel because he knew he was doing the proper work of Allah. He turned the dolly around so he could follow it down the slightly descending mine shaft, acting as a brake instead of risking having it run over him by pulling it down the tunnel. He continued farther into the mine, stepping carefully while guiding the dolly in front of him. The other two men followed with flashlights that illuminated the narrow world of pitch-black uncertainty without concern for their fate. They had no fate. They had only belief and self-indoctrinated purpose, including anticipation of Allah's ultimate reward. Karim tightened his grip on the dolly handles, still moving his lips repeatedly, mumbling the same phrases. Minutes disappeared behind them, as their cautious journey lower into the mine became well over an hour, as Karim had to urge the dolly through ruts and over stones. Sometimes the other two had to help lift it awkwardly through a few narrow passages. After more unmeasured time, they finally arrived at the end of the tunnel, soaked with the sweat of their recent exertion and anxiety despite the cool stale air. They had finally reached what could have been the eastern terminus of the mine. A few small and very narrow veins of silver remained in the rock walls at that point, shining briefly in the bright light from his LED headlamp. They ignored the few small grains of silver remaining on the floor of the tunnel from the hopeful efforts of prospectors about 150 years ago. At some point, the value of the remaining ore was lower than the cost of getting it out of the mine and extracting the silver. He set the dolly upright against the wall to his left. As the others steadied the dolly, he worked the large canvas golf bag off the lower lip of the dolly. With only relatively moderate further effort, he rested the bag on the floor of the tunnel before him. He carefully unzipped it, revealing the device that would eventually cause the ultimate punishment he knew the infidels so richly deserved–finally and convincingly. However, he did not know it would be in a manner never seen in recorded human history. In the darkness of the eastern terminus of the mine, Karim crouched over the device, reading the activation instructions from his notes in the adequate light of the LED spotlight attached to his headband. He had to execute the instructions carefully because he knew the device was equipped with a self-destruct mechanism that would explode if he did not follow the instructions precisely. After slowly entering the two five-character code groups, one character at a time, and then rechecking them for several seconds, he was satisfied that he had successfully armed the device with the delay timer set for 2100 hours, or 9 P.M. local time on Sunday, September 27, exactly 30 days hence. That gave him enough time to leave the country and hide in some distant part of the world, thereby effectively separating his presence in that part of the United States from the expected events. On that Sunday, a day of rest, a complete lunar eclipse would be visible in most of North America, Europe, Southeast Asia, Africa, much of South America, the Pacific, Atlantic, and Indian Oceans, as well as the Arctic and Antarctica. It would also serve as a sign to the entire world that he had accomplished his mission. Satisfied after 20 minutes of checking and rechecking the list of procedures that he had prepared the device according to the printed directions, Karim continued to mutter to himself as Saeed and Ahmad turned and headed back out of the mine without the dolly and the rest of their equipment. Karim checked his work once more and then turned to head back up the tunnel. About 300 yards from the device, he stopped and then removed his small backpack and retrieved a brick of C4 and pressed it into a crevice of the wall of the mine. Then he carefully inserted a detonator with a battery-powered timer. He set the timer for 85 minutes, giving him sufficient time to exit the mine before detonation. Still praying feverishly after finishing that final task, Karim pushed himself forward, hoping that his headlamp would not burn out before he returned to the entrance. He finally saw the flashlights of the other two in the distance and eventually caught up with them. A few bats flew by them, briefly startling them. The increasingly claustrophobic urgency to return to the surface of the earth gripped all of them. The journey back seemed longer than the one in, as their thighs and calves began to burn with each step. Within the next 45 minutes, they saw the small remnants of daylight at the entrance to the mine and heaved a collective sigh of relief as they hastened their pace with determination and increased effort. They finally stepped out into the periodic early evening sun, exhaled heavily, and went back toward the near side of the truck. They leaned silently against the truck for several minutes as their bodies recovered from their recent exertion.

Suddenly, Karim heard an unfamiliar voice off to his left. Saeed and Ahmad froze in fear against the side of the truck when they heard the same voice.

"Hey there! Wutcha doin'? Find 'nything…?"

He appeared out of nowhere, startling Karim. The unshaven old man was wearing dusty old dark-blue denim coveralls, a light blue denim shirt with frayed threads around the collar and dusty, well-worn, scuffed brown boots. He was carrying an old satchel with a few hand tools in it. Karim froze in his tracks as his heartbeat quickened significantly.

What is this old man doing up here in the middle of nowhere?

"Saw yer truck from back yonder…. Thought I was the only one prospectin' these days up 'round here. Been lookin' fer silver, have yeh? Ain't much up here'n these parts 'ny more I reckin…, other'n specks of it in that old mine back over there. There's prob'ly more up north 'n the panhandle…, but lotsa' *people* up there, too!"

He has been in this area before and will know whether the tunnel has been altered, or whether something of interest is in that mine if he goes in there again and will alert the authorities. I cannot let that happen. I do not know how much he has seen of our activities. It is Allah's will–I must kill him.

"Cat got yer tongue?"

I must get out of here…. I have no time to waste with this old man!

Karim ignored the old man, turned, and walked to the driver's door of his truck, opened it, and reached under the seat for his Zigana T 9mm pistol. He inhaled slowly, and then exhaled slowly. Then he whirled around and quickly aimed at the suddenly frightened man with the subtle 'click' of the safety release.

"NO! Oh God! NO!"

The old man froze in silent fright as Karim fired a single shot into the middle of the innocent intruder's forehead. The old man's legs buckled immediately, and he slumped to the ground in less than a second like a broken marionette, with his left leg oddly twisted under his right leg and his arms on the ground and slightly away from his torso. Karim stood still for several moments, listening carefully, then turned slowly full circle scanning the surrounding area, trying to determine whether anyone else nearby could have heard the shot. Satisfied for the moment that no one else was in the area and that the body had not moved, he calmly turned back to his truck and replaced the pistol under the seat.

Karim said dryly to the others, "It was necessary for the accomplishment of our mission! We cannot let this threaten our escape!"

Saeed said, "Should we not hide his body?"

"No! We cannot afford to waste any more time here!"

Karim checked his watch and said to the others, "We must leave now!"

Within 30 seconds, a small, muffled blast from deep inside the mine caused a complete blockage of the tunnel and sent a small cloud of dust out through the entrance several seconds later. Then Karim walked around the truck to the passenger side, and sent a text message to Shamir:

'It is done.'

He then opened the passenger side door and reached for the four cans of Rustoleum slate-gray paint, grasped two in each hand, and backed away from the truck as he kicked the door shut. He went around the truck and tossed two cans to each of the other two men.

He commanded, "Start painting the truck. If a search is underway, at least they will be looking for a red truck and not a gray one. At least they will not know whether it is red with some gray paint, or gray with some red paint if we do not have enough paint."

After the other two had finished spraying paint onto the exterior of the truck, Karim calmly closed the tailgate as if officially ending their mission. The other two entered the truck, closed the doors, and tossed the paint cans behind the rear seat. Karim then walked to the open driver's door, paused briefly to turn around, and again gazed out over the landscape in all directions, with one final glance at the old man's body on the ground, satisfying himself that they were now indeed alone. He checked his watch. They were still on schedule to catch their flights out of the country, each to a different destination. They would drive about 15 hours throughout the night without any further unplanned interruptions to get to the airport on time. He stepped up into the cab, closed the door, and started the engine. Then he began to retrace his route in a southwesterly direction through the sparsely populated Idaho mountain wilderness back into the open valley plain and onto US Highway 20 South to Idaho Falls. From there he turned onto I-15 South to Pocatello, where he turned onto I-86 West for a short distance. He needed fuel, so he headed south onto the nearest main commercial thoroughfare off the interstate, which was Yellowstone Avenue, also US Highway 91 running north and south through the city. Within a few blocks, he found a Common Cents Gas station on the east side of the road and drove into the fueling area to the right of the pumps, since the fuel cap was on the driver's side just forward of the rear wheel well. Within a minute, a rookie Idaho State Trooper, Chuck Mathison, driving a late model dark gray Dodge Charger cruiser with tinted windows pulled into the same gas station to the inside lane behind Karim's truck because his fuel intake was also on the driver's side. Karim could not suddenly finish refueling, because he had not yest filled his tank. If he did leave, then the police officer would wonder why he left just 15 seconds after he arrived at the pumps. The three young men endured increasing anxiety as Karim furtively glanced at the police cruiser behind his truck, but never elevated his line of sight to the police officer's face. The Oregon BOLO bulletin had not yet made its way into Idaho, at least not into the awareness of this police officer.

"Nice evening, isn't it?", the trooper said in a neighborly but mildly suspicious manner, as he briefly glanced into the bed of the truck and through the back window at the other two men in the rear seat. He noted that the gray paint areas were unusually clean compared to the red areas of the truck. He also noted the Rent-A-Wreck logo on the rear bumper.

Recent lousy paint job…. Figures.

"Yes, it is, officer!" *Police officers do not ordinarily start friendly conversations!*

"You're not from around here, are you?"

"No, just visiting. It's beautiful around here!"

Damn pump is slow! Control yourself!

The officer asked, "Relatives?"

"No…, friends from my college days back east."

Okay, copper…, we've talked long enough!

"What a coincidence! Maybe I would know one of them! I grew up around here. What's the name?"

This is enough gas for now–I'm outta here!

Saeed had dug himself into a small hole in a way that he had promised himself he would never do. He calmly took the pump hose nozzle out of the filler tube and turned to replace it in its receptacle on the right side of the face of the pump. With measured control of his growing impatience and anxiety, he turned back to his truck and replaced the filler cap, and then closed the filler door with a hint of irritation, and briefly looked at Saeed and Ahmad with obvious anxiety. They remained quiet and tried to appear relaxed and unconcerned, as they left the situation entirely in Karim's hands.

Karim turned toward the officer, and said in a contrived neighborly manner, "Good day, officer," as he walked away to the small convenience store in the adjacent Burger King building to pay for his gas in cash. He did not use a credit card because he did not want to leave any paper trails of his locations and movements.

The officer again peered into the empty bed of the truck and noticed the bungee cords anchored only at one end.

Nothing suspicious about that.

Then he glanced at the California license plate and anchored the registration number in his memory by mentally repeating it 20 times, while he continued to fill his gas tank. He also glanced at the sale amount registered on the transaction display of the pump next to the truck and noted that it was $13.71. Again, he looked at the two men in the back seat of the truck. They were staring straight ahead, ignoring him.

That's not enough fuel for this part of the country. Maybe he just topped off the tank. That's not a crime. However, most people would squeeze at least some kind of round number amount out of the pump register anyway. Maybe this guy just wasn't the typical neurotic 'neatnik.' Or maybe he was in a hurry.

Karim returned to the truck as the officer was completing his transaction with a credit card at the pump. He started his truck and headed south to I-86 West. Within a minute, the officer got behind the wheel of his cruiser, and then made written notes of his experience at the gas station, including the truck's California license plate, AHN-478. He left the gasoline station and headed for I-86 West. Out of curiosity, he took a chance that the truck might need more fuel shortly, so he continued driving west toward wherever the next gas station might be, gradually increasing his speed to catch up with the truck before it could exit from the interstate out of his sight and disappear into the vast emptiness of the West. He left his overhead flashing lights off. He did not want to alert the people in the truck to his pursuit. Other drivers would just have to notice his higher speed and get out of his way. He would activate his siren for a second or flash his high beams if necessary to goose a reluctant or daydreaming driver out of the left lane. Saeed continued to drive carefully under the speed limit west on I-84 to Twin Falls, Idaho, where he left the highway to refuel again. The Idaho State trooper had caught up with the truck by that time, followed it into the gas station, and waited in his patrol car. Saeed knew he needed to walk a tight line to avoid arousing further suspicion.

"That damned cop is still on our tail, but he does not have anything against us—no evidence. He would have arrested us by now if he had a good reason. He's just sniffing in the bushes, looking for an excuse to arrest us.... Looks like we're okay, at least for now...."

Saeed blurted out nervously, "I do *not* like this! This was *not* supposed to happen!"

"You need to pray more, Saeed!"

Karim stepped back into his truck and slowly left the gas station, then entered Route 93 South, and continued to drive to just outside Wells, Nevada, where he stopped at a Burger King just off to the left side of the highway. The Idaho State trooper had stopped following the truck at the state line and turned around. After eating, Karim took the nearby right turn onto the entrance ramp to I-80 West, and followed it all the way to San Francisco, stopping only as necessary for fuel and a toilet. Apparently, no one else on the road was suspicious of them.

Karim said with contrived confidence, "You see? Allah is watching over us. The policeman is no longer following us!"

They drove through the night for the rest of the 934 miles from the mine to San Francisco. Saeed, Ahmad, and Karim did not share their thoughts during most of the journey from Idaho. Karim was driving, staying at or below the speed limit when traffic was light, and joining the speed of other vehicles in heavier traffic in an effort to remain anonymous, trying not to stand out by going either too fast or too slow at the wrong time, or in the wrong traffic lane.

Saeed and Ahmad were physically tired but emotionally tense. They were moving their lips without emitting verbal sounds, staring far down the road ahead and further into their future, as if at least part of that future were the same for all three of them. Karim finally made his way toward San Francisco International Airport and left the truck unlocked with the ignition key in the ignition on the third level of the four-story parking garage next to South Airport Boulevard. He really did not care whether someone might steal the truck. The three men exited the vehicle and then descended the interior concrete stairs quietly except for the sounds of their footsteps and their faint echoes. At the street level, they waited with contrived patience for a shuttle bus to the International Departures terminal. About 52 anxious minutes later, they entered the main terminal and looked for directions to their flight departure areas, checked in, and settled into a series of brief catnaps before boarding their separate flights.

**** LANGLEY, VIRGINIA ****

He picked up the internal telephone receiver on his desk and barked, "Murray!"

"Sir, given various recent unusual reports, I thought you should know as soon as possible that an unknown private executive jet just recently made an unscheduled landing on a residential street in Oregon City, Oregon that used to be an airstrip. So far, no flight plan or point of origin is available anywhere, and no pilot or passengers have been identified or located. We have no clear evidence of any cargo that may have been on board, but almost certain evidence that the plane was deliberately torched after the landing—completely destroyed, according to the local Sheriff's Office."

"That's *all* you have on this?"

"Yes, sir."

"Where did you get this information?"

"I have a friend inside the FBI, sir."

Oh really?

"Thank you. Keep me informed about anything else related to this."

"Will do, sir."

While still practically strangling the telephone receiver in his left hand, General Murray cleared that telephone connection by pressing Director Miles' quick-dial button with his right index finger and waited impatiently.

About 15 seconds later, Miles answered and said in a concerned tone, *"What's going on, Richard?"*

"Well, in addition to a missing Russian nuke, we've got a new problem. I just learned that an unknown private executive jet landed on a residential street today in Oregon City, Oregon. No crew, no cargo, no flight plan, and no passengers found! *Zilch!* And the plane was torched after it landed! I'm thinking it might have been transporting the missing Russian nuke. Anyway, I can't afford to believe that it wasn't."

"Jesus H. Christ! How the hell did that happen? I don't like the way this sounds, Richard!"

"Neither do I! There is no record to my knowledge of any similar landing in the history of United States aviation. Something very unusual—and bad—is happening, and we—the guys who are supposed to know what the hell is going on—don't have a goddamned clue! I suspect that the jet was not carrying people who wanted to be in this country for an extended period of time. If they did want to stay here for more than a day or two, then they would have taken a commercial airliner and would have landed at a conventional airport. The fact that this plane landed in an uncontrolled, unmonitored abandoned airstrip almost screams negative intentions, and significant effort to hide something. If others were on that plane in addition to at least a pilot and a navigator, then I would assume they did not have noble intentions by landing where they did. The purpose of that flight was not necessarily human transportation. I think important cargo was on board. The fact that an airplane was used instead of a boat suggests some degree of urgency or that a time schedule of some sort was of primary concern. If the people on that plane were seeking asylum or safety in this country, then why didn't they use a normally visible means of doing so? Where the hell did they go?"

"How do you know that the airplane came from outside the United States?"

"No flight plan was recorded that would eliminate that possibility. If it came from within the United States, then a flight plan would be on record somewhere. Obviously, insufficient time or attention during that time hindered NORAD's discovery of the plane prior to its landing. That suggests that the plane was not flying within normal identification regulations, meaning the pilot was obviously trying to avoid detection. We might ask why it didn't land on some other coast. Why not in Florida, New Jersey, Maine, or Louisiana, for example? Lack of domestic detection in addition to having landed in Oregon suggests an origin in the Far East. Federal Aviation Agency records show no non-commercial flights from Hawaii to the Oregon or Washington State area on that date."

"So, who do we know over there who would want to operate in an unusual and apparently secret manner like that?"

"The Russians, Chinese, Japanese, or Koreans, I would guess, but probably more likely North Korea than South Korea. However, we have no reason to believe that this incident was either government-sponsored or completely private. The Japanese have the capability, but I cannot think of any likely reason they would do this kind of thing. If they have a problem that needs attention from someone over here, then I would think they would use normal or official diplomatic channels, or at least the internet or a telephone. However, Russia has a substantial number of options and capabilities to operate in secret without this kind of relative visibility. In this kind of clandestine entry, they have the advantage of Caucasian appearance that much more easily blends into most of our culture without special notice or attention. They could move easily in traditional travel and would have no need to call any attention to their behavior in this manner. I just do not believe the Chinese are stupid enough to operate this way, either. Both of those governments can be much more subtle, intelligent, sophisticated, and devious if they really want to do something nasty. The North Koreans... well, that's another matter, even though it may be only because we do not have as much information about their government and culture as we do about most others. It's the most secretive, closed society on the planet, and they are not known for their altruism. Another possibility is that whoever originated this flight was not aligned with any traditional nation or government. He could be completely independent, wealthy perhaps, and simply used the most convenient or efficient means of transportation from whatever the origin was, and at the best price."

With guarded anxiety, Miles finished the conversation: *"Get on top of this and keep me in the loop!"*

General Murray replaced his telephone receiver and stared absently and without focus into the future for several empty moments.

Marvin Miles immediately dialed the North American Aerospace Defense Command headquarters at Peterson Air Force Base in Colorado Springs, Colorado.

"NORAD. Sergeant Bowman speaking."

"Sergeant Bowman, this is Marvin Miles, head of the Central Intelligence Agency."

"I know who you are, Mr. Miles. What can I do for you?"

"Did you folks notice an unidentified business jet within the last 48 hours heading inbound toward the Pacific Northwest?"

"Just a moment, sir…. I will check on that."

About 25 seconds later, the young airman responded, *"We sent up two fighters from the 173rd Fighter Wing of the Oregon Air National Guard after a report of a small unidentified aircraft entering US air space. Apparently, the incoming aircraft disappeared before the fighters could see it, so we have no further details about that, sir."*

"Are you absolutely sure?"

"Yes sir. I'm sure."

Well, I'll be damned! "Thank you, Sergeant Bowman. That's all I need from you right now. Goodbye."

**** MOSCOW, RUSSIA ****

He picked up his secure phone receiver and said in a soft voice, "Koshelev."

"This is Ariel. The CIA believes a small Russian 'doll' is missing, and they want definitive confirmation or denial, with as much detail as possible and as soon as possible. I need to give them something, or I will lose credibility with them or value to you. I sense increasing danger. Can you help me?"

Damn! Another innocent occurrence… maybe by chance… perhaps not! Damn it–there are no coincidences! She knows I must have some information, or the ability to get it. Why could it not have been another agent? Why did it have to be someone I care about? If 'things' go awry, I might be forced to eliminate her. Viktor would never forgive me. The world is shitty enough. Why will she also have to suffer? One way or another, I will be forced to lie, and eventually, that lie might catch up to me and threaten either my career or my life, or hers…, or both. Why do I have to make this choice? Lies seem to have a way of revisiting inconveniently in the future… or requiring continuous and exhausting maintenance. Why could I not just work this my own way without involving her?

Vasily continued, "It would be extremely unwise for you to contact me again. I urge you to go deep. You will hear from me if I discover useful information or have a need for your services. Discontinue communication protocol A, and adopt protocol B."

The line was dead, and Ariel shivered with unfamiliar dread as if she suddenly discovered that she had locked herself out of her own apartment during a bitter and blinding Siberian blizzard.

He knows something, and he is warning me about something.... Go deep underground.... Why?

Later that evening, Shamir's periodic pop-up internet page appeared for the first time with a headline banner: 'THE AMERICAN INFIDELS WILL DIE IN 30 DAYS WHEN THE MOON IS RED!' He wanted to establish an extended period of maximum national anxiety and confusion with a nebulous but very real threat. He wanted to provoke maximum terror in individual lives throughout the United States for a prolonged period, while officials at all levels of government would argue blindly and wrestle with questions, plausible scenarios, and possibilities. Gradually, more people would notice the message and start to pay more attention with increasing concern. Many would spread unverified rumors and half-truths. Eventually, most people would begin to accept the message as a hoax or an empty threat, and then the inevitable jokes would appear. After the message had saturated the rumor mills without consequence, people would relax and discount the message altogether. Then his plan would unfold. One small triggering event would cause the natural forces of geological instability to run their inevitable course–the course innocently and unknowingly revealed to Shamir by Rahim Nazari in his studies at MIT–the course that Fantasia, Karina, Viktor, Vasily, Boris, and Ariel could never imagine.

To be continued... WHEN THE MOON IS RED.

CPSIA information can be obtained
at www.ICGtesting.com
Printed in the USA
BVHW051750240523
664816BV00025B/442